Flashes

A Fictional Memoir of Youth

by
James M. Bates

Robert D. Reed Publishers • San Francisco, CA

Robert D. Reed Publishers
750 La Playa, Suite 647
San Francisco, CA 94121
Phone: 650-994-6570 • Fax: -6579
E-mail: 4bobreed@msn.com
web site: www.rdrpublishers.com

Typesetter: **Barbara Kruger**
Cover Designer: **Julia Gaskill**

ISBN 1-931741-23-9

Library of Congress Catalog Control Number 2002092745

Manufactured, typeset and printed in the United States of America

No two persons ever read the same book.

—Edmund Wilson

Then something bent down and took hold of me and shook me like the end of the world. Whee–ee–ee–ee–ee, it shrilled, through an air crackling with blue light, and with each flash a great jolt drubbed me until I thought my bones would break away and the sap would fly out of me like a split plant.

I wondered what terrible thing it was that I had done.

—Sylvia Plath, *The Bell Jar*

Dedication

Marge—
My wife, an intelligent and smart woman, who has done much for me and has been helpful in many ways.

Dr. Vincent F. Romano—
Whom I first encountered at a desperate point in my life and whose attentiveness and care helped restore my physical well being. He helped make it possible to get through medical problems and back into creativity.

Dr. William F. Pharr—
Whose medical acumen and surgical skills were extraordinarily beneficial to me. He was principally responsible for restoring a vital organ to good order, further helping mightily for me to keep on with creativity.

1

Stuffy! That's what it is in here! Starting to smell sweaty—like a locker room.

The large room was crowded. The people in it—all young men—each did what he felt like doing to pass time; sat, stood, wondered, talked, was silent. Some looked nervous. Some were annoyed, some angry. Half an hour seemed too long to be kept waiting, without so much as a word as to what was next.

A hum in the room was quiet conversation, once in a while broken by snickers of laughter or a guffaw or a chorus of raucous laughing that quickly ended after a punch line, the next joke-teller eager to start.

Periodically, different anonymous voices raised a mild protest. The first one was a high-pitched complaint. "What the hell's goin' on? Huh?" He had a supporter. "Give 'em hell, pal."

When someone else got fidgety another voice hooted out of the crowd, praised by some, others shushing him.

There was general laughter when someone loudly threatened, "You don't get things *moving* here, I'm gonna change my mind! Got that?"

"SURE you will, buddy. Do it. Let's see how big your balls are!"

There was time to think.

2

He could only remember back to when he was about ten, maybe nine, but that was a guess. The guess stuck in his mind because he recalled a snapshot taken by his father, a picture of Mickey standing behind a bench on which his sister sat, in a park somewhere in the city. He wasn't very tall; the top rail of the bench back was only a little below his chest. He wore a dark-colored double-breasted suit coat—only the top part showed in the photograph—but he remembered that he had worn knickers—knickerbockers; to his mind they were still really only short pants, except they were fastened about the legs, below the knees, just above his calves; and he had had on black stockings and black shoes.

"Stand up straight!" his father ordered. "C'mon—more! MORE I said!" Mickey sucked in a breath, then another breath, pushed his shoulders up, and stood on his toes, struggling to be a half inch taller.

If you saw the snapshot you would say, "Look at that hair!" It was as blonde as it can be, practically white, just like Jean Harlow's—a towhead; combed straight back from his forehead, all the way back to the nape of the neck, plastered down flat.

Every time he went anywhere with his father he had to first go to a sink, wet his hair thoroughly, and keep running a comb straight back, over and over, until it laid suitably flat and slick. Occasionally, for longer-lasting effect, his father liberally doused oily Vaseline hair tonic on Mickey's head, massaging it into the wispy hair, working it harshly into the scalp, too.

For Mickey, his father's determined program of making certain hair was trained properly was worst at night. Then he had to suffer what he felt was terrible humiliation—wearing a homemade stocking cap. He hated his father's method to shape and tend hair. "It's the best way," the man often repeated. "Hell, I do it too! I don't know why you have to have such a fit about it." But while the small boy suffered shameful humiliation, hoping no one would ever see him—flaring at his sister with a furious rage when she laughed at him—his father seemed to think nothing of appearing before neighbors and friends with the hideous thing covering his own head, inside their own rooms or elsewhere in the building, or sitting on a stoop, or walking up and down the street.

Mickey felt he looked ridiculous the first time he had to pull on a hated stocking cap when he got ready for bed; a cap made of a discarded woman's silk stocking! He vainly argued with his father about wearing the cap that night, and cried softly in the darkness. When he thought his father had gone to sleep he pulled the terrible thing off, but his father seemed to sense the rebellious act. At almost the same time, the man threw open the door, yanking the pullcord of the wall lamp by the door, snarling, "You put that back on!" when he saw Mickey's uncovered head. Each night when his father was home at Mickey's bedtime, Mickey had to present himself in underwear and detested stocking cap for inspection, usually closed with "Keep that thing on!" or something similar, said with dire overtones. He would make himself go to sleep, worried about a sudden door opening and flood of light. He could not forget how quickly his father had appeared the first time the stocking cap came off in rebellion. Twice afterward, when his father was away working at bedtime, Mickey did not put the cap on when he went to bed, despite his sister's warnings and promises to snitch on him. Each time he was roughly awakened when his father angrily shook him from sound sleep to make him pull the cap onto his head. The first time Mickey claimed forgetfulness. The second time he said the cap must have come off when he moved about in his sleep. His father raged, "Do you think I don't know all the excuses? If I find you in bed again without it on, you'll see how angry I can really get! Understand?" Mickey felt even worse when he heard his sister snickering in their small bed when the light was turned off and the door was closed.

It was unbearable humiliation! Wearing something that had once been hidden high up inside a woman's dress—the part of a stocking that was far above a woman's knee. The part that was so close to—Mickey shuddered the first time he thought of it—*privates*!

Privates mystified Mickey. *What a funny word for that!* He wondered why everyone acted so strangely about something used for going to the bathroom, for letting water come out, for peeing. It was hard to understand why, when he asked his father a curiosity question, he was told "I'll talk to you soon"; "Some other time—not right now"; things like that.

But, once, he had seen his aunt's magazine in her knitting bag while she was in the kitchen. Quickly riffling through the shiny pages of stories and photographs, feeling guilty, feeling he should not be looking at the magazine without permission, he had seen scattered advertising illustrations of women in underwear and stockings, the long hosiery somehow fastened to underwear with long straps. The stocking tops were way up on each leg, up near *privates. That* was the part of a used, discarded stocking that was on his head for many nights.

When he had peeked through the magazine Mickey had not given more than a small boy's passing thoughts to the women's pictures. After all, he always saw his sister in her nightgown when they went to bed and knew she wore underwear beneath it. And he knew women wore stockings. The magazine only showed the stockings to be longer than he *thought* they were, going *higher* on a woman's leg than he had thought.

But with the edict about the nightcap, with recollection of the magazine, knowing that *discards* turned into caps, Mickey felt disturbed.

His father stretched out a brown, seamed silk stocking and used a pair of scissors to make a cut about six inches below the stocking top. He formed an overhand knot at the cut end, and swiftly there was a cap for nighttime. "There," he said, "how's that for a fast job? That'll make your hair grow right—nice and straight—even while you're sleeping." Mickey often wondered why his father wore one himself on many occasions because his black hair usually looked as though it was freshly and slickly combed. He, as he imposed on his son, combed his hair straight back from the brow, in a pompadour. But he would have that funny-looking get-up on his head more often than Mickey wanted to see it. He could not understand how his father could ignore its presence, but the boy never heard any visitors ask about it or joke about it. His father and they did not feel the same about a piece of a woman's stocking, Mickey decided.

Another thing that bothered Mickey about the stocking cap—what bothered him the most, what made him embarrassed, angry—was that the only others he saw wearing them were colored people. But their stocking caps usually matched their complexions, so that was sort of all right, as far as Mickey was concerned. Besides, so *many* colored boys and men wore them. He was sure they were not ever embarrassed. But with Mickey, he raged in his mind, it was *different,* it *ought* to be different. *He* should not have to wear one. It was being the only white kid he knew of who ever wore such a cap that bothered him. None of his friends had to use one, unless they were as secretive about it as Mickey had become. His father had said it was the best way to train hair—it was the way *his* hair was trained when *he* was a kid on the farm—but mercifully he only made his son wear it to bed. Remembering his father's unembarrassed appearances in front of others, Mickey had schemed many ploys for the time he might be ordered to have the despised article covering his head in the daytime, in front of other people, especially kids he knew. But his father spared him. "Nighttime's enough to suit me. That'll make your hair grow straight and neat."

His sister's laughter would infuriate Mickey when they would go to bed and his cap would have to be worn. However, though a year younger, she was sibling-wise about her taunting. She did not do it in their father's presence at bedtime. She giggled when they were in bed, and Mickey would curl his fingers tightly into small fists to control his anger, then put them behind his back. To ignore her he would turn his back to her in the narrow folding bed in which they both slept. But the narrowness left no space in which to get away from his demon. She would giggle at him loudly enough for Mickey to hear, softly enough so their father would not detect her spitefulness.

Sometimes Mickey would strike back by reaching under the bedcovers and pinch whatever part of her he could blindly find. She countered by turning onto her side and facing his tense back, worsening things for him. Not only could she combat probing fingers with defending arms and hands and fingernails, but her giggles became thunderous and screeching to Mickey. In her new position, sounds that had been muffled in a pillow and under a blanket now had the infuriating effect of being channeled directly at him. Giggling that before had filtered through an assortment of soundproofing bed fabrics now pierced his mind from only inches away.

One of Mickey's efforts to keep from pummeling her, getting into further trouble, was to roll onto his back, arms beneath him, clenched fists under his buttocks. He would press his body into the lumpy mattress, to use all his weight to pinion his own arms, to keep from violently smashing at her. But that would put his ear closer to her. She would often soften her giggle so their father would not sense that she was still lingering in wakefulness instead of falling asleep. But her taunting would not seem to soften to her brother. Mickey would get madder because she could so easily outwit him, get him mad, get him furious—doing so with so little effort.

Sometimes she would add to her torture: "Pickaninny! Pickaninny! You're a pickaninny!" That minstrel-show image flashing in his brain triggered such anger that he would unleash himself at her, unmindful of consequence. She would react in feigned surprise and indignation, and her piercing scream would have their father at bedside in short bounds. Mickey withstood many brutal shakings because of her scheming—and endured stinging cuffs to his head, arms, backside, legs, all over his body.

"Leave her alone and let her go to sleep, DAMN IT!"

Mickey sobbed himself to sleep many nights, gasping; convulsing to get air that would let him breathe again. Then he could go to sleep.

But he got even with her. He called her Maggie!

"Maggie—Maggie!"

"MAGGIE—MAGGIE!"

"M-A-G-G-I-E!"

"MAAAGGGGIIIEEEEE!"

Because she did not like it. But he only did his vengeful name-calling when their father was not near.

In the behind-the-bench snapshot both children peered intently into the lens of their father's Brownie box camera. Neither liked getting dressed fancily for picture-taking; Mickey putting on a knickerbocker dark suit, reddish argyle stockings, and worn black shoes he had to shine industriously before lacing them on; his sister putting on a white, belted dress with puffed sleeves that came halfway down her upper arms. "I hate it!" she snapped under her breath. In that picture her straight brown hair, as she always wore it when they were smaller, was cut evenly so that from one cheek on around behind her head to her other cheek every strand was the same length, draped to just beneath her earlobes. A horizontal line across her forehead formed bangs. If she did not scowl in that picture she would have been prettier. And Mickey would have looked better, too, if he had not scowled. But their father, an avid, self-taught amateur photographer, could only afford an inexpensive rudimentary boxy device made by Eastman Kodak. And the best way to take a decent picture was to brightly light the subject. His instructions to the small subjects behind the bench were to face the sun and look into the camera. He moved the camera back and forth and up and down trying to position figures in the small reverse-magnification glass viewfinder that miniaturized the subjects, while with curled hand he tried to shield the viewer from the bright sunlight. The children's eyelids narrowed against the offending light, eyebrows drawn tightly together, chins against chests, tipping heads downward slightly to ward off brilliant light. When he felt he was ready in the viewfinder he gave a final look at his offspring to see if they were doing as told. He saw pinched-vees between eyebrows, wrinkled noses, distorted mouths; and his rage rose.

"He did something to me—an' it hurts!" his sister blurted venomously.

"I didn't!"

"You did! You hurt me! You made me frown on purpose!"

Before the angry father had taken two long, quick steps, she cried out: "I didn't want to yell 'n' get in trouble—I want a good picture to show everyone—if he'd stop doing things to me—can't you make him stop doing nasty things to me?"

The compact, strong man shook his son violently by a shoulder. "Shape up—and set a good example for her—AND I'M NOT GOING TO TELL YOU AGAIN!"

Mickey measured the moment. He hissed a sharply whispered "MAGGIE!" as their father walked away to get them in the viewfinder again. It superbly agitated her and she attempted to pinch him at a thin place in his clothing. Being a year older and being a boy gave him strength to fight her off. But she knew she had an advantage. Theirs was a battle of timing strikes and parries to have the other make the mistake of moving at the instant the photographer would turn and catch the violation. Mickey's disadvantage was being the year older, with the burden of being ordered to set proper example. She had the keener sense of timing in this sort of conflict and when Mickey was yelled at—"THIS IS THE LAST DAMN TIME I'M TELLING YOU!"—she knew they were all at the brink, that she had won; now it was time to have the picture taken.

That was the picture of the two of them that Mickey remembered best. There were many more because their father was so avid in his photography, and Mickey could easily remember other picture-taking sessions and ordeals in other parks, on front stoops of several tenements in which they lived, with other people besides Margaret. But recollection of whatever became of his father's several photo albums had long since gone.

His father's interest in photography went past simply taking pictures. Some places they lived had the bathroom soon converted into a part-time basic darkroom. Up would go a curtain rod on the top of the door frame inside a small bathroom and a long sheet or blanket would be draped over it to keep light from leaking in through tiny crevices around the closed door. And he would keep a red light bulb in a water glass on a shelf in the medicine cabinet, ready for exchanging with the white sixty-watt bulb in the socket the rest of the time.

*   *   *

Maggie was really Margaret—on her birth certificate, and as their father called her by name. But she liked to be called Peggy. She did not object to Peg occasionally, particularly if said by a close friend, but it was Peggy she preferred. Mickey never knew why she wanted that name, and she would never explain, even when he asked. There were no celebrities of the time with that name; but she threatened repeatedly that as far as *he* was concerned, he was simply to accept that *Peggy* was what she wanted to be called, and he WOULD call her that! But Mickey resisted. He saved the infuriating *Maggie* as his ultimate weapon against her, but he would not submit to the *Peggy* she craved. *Margaret* would be the best he would give her, if he called her by that name at all. *I'll show her,* he thought each time they shouted at each other about her name.

Feelings between them—never really bad, never really good—might have been better if he had done what she wanted about her name, because with others he called them by what they wanted to be known. Mickey often wondered if he could have kept out of trouble with her and away from confrontations with their father if he gave in to her will about her name choice. *But then she'd find some other way to keep me in Dutch with him, to keep on bein' his favorite. An' she's a girl an' I'm a boy, an' she's younger, an' I'm s'posed to be an example all the time—and I can't win against all that!*

*   *   *

The tighter Mickey gripped Margaret's hand the more she resisted his admonition to do as he ordered. She did not like going to church. Neither did she like getting dressed so fancily just to go to church. But Aunt Ellen said all other little girls her age liked getting dressed up and she did not understand Margaret disliking to do so. She told that to Margaret over and over as she stubbornly dressed the stubborn child. Ill-humoredly Margaret gave in to insistent persuasion and greater female will, submitting to fresh underclothes, a knee-length pinkish-colored dress, black patent leather shoes, calf-high white cotton stockings, and a barrette pulling her dark brown hair to one side as a change from the bangs she always wore draped over her brow.

They were going to be late for Sunday school if they did not hurry. Mickey knew it and kept telling her so. His walk became faster and he tugged vigorously at Margaret's arm to make her keep pace. But she took out her bad mood on him. She told herself that he had had nothing to do with making her get up early nor with getting dressed in dressy clothes, but *she* could do something about being on time for church, just the same! She would show them! She would get even with *someone!* She held back and would not walk faster. She pouted and shouted that he was hurting her arm, that he was making her trip and almost fall down, that it would be his fault her new shoes would be ruined, but Mickey persisted in trying to be prompt for Sunday school. His father might somehow, Mickey thought, find out they were late and he'd be in for it again. He fumed over how his father always seemed to learn things that led to Mickey being yelled at, that led to punishment. He kept tugging at his sister with determination. *She ain't gettin' me in trouble this time!*

The four-block walk north on Broadway took longer than usual but the strength of his grip kept Margaret from pulling free to peer into the magic worlds of store windows along their route. At Eighty-Sixth Street the light was still green for them to cross that wide street to the far side. From there they would make a left turn, go down the steep grade for one block, be at Sunday school on time. As they stepped off the curb, the yellow caution light blinked on, but, Mickey calculated, looking about at standing and moving traffic, they could easily make it to the other side. He pulled angrily at Margaret. She fought, then acceded. They dashed across the wide four-lane street.

"Oh, G-E-E-Z!" she screamed.

Like a gigantic Times Square billboard sign of thousands of light bulbs flashing at incredibly fast intervals, a warning exploded in Mickey's consciousness as they darted headlong ahead—then he shouted what he saw: "THE LIGHT'S RED!"

In confidence, sure that she would move easily with him, Mickey had relaxed his strong grip on Margaret as they scurried for the opposite sidewalk. The red light made Margaret suddenly pull her hand loose from his as he charged from an easy run into an anxious lunge for the curb. He was stunned when he realized she was not running with him.

Everything in those moments took place with extraordinary slowness, a sensation Mickey had never had. Margaret darted alongside him momentarily, then spun away. Helplessly he watched the skirt of her dress fly wildly in a spin, body angling sharply away, slippery-soled shoes hammering furiously at the black asphalt pavement trying to grip the oily surface. Her roller-skating balancing skills welled up and before her hands touched the pavement, she started her recovery from the abrupt, dizzying turn. Now she faced back from where they had started. Without a chance to react, Mickey watched her blindly run to the distant sidewalk they had left. She was looking over her shoulder toward him. In her extraordinary fear she did not seem to understand what was happening. Her eyes frantically searched Mickey's, questioning why he was *standing* as she was running.

"MARGARET! LOOK OUT!" Mickey implored—a loud, anguished, forlorn scream she did not hear.

She did not see the front of the taxicab plunge quickly downward, only feet away, as the driver jammed the brake pedal as far to the cab floor as leg strength would let him. Margaret saw none of the cab, even as it lifted her from the ground. It did not hit her with severe impact, but forcefully enough to lift, twist, and spin her in the air. The back of her head struck the car and she was instantly unconscious. Mickey, tears burning his eyes, watched her flip about, legs flailing up, watched her slow-motion arc above the hood, her brief contact where the hood joined the windshield, saw her slide from the hood to the pavement alongside the driver's door. Mickey could not move, his fear was so great.

People were running to Margaret as he stood, pushing Mickey aside as they hurried. He lost sight of the cab in the rush of people as the driver opened the door, looking down, an expression of terrible pain on his face. Mickey could hear shouting but he could not understand words. "What should I do?" he cried out in terror, pushing through the crowd surrounding the cab. Tears kept welling in his eyes, burning his vision, sliding down his cheeks. He tore at arms and legs, at trousers and skirts, at anything in his way. He sobbed at people's backs pounding at the backs and legs and arms. "I *hafta* get through!—she's my *sister!*

*   *   *

"JESUS CHRIST! SHE COULD HAVE BEEN KILLED! HOW COULD YOU LET THIS HAPPEN? DIDN'T I TELL YOU—" was all Mickey heard, it seemed for the hundredth or thousandth time, before he closed off listening anymore. He cringed in a corner of the Schulte cigar store near the street intersection. He screamed, "Isn' anyone gonna let me alone? It wasn' my fault! She pulled away before I could do anythin'. Don' anyone believe me? You don' know what she did! Lemme alone!—please—PLEASE!"

His father walked from him to where Margaret lay on the glass-top cigar counter, with someone's thick sweater rolled into a pillow under her head. Aunt Ellen took her arm from about Mickey's shoulder. "I'll talk to him. I'll get him to stop."

Someone in the crowd had been able to get their names just after the accident. Margaret moaned and tried to move in her unconsciousness and Mickey was told she was not seriously hurt, that it looked like something was wrong with her shoulder. Then a policeman said it was okay to move her from the street so traffic could move and so an ambulance could get through. When Mickey told the policeman they did not have a telephone at home, the officer drove off to the family's basement rooms with a spectator who offered him a ride. Mickey wished, at the moment the officer said he would go get someone from home, that he had not said a word about no phone, that he should have said he did not remember the number, or that no one was home; or something else—*anything!* He was terrified by the thought of seeing his father. "Don' let him hit me!" he sobbed.

In none of the ensuing days was Mickey struck as punishment for Margaret's broken collarbone. He was sure it was only because Aunt Ellen would not allow it, that his father heeded her this once. But Mickey was punished. Margaret was the center of attraction for visitors, and Mickey felt he was pointed out accusingly to each visitor—"AN ACCIDENT THAT COULD HAVE BEEN AVOIDED—SHOULD HAVE BEEN—AVOIDED—DAMN IT!" The torturous accusations would never stop, it seemed to Mickey. He prayed for his father to leave for work each day, prayed he would be late each night, prayed Aunt Ellen would always be at hand when his father was home.

One afternoon Margaret said to Mickey that she had told their father the accident really was not her brother's fault. "I told him I got scared when I saw the light turn from yellow to red—that you didn't have a chance at all to keep me from doing what I did." But Mickey did not believe her. Then he did believe her. He vacillated between belief and disbelief over several days. He warned himself, *That's not the way things are between us. Why would she tell me that?* He thought that again and again, sibling-suspicious.

Days later his father railed: "THIS IS THE LAST DAMN TIME I'M
GOING TO SAY ANYTHING ABOUT THIS! BUT JUST MAKE DAMN
SURE YOU WATCH YOUR SISTER BETTER FROM HERE ON!"

Mickey, struggling to keep his face expressionless, looked at his father across
the small table, fearing that something would excite the angry man further. Aunt
Ellen and Margaret moved food with their forks from one place to another on
their plates.

Mickey sat at the table wordlessly when he had been summoned from outside
for supper. He could not remember anything of the little that had been said since
the meal began. He had no idea how the subject of the accident had been brought
up as they ate. He abruptly was aware that his father had raised his voice and
harshly made what he said would be his final say on the matter.

His father kept glaring. Mickey wanted to scream at him, but only returned
his ominous look with a vacant-eyed stare, desperately striving, without
whimpering, for an appearance of utter subservience. Mickey knew that was all
that would appease his father. He could see his father's thin lips purse tightly into
a thin angry line, could see the flesh covering his jawbones rippling as he clenched
his teeth rapidly.

His father looked down at his own meal, then noisily attacked a thin piece of
meat with knife and fork slashing and clattering together and against the plate.

Mickey worried, however. *He still don' b'lieve me—I'm sure o' that—or b'lieve
Margaret, if she tol' him, like she said she did—I'm sure o' that too. He never said he
was sorry for accusin' me.*

But, after that, Mickey was left alone by his father about the accident.

3

That kid—the red-head. What the hell was his name? The one with the sister —

Buddy?

I think so. Yeah—Buddy. And her name was Patty.

Poor Patty. I wonder what ever became of her?

4

Buddy Casey whispered in Mickey's ear, "I'll make my sister Patty show you hers if you'll show her yours."

"My *what?*" Mickey asked, and Buddy answered, "You know—" smiling an odd smile Mickey was sure hinted at something wicked. He was afraid he would be in for trouble, knowing Buddy. But he did not want Buddy to think his offer was not really understood—it was not—so he arranged to meet him late in the afternoon over near P.S. 81; still in their neighborhood, but several blocks from where the three lived.

Mickey saw no sign of Buddy or Patty when he got to the meeting place on time. For some minutes he sauntered along the sidewalk, past several tenements on each side of the designated number. Then he spotted Buddy peering from an alley between two of the several-story apartment buildings, beckoning Mickey toward the alley. Walking hesitantly to him, Mickey heard calling in a hushed voice: "Hurry up! C'mon!"

Buddy shushed him each time Mickey asked where Patty was, leading him into a long, narrow space. In another fifteen minutes the sun would go down beyond the Hudson River and darkness would relentlessly and quickly chase light from the streets; even more quickly from between-building alleys that gave access from streets to high-fenced backyards. It was as dim as a coal cellar in the high-walled passageway. Ahead, something seemed to be blocking the alley, but Buddy hurriedly led Mickey on.

Mickey thought: *If I didn't know this red-headed bastard as well as I do I'd be nervous enough to shit my pants—being in a place like this—and almost dark!* Something was slanted across their path. He slowly recognized it as a long, broad, battered metal cement-mixing trough, standing on a long edge, tipped into the corner formed by a building wall and the alley floor; the upper edge resting against a second building, creating a lean-to more than six feet long.

He swore at Buddy: "What the Christ is goin' on?" Buddy shushed him again and knelt down, peering beneath the lean-to, motioning Mickey to do the same. Over his thin friend's shoulder Mickey glimpsed ten-year-old Patty seated on the ground, leaning her back against the brick wall, knees drawn to her chin, hands at her sides. Buddy slid aside, turning to Mickey. "Go ahead, get in there with her. It's OK, she wants you to—go on."

"Why should I?" Mickey refused.

"You made a promise," Buddy snarled, "and you better fuckin'-A keep it!"

"I don' know what you're talkin' about—an' you better tell me—quick—or I'm gettin' outta here!"

Buddy insisted and Mickey resisted. Persistently, in hurried, hushed tones, Buddy argued, "You gotta keep your word! I promised Patty candy an' some money to get her out here—an' you ain't gettin' me in Dutch. Nobody else acted the way you're doin'."

Buddy berated his sister, "What are you waitin' for?" then ordered, "Mickey, jus' wait a second!" He punched her shoulder and her face scowled with pain. A second, harder punch brought tears to her eyes, visible in the shadows and growing dimness. His whisper became harsher. *"Go ahead,* I said!" He looked at Mickey and watched his face steadily.

Patty bent her head down, hiding her eyes. She raised her hand holding the skirt about her ankles, lifting the dress slowly toward her tightly pressed knees.

Mickey was puzzled. *Jesus! What's she doin'?*

He glanced curiously at Buddy, staring intently at Mickey's face from within the deep shadow of the lean-to. Without looking at his sister, Buddy snarled in a whisper, "Get goin', Patty—I told you!" Seeing no reaction by Mickey to his sister's movements, he yelled hoarsely, still looking at Mickey, "GET GOIN'!" His voice rose uncontrollably. "You know what you're supposed to do!" He gave her another powerful shoulder punch. Anger flared in her downcast eyes. She slowly let her hand slide back down to her ankles, easing the skirt over her shoes to the ground.

Buddy turned to look at her, then thumped her shoulder again, viciously, without saying a word. Patty closed her eyelids, squeezing tears onto her cheeks, both lips between her teeth, biting hard. Her hand rose to her knees, lifting the dress. Buddy whispered hoarsely, "Do it, dammit!" She lifted her dress higher above her pressed-together knees, letting it go to drop down her thighs to her stomach. "Hurry up!" Buddy growled. "Slide your fanny down so he can see better—an' turn aroun' some more. Get away from the damn wall!" She twisted toward Mickey, shuffling her spread feet to point to him, her knees still pressed together, her arms behind, weight on hands pressed to the dirty cement. She lowered her chin and Mickey could no longer see glistening drops on her cheeks. Hesitantly, an inch at first, then two inches, another inch, a half-inch, two inches, starting to bring her knees together again, then afraid of another punch, a worse punch, she spread her knees apart, until each was beyond the width of her shoulders.

Mickey stared in amazement and disbelief at the crotch formed by her thighs and hips. "She ain' got no dick!" he blurted. In the fast-enveloping shadows he stared harder to be certain of what he saw, of what he did not see. Reluctantly, mistrusting, he leaned forward for a disbelieving closer examination. "Jesus Christ, I'm right!" Mickey said softly, more to himself, shocked at his discovery. "She *don't* have a prick!"

"Hurry up!" Buddy insisted. "Show her yours!" But staring intently at the small, smooth, puffy mounds of flesh with thin vertical lines, Mickey's astonishment numbed his mind and reactions.

"Jesus, she's got no dick?" he asked aloud, unsure.

Mickey had known there was a difference between boys and girls, differences in the way they looked and felt to the touch, ways they dressed, ways they were treated by adults, games they played, their toys, amenities accorded them. He had always known these and other differences, coming to accept such differences. It made no matter to him that he did not understand the reasons. But never before this stunning moment had he realized, fully, that a penis was one of the differences. Girls looked different with their pretty faces, clothes, and hair that was *supposed* to be let grown long. And they played with dolls, acting like mothers and aunts with them. They were allowed privileges boys were not. And boys were not supposed to hit them or yell at them. The boys would not let them play stickball with them, even if now and then a girl wanted to, and no girls could join secret clubs. They were told not to go to rough, dangerous places boys went; and boys would not let them, even when some of them pleaded. Girls and women had large soft chests—"They got tits," older boys told younger kids, who, despite that explanation, did not really understand what the older boys meant. "And they got something else we ain't got," older boys said, not saying exactly what. "But you'll find out—someday! And, boy—then—look out!"

But this? Mickey pondered. *Jesus!*

Buddy's voice was frantic, demanding. "You hafta show her yours now, ya sonofabitch! C'mon—sonofabitch!"

Mickey could not understand the sudden warmth that flushed his mind, then surged through his body. He pressed doubled fists into his groin, trying to suppress his swelling and stiffening penis. Mickey worried. *What's happenin' to me?*

Just 'cuz o' what she's doin'? he fretted.

Mickey had had erections many times, with no idea as to why, and made himself accept what he steadfastly thought was simply one more problem he had to suffer—like the nosebleeds. But he kept this problem a secret. It was a problem with which he would have to cope. Alone. There was not any help.

But recently, offhandedly, in hushed lurid talks, when there was little else to do or talk about, he learned friends had also experienced the same phenomenon, that each had also at first kept it to himself, afraid, desperate. One boy said "hard on," and another boasted, "You guys shoulda seen the one I had the other night! It would not go away! It was like *this!*"—gesturing with his right arm, upper arm tightly pressed to his side, rigid forearm and white-knuckled fist angularly pointing upward and out from his body. He smiled. "But I got rid of it!" he said triumphantly. Some boys snickered. Mickey knew they understood what had been said, and *unsaid,* though he did not.

He enjoyed the sensation of the erection, and other curious sensations in his body; and the strange wandering, wondering thoughts; the heated flush that spread over him.

He became more at ease with his unpredictable physical predicament. But he still felt it was an inexplicable shame, *his* shame, his alone. He did not think there was anyone his own age, or even a little older—never mind someone close to being a grown-up—who could give him answers, who could help in any way. He certainly did not want to reveal the plight to his father, who could not be of much help, Mickey was sure. And Aunt Ellen, nice as she was, who always helped, could not have answers, he argued to himself—even if he could bring himself to approach her. So why bother? He persistently wondered: *Why do I hafta go through such a thing?*

The sight of Patty's curious-looking fleshiness agitated Mickey. He almost said aloud, *That's why they say girls got a gash!*

"Jesus, will you hurry up!" Buddy berated Mickey, who did not know what to do, his mind whirring, his body reacting to primal feelings he did not understand. Patty sobbed convulsively, softly, her face turned away from Mickey. Mickey glanced at Buddy, then felt Buddy's hard punch to his left shoulder, sharply hurting his collarbone. As he kept kneeling, he straightened his back, rearing away from the frightened girl. He understood what Buddy wanted. Staring at Patty's crotch, his hand moved to unbutton the fly front of his knickers. *He wants me to show her my dick.* Flustered, he glanced at Buddy, eyes following Mickey's hand movement.

Mickey's penis was sore from the sudden engorgement, quicker than it had ever happened before, sore from the confinement by underwear and knickers. Fascinated by Patty's crotch, by absence of a penis, he was puzzled. *How could it be?*

His glances jumped between Patty, sobbing, and Buddy, eagerly watching as Mickey's hand worked into his knickers. Mickey felt for the opening in his undershorts, grasping his penis that was reacting to new sensations. Patty's sobs were louder, Buddy's hoarse whispering more insistent. "C'mon, ya sonofabitch, you promised!"

Is that what Margaret looked like? Mickey thought. *It must be! She's a girl— and about as old as Patty.* He had seen his sister in her underwear many times, ever since he could remember, but he had never seen her naked. He could never go into the bathroom when she was in it, his father ordered, and always had to have on a bathrobe or pants of some kind in her presence. His father sternly warned him, without explanation, that he was always to have clothes on if Margaret was home. Mickey wondered about the fuss his father made, but gave little thought to what had an overtone of a threat. Even if he had not warned him, Mickey would have worn something anyway. He was so uncertain about his penis that he never wanted Margaret asking questions if he was uncontrollably stricken by his problem.

Buddy did not whisper again. He yelled hoarsely: "Do what you said you'd do—better keep your promise—punk yellow cheatin' sonofabitch!"

Mickey sprang to his feet, pulling his hand out of his knickers. Stunned, Buddy glared up at him from his squat. An enormous sympathy for the beleaguered, crying Patty had come over Mickey. He was worried about why he had a sudden erection merely at the sight of Patty's whatever-it-was, astounded that she had no penis herself, as he did. A surprising thought struck him: *How does she piss?*

But her tears affected him most. He was angry at Buddy for his viciousness with his sister. Mickey's punches at his own sister were just in defense if she lashed at him or in revenge if he was sure, or suspected, he had been the victim of her deviousness. But he had never hit her for something like this, just to make her do something she did not want to do, something that suddenly seemed *nasty.* Mickey's uncertainty was increasing. *How can Buddy make her do somethin' wrong?* But Mickey was unsure of what made him feel it was wrong.

He fumbled at his fly buttons as his penis became flaccid more quickly than it had become engorged. He was terrified of what might happen if they were caught, unlikely as it was in the deep, narrow alley; Patty sheltered by the cement-mixing trough, the setting shrouded in the last vestiges of dusk.

He had only fastened two buttons at the front of his knickers when he spun about and blindly ran the length of the alley, stopping to look back only when the alley joined the sidewalk. There was blackness behind him. He could not see the tilted trough or the figures of Buddy and Patty.

He walked along the sidewalk, puzzled, worried, wondering what to do next, where to go, what he should do about what had just happened. He silently questioned himself, arguing his position in this dread situation. *Wha' could I do? For Christ's sake, I didn' have nothin' to do with getting her there. What do I have to be scared about? But who's gonna believe me?* As he wandered, he decided the only place to go was where he lived.

He planned and worried about being at home. *I'll just go in like nothin' happened and nobody will say anythin'. How will they know?—I'll bet Margaret will know. Oh, Jesus—and if SHE knows then HE'LL know! Jesus Christ! What am I gonna do? That fuckin' Buddy!*

No one was in the basement apartment's small rooms. When his father came in, Mickey was sprawled on the sagging, threadbare couch. He had relaxed, occasionally dozing, otherwise reading and rereading a coverless, torn-page comic book, half listening to the radio blare serial adventures of *Renfrew of the Royal Mounted* and *Jack Armstrong.*

"Comic books and laying down," his father muttered, passing through the dim front room, past the table with four unmatched chairs, one on each side, grouped in a corner near the kitchenette area with a gas stove, icebox, and a large white double-door metal storage cabinet, all of this really in the front room too.

"You'd better have your homework done!" he growled, facing the boy in a hostile, hulking pose. "HAVE you got it done?"

Mickey—Buddy and Patty nearly gone from his mind—sprang upright, twisting to put his stockinged feet on the linoleum floor. "Yes—sir; yessir, I do. It's all done. There wasn't much." He hoped he would not be asked to show it. There was always that fifty-fifty chance. *He'll whale the shit outta me again for not havin' it all finished.*

His father opened the icebox. "Did you empty the water out of this thing like you're supposed to?" Mickey answered yes quickly. His father took out butcher-paper-wrapped packages, slamming the thick, oak-wood icebox door with a knee, roughly jerked open a door of the metal storage cabinet that served as a pantry, pulled out a half loaf of white bread with the opened end of the waxpaper wrapping twisted and tied with a rubber band, slammed the door shut with a knee thrust, and started making sandwiches on the small linoleum-covered counter next to the sink.

When Margaret got there she was as brusque as usual with Mickey and only talked with her father. Mickey did not care this time, as long as she did not *find out!* He carefully avoided looking at her. He worried that he would be caught looking at where her privates were, worried that heated blushing would brighten his face unexplainably. He worried about having an erection that would show—not just the pulsations that sometimes happened quickly, receding just as quickly—but an erection that would not be missed being seen if it happened at the time his father might order him to get more milk from the icebox or do some other midmeal chore—an erection that could not be dismissed simply by willing it away. All because—dammit—he could not rid himself from flashing images of Patty or her curious-looking slitted, puffy folds of pink flesh where he had expected something different. He was uncertain as to what to expect anymore, about anything.

He was glad he and his sister were not allowed to talk at any meal-time, unless spoken to. Now he could not make any mistakes or say anything so either of *them* could figure out things for themselves. He avoided meeting her eyes throughout the meal. And he did not sense that she looked at him suspiciously, that she *stared* at him. *Good, she don't know!*

The boy and girl busied themselves at opposite places of the front room as their father spread out on the couch, read a newspaper, listened to the radio playing hillbilly music, now and then dozing and snoring.

Mickey was satisfied when they were sent to bed early because their father wanted to go to bed early. His ordeal was over.

5

What a dirty little bastard that Buddy was! I'll bet there are more guys like him. Damn!

And I guess I'll run into them wherever I'm going from here. Maybe they won't be showing off their sister's privates, but they'll be dirty bastards just the same!

Too bad Buddy wasn't like that Cartwright kid.

6

"Get off your behind. You're going with me."

"Where?" Mickey said, looking to the kitchenette table where his father sat, just arrived home from work, rustling through the *Daily News*, quickly flipping pages, looking for something specific. With no answer, Mickey hesitantly inquired again. "Where we goin' tonight?"

The newspaper rustled more noisily and Mickey decided he had better get to his feet quickly. He crossed the room past his father holding the tabloid high in front of him, sorting pages. Mickey went into the tiny, crowded bathroom, barely roomy enough for an undersized tub, a discolored commode with a cracked-paint seat without a cover—only its rusted fittings remained—and a small, once-white sink standing on two iron-pipe legs. The sink's porcelain glaze was crazed into patches of tiny patterns of brownish lines that made the sink yellowish and dingy.

The smallness of the cubicle—it was hardly more than that—caused the door to be hung so it opened outward rather than into the bathroom where there would have been no space for it to swing back and forth. He turned the HOT faucet on and let the water run, hoping for it to at least be lukewarm, but only cold water poured out, getting colder as it ran. Mickey leaned down, his face nearly into the bowl, and splashed cupped, double-hand pools of water quickly up onto his face, flinching and grunting at the chilliness, rubbing both cold hands on the back of his neck, huffing and whooshing at the shock to his skin. Twice more he quickly did the same freshening routine, trying to wake himself from the drowsiness that had engulfed him until his father spoke. He ran wet hands through tousled hair, hastily swiping at his face and neck lightly with a thin hand towel that had little absorptive pile left, leaving glistening wet stripes on his skin.

He used a snaggle-toothed black comb from a back knickers pocket to untangle his blond hair and pull it from brow to the back of his head. He was thankful that his father was satisfied Mickey's hair was sufficiently trained that he no longer had to wear a nighttime stocking cap. He pulled at the chain of the ceiling fixture, turning off the light he had left burning since getting home from school, relieved that his father had not discovered the infraction. He stood outside the bathroom, looking at the man, who had spread the paper on the table and was filling in small squares of a crossword puzzle. "Do I have to change?" Mickey said.

"Yes, you do," his father said, not looking up from the crossword. "Put on your long pants, the dark blue ones—and get a clean shirt—one that matches. "You're not color-blind, so do it right!"

Mickey smiled when he heard *long pants*. He was tired of wearing knickers when other kids were wearing trousers all the time now. He and two others were the only thirteen-year-olds still wearing knickers after school. But his father said he could only afford a blue pair and a brown pair of long pants and they would only be worn to school and to church and when they visited certain people. The rest of the time it was to be knickers. "You're not the one who has to come up with the money for new ones if what you've got gets torn," his father sternly pronounced. He warned further, "God help you if I find either pair ripped or even torn a little bit after school. That means no rough-housing when you've got them on—and I don't want to hear any song-and-dance stories about something being *somebody else's* fault. You just stay out of trouble and get away from any rough-house stuff if it gets started. You hear me?"

Mickey answered the way he had to and was lucky on the two occasions he neglected the promise—once in a fast, broad-ranging game of tag in the schoolyard; once in a stickball game two streets over from where he lived. The trousers remained undamaged both time, only getting a little dirtier a little quicker.

Mickey rummaged through the cabinet—a chiffrobe his father called it—near the bed and found the trousers on a pants-hanger, dangling from the cuffs. He took a light-blue checkered shirt off a hanger and got clean black socks from a chest of drawers next to the chiffrobe and found shined black shoes under the chest of drawers. He said, "Is she goin' with us, too?"

"Your sister's name is *Margaret,* not *she;* and you *call* her Margaret, not *she*— and no, she's not going. She's staying at her girlfriend's place. *I* know where she is and what she's up to. Just get *yourself* ready and don't worry about anyone or anything else!"

On the subway south Mickey still did not know where they were going. Then they transferred to a cross-town line, and transferred again to a northbound express. After a half dozen stops, with long, hurtling rides between, they changed to a local train that made another several stops. On the northbound express Mickey guessed at where they were bound. "We goin' to the Cartwrights?" he said. His father, rereading the newspaper he had folded and thrust into a suitcoat pocket as they left home, grunted, "Uh, huh," not looking away from the paper. After a pause he added a trace of sarcasm. "OK?"

Walter Cartwright was a colored boy, the only colored kid Mickey knew on a talk-to basis. His father was a taxicab driver, and that is how Mickey and Walter became acquaintances that became budding friendship when Mickey set aside reluctance and uncertainty. Their fathers worked for the same livery company in downtown Manhattan, in the upper West Thirties.

Mickey never saw Walter anywhere but at the boy's apartment home. The first time was when his father had taken him for a supper meal at the Cartwright's place, giving no explanation, only a gruff "Get washed and dressed. You're going with me for supper and visiting with someone I know—and watch your manners!" They had gone from their tenement basement rooms to the Bronx by the now familiar subway route. Mickey was surprised to see that the family—the father, mother, and Walter—lived on the fourth floor of a building where they were the only colored people. He had thought all colored people lived in Harlem. And he was surprised they lived in four rooms—bigger rooms than where he lived, much neater and cleaner; and Walter had his own room; and the bathroom was twice as big as theirs, and the tub did not stand on four small curved legs. It had a long, flat, smooth side extending between two sidewalls, going all the way to the linoleum floor. Perched atop the tub edge were sliding glass doors he had never seen on a bathtub before.

On that first visit several months earlier, the two boys—about the same age, about the same size and build—only spoke *hello* when introduced. Walter seemed relaxed, but Mickey felt tense, unsure of what to do or say to the other boy. After the most satisfying meal Mickey had had in weeks, during which Mickey looked at his plate most of the time, now and then glancing at the boy opposite, making himself not stare, their eyes not meeting, the adults sent the boys to Walter's room while they talked and had drinks at the dining room table and then in the living room. Mickey had difficulty talking with Walter when they were first alone, overwhelmed by annoying, sudden embarrassment. Talking on sociable terms with a colored boy was new to Mickey, something he'd never expected. He had never had a conversation with one before, only random words and phrases during chance encounters with an aura of hostility, especially if he was in the company of friends wandering out of their neighborhood. If he was by himself and saw a colored boy he avoided a chance of confrontation. If he saw two or three or more, he kept a distance he thought safe because he'd been told by other boys, "Watch out if you see a bunch of 'em! Get the hell away or you'll be in trouble, that's for sure!" He always followed that stern advice, uncertain about the reasons for hostile reactions between white kids and colored kids.

Mickey thought, facing Walter, *I got to remember not to say nigger by accident,* recalling his father's forceful some-time-ago admonition that he had better not hear that word out of his son, anywhere, anytime, for any reason—or he would get a swat in the mouth—quick!

Walter eased the opening moments, showing Mickey his reading books and new comic books. He tried to interest Mickey in Monopoly, but Mickey said it looked too complicated. Mickey marveled that he was so close to an actual colored kid, who talked English the same way he did, not funny-sounding. Paying closer attention to Walter's parents speaking as they all ate, he realized they sounded different than most colored people he had heard. He had thought most of them spoke a language other than English, often garbled, annoyingly unintelligible, though much of it did resemble Mickey's language except for being pronounced differently.

That first evening visit had become enjoyable to Mickey by the second hour. He relaxed as Walter simplified differences between them and they were two boys with things in common. On the subway trip home, Mickey drowsily and happily remembered the meal, a stomach-bulging feast. Vegetables seasoned with flavors Mickey did not know. Baked ham dotted with small dark objects he was told were cloves after he had crushed one in his teeth and his tongue was briefly but agonizingly seared. There were small pieces of roasted chicken with skin done to a crisp and browned with glazed sugar. The home-baked bread was made that afternoon in the kitchen, the woman answered Mickey's question about the warm slices. And there was a large, high, warm apple pie that Mrs. Cartwright slid from the oven when they all agreed they were ready for dessert, bringing o-o-o-h and a-a-a-h compliments. Mickey smiled as the nose-tantalizing wedge almost filling a small plate was put before him. *I wonder how they can eat so good? We never do. And his old man and my old man are cab drivers. They're just like each other, doin' the same kind of work. We only get somethin' special if Aunt Ellen shows up—but nothin' like this even then.*

Mickey and Walter had other good, shared hours occasionally after then. And Mickey feasted on each visit, often taking home a bulging bag of cookies as a treat for later.

Mickey did not know Walter for a long time. No more than half a dozen times in little more than several months did they spend more than three hours together. But Mickey decided firmly that he knew Walter as well as he needed, well enough to wonder about the stern advice, "Watch out! Get the hell away!" Walter was the only colored kid he had talked with as a friend, and he liked him. *I'm learnin' Monopoly, too.*

Mickey was disappointed when his father told him at a supper meal at home that the Cartwrights had moved to New Jersey. "They bought a house, one with six rooms on two floors." Mickey did not understand what his father meant when he said, "I hope you learned something by knowing Walter."

Slight tears moistened his eyes as he fell asleep later, his mind on Walter.

7

*N*ot a bad kid, that Walter. In fact, a good kid. I wonder why I never called him Walt? Guess it didn't fit him.

Wish I'd had more friends like him—at that time—even one.

I'd have stayed out of things that made it easy to get in trouble back then.

8

Money for Mickey's pleasures was always a problem. For candy and soda, for movies, for subway rides, for pitching pennies and nickels and dimes against walls and steps, trying to win from other kids. He could get by without most of the things for which he wanted money, but his great desire was getting money for subway rides. He wanted to avoid risky running and ducking under turnstiles, waiting impatiently for a moment when a subway guard was not looking.

Subways were a means of getting away from his neighborhood, into new neighborhoods, into great crowds. Subways hurtled and roared and clattered and shook—like a horizontal roller-coaster—headlong into pleasure and excitement and adventure. Subways were a way of postponing chores and evading school.

Snitching subway rides was usually easy, if he paid careful attention to what he was doing, but it often meant taking a nerve-jangling chance. The first move was to peer down the flight of steps from a street-level entrance to determine how far down into the ground the train platform might be. That decided his next move. If steps descended beyond his vision, with no platform seen or without a sharp turn to either side, he would wait, lingering so he could enter the subway maw trailing closely behind an adult—two was better, three or four was better still. He hoped for oblique or sharp turns at which he could drop back, pause, peer around the turn, scan the area ahead. Turnstile assaults were best made in a local-stop station where there probably might not be a guard, where the small change booth with its barred window would limit the attendant's vision. That setting was best for sneakiness, for speed and surprise.

But Mickey seldom had the luxury of choice when he wanted a ride, particularly if it appeared he might be risking his father's wrath by getting home after a mandated time. Most times he could not wait for an adult to go down stairs first. More often, he had to descend alone to begin making further decisions, risk being seen by a platform guard. That might mean having to retreat above ground; think about how far the next station was; or plan another way to get home in a hurry. He never wanted to walk all that way—took too long. The thought of hanging on the back of a bus, out of a driver's sight—sneaking a hitch—worried him, *frightened* him.

If stairs descended from street level past a change booth and led directly toward a rank of turnstiles, Mickey altered his technique, depending on the station layout that materialized, ready for an important, hurried step—spot the guard.

Usually, a guard would be on the passenger platform close to the turnstiles, staying visible to discourage the likes of Mickey. Mickey's tactic was to stay out of sight in stairwells until a rumbling train was close or could be seen pulling into the lighted station from the tunnel's pitch darkness, holding back his assault until the train screeched almost to a stop. With an open-door car standing at the platform, with people hurrying in and out, the guard would have his attention diverted. Mickey waited for an instant he was sure he would not be seen, the moment to strike out from hiding. He would make a bold rush at an unblocked turnstile, doubling over to charge below the thick, hip-high wooden crosspiece blocking the narrow entrance slot, carrying on with the headlong bolt at an open door, praying for it to close before a guard was alerted. Mickey had not been caught in more than a dozen attempts, but there had been more than one harrowing escape from furious guards. It was a stroke of good fortune when he chanced on a station without a guard, but that had happened only twice. And neither time did Mickey have the pressure of punctuality-or-else, making the victories seem tainted.

Mickey reasoned, on each contemplation of a free subway ride: *If I had money I wouldn' have to take such chances.* He rationalized that with an allowance he could travel at his convenience rather than rely on fortunate timing, craftiness, and stealth. But he was not given an allowance "I haven't got money for you to fritter away on comic books and candy," was his father's annoyed reaction to Mickey's first and only request. *"I* never got an allowance!"

And being able to pay admission to a movie was simpler than trying to find an unlocked theater exit. Having money meant less wasted time standing outside a theater and pleading, sometimes whining, to moviegoers about poverty, begging for someone to pay his way. "Please, he's my favorite actor—he's so good—an' we don' have enough for me to go to movies much—please—"

His favorite actor would be whoever was in a movie he was trying to see. Standing out of sight of the ticket booth, he watched for a kindly appearing person heading for the box office, someone he calculated might believe the plea of a small boy. Giving promises, seeming to struggle with shyness—an appearance he developed as something else to work in his favor—he was successful at seeing many movies free. "I ain' begging for money—I jus' wanna see the movie. I don' want nothin' else, I promise—an' I'll behave—I won' be no trouble to anybody inside. I only wanna see a movie—honest!" When he learned to watch for couples and make his appeal to the woman, wiping at his eyes to stave off carefully worked-up tears, he was even more successful.

As a desperate resort at nighttime—if moviegoers were unsympathetic to ticket-begging, or he was chased away by an angry manager—he searched alleys and fire escapes for unlocked fire exits; but he only succeeded with two nervous attempts at night movies. In most tries a clamor was raised by patrons, angry at someone sneaking in to see what they had paid for, or he was foiled by a shouting usher rushing down an aisle toward an opening revealed by a long vertical stripe of exterior night light filtering into the darkness, an alarm as good as any bell. On one frightening escape he was grabbed by a wrist as he started into a narrow door opening. For terrifying seconds he struggled violently with an unseen opponent before pulling free from the quick but slippery grasp.

Stealing empty deposit bottles from outdoor vestibules, if gates were unlocked, or from unsecured under-stair closets in building hallways was productive in a small way. But it was tedious, time-consuming, tiring. Up and down flights of stairs in several buildings, always nervously alert for someone discovering him rummaging in their storage area, in their property; fearful of every bumping, clunking, banging sound he made; afraid of a pummeling from an irate tenant; dreading being held prisoner by a cop who would turn him over to his father after detention at a precinct station. After open-hand wallopings and razor-strop whippings for simple disobedience of his father's rules, Mickey knew the risk of being caught at something that bore the suspicion of stealing. But he was certain his skills, cleverness, running speed, and agility would let him roam freely and avoid confrontation or capture, so he persisted in searches for deposit bottles. There were close calls in those thievery tries, but he won each time, and his wiliness improved with each venture.

One late afternoon, in the gloom of a bedroom with a drawn windowshade, while his father slept between shifts of cab-driving, Mickey looked to see what waking time had been set on the big, noisily ticking alarm clock, wondering about supper, if it was to be fixed for him or whether he would need to make his own meal. Squinting at an object on the floor by the head of the bed, he wondered what it was. *Uh, oh—it's his wallet.*

It had slipped from beneath the pillow and its bulgy thickness—newspaper articles, membership cards, business cards, money, photographs, slips of paper bearing scrawled information on numerous subjects—had pried the folds ninety degrees apart and it stood on edge. When Mickey picked it up the sight of protruding corners of bills gave him a quick shiver. *How easy it would be,* he thought. The wallet took on a sudden heaviness. It felt warm in his palm, like suddenly found money burning a figurative hole in a pocket. He changed his grasp to hold it by fingertips.

His thought about easy pilfering only lasted a flash before he realized he would certainly be the first suspect. He looked at the sleeping figure, flat on his back, head faced slightly away. His mouth was open and he snored softly. Mickey squatted by the bed so as not to be seen if the figure suddenly turned and opened his eyes. He glanced swiftly back and forth between the wallet and the profile. The figure did not stir; the snores had a snuffling sound. The boy straightened the half-folded wallet and riffled through the compartments, counting two tens, two fives, and fourteen singles crammed among papers and cards. *Jesus, what a time I could have with this!*

The thought only lasted a second or two. Mickey decided against the foolish risk and gently pushed the wallet beneath the pillow. With his hand poked deep inside the bedding, he paused, then carefully withdrew the wallet, heart pounding, holding his breath, hands trembling. But his father did not stir. Mickey clumsily drew a one dollar bill from among others, fearing that the one he chose might be new, that it might crackle in the silence and wake the sleeping figure. But there was not a sound. The setting was not an ambush. He slid the wallet under the pillow again, then stood carefully, stuffing the bill in a knickers pocket, backing quietly through the doorway, closing the door gently, trying to remember if it squeaked, praying it wouldn't. *At least not THIS time—PLEASE!*

Even with the door closed between them Mickey was terrified. He worried. *What made me do that? I didn' think my balls were that big.* His heart kept pounding, and lungs were gulping air after having held his breath for long periods in that room. He pleaded to God that his father would not remember exactly how much there was in the wallet when he had gone to bed, that he would not for some reason count the money when he woke up. Tears of fear wet the boy's eyes, stinging.

He jerked nervously when the clamorous alarm sounded on the other side of the door. *Shit, I never did look at what time the alarm was set! Suppose the damn thing went off with me in there?* But he had time to compose himself. The annoying jangle was quickly stilled, and his father was always slow to wake. Mickey washed his hands and face at the kitchenette sink, thinking repeatedly, KEEP CALM, KEEP CALM, went into the bathroom to urgently urinate, then turned on the radio in the front room, twisting the dial to tune in an adventure serial. *Keep calm! Take it easy!* In the bathroom he had put the folded dollar bill under the sole of his right foot, between the skin and the stocking, drawing the sneaker lacing extra tightly, securing it with another knot atop the regular bow. He sprawled on the threadbare couch and was reading newspaper comic pages when his father appeared sleepily, eyes sweeping the room to see if his son was home.

By the next afternoon, his father sleeping before his next driving shift, Mickey knew he had succeeded in his first direct theft of cash from someone. He was awed, and a dollar richer; richer than he remembered. He could have a good time for a week; and it had been easy to get that buck.

More and more often Mickey became angry about having to duck under turnstiles, dodging subway guards, dodging building tenants—all for free rides and getting pennies and nickels for spending money, he sulked. *I'm tired of borrowing nickels and dimes from other kids, then breakin' my ass to pay 'em back!* With each anger he was tempted by the concealed wallet. *How easy!* But he needed the right time and compelling desperation to pass beyond the thinking-about-it stage. To risk his father's rage was a powerful deterrent, sufficient that three weeks passed before the simplicity of having taken that first dollar bill overwhelmed him.

He counted on his father being such a heavy sleeper that he would not have difficulty getting to the wallet without disturbing him. He would closely check the alarm setting as his first precaution after entering the room. And he artfully worked out a reason why he should be in the room, so close to his father's bed, if the man suddenly woke and found the boy over him. If he woke unexpectedly, or if movements nudged him awake, Mickey planned to shake him gently as though trying to bring him to consciousness to ask a question, something like, "Is it OK if I go to Johnny's house tomorrow after school instead of coming right home?" or, better yet, "Is there anything special you want me to do after school tomorrow when I get home?" That would put him off guard. When he had his deviousness contrived and mentally rehearsed, he waited for his next opportunity.

His father's cab-driving schedule was erratic—random-length periods of daylight hours or the four-to-midnight time or the ominous-sounding *graveyard* shift. On any of the schedules he sometimes went to work earlier to fill in for someone or he would work later to make more money. Occasionally he would work a double shift for both reasons, or for reasons Mickey did not pay any attention to if his father said he would not be home at an accustomed time. He would think: *So what? Who cares? An' Aunt Ellen only shows up to make meals when he ain' workin' so much anyway—and she don' stay over so many nights anymore— with him workin' like he is.*

Mickey seldom paid attention to his father's absence. The less his father was at home the safer Mickey knew he was from impulsive anger and sometimes towering rage; the greater was his freedom. He and his sister had long since learned to get themselves off to school if their father worked through a time for them to be gone. Seeing to it that they both got up at the alarm and fed and on the way on time was another of Mickey's assignments; as his father put it, his *chores.* Many times he had only to feed himself to tend to because Margaret would stay with Aunt Ellen for two or three days and nights. Mickey now and then thought: *It sure is lucky that Aunt Ellen lives only a few blocks away wherever we move; that way Maggie stays with Aunt Ellen and keeps outta my hair!*

But his father's schedule became of interest as Mickey lost enthusiasm for scrounging bottles as a prime source of money. Mickey proposed to himself: *It takes hours to get a buck that way; it only took two or three minutes the other way.*

It was a week after he had ventured that proposal to himself before he made a wavering decision to resort to the quicker money-making method. Every day he weighed risks and argued with himself that each risk amounted to nothing, really; that he could eliminate anything that posed danger. Two days later he made a firm choice. He *could* get away with a stealthy sortie into his father's room—when the time was right. He *knew* he could.

His father woke Mickey for school when he got in about six-thirty one morning and was in bed by the time the boy had washed and made toast for breakfast. Mickey started into the hallway from the apartment, then instead went to the ajar door of his father's room. He could hear snuffling snoring. He composed a question to have ready if he should need one, then knocked on the door firmly enough to be heard if the man wasn't deep in sleep. He poked his head through the opening and peered into the room darkened by a drawn shade, rapping on the door more vigorously, to be certain the blanket-shrouded figure was soundly asleep before he trespassed further. Sprawled on the bed, his father had the blanket pulled up to his chin, mouth open. The fidgety boy crouched defensively by the head of the bed, two textbooks and a notebook in his left hand, cautiously slipping the other hand beneath the pillow, gingerly feeling for the wallet. He worked his fingers around the shape of the top of his father's head, praying the wallet would not be under his head or neck, or so far past his head that he could not reach it—then his fingers were on it!

He eased it to him, fingers aching from tension, arm nerves and muscles twitching as fear built. He wanted to put the books on the floor to manipulate the wallet and search compartments more easily, but worried that his father would not see the picture Mickey wanted to portray if he abruptly awoke, that he would become suspicious, that he would react violently. He rested the wallet on edge on the floor and one-handedly fingered the bills he could see in the dimness. Riffling quickly, he got excited. *There's more 'n' the las' time!*

He slipped a worn dollar bill from between others, stuffed it into a shirt pocket, then gently pressed the wallet far under the pillow. He left the room quietly, steadily moving sideways, watching the snoring prostrate figure, dreading he might suddenly waken and see the clandestine exit. But Mickey was safe. He rushed noiselessly out of the flat, then pattered along the hallway and down the dozen brownstone steps, not stopping to calm nervousness until reaching the corner, a half block away. Looking back, his father *was not* coming after him, not even looking at him from their building doorway.

Less than a week later Mickey had the urge to get another easy dollar. He had not searched for bottles nor borrowed money in that time, and the easy money was gone in three days. He was briefly satisfied, though, by indulging in paying admission for two movie matinees on two alternate days of playing hooky, buying sweets at lobby candy counters, enough the second time to make his stomach rebel at excess chocolate.

He did not need money yet, but would in another day or two, he guessed as he contemplated his finances, what with his increased spending, thrilling in the unfettered pleasure of being a spendthrift. He calculated it would be simpler to have extra cash ready rather than to have to hurriedly carry out another assault on his father's room, but he wanted the time to be of his choosing.

Mickey's third act of early-morning thievery was carried off confidently and smoothly, without appreciable nervousness, free of physical tremors, without hurried exit or passage to the corner and to school. Poised beside the bed, books in hand, in brightening, shaded morning light, working quickly, efficiently, he was amused by his presence and calmness within inches of someone he so feared. He thought of doubling the amount filched, trying to persuade himself his father would not miss another dollar. But he cautiously took only a single bill.

Mickey's thievery stood at three dollars, two-thirds already spent. *So simply got, too!*, he thought. Fears and trembling of the first and second forays were soon overshadowed by successes. At random times in the early mornings of the next three weeks he filched other dollar bills. He liked the sound of *filch* instead of *steal* since a short time ago when he had heard an adult say it, then explain in answer to Mickey's question about meaning. Each time he persuaded himself not to let greed get the best of wisdom by adding a second dollar to his pockets. He had tripled, then quadrupled weekly pocket money from what it had been from picking up—filching—deposit bottles. He did not want to imperil newly-found good times. He was having a splendid time with each purloined dollar.

The seventh attempt was fruitless. His routine and technique were flawless and swift, but there was no wallet under the pillow. He thought of searching in trousers draped over a straightback chair by the window, but discarded the idea as foolish and risky, *too* risky. On each recent theft venture he had had a plausible reason prepared for being by the bed if his father woke to find him nearby, but he would not have one for being at the chair on the far side of the room—and *absolutely* no cause for handling the trousers.

Retreating disappointedly, he reasoned that the wallet this time had been directly under his father's head, out of feel, out of reach. He began planning another try the next morning, or if that did not work out, the one after that. There was no reason to rush. He still had several coins.

Three days later Mickey was again luckless. In another four days he once more left his sleeping father's room empty-handed. He sulkily resorted to searching yards and hallways for bottles, but pickings were lean. He began sorting through garbage cans in backyards and on street curbs, but bottles were scarce. Periodically, on a school day, without money in his pocket, angry and frustrated, he played hooky.

Recklessly ducking under turnstiles, not bothering to first carefully spot a guard, he took the chance that the sound of an arriving train would be one going in his direction. If it was traveling an opposite way, tracks and support columns were a difficult, hazardous maze separating uptown and downtown platforms. But he defiantly prepared himself, if he was spotted, to leap down onto the trackbed and escape into the forbidding columns, tracks, shadows, and pitch-black darkness. He feared an unseen rushing express the most—its sounds masked by the arriving local train—if he had to dart away from a pursuer. The trackbed would be too intimidating for the likes of most guards. The thought of the third rail carrying high-voltage electricity was frightening, but he knew exactly what they looked like and where they were located along the trackbed. It only took reasonable care to avoid that threat.

But he did not encounter a guard on those assaults. There was no need to challenge the underground dangers of darkness and hurtling trains and electrocution. He took long subway rides up and down and back and forth much of the thirteen-mile-long island. He window-shopped the Times Square area. He begged movie entry money in the bustling Forties midtown region. But begging was fruitless. People were not willing to gratify a suspected hooky-player when a boy his age obviously belonged in a classroom on a weekday that was not a holiday.

On a morning that Mickey started from the front room on the way to school he heard his name called from his father's room, then called a second time, insistently. The tone of the summons worried him. Mickey was apprehensive about going to him, thinking of continuing into the hallway and out of the building. Later that evening, if his father complained, he could say he had not been there to hear the call. *But would he have called me if he didn' already know I was still here? S'pose he heard me moving' aroun'? S'pose he looked out first and saw me? I better get in there!*

Nervous, he entered the bedroom. His father sat on the edge of the bed, feet on the floor, a blanket pulled across his thighs. Dark, abundant, curly hair showed at the top of his white undershirt. Black, straight hair on his head was rumpled; he rubbed his eyes and yawned. Mickey stood barely inside the dimly light room, thinking of escape if he was confronted about the missing dollars. But his father only asked Mickey what time he would be home from school.

"I want to take you with me tonight. I'm visiting friends." He stretched, arms high above his head, then bending them at the elbows, locking fingers behind his neck, twisting from side to side at his waist, grunting softly as he made waking-up pulls and turns.

"I dunno," Mickey answered. "Right after school, I guess—" His father pulled the pillow into his lap, "—as usual—" thrusting a hand deep into the pillowcase covering the thick headrest, "—I got homework—" slowly withdrawing his thick, black, folded wallet.

"Have homework, not *got,"* his father corrected, in a quiet, calm tone, contemplating the wallet, holding it loosely, then looking up at his son. Mickey felt there was something ominous in his father's quiet voice. He had never so patiently corrected his son. Mickey wanted to bolt from the room.

"There's a *lotta* homework I *gotta* do—I *have* to do!" he said quickly, feeling his face flush, waiting for a sudden lunge and hammering blow. "Two teachers gave out extra work—"

He thought his voice quavered, then cracked, but his father gave no sign of suspicion.

"—an' we're s'posed to—"

He did not know what to say next—then thought of something.

"We hafta have it for tomorrow." He imperceptibly sucked in and bit his lower lip on the inside. He hoped the painful, distracting bit of defensiveness would not be seen by his father. "But if I start right away when I get home—"

His father's wallet-holding hand dropped, softly, a plopping sound on the pillow, a sound Mickey fearfully sensed as threatening.

"I can get a lot of it done—I can get all of it finished and still go OK—" Mickey thought he was talking too fast, that he was going to stammer. His stomach ached abruptly. He felt shrouded with terror, seared by the prospect of brutal punishment. He was about to say he did not mean to steal from him; to plead to be spared; to defiantly yell that he would run away if he was hit. His father lifted his hand, swung it to the left, dropped the wallet on the head of the bed, and tossed the pillow over it. He stretched himself the length of the bed, pulling the blanket to his neck. "I'm going back to sleep." He paused. "I'll see you after school."

Mickey mentally scrambled to analyze his father's stare, fearfully expecting the prostrate figure to explosively lunge from beneath the covering to ferociously pounce on him, but the voice carried no menace. *That ain't like him.* Mickey was worried, cautious. His father still looked intently at him. Mickey's mind clamored. *What's he thinkin'?* The man rolled onto his side, his back to Mickey, pulling the blanket closer about his neck.

Worries formed and filtered rapidly through Mickey's mind. *That's why I didn' find the damn wallet the last few times—it was INSIDE the pillowcase!*

He left his father's room and the apartment, slowly walking the detested route to detested school. He mulled a question repeatedly: *Why'd he call me inta his room?* Questions plagued him, frightened him, as he wondered what his father's next step would be. His pace slowed as he carried on steadily arguing, defending, cajoling, persuading himself; projecting himself into his father's position, then coming back to planning his own next steps; alternating between internal frantic and calming words and phrases, then complete sentences said aloud, only loud enough for himself to hear. The soft, spoken words were more reassuring than thoughts only.

He was puzzled. *Other times he always only left notes to keep me home after school if he had somethin' for me to do.*

An' the look in his eyes with that wallet in his hand on the pillow. Geez, I thought for sure I was gonna be walloped or somethin'. I don' get it!

When he recalled past thrashings for small acts he became exhilarated over having come out of the room scot-free. He puzzled more over the bedroom scene as he plodded toward school. *Why'd he take the wallet outta the pillowcase like he did? But then he only asked a dumb question! He shoulda said more—but I know what he was up to! He was tryin' to catch me off guard—get me off balance—to knock me on my ass!—make ME knock me on my ass MYSELF! He was tryin' to trap me!—and that look in his eyes—he KNEW somethin'—he hadda!*

Three-quarters of the way to school Mickey persuaded himself he had outwitted his father. He reassured himself: *He didn' know what I been up to—but I ain' positive—not that positive! I better take it easy!* Farther along his plodding course, intelligence welled up, to make him reluctantly admit he had perhaps been outsmarted by his father. *The old geezer guessed somehow, some way. He musta counted his money one time before going to bed and when he got up. What made him do that? Wonder if he heard me goin' out of his room once?*

That last fleeting idea drifted to another part of his brain, then, like a thunderclap, exploded to bulge his mind. *Christ! He was WAITIN' for me! Oh, shit! The son-of-a-bee was waitin'—but he missed! That's all that saved my ass!*

Mickey pictured his father counting money in his fat wallet, then recounting; pictured him thinking and scowling; pictured him scheming, setting an early-morning ambush in a darkened room, thick fingers poised to close like a steel animal trap onto a skinny wrist; pictured his looks of triumph and rage.

Mickey sat on a brownstone step, shaken by thoughts and images. Calmed in moments, he thought through the near mishap. *What saved me? It's a good thing I didn' whack him for a buck every day. Sure as shit he woulda caught me! He musta foun' out just after the last time I got somethin'!—an' started puttin' the wallet INSIDE the case instead of only under the pillow. Ain' I fuckin' lucky. He musta fallen asleep while he was waitin' for me those last two times I was in there an' couldn' find the goddam wallet! What screwy good luck I got!*

Mickey was mystified by his father's control of an easily aroused temper; thankful that this time rage had been contained for some reason. His final conjecture on that walk along chilly streets was that he had been given a warning. Though Mickey had no comprehension of the word subtle, he did have a profound appreciation of the circumstance he had been in; that for a peculiar reason he did not understand, his father altered his way of doing things, his way of controlling his family. Mickey did not care why a change had been made; any reason was good enough. He simply mused over his fortune. *He DID give me a warnin'. I'm sure o' that! It hadda be! Why else—?*

As his confidence returned, youthful certainty gained headway, too. *He don' KNOW what I did! The best he could do was guess! I DID outfox him!* Mickey did a joyful series of hop-and-skip near-dance steps along the sidewalk to celebrate what he perceived as his victory, then decided, with burgeoning confidence, swelling to arrogance, that all along he had been extraordinarily ingenious.

There was no visit with his father's friends that evening, but Mickey was not told so even after he had finished his skimpy homework and waved several sheets of paper near his father. Not until after supper, when Mickey asked, did his father say, "I changed my mind! That's all *you* need to know!" Then he stretched himself on the couch, arranging a newspaper in folds like subway readers do for easy reading. "Find something else to do!"

Mickey did not venture into his father's room again, heeding his advice to himself, heeding the warning he felt surely had been given to him, resigning himself to humbly searching for bottles or borrowing from friends. The next afternoon, after a cheerless, fitful, annoying school day, he entered the M. & A. Weinstein Pharmacy, a half block from where he lived, deciding it was a good place to spend his last dime on an ice cream soda and a good time to start planning a quicker way to get money than filching deposit bottles, a safer way than stealing at home.

9

I never could figure him out that morning, doing what he did—and the way he did it.

But I should have paid better attention to what went on in that room. I mean I should have remembered it. What a break I got!

Good luck—yep! That's what it was. I could have used more afterward.

Nah! Luck had nothing to do with it, dammit! You should have used your head. Stayed out of trouble.

10

The boy was the only customer in the drugstore as tall, slender Mr. Weinstein mixed Mickey's chocolate drink at the soda fountain. As the final step in concoction, Mr. Weinstein gave a light push at the fountain handle to squirt a brief high-speed stream of carbonated water into the mixture in a tall glass. After several swirls of the contents with a long-handled spoon, and with a slight smile and pleased expression, he placed the foam-topped glass in front of Mickey. As the man started toward the back room of the store, Mickey reached for the bottle of straws, eyes feasting on the tall glass of soda, anticipating the taste, fingers of one hand fumbling at the knob handle on the metal cover, other fingers picking a paper straw from the jar.

Mickey lingered over the rich, chocolate-flavored soda water, using the long-handled spoon to slice slivers of ice cream from the two extra-large scoops the druggist had packed into the tall glass. Mickey thought: *I'm glad this Mr. Weinstein is workin' insteada the fat one. That one always makes little scoops—really small— nothin' extra past the edge of the scoop—uses a lot less cream, too—puts in more carbonated water than this Mr. Weinstein does.*

He alternated between sipping the soda through the softening paper straw and scraping bits of thick chocolate from the thawing scoops and letting slivered ice cream melt in his mouth. He sipped the soda more slowly; turned languorously on the swivel stool; sipped more soda; repeating the slow routine so he could linger over his treat as long as he could.

His befuddled mind could not develop a safe way to make pocket money, except to work in a grocery store sweeping the floor and doing other small tasks. But he did not think any small store in a dozen blocks in every direction from where he lived would hire him. In all the tiny stores owned by older people, the women always did the sweeping and dusting and the man did everything else. They were not busy enough that they did not have time to do their own work, and were not rich enough to even pay a kid for part-time work. In other stores, owners put their own children to work or only took on older, bigger, stronger boys. Mickey's thoughts were angry. *Why do I have to be so little and skinny? Other kids my age ain' my size. How come they're bigger?—got more meat on 'em?*

He slurped the last of the soda through the straw, pulling the long limp paper tube from the high glass. The upper end of the straw was scarred and misshapen, clamped repeatedly by teeth, squeezed by tightly pursed lips. He had vigorously slapped an end up and down inside his closed mouth with his tongue tip as he carefully made the soda last as long as possible by preventing liquid from passing up the straw even as he siphoned. He peered into the bottom of the heavy, ornately shaped glass, then tilted it high to let the remaining drops trickle into his throat.

Satisfied he had every trace, he sat with his elbows on the counter, chin cupped in both hands. His stool was the second from the store front in a row that was perpendicular to the plate glass window, the row going toward the rear of the store. He sat with head slightly tipped sideways, watching street activity as a distraction, peering between taped-on sale posters on the high, wide expanse of glass, watching people and traffic pass, looking for a friend. In his reverie, mind searching for solutions, for tricks, for *some* way to get money, he uncomfortably sensed he was being watched.

Slowly, to not convey a sense of guilt or worry, he twisted his stool to the right, wanting it to appear as a casual movement. The ice cream soda-maker, stood nearby, looking at him from behind the end of the fountain counter. Mickey waited to be berated for loitering, as he had seen the other Mr. Weinstein do to kids, but there was a kindly look to the man's face.

Both Mr. Weinsteins had mustaches. The short, fat Mr. Weinstein was nearly all bald, except for a band of thin black hair from one ear round the back of his head to the other ear. He was the *M.* of M. & A. Weinstein Pharmacy—M. was for Morton. The Mr. Weinstein looking at Mickey, inches taller and four years older than his brother, was the *A.* of the drugstore's name on the store window, A. for Arthur. Mr. Morton Weinstein's mustache matched him, Mickey thought, amused—thick, like his belly; broad, like his behind; dark, like his mean-looking eyes; stiff and scratchy-looking, like the way he was with everybody, as Mickey was to later learn. The mustache made his round, constantly scowling face appear fierce, angry, unforgiving.

Mr. Arthur Weinstein's mustache, Mickey decided, fit him well also—full, wide, gently curling at the sides; soft; of brownish-red hair, with thin lines of gray scattered throughout; going nicely with his full head of hair; making him look like a *nice* man, like all the nice fathers and uncles Mickey had seen in films.

Arthur Weinstein didn't berate Mickey or chase him away. "I wonder if you could tell me something, young man?"

Mickey was surprised; no one had ever said *young man* to him before. "Uh— whadda ya mean, Mr. Weinstein? Like what?"

"Would you know," Mr. Weinstein said, "if there's a boy in the neighborhood, maybe one of your friends, who wants to make a little extra money after school every day, and sometimes on Saturday morning? Or maybe you would like it yourself?"

Mickey had always liked Mr. Weinstein's voice. *His Jewish accent is nice—just a little bit of it in some words; not all of 'em; not in everythin' he says—not like his brother's at all! Like Mrs. Scalise's Italian accent is—soft, makin' words sound differ'nt than other people say 'em.*

"Doin' what?" said Mickey.

"It won't be hard—delivering prescriptions and other things. And once in a while doing other things around here. There won't be any money as pay from the store, but there *are* tips from customers for whoever takes the job. We have a lot of deliveries, and whoever wanted to do the deliveries would get to keep all the tips."

Mickey quickly considered himself for the job, but almost as quickly became unenthused about working for someone else only for tip money. *Sure—he SAYS there's lots o' deliveries. But I'll bet there won' be if I do start.*

Mr. Weinstein went on: "I think you would be good here. I've seen you a few times in here and you seem like a nice boy, and bright. If you wanted the job I would like you to have it."

Mickey felt trapped. *Come in here EVERY day? The same place all the time?* Mr. Weinstein added, "And it would be a good place to keep busy—maybe avoid trouble."

Mickey thought of the other Mr. Weinstein. He was not sure he would like being close to him, even briefly, much less work for him. The pause seemed long to Mickey, but the druggist stood patiently, not appearing to be in a hurry for an answer. "Gee, Mr. Weinstein, I don' know if my father would let me. I'd hafta ask him first. He says I first of all hafta do homework before anythin' else—and he's always after me about it. I don' know."

But getting only tips and no regular pay was his real cause for reluctance. He did not think he would earn enough that he should have to endure constriction and confinement. The neighborhood was not well-to-do, though neither was it poverty-stricken. Mickey had often lived in much poorer sections and when his father had moved them here Mickey felt he was finally lucky to be somewhere better than what he had been accustomed to for so long.

"But, I guess I'll do it if it's okay with my father." He put his faith in Mr. Weinstein's claim that there would be a lot of deliveries. He could be away from the drugstore most of the time if it was true, and, he schemed, when he was not making deliveries he could be out of sight in the store and read the latest comic books in the magazine rack without having to buy them. *Besides, I could still check hallways for bottles while I was makin' deliveries. People won' look suspicious at me cuz they'll get to know I work here—an' they won' bother me—and it'll be easier to lift bottles. If I get a nickel tip from everybody that's more than for any bottle!*

Mickey's father talked with the same Mr. Weinstein soon after he woke that early evening, before their supper. He had the boy go with him as he confirmed his son would be putting in time for the store only for tip money. The father, like Mickey, was not enthused about the uncertain income, but when he calculated potential tips—"Every little bit will help in the house!"—he agreed that a kid his age would at least be under Mr. Weinstein's and his brother's wings for a while each day, and that was better than him hanging around on street corners.

"It's all right with me—and you can start tomorrow afternoon. But you're only doing it as long as I know you're doing your school work—and that means being ready to show it to me if I tell you to. And it means passing grades—or you're out of a job—this one or any other one as long as you fail anything!"

Mickey thought, eyes averted, looking at orderly rows of cans, bottles, and cartons on shelving on a wall in a far corner: *Geez, here comes another lecture—every time, another sermon. Why don' he just ever say anythin' quick—or just say nothin'—just say yes or no!*

"You paying attention?" he heard his father saying, wondering, from the irritated tone, if he had missed something said.

"Yes, I'm—yes, sir—I'm listenin'. I jus' don' know—"

"Well, keep listening—if you want this job. I'm not through—and I want Mr. Weinstein to know that you are to do things you're supposed to—and do them right!—and to tell me if you don't—and—"

Not *more*, Mickey thought, hoping the wince he felt didn't show visibly.

"You've got chores at home, too!"

Why does he keep callin' 'em CHORES? He keeps talkin' like he's still on that damn old farm—like she and I are both goddam farm kids!

"Got that?" his father said, and Mickey answered, "Uh, huh—uh, yes sir."

"It's good then, Mickey," Mr. Weinstein said. "It's settled. And you'll be all right here." To his father he said, "He'll do just fine. He's a nice boy. I've seen him in here a lot of times, and he never was any trouble. And he was polite whenever I talked to him. A lot of boys who come in here aren't so nice, believe me."

At home, Mickey's father said, "There's something else,"—*Oh, God, he ain't done yet!*— "don't think all the tips you'll get are for you to keep. You're wrong if you think so. We need that money for the house. You and your sister have to have clothes and shoes. Money isn't that easy to get! It doesn't grow on trees!" The boy fretted: *Hurry up, will you?* "But you'll get a weekly allowance because you're working. I think a quarter—a—quarter—yeah, I think a quarter should do."

That decision shocked and disappointed Mickey. He wanted to quit before starting, but it was too late to do anything. He thought about firmly saying he had too much homework, that he needed more time to do it and do it right, so he had better not take the job after all. *But he won' believe that story now. I was too good when I told him about the job in the first place, thinkin' about all that money in my pockets!*

Any reason he contrived agonizingly to himself during and after supper he rejected as either stupid or unbelievable by his father. But he felt better by the time he went to bed. *I know what I'll do! I'll start tomorrow but I jus' won't give him all the tips! How's he gonna know the difference? If I get more than a nickel from somebody I'll say I only got a nickel and put the rest away somewhere. I'll show him! Besides, I could still find bottles—and I could still see all the latest comic books.* He persuaded himself he could not lose, and slept well that night.

Hurrying, to make a good impression on the friendly Mr. Weinstein, Mickey's first prescription delivery four blocks from the drugstore brought him a quarter—*Holy—that's a whole week's allowance*—from an elderly woman on the third floor of her building. Trotting and walking two blocks south he made another delivery and received a dime; then two blocks away, on a building's fifth floor his tip was fifteen cents, and he discovered two two-cent deposit bottles inside an unlocked hall closet. He rushed back to Mr. Weinstein's for the other prescriptions the druggist said he would have ready, stopping at a grocery store to cash in the bottles. Trotting again to the drugstore, he thought of a scheme to show his father his diligence and stopped to make notes on a piece of paper. He wrote:

> Mrs. Meyers —5¢
> Edwards —5¢
> Gaines —10¢

He was pleased with the last entry—a smart idea, he thought—showing a dime received at one stop. It would point up his straightforwardness. He decided then to occasionally insert other higher figures here and there as deliveries went on, depending on how he fared. He was excited. He joyfully thought: *I can't believe this!* Mickey went over his money and calculations a second time. In less than half an hour he had put thirty-four cents in his pocket, and had twenty cents and a tally sheet to turn over to his father.

He grinned at Mr. Weinstein as he entered the store, and the druggist smiled in return as he waited on a customer. After several minutes he gave Mickey four small paper bags with billing statements stapled to them.

The gleeful boy was back in forty minutes. His tally sheets bore additions for Smythe—5¢

but he kept fifteen cents;

Mrs. Harris—5¢

but I kept twenty cents, he mentally crowed as he wrote;

Mr. Klipstein—15¢

keeping a dime on this;

Schmidt—5¢

splitting evenly, keeping a nickel.

There were no more deliveries nor small tasks to do at the drugstore. Mr. Weinstein told him he could leave, that he had done a nice job that day, a really nice job. "Oh," he said, "I won't be here all of tomorrow. I've already told my brother you're delivering and will maybe do other things here once in a while, and he'll be here from two o'clock until closing." Mickey only knew the other Mr. Weinstein by sight and wondered, as he had once before, if the other druggist was as mean as he was ugly, then forgot about him.

Mickey was satisfied with how things had gone for him. In an hour and a half he had fifty cents for his father, and eighty-four cents for himself. Not bad, he kept thinking as he walked the short distance home. Several times he smiled. *That was easy work—an' that Mr. Weinstein was nice—meetin' customers was nice too—and that eighty-four cents was easier gettin' than raidin' my old man's room in almost dark—just for a buck—a lousy buck—that would have to last a week. I don' have to think about that wallet no more—no sir!—that's easy money at the Weinstein store.*

Mickey knotted his undeclared coins in a corner of a grimy handkerchief and buried the wad in the backyard between a clothesline pole and a fence before going up to their first-floor apartment. His father reacted suspiciously to the fifty cents in coins happily handed to him, scowling at the small sum in his palm, taking them nonetheless. "I would have thought you would do better in this neighborhood."

Mickey knew he had to persuade him so he acted cowed, extending the folded, crumpled tally sheet as evidence. "You mean," said his father, studying the paper, frowning, "that for seven deliveries all these people except one gave you *nickels*? In this neighborhood? It's not a rich one, I know that, but it's not that poor either—I know *that*, too!"

God, another lecture? Why don' he jus' take the damn money and lemme alone?

"We're getting better places to live every time I can. That's why we moved up here. It isn't great, sure, and we're not in the best part of the city, but it's better than the last dump." Mickey wondered: *How come the Cartwrights had such a nice place? That kid's ol' man and mine both work for the same cab outfit!*

His father's voice droned on. "I know that last place was a dump—and this one, good as it is compared to that other one, is only for a little while. We'll get something better." *That's what he thinks—this section o' town ain' that much better— it's only a few blocks up from the last place—and there's still gangs and fights goin' on. It's just him THINKS it's better.*

His father jammed the coins into a trouser pocket, saying, "You get the allowance on Fridays, after you get home from the store."

Mickey's second afternoon at the drugstore did not go as well as the first. Morton Weinstein was nothing like his brother. Mickey had to work harder and longer. The fat Mr. Weinstein quickly put the boy to work doing things in the store and was seldom satisfied with how Mickey carried out a task. Less money was taken to his father because of fewer deliveries—and he did not make as much for his own pocket.

None of the times working with Morton Weinstein were enjoyable. Mickey soon learned that even when both brothers were in the store the younger one dominated the partnership, acting as though he were the elder, the one in charge, that he had a *right* to be in *command.* And the pudgy one always yelled at people that his name was Wine-STYNE, not Wine-STEEN! The older brother never corrected anyone about how to say their name.

Mickey thought about working only when Arthur Weinstein was in the store, but he could not learn their schedules. Their hours and days were haphazardly arranged, just as his father's were; each working alone from one to three days successively; sometimes together for one or two days. Mickey resigned himself to turning a deaf ear to Morton Weinstein; and he took longer than needed to make deliveries on days that brother worked, whether alone or with Arthur. He wanted to stay out of the fat man's sight as much as he could.

Mickey also quickly learned that the fat brother was easily irked by seeing the boy idle in the store And he had become infuriated when he found Mickey reading comic books at the magazine rack. He relentlessly gave the boy one task after another—spreading damp sawdust on the floor and sweeping; washing glasses and spoons behind the soda fountain; using a feather duster in the customer's part of the store; making him endlessly pass that duster over quart, half gallon, and gallon medicine jars on long, high shelves above a counter in the back room where prescriptions were prepared. Mickey thought it curious, after two weeks of working for the Weinsteins, that there were always more deliveries to be made for the slender, older brother than when the short, fat brother worked. Once, when both brothers worked, Morton had Mickey start sweeping the sawdust-sprinkled floor while he put on his overcoat that had been folded and put on a fountain stool. "Do that instead of working around the ice cream at the fountain!" Morton took a large closed paper bag from the fountain counter near the front window and left the store. When his brother came from the back room and asked where Mr. Weinstein was, he seemed puzzled when Mickey answered that he had gone, taking the bag. He scowled, returning to prescription-making. It was the first time Mickey had seen a frown on his face.

In less than half an hour the absent Mr. Weinstein returned, face flushed. He hung his overcoat on a wall hook near the back room, and in puffing breaths gave Mickey instructions to dust shelves out front. "And then you can wash and dry the glasses and silverware behind the counter. I don't know why you haven't done these things yet!—why you have to wait to be told something!" Before he could protest, the other Mr. Weinstein, in a firm-sounding voice, called Mickey into the back room, handing him a large, full bag—one like Morton Weinstein had carried away—telling him to deliver prescriptions instead of doing anything in the store. "Take your time, Mickey—there won't be any more deliveries this afternoon." As Mickey left he heard angry voices in the back room, the bald Mr. Weinstein's voice by far the louder.

It was almost a month before the brothers again had angry words while Mickey was in the store. He heard them saying things in the back room, only making out scattered words in their hostile argument. Morton Weinstein's high-pitched whininess bearing down on Arthur's quieter tones; Morton's flood of angry spewing inundating Arthur's attempts at more even-handed discussion. As sharp in tone as words and phrases were, the sharpness was muffled by the closed door and the partition dividing the rear of the store. The sliding glass window in the center of the ceiling-high, store-wide partition, rarely closed, *was* closed.

Their squabbling started when Mickey entered for a weekday after-school stint and a moment later short, black-mustached Morton Weinstein entered behind him, immediately going to the back room, shaking off his overcoat from thick, broad shoulders as he passed the boy in a front aisle. He strode into the sanctum in the rear of the oblong-shaped store, but it was minutes before Mickey heard sounds of anger. Surprisingly, the elder Mr. Weinstein's was the first irate voice Mickey heard. But the wall and distance from where they faced each other to the front of the store where Mickey stood perusing pulp-paper comic books muffled their growing stridency. It was simple to comprehend they were both angry, but *about* what Mickey could not decide, and did not care, as long as he was not the crux of the matter. Adults, Mickey thought, distracted from his idling, embarrassed by their arguing, always seemed eager to fight about something, anything.

Fatso Weinstein is always mad—at me, people in the neighborhood—even his own brother. Mickey's eyes were on the comic book pages, but his mind was on the brothers. *My Mr. Weinstein is older. He oughta know a lot more 'bout a lot of things than that UGLY shit!—the way he waddles—the fatass!*

Mickey reassured himself that the fight had nothing to do with him. In the weeks between the two arguments Mickey felt that he had at least proved himself to Mr. *Arthur* Weinstein, the *important* brother, in his estimation. The drugstore's business was good; Mickey made many deliveries; he increased the amount he gave his father, artfully and gratuitously providing a daily tally sheet to show his integrity; and he played less hooky. His mood had changed. He became less refractory in school. When Mr. Arthur Weinstein was working alone and if he was not busy in his back room and there were no customers, the boy and the man would sit side by side on swivel stools at the front of the counter, sipping sodas or nibbling at sundaes the man had made for them. They talked of things that interested both of them and the man asked about things that interested the boy.

When the muffled argument subsided the older Mr. Weinstein had a scowling face as he called and motioned Mickey to where he stood by the ancient cash register on the end of the counter that extended almost the rear width of the store. He took a large bag of smaller bags with invoices attached from beside the huge, ornate gold-colored register. As he swung toward Mickey the bag caught against the machine, tearing a long hole in the heavy paper. He pressed the gaping tear against his chest, trying to slam the drawer shut at the same time with an elbow. Failing, visibly greatly annoyed, he went into the back room for a new bag. Mickey had never seen him so angry before.

The register drawer had been vigorously elbowed but a broken mechanism kept it from locking, even closing fully. However, the spring that snapped the drawer open in normal use, whenever a key was depressed to ring up a sale, did function perfectly, keeping the drawer open three to four inches at all times.

It was a sharp corner of the protruding drawer that snagged the bag, delaying Mickey's exit. *Just when I wanted to be out of here in a hurry, the way Fatso is hollerin'.* He could hear the brothers again saying curt, angry words as he looked about to distract himself from deciphering their anger, his wandering eyes gravitated to the open drawer. He leaned sideways to look at the compartments filled with coins—pennies at the left front of the drawer, then, nickels, dimes, quarters, and half dollars to the right. He looked away quickly when he realized what he was thinking: *Holy—why didn' I think o' this before?*

The Weinstein's cash register was a wondrous machine, Mickey judged, especially comparing it to others. It was the largest and most intricately embellished one he had seen, so large that its base was below the surface of the store-width counter. It was positioned on a special cabinet a carpenter built low enough so the double-sided, glass-enclosed, one-above-the-other transaction windows—one side for the customer to verify a sale amount, the other side for the register-user to see—would be at the short Morton Weinstein's eye level. When Morton announced to Arthur that he was hiring a carpenter, Arthur had not made a single protest that *he* would then need to bend his knees uncomfortably to also see the windows, or have to stoop and aggravate his back problem.

An ornately shaped, thick metal panel perched at the top of the ponderous device, rising six inches at the peak of its curved, curlicue-ended form above the upper oblong window that flashed CASH or NO SALE when transactions were done at the register. And the window below had its own index-finger-pointing hand symbol that showed dollars and cents amounts of purchases. Otherwise, large zeros showed below the NO SALE signal if the register was opened. The side of the plaque facing customers was emblazoned with bold lettering carved into the metal:

M. & A. WEINSTEIN

PHARMACY

When they purchased the machine, Morton had said he would be glad to take care of details of installation, ordering the engraved nameplate that was included in the purchase price; things like that, as Morton put it; so Arthur would not have to bother himself with small matters. Thus, besides the special cabinet to accommodate Morton's stature, the register's nameplate had initials M. & A., not A. & M.

The register had two drawers, Mickey noted; one smaller, above another, both with locks. He thought: *All the other registers, in other stores, they only had one cash drawer.* He realized, standing beside the very large machine, that he had, unconsciously, studied registers in other stores. *Why did I do that?* He remembered that detail suddenly. It had become habit to scan every store he entered in hope of getting part-time work, eyes searching every part of each new place. As his habit developed he never wondered *why* he paid such attention to seeing things. But now, looking over this ornate register, he remembered flashes of details of other store registers clearly, he remembered that he had given this register a quick once-over on his first day of work, back when the machine was in proper working order.

There was an elegant-looking shelf at the front of the Weinstein's register, between the top and bottom drawers, made of thick white marble, four inches from front to back, extending the width of the gilded bulk. The whiteness of the marble was delicately veined with haphazard whorls, crazed-patterns of faintly visible gray lines. On the right side of the register was a long-armed crank handle with a bulky, free-spinning wood knob. It was the "key" to the machine, the way of opening the spring-loaded drawer that would surge open with loud sounds of released springs and ratchets to an accompanying loud single-tone bell. On the left side was a complicated attachment Mickey had not seen on other registers; a thick, high box, heavily embossed with entwined leaves, gold-painted, capped by a rounded box with vertical slots and protruding levers. Mickey stood enraptured. *That's new to me—won'er what it's there for? Won'er what it does? But—the whole thing is a beauty!*

Mickey contemplated this "beauty": *It's not new. There's lots of stores with new machines—most are plainer—not as big—and that little hand in the window with the pointin' finger is gone on most of 'em—and they open with one of the button keys instead of a handcrank—and all the curlicues are gone, too—you don' see 'em anymore, much—just plain old things now—smooth all over—one drawer—a lot smaller—no glass at the top where the numbers and CASH and NO SALE can show. Well— everythin's differ'nt all the time now.*

Mickey became more impressed as he looked more closely. *This one is beautiful-looking—s-o-o BIG! Look at all that fancy stuff carved on it!* He traced fingertips across the broad front panel that faced customers, wondering why the makers went to so much trouble to make something so fancy just to hold money. He ran fingers over swirled embossed and carved patterns on the side of the machine, and moved to stand more in the narrow side aisle that connected store front and back. He edged farther to the back so he could see the opened drawer and bank of keys. *How much is in there?—jus' in the open drawer? How about in the drawer that ain' open?—right now, this very minute—while I'm standin' right here!*

Mickey gazed, fascinated, at the entire bulk of the glittering machine, not seeing particular features now. Then his eyes shifted to the plaque perched above his head. The plaque, on this side, also had deeply carved letters:

M. & A. WEINSTEIN

PHARMACY

Why the hell they got it on both sides? Some registers he had seen only had AMOUNT PURCHASED instead of names. *They know who they are! Why do they need a sign in front of their eyes every time they use this thing?*

Across the curved, sloping front of the cash register there were five vertical rows of keys rising from the upper drawer to the window at the top. Four rows had ascending numbers on the round keys, some with dollar symbols. The row at the left had letters, A at the top, down to B, D, E, H, and K, plus three other special push keys, R. ON ACC'T, CHARGE—a red key—and PAID OUT.

Scant few square inches had escaped the designer's penchant for embossed and carved filigree; elaborate leafy forms, swirly shapes culminating in curlicues; horizontal patterns; vertical designs; on panels on every side and on drawer fronts; between rows of push keys; surrounding the thick-glass windows; with all the metal gilded by gold-colored paint carefully applied. Mickey thought the machine was beautiful when he had first seen it and now thought it even more beautiful— no, handsome!—now that he could study it so closely. *Even if the drawer don' work the right way—they can get that fixed.*

Sounds of rustling paper and glass clunking against glass came from the back room as the boy stepped away from the register to peek in at the brothers. Both had their backs to him, busy at opposite ends of a work counter. Mickey moved back to the open drawer, then looked at the small viewing window in the center of the wall separating the store's two areas. He hoped the bald Mr. Weinstein hadn't, in the last second, suddenly moved to look through the window into the front of the store for customers, or to watch him. He swiftly pulled the cash drawer open, hastily studying the oblong large slots holding bills, two stuffed with ones, each of the others containing, fives, tens, and twenties. The compartments of five-dollar bills and larger were at least each half full, the money held compressed by hinged weights. His eyes widened at the treasure. He had never seen so much money in a single place at one time. A greedy urge came over him to scoop up all the coins and bills. His mind raced.

I'll run from here—so fast they can't catch me—never catch me—away from home—from the whole city! No one will ever find me! I'll be so rich! I'll show that fat sonofabitch!—for bein' a mean bastard!

Then he imagined a disappointed look on Mr. Arthur Weinstein's face, turning into a sad frown. Mickey stepped back from the fully open drawer, closing his eyes, panic-stricken, flushed with shame, denouncing himself. *Why'd I do such a thing? He's so good to me.* Tears burned his eyes. Not wanting to, dreading it, he slowly opened his eyelids, squinting at the cloudy mental image of the man he had momentarily betrayed in his mind.

Mickey stood *alone* between the register and the back room opening, hearing paper-rustling and glass-bumping noises. *Thank God!* He looked into the work room; the brothers still worked busily and wordlessly at the counter. He felt relieved, puzzled. *I can't b'lieve it! I only IMAGINED Mr. Weinstein standin' there!* Mickey's mind had never conjured so clear a vision, an image so confounding, so stirring. He warned himself. *I shouldn'ta opened that damn thing!* He pushed the cash drawer in as far as it would go, the broken mechanism keeping the drawer four inches from closing, leaving the spacing as he had found it, then leaned casually against the back room door frame, hands in knickers pockets, eyes on the floor, softly whistling unmelodiously, striving to appear to be patiently waiting for the new bag to be packed.

Over the early part of the route, the whole trip taking more than an hour to cover several blocks in more than one direction, to climb stairs and go back down them, along the way trying doorknobs of storage closets for bottle searches, Mickey worried about the apparition of his Mr. Weinstein. It was so *real*, so *close*. Even now it was so clearly apparent that he could not hold back fright, shame, occasional teary eyes. But as the route lengthened and became wearying, the image became fuzzier, then remote, then unseen, forgotten. By the time he arrived at the drugstore, eight parcels delivered, an even dollar in his pocket to take home—the largest amount yet—plus seventy cents to add to his backyard hoard, he had dismissed the event with reckless ease. An hour earlier—an eon of youthful attention span—he had been awed by a pile of coins and stacks of bills within easy reach, then forgot about them. Now, an hour later that awe returned, but with it he felt edgy as he greedily thought about somehow dipping into that till.

On many occasions in the store thereafter, Mickey paid particular, sly attention to the register, sure that one day he would get to the Weinsteins to find the venerable machine repaired to perfect working order. Sometimes, when he could do so unobserved, he even touched the slightly open drawer, made gentle pushing tests, seeing if the malfunction continued to exist. He periodically studied the positions of exposed coin compartments, and on some afternoon or Saturday morning trips to the drugstore from home, his first objective was to go by the register to covertly check the levels of the coins. When he would go into or leave the back room, he would flick an arm across the front of the machine above the protruding drawer, testing how far, how rapidly, how smoothly he could stretch a hand and retract it. But he only practiced those stealthy movements and improved his dexterity when the ill-tempered, belligerent, unfriendly Mr. Weinstein worked alone.

Customers came to know Mickey as a cheerful boy and became more friendly. Mickey had quickly learned secrets of dealing with people on whom he relied for money, for income. Women gave him cookies and candies; and tips from everyone were larger than when he had started the job. He learned to rid himself of sullenness before getting to the first delivery stop, sullenness brought on by the morose, irritable brother. The man never greeted him when he arrived, whether he worked alone or with his brother, and seemed always ready with a long task for Mickey inside the store. When the pudgy Mr. Weinstein worked alone he did not have deliveries ready to be made when Mickey reported for work, deliveries the older brother had said would be his primary duty. When Mickey was sent out it was usually to make from two to four deliveries nearby and he was told he should not have to take more than fifteen or twenty minutes. Each time he was admonished to hurry back, but he never did, finding excuses to linger, improvising clever explanations for delays.

Mickey became increasingly angry about having to do dusting, sweeping, washing, and arranging shelves for Morton Weinstein, fed up with working for nothing. With differences apparent to Mickey in the number of deliveries when the brothers each worked by himself, the boy grew suspicious that somehow the fat, angry brother was carrying parcels to customers instead of leaving them for him. He grew sure the two large paper bags that Mr. Weinstein had twice gone off with while Mickey labored about the store without payment were the cause of the heated arguments with his brother, feeling that only something like that would have made his Mr. Weinstein so angry and scowling.

But he could not substantiate those suspicions. Mickey made fewer deliveries each time the fat brother worked, but still, Mickey could not fathom when Mr. Weinstein could possibly find time during the day to leave the store when he was alone, and Mickey did not think he would do that. *He never left me alone to take care of the store because he don't trust me, that's what I think. He's always watchin' me move, watchin' where I am when we're here together.*

There were no loud arguments again, but the brothers seldom spoke to each other. Mickey's Mr. Weinstein patiently took the initiative with his brother, but without noticeable success. Pudgy Morton Weinstein resisted gentle talk, small talk, subtle persuasions. He ignored Mickey except to growl instructions or to express annoyance at some thing the boy had or had not done.

Mickey disliked the way the portly brother treated customers; gruff with man or woman; mean with children, no matter what age; specially mistrustful of youths. More than once Mickey heard Morton Weinstein warn his brother sternly: "Watch those kids close—they'll steal us blind!" Yet people in need of prescriptions and patent medicines were compelled to do business with M. & A. Pharmacy; it was the only drugstore in the widespread, populous neighborhood. The stocky Weinstein brother was keenly aware of the relationship and made no effort to create good will, to even display simple courtesies. Mickey thought he was the greediest person he had ever known, often listening as he talked continually about making money, saving money, increasing profit; about selling the store and moving to another neighborhood—a richer one; about opening a second store—and someday, who knows, maybe even a third one?

He watched him often wheedle customers into buying something more than they wanted, another this, another that. Mickey detested him most when he persuaded elderly customers—people with meager money to last from month-end to month-end—to spend some of their small amounts as soon as he cashed their monthly checks for ten cents. Toward the end of a month he would gather items, a hodgepodge of what did not sell readily, putting them on the sales counter close to the cash register. Counting bills and coins in return for checks he would unctuously make his sales pitch, touting one extra-special—as he emphatically termed it—sale item after another. Many who could ill-afford even slight extravagance would yield to him, leaving the drugstore with less money than they had planned.

Mickey thought selling Mrs. Scalise bars of perfumed soap showed he really was a *devil.* Mickey wanted to shout at the woman before Mr. Weinstein could deduct her soap coast from money in his hand, to stop his unmerciful lusting for her meager dole. But he did not; he wanted to keep his job.

"It's nice, Mr. Weinstein," Mrs. Scalise said, soft traces of Italian speech shading her words, carefully watching him lift bills and coins from the drawer. "But you know—it isn't—"

She was sixty-six years old and nearing the end of her second year of widowhood. Her unfortunate husband, only two months retired, forced to move slowly because of arthritis in one knee, did not move quickly enough as he forgetfully started across Columbus Avenue without worrying about traffic weaving in and out around thick, high metal columns supporting the elevated train tracks. A roaring express overhead obscured every other neighborhood sound and a reckless driver's vegetable truck bumper caught the ambling man from behind, lofting him headfirst from his careless path directly at a steel column. He died instantly without any sensation of having been struck and hurled into oblivion.

Mrs. Scalise endured her anguish for weeks, wanting to die. But she endured further, staying in the neighborhood where she and her husband had lived more than thirty years, subsisting on their small savings shown in her dog-eared bank passbook and a small monthly check from the government's new Social Security program.

Mr. Weinstein stopped selecting money from the drawer, the cash in his left palm, stepping sideways to face Mrs. Scalise directly, lifting a pink-paper-wrapped small bar of soap from a stack next to the register. "This is *really* good soap, Missus—with a good price—that we bought ourselves from a downtown importer—so we could have the best—because our customers are special—"

"It is nice; I can smell it," she said, looking at the bar in fingertips he moved closer to her, "but I have to get some not so expensive. And look, Mr. Weinstein, look at my hands and face. Can they be helped with perfume? My fingers have knots. My face is old, with these lines, with wrinkles. Cheap soap makes me clean. To be *clean* is what I want."

"Think, Mrs. Scalise," Weinstein said, "to when you used to use something like this—how nice you felt after—the nice smell, a wonderful smell." He moved the bar closer as she waited for her money, slightly moving the soap in his fingertips from side to side to spread aroma in the air near the old woman.

Mickey flicked the long-handled feather duster at stock on shelves as he stood near them, drifting the duster back and forth over small sections one above another, careful to stay in the same location yet appear disinterested; now and then squatting to rearrange things that didn't need rearranging; occasionally turning to other sections for more dusting and unneeded rearranging.

Morton Weinstein tantalized Mrs. Scalise with words, putting the soap on the counter between them, closer to her, then inching the bar to her edge of the counter, easing his other hand toward his side of the counter, sliding a bill and some of the coins from her cashed check toward him. "You are a handsome woman, Mrs. Scalise—and I know you were beautiful as a girl—as a lady—with lots of young men who wanted your company where you lived in Italy. It must have been unendurable for them."

Mickey perceived a remarkable change come over the homely, small Mr. Weinstein. The sensitivity he showed toward Mrs. Scalise astounded the boy. She was enthralled by the man's evocative words, and Mickey, idly flicking the duster, was surprised and captivated by his phrases and descriptions. Weinstein quickly and persuasively talked of the pleasures of long, aromatic, bubbly baths, smoothly heaping one word on another, creating soft enticing phrases, all in brief moments. His eloquence caused Mickey to turn his head to study the druggist appealing to the small woman. His face was not the one Mickey always saw as he said, "If I had been one of your young men the others would have had to deal with me for your attention!"

With each word Morton Weinstein's eagerness mounted. Mickey could not believe how gently the man could speak, the affection he expressed. The druggist tried persuading Mrs. Scalise that the bar wrapped in pink paper would certainly please Mr. Scalise each time she used it. He was not dissuaded when she softly told him, "Mr. Scalise, God rest him, died two years ago." He deftly switched to again describing the effects of the soap on her. She was enraptured by his almost poetic softness and vividness of speech.

Mickey would have continued to be, also, if he had not seen thick fingers curled tightly about the bill and the coins Weinstein had now picked up, the hand resting near the back edge of the counter, top knuckles white from his clenching grip. Weinstein leaned heavily toward on the wide countertop, resting on his right forearm, the small bar of expensive soap protruding from the casually extended stubby fingers, holding the temptation near Mrs. Scalise. His voice dulled to a murmur and anger built in Mickey. *The sonofabitch—the fat no-good bastard—he's teasin' her!*

Mrs. Scalise said she would take the soap, but protested against a second bar the druggist tried to press on her, less diligently, but still eager, still hopeful. Mickey's anger distracted him from paying attention to the dusting chore. Tipped and dislocated by irritable swipes across shelf stock, several small cans and bottles clattered and clunked onto the linoleum-covered floor. The bottles luckily stayed intact and Mickey had most of the items in proper places before glancing at a glowering Morton Weinstein and a sympathetic, sadly smiling Mrs. Scalise. Looking from the man to the woman, Mickey had a burst of greater anger. *I hope somebody gives it to him good someday!*

Mrs. Scalise, smiling, murmured something unintelligible to Mickey as she passed along his aisle toward home, clutching her purse and the pink-wrapped soap to her chest.

Mickey fumed. *The cheapskate didn' even put it in a paper bag for her—not even a little bag!*

After she left the store Morton Weinstein nudged Mickey aside to examine the material replaced on the shelves, making unneeded adjustments, growling, "You'd better be more careful if you want to keep your job—and get back to work! There's plenty to do!"

11

Murmuring in the large room had steadily become louder, bouncing off the pale green walls and the high, once-white ceiling, the sound becoming an increasingly higher-pitched drone.

A head appeared from outside the room through a slightly opened door, calling out loudly, "Hey!—listen up!" Few stopped talking to listen, most of them because they did not hear the command. The drone barely lowered in tone.

"HEY!—" the head shouted, stretching out the short word out to a long command. "I said LISTEN UP!" The head's strong voice thundered, drawing out the last word. "You people hold it down! You're too noisy! We've still got things to do in this other room—then you'll all be moving on. Now hold it *down!*"

It became much quieter, making it easier to think again.

12

Several days later, during which the brothers worked simultaneously, Mickey entered the drugstore and saw the chubby Mr. Weinstein was the only brother working. The boy pleaded stomach illness, saying he could not work that afternoon, then loafed with other boys blocks away, went home in time to listen to *Renfrew of the Royal Mounted* on the radio, later did some homework, but not all of it; enough to satisfy himself he could give a truthful answer if his father asked, "Did you do homework?"

The next afternoon, to see who was working, he stealthily peered through a corner of the store's front window, peeking through the camouflage of haphazard advertising posters taped to the inside of the window. He persuaded himself only the troublesome Mr. Weinstein was in the store and sacrificed another opportunity to increase his hoard of money. Both times he explained to his father that he'd had a lot of homework to do, that he had stopped by the drugstore to explain his absence beforehand; that the brothers had said it was fine, that schoolwork always came first.

On Saturday morning he did not go near the pharmacy, thinking he would rather bet that Fatso Weinstein *would* be working by himself. Later, if he learned that *his* Mr. Weinstein had been the one working, he would just say he was sorry, that he could not come in because he was still sick that morning. *I don' like doing that to such a nice man, but it's better than goin' in first and find out that the other one IS there alone and I'll maybe get rooked into stayin' to do sweepin' and other lousy stuff.*

On Monday afternoon Mickey made himself report to work. He was worried his father would be suspicious of another excuse of doing homework and Mickey could not dream up another reason. He was happy to see the smiling Mr. Weinstein working by himself, then even happier when he learned his Mr. Weinstein would be there for the next few days, too.

"Mr. Weinstein," Arthur Weinstein said, "left on the overnight train to Chicago, just after lunchtime today." He hesitated.

"He's going to a convention—for three days—for pharmacists from all over the country. He'll be gone all today"—Mickey smiled, hoping he didn't appear satisfied—"for traveling, for eating in a fancy dining car—and sleeping in a sleeperette, he says it's called; getting there fresh as a daisy, he says.

"Then Tuesday, Wednesday, and Thursday will be for their convention. I hope he'll go out at night with some of the others to have a good time." Mr. Weinstein paused. "He deserves it—and needs it. He works hard—doesn't take enough time off—" He stopped his analysis, then said "Friday, sleep late, and a little sightseeing maybe—he *should* do some good-time things. Then he'll take the return train from Chicago, eating and sleeping while he's rolling high-speed across the country. Of course, Saturday he'll need to rest up. All week before then he'll be going through things he's not used to."

Mickey did not know if Mr. Weinstein kept talking; he had stopped listening—counting the days, saying the names of the days to himself, counting again, thinking ahead. *THIS afternoon—and four more like it!—and Saturday, too!—maybe all day!*

As Mickey went about his deliveries he looked forward to getting out of school during the coming week so he could get to the drugstore. He promised himself he would do his homework quickly and well each night so there would be no complaint from school or by his father. *I'll up the amount I give the ol' man every night—not so much that he might get suspicious about extra money, but enough so he'll be tickled and won't mind me spendin' so much time runnin' aroun' makin' deliveries.*

It was a week of sheer enjoyment for Mickey, charging swiftly about the neighborhood, hustling to make deliveries, running up long flights of stairs, bounding back down two and three steps at a time; anything to return to the store soon after he left it; not taking time to search for a single bottle for the two or three cents it would bring. He lost interest in building his backyard cache. He had more money hidden there then he had ever had at one time, with no plans for spending any of it. However, with his Mr. Weinstein working each day he had more deliveries to make, and his quickness and boundless good spirits with the customers resulted in greater tips each time he worked. Almost reluctantly he kept adding to his hidden store, a trove now composed of four metal cans—slender, rectangular hinge-topped, red-colored Prince Albert tobacco cans packed with coins, all the cans wrapped together in a large remnant of yellow kitchen-table oilcloth.

He had seen dozens of discarded tobacco tins in his quick bottle searches in trash and garbage pails, paying little attention to their possible second-hand utility value. He had no need for a can like it—three inches wide across the front, four and a half inches high, by three-quarters of an inch thick. He had nothing to protect then. The first time he came across one, he wondered: *Who's the bald-headed guy in the picture on the front, with the funny-lookin' coat, and a cane.* Across the front of the can, at the top, above the oval picture, high capital letters proclaimed

PRINCE ALBERT

Beneath the black and white three-quarter portrait, there was other printed labeling:

C R I M P   C U T

LONG BURNING PIPE AND

CIGARETTE TOBACCO

He don' look very comfortable—standin' stiff-lookin' like that—an' he's kinda pudgy too—but at least he ain' a lardass like Fatso Weinstein is. I won'er what he's a prince of?—if he's a real prince?—even if he's a real person. I thought princes were s'posed to be handsome. Bein' bald don't make him handsome—nosirree!

The back of the can extolled the product:

PRINCE ALBERT

TOBACCO IS PREPARED FOR SMOKERS
UNDER THE PROCESS DISCOVERED IN
MAKING EXPERIMENTS TO PRODUCE
THE MOST DELIGHTFUL AND
WHOLESOME TOBACCO FOR
CIGARETTE AND PIPE SMOKERS.

PROCESS PATENTED
JULY 30TH 1907.

R.J. REYNOLDS TOBACCO COMPANY.
WINSTON SALEM, N.C. U.S.A.
DOES NOT BITE THE TONGUE

His four coin-filled cans, all in good condition, one still bearing most of the *2 OUNCES TOBACCO* blue paper seal across the lid from side to side and extending down each narrow curved side, were quite heavy, even singly. Their consolidated heft excited him while holding them all in one hand. As reluctant as he currently was, he nonetheless kept adding to his secret store. *I have to do SOMETHIN' with all the extra money I'm gettin' every day, don' I?*

He considered slightly increasing his father's share of the tip money, but decided against it. *Naw, I'm gonna be making' a lot less when Fatso gets back!—and I don' want the ol' man to won'er how come so much this week and why a lot less next week.* His hidden wealth increased slowly and steadily.

But his greatest happiness of the week was because of the time he had with the brother who smiled, *his* Mr. Weinstein. *He treats me like a son.* Mr. Weinstein only had Mickey dust the store's front shelves once during the week, telling him it wasn't necessary to make *several* passes over each section before going on to the next. When Mickey asked about the shelves in the back room—"Mr. Weinstein always has me dust there every Monday, Wednesday, and Friday"—Arthur Weinstein told him, "No need to bother. I always do it myself at the beginning of every week, and once a week is adequate."

Each day, after school, Mickey found his Mr. Weinstein busy behind the soda fountain, cleaning and drying glasses and utensils, melodiously humming or softly whistling along with strains of music from two small radios. He would smile at the boy, say his name, ask how everything was going; was school all right? Three days that week, the druggist had Mickey sit at the counter and served him what he requested, as though Mickey was a customer. "It's my treat," Mr. Weinstein said as he pushed back Mickey's coins the first time he laid them on the marble counter. And Mr. Weinstein said the same the next two times also.

Anything Mr. Weinstein asked the boy to do he did eagerly and intensely. And the man said thank you when each task was done. Mickey's spirits were so high that Margaret asked him why. His father was curious too, but did not say much other than ask what he was so damn happy about all of the time, all of a sudden.

Everything about the store was different than it had been. Mickey was chipper. Customers' moods changed. They called out cheery greeting after the first two days of the week when they learned Mickey's Mr. Weinstein would be tending the store the rest of the week. Sunlight seemed to flood the streets between the brownstone and brick buildings, pouring between the scattered, various-shaped posters taped to the inside of the high, wide plate glass front window, the sun filling the long rectangle of the drugstore with unaccustomed brightness. Tuesday afternoon strains of classical music unobtrusively suffused the store area.

Mickey's Mr. Weinstein enjoyed listening to music and kept a small radio on the back room work counter, pushed into a corner at the place he did his work. He kept the volume turned low, to play his music softly, to avoid his brother's complaints from several paces away, where he was always roughly clattering and clunking bottles, cans, and measuring and mixing implements. That radio was now on the front customer service counter, at the end opposite the cash register, and Mr. Weinstein had placed another small radio at the front of the store, on the soda fountain marble counter, close to the window. Neither radio played loudly, but the oblong room was filled with soothing musical strains. Customers looked about when they entered, puzzled at the new environment. They smiled and complimented Mr. Weinstein; and Mickey hummed and whistled softly to sounds to which he had seldom before paid attention.

Friday afternoon's after-school work started promptly with six deliveries to be made. They were all in a large bag containing small bags neatly stapled closed so only the customer's name showed in neatly typewritten lines on a label. *Boy, he sure does things nice. These ain't like the ones Fatso gives me—names and numbers I sometimes can't even read when he writes them—worse than my old man's handwritin'—and that always means I gotta read the names and addresses before I get out or I'll waste my time once I'm out—then he gets mad when I ask him what he wrote—the shithead!*

Mickey returned without wasting time and Mr. Weinstein said, "I wonder if you would mind watching the store for a few minutes?" Mickey was confounded, sure he had not heard correctly. "I want to go shopping—I *have* to go shopping at the delicatessen for a few things."

I can't believe he's sayin' it! ME watch the store?

"Mrs. Weinstein just telephoned and wants some kosher food for our meals this weekend. You know what kosher is, don't you? It has to do with food we Jews—something like Catholics not eating meat on Friday—maybe not quite the same—well, never mind—I have to do the shopping; Mrs. Weinstein isn't feeling too well today. The deli is only two blocks away." Mickey hemmed and hawed, so softly that Mr. Weinstein found his words unintelligible.

"You don't have to worry," Mr. Weinstein said as he put on his light overcoat. "I'll only be gone fifteen or twenty minutes—maybe not that long if the deli isn't busy."

I can' believe he'd lea' me alone—for fifteen minutes—that he'd trust me. How come he don't sen' me with the shoppin' list? The other one would. Fatso wouldn' lemme be alone in HIS store!

"You can sit here on a stool in the front—and look at whatever you want from the magazine rack—and just tell anyone who comes in that I'll be back soon and they can come back then, or they can sit with you and be comfortable waiting." He moved toward the front of the store, opened the door, turned, smiled, waved a hand, and closed the door behind him.

Christ! He DID it! I'm the only one here!

He was in a small, suddenly-turned-more-wonderful world of shelves along one wall stacked high one on another from floor almost to ceiling, packed closely with colored items of an enormous array of sizes and shapes. And all about him were six-foot-high, back-to-back standing rows of shelving, twenty feet long, similarly crowded with every rainbow color and every shade between. Everything looked brighter and shinier and prettier and more colorful now that it was his domain, no one else's. It had been given to him, at least for a short while.

He sauntered through the aisles, taking new looks at his possessions, seeing things he had not seen when simply required to dust and rearrange. He checked each of his swivel stools to be certain they all worked properly and quietly. Behind his soda fountain he pushed firmly down on the Coca Cola pump handle and squirted dark brown, rich-smelling liquid chocolate into a gracefully shaped Coca Cola glass, then filling it slowly with carbonated water, noisily swirling and rattling a spoon around inside the glass to blend bubbly carbonated water with the soda concentrate. With the mixture near the top of the glass, he pushed the fountain handle in the opposite direction, holding it firmly away from him. The gently flowing carbonated water turned into a high-pressure stream, furiously agitating the mixture into foamy-headed bubbliness, rising and spilling completely around the rim, pouring in a torrent over his fingers. Fascinated, listening to the high-pitched sound the thin stream made, he watched the high-speed water roiling the contents. Satisfied the concoction was correctly formulated, he turned off the water, inordinately proud of the first soda he had ever mixed. With an insolent air, he casually tossed the mixing spoon into the sink for someone *else* to clean.

Sipping soda through a paper straw, he sauntered through the long aisle paralleling the soda fountain, then through other narrow center aisles, finally through the one by the near-ceiling-high wall shelves, acting like a ruler surveying a kingdom. He went to the magazine rack, intending to use all his undisturbed time perusing every one of the ten or twelve different comic books. But after quickly scanning two of them, flipping pages back and forth, staying only a few seconds at some pages, he no longer felt inclined to idly read funny-books. He wondered why he suddenly felt disinterested in what usually was favorite reading.

He loitered about the front of the store, peering between posters on the large window to study people and vehicles on the street. He wandered to the rear of the store, feeling restless, wanting to do something better to pass the time. He detested housekeeping tasks—they were *chores*. He had an idea. *I'll surprise Mr. Weinstein and clean whatever needs cleanin'—or I'll dust somewhere—or make sure everythin' in the store looks neat. I'll do it for Mr. Weinstein.*

He went back to the seltzer water spigot and retrieved the spoon from the sink, rinsed it under hot water, and put it in its rightful place. He felt better about his slovenliness. *Mr. Weinstein don't deserve me makin' a mess of his place.*

He wiped a damp cloth over the mottled gray-and-black marble serving counter and polished it lightly with a fluffy white towel. He dry-wiped the flip-top covers of the four gallon-size compartments in the ice cream cabinet, filching spoonfuls of chocolate, strawberry—*M-m-m, this one's my favorite*—vanilla, and black raspberry ice cream. He refilled his glass with Coca Cola and carbonated water, adding extra syrup to give the drink a stronger flavor, to perk him up a little more.

He was pleased with his brief clean-up effort, with the shining proof of his industriousness. He decided that the rows of stocked shelves needed no attention. *Mr. Weinstein must really be takin' care of 'em during the day while I'm in school—jus' like he says he does.* He contemplated the store, searching for what to do next. *Maybe I'll do the back room, if it needs anythin'.*

As he passed the cash register he saw that it had apparently not yet been repaired. The drawer still protruded several inches. He pushed it in firmly but the locking mechanism was not working. Lackadaisically, he tried shutting the drawer several more times, vaguely expecting that something might catch as it should. Then, suddenly worried that something *might* catch and lock the drawer permanently, that Mr. Weinstein would then know that he had been at the register, he left it alone.

Stop staring at the damn money!

He pulled the drawer open until all the coin and bill compartments were exposed. "Jesus!" he said aloud.

He fingered the quarters and half dollars, then the bills. Lifting one out, he held a crisp, crinkly twenty dollar bill in fingertips of both hands, imagining what he could buy with it, the things he could do, thinking about places he could go and the things he could see. *Geez!—maybe I could go for a boat ride and go out and see the Statue of Liberty.* He carefully placed the bill back beneath the weighted arm in its compartment.

There were eleven fifty cent pieces in the drawer. Five dollars and fifty cents, he totaled mentally. He stacked them in the palm of one hand, visualizing candy bars and cookies—and lemon pies from the bakery. *Big lemon pies, not jus' the little ones wrapped in that thin gray wax paper that I always have to get cuz I don' have enough money for a big one from the bakery.* And he saw Errol Flynn lettered on a marquee at the theater and the poster in the lobby showing him leaping and swinging agilely as a monkey in the rigging of the towering sails, staving off swarming pirates, slashing them, slaying them dexterously or knocking them overboard from the end of his rope pendulum.

Fifty cents won' be missed—jus' one of these—'nough for a movie tomorrow afternoon if I skip school—plenty left for candy—I wouldn' have to touch nothin' in my Prince Albert cans. Forming a shallow scoop with both hands cupped, he jiggled the stack of coins to make it collapse, then let the coins trickle through a hole he opened in the bottom of the scoop, clunking softly back into their compartment.

Coincidentally, the quarters, twenty-two of them, also totaled five dollars and fifty cents. He balanced this taller, more slender stack in one palm as he thought of Errol Flynn again. He let the coins tumble into cupped hands, then made a chute of fingers, reluctantly letting the coins dribble slowly into the empty quarter compartment.

He felt angry. *I shouldn' be thinkin' about takin' Mr. Weinstein's money! Not my Mr. Weinstein! I got my own buried treasure where no one can find it. I don't need no more money—especially not his!* He shook off his trance slowly, pushing in the cash drawer as far as it would close without locking.

He went into the back room and stood examining the area for something to do that would be useful to Mr. Weinstein, still damning himself for thinking about rifling the cash drawer. Starting from his Mr. Weinstein's workplace he walked along the twelve-foot-long counter covered with linoleum, trailing an index finger on the surface, searching for dust or grime. As he passed the glass window in the partition between the store rear and front areas, he took a long look into the front, examining for customers. He had not heard the bell mounted above the door jingle to signal an entrance, but he looked through the window nonetheless. He ran a finger around the inside of the metal sink in the center of the counter, but it was as clean as everything else. He finished probing for dirt, ending at the fat brother's work station. He had no reason to pass a dustcloth over anything. He contemplated turning on the small radio to listen to a radio adventure serial, then remembered it had been moved out front. *Anyway, I'm s'posed to be watchin' the front of the store an' takin' care of the customers, not sittin' on my duff in the back room.* He stepped back and studied the wall shelves reaching high above his head. Everything was in order, clean as a whistle, neat as a pin.

The tall Coca Cola glass was nearly empty. He slurped the last few drops through the soggy, collapsing paper straw. He rinsed the glass and looked for a trash pail for the useless straw. But there was none in any corner, no waste receptacle on the counter. He tugged open several cabinet doors beneath the work counter but no trash bucket was handy. In the last cabinet, at the pudgy Mr. Weinstein's end of the work counter, he discovered two stacks of cigar boxes in the dim space stored alongside and slightly behind bottles of cleaning liquids and small cartons of soap powders.

Now there's somethin' I ain' tried—a cigar! He tried remembering who smoked cigars. He had never seen either Mr. Weinstein with one. Nor had he even seen one of them with a cigarette or a pipe. One of his father's friends seemed as though he always had one in his mouth. *Yeah—he never took it out—but I guess he did at least when he ate—but I never saw him eat—an' who knows with that guy—and he talked with it in his mouth all the time—an' that Italian kid Joey always looked funny doin' it—looked dumb—he don' know how to smoke 'em, that's what's wrong with him. Besides, these here gotta be real cigars—not them skinny, crooked things of Joey's—can't be any worse than cigarettes—at least not to just try one—to see what it's like.*

Mickey had smoked cigarettes several times, but never got to putting up with the sharp, biting sensations searing his throat, tearing at his lungs. The first two times he had coughed so violently he thought he would vomit. His most recent smoking escapade had been a few weeks ago, in Central Park, out of passersby sight, away from prying adult eyes, crouched with friends between the perimeter stone wall and a wide cluster of thick, tall bushes. The cigarette smoke was more bearable by then, but not enjoyable. Mickey did not smoke except when ridiculed or challenged by friends in small groups. Then he did it for appearances.

Squatting by the open cabinet door, he felt differently. *Maybe I'm more used to smokin' by now. And it wouldn' mean anythin' if I helped myself to just one cigar. I could puff on it in the backyard the next time I put money away. I wouldn' have to inhale, that's all.*

One after another he pulled several various-shaped boxes from the cabinet, most boxes made of thin wood, some boxes made of thick, rigid cardboard. He lifted lids to compare sizes, shapes, and bulks of the different brands, searching for the biggest and best-smelling cigar. *I remember somebody callin' 'em—what was it?—cheroots?—or somethin' like that.*

When he pulled up the lid of the last box, he had to tug at it hard to get it open; the box was held closed with a short, slender brad, with the head protruding a bit. Mickey stared curiously at the contents. Rolls of tightly wound paper stood on end at one side of the deep six-inch-square box, finely constructed of strong, light-brown wood. Most of the rolls were almost an inch in diameter, some of them only a half inch or so across. Mickey started counting. There were thirteen vertical, rolled, elastic-banded cylinders of paper crammed next to the horizontal layers of thick cigars. Tipping the box to study the rolls, he saw a large number on a corner of rolled paper. *20!—money!—paper money!—holy Christ!*

He nervously picked at the slimmest roll, trying to pull it up, numbers flashing in his mind, guessing at how much he might be holding in his shaking hands.

Mickey suddenly thought of Mr. Weinstein, *his* Mr. Weinstein, finding him at nosiness, at stealthiness. In panic he put the box on the floor, stood up and frantically looked at the door opening between the two rooms of the store, then grimly stared through the partition window, looking along the only two aisles that could be viewed. He desperately listened for sounds of movement or someone calling out. He sighed. *No one! I'm safe!*

He squatted, staring at the open box on the floor. The smallest cylinder had remained protruding up. He twisted the roll to see the corner numeral again. *I was right! Twenty dollars!* He jerked the tube from the box and violently tore off the elastic band, unrolling the money enough to count all the corners he could. *Ten bills! All twenties! All in one little roll! Jesus! That's—holy!—two hundred—oh, boy—that's two hundred dollars!*

As he counted, inner tremors and mental excitement turned to actual trembling, to weakness and tightness in his legs in the uncomfortable squat. He shifted to a kneeling position, pulling out other tubes of money, checking denominations. They were five-dollar-bill and ten-dollar–bill packages. He wanted to count every bill to see how much *could* be all *his.* He felt as stunned as if he had been hit solidly on the chin in a fist fight. His head pounded and he saw faint stars and bursting colors. It was the baseball game at Bear Mountain Park again, but a lot less. It was almost the same as when the bat in the hands of a wildly swinging hitter had missed a pitched ball by a wide distance and the fast-moving circling bat smashed into and broke Mickey's nose, knocking him senseless for several minutes.

His fingers were like thumbs. He had to recount the corners because of his awkwardness and confusion. *I'm right! Two hundred bucks!*

He became clumsier and more rattled, worrying that Mr. Weinstein *had* returned, was in the store that very moment, would reappear in seconds. *He's gonna catch me! Oh God, suppose the OTHER Mr. Weinstein is back from Chicago? He'll kill me!—just seein' me like this!*

The image of his own Mr. Weinstein ambling slowly, unexpectedly, along an aisle toward the back room terrified Mickey. But he fought off the paralysis caused by his fears and put rubber bands back in place, jamming each cylinder into the cigar box.

He was unable to comprehend the amount of money at his knees. A thousand dollars had once been decided on as he and friends chattered about what sum would make up a *fortune,* a real fortune, one that would last forever. Well, maybe not *forever,* they redecided, but a thousand dollars *would* last a long time—years even—and it would buy nearly everything anyone would *have* to have—and a lot of things anybody would *want* to get, just because they felt like it!

Almos' that much musta been in my hands. Hadda be! There jus' hadda be that much just in some of the bigger rolls I didn' get a chance to look at—and how 'bout all the other rolls?—some of 'em really fat! Despite his anxiety he could not resist tugging at other rolls and pulling them up, but he did not take any of them fully out of the box. *How much is in this one?—and this one?—this one?*

He had an urge to grab the three largest rolls and run. Then he decided he might just as well take the whole box, cigars and all. *But then go to WHERE? No one will ever lemme get away with this much! I know in all those movies the G-Men track crooks to any place they hide! I don' know what to do! Damndamndamn! Where could I go?*

He jammed the three rolls back down into the box, closed the lid, and pushed the brad firmly back in place, then put the brown box against the rear of the cabinet where it had been. In reverse order from which he had removed the boxes of cigars, he carefully replaced them, one stack in front of another. *Just the way I found 'em!* He pushed other things back in place, concealing the double stack of boxes as they had been before. With a sudden flush of relief Mickey closed the cabinet door firmly The work room now seemed to be shrinking in size in a rush, becoming oppressively small. He was afraid he would have no place to go, afraid he would not be able to get out at all, afraid his Mr. Weinstein would discover him, terrified that Morton Weinstein would loom over him. He rushed out of the work room and sat on a swivel stool at the soda fountain, struggling for calmness before Mr. Weinstein returned.

He sat mournfully, swearing silently at himself because he had not taken the money and run far away; cursing himself for the terrible thing he had almost done to his Mr. Weinstein; berating himself that he had been so nosy in the first place, for thinking about stealing cigars he would probably throw away after a few puffs, even without inhaling. *My God!—the glass. What if he finds it?*

He ran into the back room and to the sink and snatched the tall glass from the work counter, pulling a cleaning cloth from his back pocket and wiping the water ring from the dark linoleum covering. In the front of the store, he put the glass on its shelf along the wall behind the soda fountain.

He was safe again, assiduously sorting and straightening magazines and newspapers in the long, high wall rack when Mr. Weinstein returned. As he pushed open the door, with a large bag of groceries in each arm, he apologized for taking so long. Mickey stopped soft whistling of a cheery tune to smile at Mr. Weinstein.

At home, doing homework after supper, Mickey was continually distracted by what had happened.

Damn!—God!—all that money!

13

*M*oney—*money! What trouble it can be—it can CAUSE.*

How does it go? Money's the root of all evil? No—MONEY isn't—not money itself.

Remember the right way the saying went? The LOVE of money is the root of all evil.

14

Mickey's Saturday was tinged throughout by dismay. He rushed to the drugstore early, eager, happy with the warm sun, happy because of his Mr. Weinstein, happy with prospects for the day.

Rounding the last street corner, the drugstore in sight, he was struck with the thought of which day it was. The last one he would work before the other Mr. Weinstein was back again. The last day of music. The last one of smiles. Less friendliness.

When Fat Stuff gets back there's gonna be more slammin' and bangin' in the back room—everywhere in the store—an' he's always gonna be mad—always snarlin' an' yellin'.

Mickey still could not understand why the older brother could let the younger one be the boss, deciding how everything would be done in the store, in the business. He thought about quitting.

The open cash register drawer, passed more than a dozen times that Saturday, was given only a casual glance now and then by Mickey. The third time, he congratulated himself that he had gotten rid of any thought about pilfering from the drawer. Twice later, randomly, he was pleased with himself again. *Nice goin'. See how easy it is?* Then later in the day, he smiled slightly as he went by the open drawer. *See? Nothin' to it. Besides, you got enough.*

But more than once that day—and several days after—Mickey was nagged by curiosity about the hoard hidden in the absent brother's cabinet. When work was finished, with a layer of coins spread on the soda fountain counter, he counted his tips. He divided coins for the backyard trove and for his father. He felt disappointed about how insignificantly his total for the day compared with the slim roll of bills he had counted, the roll not much larger in size than a cigarette. *What a fortune I had in my hands then!*

The cache of Prince Albert cans had grown to four, three packed full with coins, each bound closed with a thick, doubled rubber band around top and bottom. The fourth can had filled more slowly. Mickey's pleasure with working for Arthur Weinstein led to being at school when he should, spending more time in his room doing homework. His expenses were now small, and already funded. For the whole week, each day, he put more coins into his father's portion than his own. He was satisfied with what he had put away; satisfied that *something* was added every evening to increase his treasury.

Today he impulsively was more generous, counting and recounting into two clusters of coins, making a small third group of pennies and two nickels. Mr. Weinstein smiled as he exchanged one cluster for a fairly new dollar bill; then handed Mickey a newer paper dollar for the second handful of tip money.

Mickey carefully folded the two bills in half, gathered up the pennies and nickels, putting them all in his shirt pocket with the artfully scribbled, artfully crumpled tally sheet he continued making each time before going home.

In the backyard, he tugged the large rock that partially filled the hole in the ground between the clothesline pole and the six-foot-high wood fence. He untied corner knots of the oilcloth bundle and added a single dollar bill to the fourth, partially filled tobacco can. It was the first time that he had secreted paper money, worried that dampness might harm the paper. Segregating money on the soda fountain counter, however, he decided the ground was never *that* damp, that he had plenty of protection, what with a closed tin can wrapped in a lot of thick oilcloth. As he redid the bundle, he thought what a small sum he really had. *Nothin' like Fatso Weinstein's got stashed away!*

It mus' be him! The other Mr. Weinstein wouldn' keep money hidden away like that!—bein' so sneaky!

His father, with a half smile, said, as Mickey gave him the dollar bill, two nickels, and several pennies, "It's about time. I knew you could do better at that place—in this neighborhood." Without looking at the fabricated tally form Mickey handed to him, he crumpled the paper and lobbed it several feet away into the trash pail by the kitchenette stove. Mickey sighed, inaudibly. *Good! I won' hafta do THAT no more!*

Only minutes after starting work at the drugstore on Monday afternoon, Mickey felt as though Morton Weinstein had never been away.

The first thing Mickey looked for—testing the mental bet he had made with himself as he reluctantly plodded home—was what made Mickey so certain. *I won the damn bet—dammit! The radio out front is gone!* It was a bad omen.

The fat Mr. Weinstein's temperament was not brightened in the least by his week away to a new environment. Mickey was disappointed that nothing had changed. If anything, he thought the man looked darker-faced, scowlier, in worse temper. *I woulda thought a week of good times—a whole week of bein' away from the same old thing every day—woulda made him feel better at least for a few days after bein' back—maybe even for a whole week.* Mickey gritted his teeth each afternoon he reported for work from school, finding Morton Weinstein in the store, hoping it would be the kindly Mr. Weinstein's turn to work. Mickey's tips were meager. He seldom left the store, over and over sweeping the floor and dusting shelves. Ice cream dishes and soda glasses and spoons accumulated at the soda fountain during the day.

Twice Mickey saw customers to whom he had often made deliveries now appearing in the store, picking up prescriptions. *I won'er why they're doin' that. I never did anythin' to make 'em complain about me. Fatso woulda let me know if I did—maybe even fired me.*

The third day without Arthur Weinstein at the drugstore after school, Mickey saw Mrs. Crabtree. Mickey had sullenly dusted shelves, made one delivery only two blocks away, and spent almost an hour at the soda fountain sink, shirt sleeves rolled above his elbows, brushing and rinsing glass after glass, spoon after spoon.

What's she doin' here?

She closed the door after entering, doing it awkwardly, slowly turning about to face it, shifting a cane from one hand to the other to work the doorknob, shifting the cane to the other hand again, then turning toward the back of the store.

She shouldn' be out—shouldn' be comin' down those stairs where she lives. Did she walk all the way here?

Mrs. Crabtree walked slowly, glancing at Mickey where he bent over the sink, watching her curiously. She raised a hand at him, waggling fingers in recognition, and smiled slightly.

The cheap bastard is makin' people come in for their own things!—keepin' me in here workin' for nothin'!

Mickey wanted to quit the job again. He swore under his breath at the face in the partition window, peering out to see who had made the signal bell ring, glowering at Mrs. Crabtree. Mickey wanted to rush into the back room and call the man some vile name.

Morton Weinstein always stood on his toes to see out the sliding window, though he could manage looking through it without raising himself. But he had once noticed his reflection in the glass, eyes only an inch or so above the sill. He thought the image made him look silly, imitating the ubiquitous cartoon head scrawled on public bathroom doors and walls, seen in subways, on buildings, billboards, everywhere—the bulbous head peeking over a fence, bulging eyes just above the top edge, oversized nose hooked onto the fence, draping heavily. And two misshapen hands clutched the fence top at each side of the head, seeming to add support for the nose in holding the inquisitive head high enough to see what went on elsewhere. With that vision of himself, Morton Weinstein took to stepping to one side, to the open section of the window, away from glass. And he took to stretching himself up so at least his chin was above the window sill. Even if he did not see his reflection, he did not want customers to see only half his head, looking like the cartoon.

Look at him there—lookin' out again. Looks like a pumpkin in a window at Halloween!

Morton Weinstein brusquely tended to Mrs. Crabtree, without speaking, not even saying hello; pushing a small bag from his side of the counter to hers, standing silently as she delved through a change purse brought slowly from her pocketbook. He stood at the register dropping her assortment of coins into compartments, ignoring her thank you and good-bye, only glancing indifferently at her, ignoring the shadow of disappointment. She did not look at Mickey, watching her, as she passed again, walking slowly, looking tired.

Mickey several times forced the picture of her visit from his thoughts as he mindlessly puttered about, doing detested tasks, seething emotionally.

Trying to seem casual, he asked how Mr. Weinstein's brother was: "—cuz I haven' seen him since Saturday." The grumbling, irritated answer was terse, interpreted by Mickey as "—being home sick, he says. Should be in Thursday."

Thursday, when Mickey sporadically peeked through the front window over a few minutes, he saw only his antagonist each time. Mickey decided he would plead his own illness, to get out of working with the man. *That'll serve him right!* That would be better than not appearing at all. That might mean summarily being fired.

Mickey went around the street corner to work up his credible excuse. He poked a finger down his throat, stirring it about, gagging, gasping for air, almost vomiting. Complexion flushed, eyes watering, he entered the drugstore, passing through a long aisle toward the rear, appearing to walk unsteadily. His scheme was to quickly appear recovered if Arthur Weinstein was there; or to carry out his deception if Morton Weinstein still worked alone. Mickey actually felt ill when only the short, fat figure materialized, then felt better when the druggist grumbled, "Just make sure you show up tomorrow! I can't keep on doing everything alone!" He angrily slammed the cash register drawer twice, but each time the broken mechanism sharply bounced the drawer back at the man, the second time thudding into his body as he spun away from Mickey. The boy smiled at the man's grunt.

Friday, again, only Morton Weinstein worked. He became even angrier than on Thursday when Mickey begged off staying with another performance of illness. This time he had not prepared himself before entering the store, assuring himself that his Mr. Weinstein *ought* to be back by now, *would* be back. When he saw Morton Weinstein's head in the partition window—the pumpkin image—Mickey quickly turned as though to look over his shoulder at something, poking a finger at the dangling uvula in his throat, gagging and retching as quietly as he could, feeling his eyes water. Facing the pumpkin head again, he saw it rotating slightly from side to side. The head leaned closer to the window. "So—you're going to tell me you're not feeling good enough yet to *work*, huh?" His emphasis made Mickey suddenly aware how the man always pronounced it *woik*.

"Am I right?"

WOIK? Hah! Even I say it right!

"I don' think I better, Mr. Weinstein. I'm still feelin' terrible. It was bad enough so that my father lemme stay home from school today. I jus' got up a little while ago—that's how bad it was. I jus' came over now jus' to tell you so you wouldn' be wonderin' or worried 'cause I didn' show up."

Morton Weinstein grumbled unintelligibly, lowering from his tip-toe stature, looking back at his task, only the bald top of his head visible to Mickey. The lie of not going to school seemed to ease the man's grudging acceptance of the excuse for not working.

As he had done on Thursday, Mickey loitered with other boys at far reaches of the neighborhood, out of sight of next-door-neighbor acquaintances of his father who might accidentally tell that Mickey had not worked. Home again each day, he went to his backyard hoard, removed coins from a tobacco tin, then turned them over to his father as that afternoon's tip rewards. Each time the man took them without comment. Mickey was glad he did not have to spend time fabricating tally sheets. The ritual of turning the money over to his father had become an annoyance. He had tried leaving the money on the kitchenette table for his father to find, but he was sternly directed, "When I'm home I want you to *hand* it to me! I don't want it just laying around like that!"

Mickey argued with himself Saturday morning, still in bed, feeling lazy. *What the hell—I can put up with Fatso's crap for one day—can' I?* It was quiet in the apartment's rooms. He remembered his father saying last night that he would be leaving for work at six this morning. Mickey looked at his clock on the seat of the wood chair on which he draped and piled clothes every night. Seven-fifteen or so, the face showed. *Margaret? Don' hear her. Probably still sleepin'. She's lazy anyway.* Then he remembered. *I know she went over to that skinny Catherine's last night. They can' stay away from each other—always gigglin' and whisperin' and more gigglin'.*

Mickey could not find a reason to stay away from the drugstore. *Fatso won' believe me if I still tell him I'm sick. Anyway, I'm tired of that baloney story.* Mickey struggled with one idea after another. *I don' think he'd fire me, though. He's got somebody doin' free work. He ain't gonna find another one like me again—a dumbbell like me.* Then he decided his Mr. Weinstein *could* be working today; that he must be better by now. *He's never been out this long. He should be there. I just know he'll be in.* The preponderant go-to-work motivation was fear. *I'll be in for a good lickin' if the old man finds out I didn' go to work for no reason. Then he might find out I didn' work the last two afternoons either. Then he'll kill me, for sure!*

Yeah—I can put up with Fatso for one day. I jus' had a vacation from him.

Mickey sauntered into the drugstore positively, praying to himself that his Mr. Weinstein would be there. *He don' have to be workin' alone—what with bein' sick and all. I don't care if the fat guy's here too. What difference does that make, huh?* But for the sixth day Arthur Weinstein was absent.

Mickey went into his usual starting routine: "Hi, Mr. Weinstein—I'm here." He put his head just inside the back room door to look at the man, then slowly shook his head in disgust at the sight of the stocky figure at the work counter, glowering out the partition window, a long, dark cigar jutting from his mouth. Acrid bluish smoke floated in the still air. The man muttered something.

"Whadja say, Mr. Weinstein?"

"You should have *heard* me the first time I said it." The *heard* was said *hoid.* He did not look at Mickey. "If you pay attention, I won't always have to say things twice—like you always make me do!"

Mickey cut him short. "How's Mr. Weinstein? Is he all better yet?" Morton Weinstein kept staring out the window. "Pneumonia. He's had a little pneumonia all week—so he's still out."

Mickey remembered he had interrupted him. "What was it you said before? You got somethin' for me to do?"

"I told you—deliver those—in the bag out front." It was rare, but this time Morton Weinstein did not do what Mickey had expected. It was not like him to send Mickey delivering as soon as he got to the store. But walking along the street to the first delivery stop, Mickey speculated. *He must rather have me out here doin' this than stayin' alone in the store while he got rid of these hisself.*

When Mickey returned he was disappointed when the druggist told him he would have to work all day, until four o'clock instead of getting off at noontime as he usually did on Saturdays. The boy's only respites from the man's oppressive mood were two more brief delivery trips. Sweeping and dusting and other make-work jobs given to him roused his anger to again thinking about quitting. *An' this time for good—an' I goddam mean it!* But the thought of his Mr. Weinstein's return on Monday kept calming his annoyance.

Monday, the brother Morton seemed to be a greater demon to Mickey. He looked fatter and uglier as he came from behind the cash register, towering ponderously over Mickey, scowling and growling. His voice was raspy and angry, demanding Mickey to be on time every afternoon right away after school—and Saturday too! He kept jabbing an index finger in the palm of his other hand as he emphatically warned, "You'd better show up every afternoon or some other kid could have this job—and like I said—be on time! That's all there is to it!"

It was a terrible week for Mickey. Morton Weinstein kept him in the store most of each work session after school, limiting deliveries to only one round each day, never with more than three stops. Again, Mickey saw customers who usually had deliveries made to them now stopping by the store. Now his routine was tending to the full sink of glasses and utensils, floor-sweepings, repeated dustings, and moving items from one shelf location to another, one aisle to the next. Mickey wondered why Mr. Weinstein kept having things moved from one place to another.

His father questioned the diminished tip money, more suspicious each evening. On Wednesday Mickey decided he would try to beg off from after-school work for the rest of the week, saying to his father, "He's always got me doin' things *there*—in the store—all the time—you know the things I mean—dishes an' silverware an' stuff—an' sweepin' every day—hardly any deliveries at all. It isn' my fault I'm not makin' tips."

Mickey pressed, hoping his father would get angry at Morton Weinstein "Gee, I could be here doin' my homework insteada—" He hoped his father would storm off the drugstore to see to it that his son would not have to be working free for someone. For once Mickey wanted his father at the store, to be there to challenge the fat man. But his father suddenly seemed only to mirror Morton Weinstein, scowling, raising his voice harshly.

"Stop whining!—and just do whatever you're told to do by whoever's at the damn store! DAMN IT!" Mickey was stunned. "I don't want to see you getting canned and losing that money just because you don't like doing something constructive!"

I won—I won! Mickey exulted in what he felt was a victory on Thursday.

When Morton Weinstein called him away from scrubbing the stainless steel covers of the ice cream compartments and into the back room, Mickey defiantly practiced a rapier-thrust stretch to the far side of the protruding cash drawer with his right arm as he passed the register. Such darting movements over the money drawer had become a habit, done whenever he passed the register—a challenge to himself, something he could do simply because he *felt* like it, a whim. But he only practiced when the younger Weinstein brother worked alone. *How easy it'd be to snag somethin' outta here—jus' like nothin'!*

He practiced with his right arm when going into the back room, and with his left arm when going from back to front, his hand moving—he persuaded himself—*with the speed of a lightnin' stroke, almos' faster than anybody's eye could see.* But Mickey knew that he would be slower than in practice if he actually filched a coin. Slashing a hand out and back without a pause was one thing. Stopping for even a fraction of a second to pick up a coin from a drawer slot without a sound of the drawer being touched, no matter how slightly, or without accidentally dropping a coin, that was another matter.

Morton Weinstein pointed to a mortar and pestle and several metal spatulas in the work counter sink. "Get busy cleaning those! I've got something important to find somewhere among those shelves," waving an arm about, grumbling as he walked away. "And no back-talk about it, hear?" Mickey washed and dried the implements while the druggist clinked and clunked jars. A few minutes later, when he left the back room, Mickey made another cobra-like arm lunge across the open, wide drawer, lightly, noiselessly plinking fingers across compartment dividers as he retracted the arm, like rattling a stick along a picket fence. Without thought, he deftly plucked a fifty-cent piece from the nearest compartment. His fingers curled into a loose fist, the half dollar seeming to instantly burn his palm. With a smooth motion, as quickly as if he had done it for years, he transferred the coin to his other hand as he walked quickly to the soda fountain, then slipped the coin into a small pocket of the knickers, below the belt near the right pocket. He walked slightly sideways, peering over a shoulder at the back room doorway, then at the partition window. He felt an exquisite exhilaration.

I beat the fat bastard!

Mickey whistled a happy melody as he cleaned the soda fountain syrup pumps and water spigots. When he was called into the back room again he thought how many times the druggist always seemed to know when Mickey had only a few seconds remaining on a task. But this time Mickey did not linger, purposely slowing his movements, just moping along, as his father would say. He trotted eagerly to the back room, practicing his smooth right-arm–flick on the way in. Leaving the back room a moment later, seeing Morton Weinstein's back toward the door, Mickey deftly snatched another coin from the drawer—a quarter.

Fuck you, Fatso!

15

Boy, *that sure made me feel good! The son of a bitch deserved it!—even if it was a wrong thing to do. What I did was STEALING—that's what it really was—plain and simple!*

But my Mr. Weinstein didn't deserve it—me stealing. Well, at least I wasn't thinking about him when I did it. It wasn't anything he had ever done. But if only he had been there that day—

Thinking back, snitching that money didn't make much difference. Fat Stuff didn't know I'd done it. So what good was that? To get even with him—to make him treat me right from then on—I should have done something that he KNEW I did—not just something sneaky that nobody knew except me.

But I don't really know what I could have done. I wasn't smart enough about things like that back then.

16

The two coins, cool to the touch, no longer burning his fingers, went into the Prince Albert tobacco can. He had not taken another coin, not even a penny, though he had an opportunity with every trip by the register, back and forth a dozen times or more in another hour and a half. As swift as his arms and fingers were, he craftily decided it was better to be sensible. *Might be I'd be pushin' my luck this first time. Besides—I don' need no more right now.*

On Friday afternoon the coin compartments were as full as the day before. Impelled by the courage born of success, Mickey filched a half dollar and two quarters.

Before he got to the store he planned: *It'll depend on how things look aroun' the place*—to take no more from the register than he did the first time—*I don' even know if there's gonna be as much in the drawer as there was yesterday*—if he was going to take anything at all. *It depends. I gotta think about it.*

He had to clean the day's sink accumulation at the soda fountain. He did it without first asking Mr. Weinstein what he wanted done. Lately the sink always was full when Mickey arrived, and by now he knew he would only make one delivery trip sometime during the two to three hours he worked each day. In the first part of Arthur Weinstein's absence, Mickey lingered along the delivery route, dallying at the slightest reason for delay. But he grew tired of the other druggist's anger when he returned from out in the neighborhood. Mickey stopped letting himself be distracted too often, stopped seeking distractions. *I'll just hafta put up with Fatso's crap!*

There seemed to be a greater accumulation in the sink today. Two customers who were still seated at the counter when Mickey started washing finished their sundaes and left about the time he had half completed the chore. Washing, drying, sorting, and storing the dishes and utensils had become that to Mickey—a *chore*—an inescapable, not-to–be–forgotten-dammit!-bit-of-work that was the start of his regular daily drugstore routine; tedious, boring, detested; causing spitefulness.

Mickey's right hand moved quickly as he passed the cash register, heading into the back room to let Mr. Weinstein know the sink work had been completed, fingers delicately and quietly probing the nearest coin compartment without looking, clenching a fifty-cent piece with thumb and forefinger, halting his step for a fraction of a moment to slip it into a pocket, stepping ahead again.

"Mr. Weinstein—I got the sinkful of things done. What should—"

Morton Weinstein, crouched down at the low cabinet beneath where he usually worked at the counter, glared at Mickey from behind the open door. The door was swung open toward Mickey and the druggist's face from the eyes upward showed over the top edge. His balding head suddenly seemed greatly balder to Mickey than it ever had been before. The man's forehead was heavily creased by his abrupt anger, his dark eyes seemed to rage beneath heavy eyebrows. "Out! Get OUT of here!" He rose up slightly, moving closer to both the cabinet opening and to the door swung out between them, turning enough to rest his right arm on top of the door. His thick body completely blocked the cabinet opening. "Find something to do out there! You know what needs doing! I'll call you if I want you!"

Mickey shrugged his shoulders, backing quickly out of the doorway, turning, shaking his head side to side slowly, perturbed. His left hand darted to the register drawer, fiercely clamping fingers onto a quarter. *That's for yellin' at me for nothin'!*

As Morton Weinstein later argued loudly with a customer at the front of the store about a can of foot powder with two different price stickers on it, Mickey pocketed a second quarter. *This one's for that lady! What the hell are ya yellin' at her like that for?*

Saturday was a lucrative tip day for Mickey. Saturdays were always busier when both brothers customarily worked. On most after-school days Mickey never knew which brother would work or if they both might work. But he had come to count on both brothers putting in a long day on each Saturday. Today, however, his Mr. Weinstein was still at home. *I sure hope he's better soon.*

Between brief spells of chores in the drugstore throughout his nine a.m. to six p.m. work day, Mickey made four delivery trips. Each was a relief from the irritable brother, steadily busy with customers and formulating prescriptions. The druggist was so busy that he told soda and ice cream customers that the fountain was closed. Mickey smiled each time he heard that.

Mickey expected troublesome moments with Morton Weinstein as the day went on. The man seemed more intense and edgy each time the boy returned to the store.

Late in the day he saw Morton Weinstein take twenty dollar bills from the cash register drawer, shifting tens to that compartment, and more tens and fives to other slots, dividing the increasing bulk of singles into two openings. He took the twenties into the back room. *What a pile of money! I wouldn' keep that much aroun' in a place like this!* He remembered overhearing the brothers' story told to a customer about a robbery years ago.

"Only a little while after we opened up, that's when it happened," Morton had said. "Morton, it was almost a *year* after the opening," Arthur said. Morton glowered at his brother. "So? That's only a little while! What's a *little while?*"

Even with dividing the dollar bills into two stacks, both compartments were nearly full, Mickey discreetly noted as Morton Weinstein pushed the drawer shut as far as it would go.

While he talked on the telephone out of sight in the back room, Mickey turned away from the doorway to the register, pulled the drawer open slowly, rapidly sorted through a stack of ones, and slipped a well worn note from the middle of the sheaf, easing the drawer closed as far as he could. Mickey padded lightly to the soda fountain and noisily got busy washing already clean glasses and silverware, blithely whistling.

He turned over all of Saturday's tips to his father, and used Friday's coins and Saturday's dollar bill from the register to increase his tobacco can wealth. *This week turned out better'n I thought it would at the beginnin', figurin' back to last Monday. But I sure wish my Mr. Weinstein would come back.*

17

Took you long enough, didn't it? To figure things out?

Well—I never really gave it much thought before. In fact, I never gave it ANY thought. Didn't have reason to.

But now you think about it?

Sure—that's because everything is different now—and I mean EVERYTHING! You know that. I've got a lot ahead of me—if I make it through OK.

Isn't it funny?—I guess I mean strange—not funny. I didn't know then why I did what I did. It was just a reaction—because the opportunity was there, I guess.

I sure as hell didn't want to cause MY Mr. Weinstein any anguish. It was just—well—I guess—no, I KNOW—it was that son of a bitch of a brother!

18

Arthur Weinstein looked so thin to Mickey that the boy wanted to cry. The man looked so tired, his face so drawn, his shoulders seemed to sag. He saw Mr. Weinstein standing behind the counter, handing change to an elderly man while another customer waited her turn. Mickey stood at the front end of an aisle for moments, pitying the druggist for how he looked. Arthur talked softly to the man at the counter, then looked at the woman, raising a hand, holding up the index finger, signaling he would be with her soon. She waved a hand slightly in acknowledgment.

Poor Mr. Weinstein. But he's back!

Arthur kept speaking quietly to his customer, patiently explaining an answer, reaching out to pat the man's hands resting on a cane. Arthur glanced over the old man's shoulder, aware of a figure down the aisle, adjusting his glasses higher on his nose to see better. He smiled a wide grin, standing a little straighter, raising an arm shoulder high, wiggling his fingers slightly in a wave when he recognized Mickey.

There—he looks better—smilin'. His face don' look so bad now. Boy, am I glad he's here again.

Mickey walked along the aisle, turned left, went into the back room, hung his thin jacket on a wall hook behind the door, and went back into the front of the store. Passing the counter, looking at Arthur, he saw another smile flash across the man's face, flushed with reddish color, then Mr. Weinstein quickly gave his attention to the woman, who had stepped forward to the counter.

Mickey felt excitement rising higher as he went to the soda fountain to do housecleaning tasks. *Things will be differ'nt now with Mr. Weinstein back again. Maybe not a whole lot different cuz Fatso is still aroun', but things'll be differ'nt for me, anyhow. Now it's easy to come inta this place.*

The sink was empty—and shiny. Turning to the mirrored wall behind him, he saw that the two long shelves were full with three sizes of soda and sundae glasses and various-shaped metal sundae dishes that had been washed and dried. Six tall metal milkshake mixing containers seemed to sparkle. The milkshake machine glistened, too. Mickey took the two mechanical ice cream scoops from the deep circular water-filled rinsing tub. The water was clear, and Mickey could see it was circulating slowly, spilling over at the top, flowing through a small drain into the sink. *Sonofagun—the thing is fixed—and the scoops are clean for a change.*

Mickey marveled that with his Mr. Weinstein back only one day in the drugstore there was already this difference. The boy had mildly complained to

Morton Weinstein about the malfunctioned water circulating device, the discolored water, and the messy scoops, but the man growled, "It's only ice cream. Get busy!"

Arthur Weinstein had made another change. A cluster of bright yellow, fresh-looking bananas rested on a large oval plate on the counter. *That makes things look better, too.*

Mickey watched the woman customer leave the store, then Mr. Weinstein come behind the soda fountain.

"I was just gonna clean up around here—" Mickey said, "like I been doin' every day the first thing."

"Shoosh, shoosh," Arthur said, standing near the boy. "You won't have to bother. I had a little time today—and I wanted something to keep busy."

Mickey thought, seeing him closer now, how tired he really does look. *His face does—but his eyes look OK. His eyes are always so friendly lookin'.* Mr. Weinstein smiled, looking down at the boy, three feet away. He kept his lips together, but Mickey could see his mouth widening, slightly at first, then broadly. *Now he looks better.*

Mickey said, "Is there anythin' you want me to do right now—anythin' special?"

"Yes—one thing. Now you go right around from out of here and sit wherever you like on one of those stools on the other side. There's something I want to do."

Mickey hesitated. "I'll be glad to do it for you, Mr. Weinstein—do whatever needs doin' aroun' here."

"No, no, it's nothing you can do. It's something I've thought about while I was home. Now you let me in there, and you go take your seat." Mickey was puzzled. What had he done, he worried, that he had to get out from behind the soda fountain? There was nothing he knew of that should make Mr. Weinstein act this way.

Oh, God—maybe he knows about the money. He could sense his heart beating faster, noticeably thumping in his chest. He look quizzically at Mr. Weinstein, searching for something suddenly sinister about him. But he was smiling again.

"No, no, it's all right." He patted Mickey's shoulder. The boy flinched at the touch, waiting for the worst, sure there would be a hard blow. *Somethin's fishy! If it was the other guy and things were like this I'd keep my eye on him—make sure I didn' get a fist in the back of the head.*

The man moved aside. "Mickey, go take a seat. I have things for you to deliver, but first—" Mickey eased past him, trusting he was not wrong about Mr. Weinstein, tightening muscles across his neck and shoulder blades, mentally flinching, moving away from the man more quickly until he sensed he was out of easy reach.

Selecting a swivel stool, he sat on one opposite Mr. Weinstein standing at the ice cream compartments, to one side of the water spigots. Mickey was still puzzled.

"What would you like, Mickey? You pick out whatever—no, I have a better idea. I will surprise you. I know you're not fussy—choosy. You like everything we have here."

Mickey slumped on the stool, suddenly relaxed, feeling weak. He smiled quickly at Mr. Weinstein for a brief moment.

The man rubbed his hands together, acting gleefully, then lifted the ice cream compartment covers one at a time, peering down into each space before going to the next one, deciding. He stood straight, one arm across his chest, supporting the other arm, forearm vertical, hand reaching to his face, lightly touching his chin, squinting, looking dreamily past Mickey. The boy smiled briefly again. *He looks just like Jack Benny, standin' there lookin' like that.* "Let me see—I could—no—I think I will—no, no, I have a better idea—h-m-m-m-m—"

He's just teasin' me. I won'er why?

Arthur Weinstein turned to the shelves behind him, studying their contents, plucking a long oval metal sundae dish from the lower shelf. He pulled a half-round ice cream scoop with a movable thumb lever from the rinsing container in the sink. He lifted a compartment cover, reached down into the hole, and dug into a one-gallon tub, scraping up a hugely oversized ball of strawberry ice cream, balancing it on the upside-down scoop until, with a sudden flourish, he flipped it over with a quick twist of his wrist, firmly placing the ball into the center of the dish. He bent forward again, probed in another compartment, and scraped up more ice cream, again rising with an overflowing scoop, this time dark chocolate, again grandly pressing the ice cream onto the dish balanced on his fingertips.

Look at the size of 'em—both of 'em. Fatso would kill Mr. Weinstein if he saw that!

Arthur Weinstein flipped the two compartment covers down briskly, the sudden thumping startling Mickey's reverie for an instant. "How does that look, Mickey?" The boy nodded approval.

"And," Mr. Weinstein said, "I'm not through." With a theatrical flourish he put the sundae dish on the counter, in front of Mickey, but only for a brief moment before taking the dish back and positioning it in his left hand so that the small pedestal base of the dish rested in his palm and his fingers reached up to just touch the underside of the dish. Mickey held his breath briefly, afraid Mr. Weinstein might drop his creation. Though the dish seemed perilously balanced to Mickey, the druggist kept working on, confident of his grip. He jerked up a third compartment cover, plunged an arm into the space, and came up with a third great ball of ice cream, hard and white. "Here's vanilla!"—flicking the thumb lever to free the scoop into the dish. "And now—" He bent and rose again, holding the upside-down, overflowing scoop toward Mickey. "Know what this green flavor is? It's the first time we've had it—and it's quite good, I must tell you." He twisted his wrist and pressed the ice cream onto the already crowded oblong dish. "Pistachio—that's what it is."

Mickey wondered what the green-colored pistachio would taste like, telling himself it would have to taste just like the red-shelled nuts he liked—liked except for having to take time to break open shells— *'cuz chocolate ice cream tastes just like reg'lar chocolate, an' strawberry ice cream tastes just like strawberries.* But being green made him think it might taste something like peppermint.

Arthur moved to his right, the dish still held waiter-like on splayed fingers, his arm extending to Mickey; smiling, looking at his sundae handiwork, seeming to admire it. He stopped in front of the row of metal covers with spoon and ladle handles sticking up through holes. With theatrical deliberation, he lifted each cover and placed it carefully on the counter. Mickey smiled at Arthur's contrived movements. One cover after another made a light ringing sound as it was lifted upright and placed on the counter, until all six were in a row. Arthur methodically peered into each container opening, deciding his first choice.

He lifted a small ladle of thickly viscous syrup from a container, tipping chocolate sauce along the length of the dish, lightly drizzling it onto each flavored mound. "I don't want *too* much of this, good as it is. But I don't want the whole thing to taste only like chocolate. Do you?" Mickey casually shrugged his shoulder, sure that Mr. Weinstein did not really expect an answer.

Arthur lifted a second ladle, saying, "This is butterscotch—and—" slowly circling the ice cream, speaking in pauses as he let yellowish syrup dribble from the ladle "—this goes—in very small measure—right—around the edge of—the chocolate—mostly for looks—for appearance—help make it pretty. See now?—a pool of brown with a ribbon of yellow all around the edge. Nice?" Mickey nodded. Each side of his jaw tingled at the corners as he anticipated all the tastes.

With a third ladle Arthur Weinstein placed two dabs of chunk-filled sauce at each end of the dish. "A touch of red for more color, with bits of strawberries for another delicious flavor!—and now these." He lifted a long-handled spoon from an opening, balancing a heap of chocolate chips, sprinkling them lightly over the four mounds. "But—easy—just a few. As I said, not too much chocolate."

Next he spread a thin layer of small bits of walnut along the ice cream tops. Arthur contemplated his creation, then lightly put it on the counter, standing with his arms folded across his chest, squinting at his work. Mickey stared at the full dish.

The man snapped his fingers. "I know what else. I almost forgot I had—that I brought them in this morning." He slid the sundae along the counter toward Mickey, and plucked a banana from the cluster on the plate near the boy, holding it upright, then slowly peeled down the skin strips. He cut off the fleshy ends, sliced away thin strips of discolored fruit, and scraped off thin, unsightly strings. He carefully sliced the banana in two, lengthwise, placing each half along opposite sides of the ice cream balls.

"Almost—my boy," the man said, sliding the dish away from Mickey, back along the counter to the ice cream and topping compartments. He knelt, opening the door of the small refrigerator, standing again with a slender, tall metal cylinder in both hands, shaking it vigorously up and down. "Now, the next-to-final touch. But—let me ask you this: Do you know the word *penultimate*, Mickey? Well— that's where we are right now—the one before the last—the next to last step." He smiled as Mickey's face took on a puzzled appearance, then bent over the sundae, pointing the cylinder nozzle at it. With deft squeezes of a small lever at the top of the cylinder, he squirted small globs of fluffy white cream at both ends of the dish and at places along two side edges. "I have to do this like an artist does little things to a painting when it's almost done. Gently. Not too much—a touch here—another there. I don't want to cover up this little yellow butterscotch stripe I so carefully put around the brown of the chocolate." He stood straight, smiling at Mickey. "Like it?"

"Gosh, Mr. Weinstein—"

"You'd think," the man said, "that that's all—that I'm finished—wouldn't you, Mickey? That I am done. But—watch this!" He lifted a ladle from the last topping compartment, reaching for a long-handled spoon with his other hand, using the spoon to pluck a bright red cherry from the ladleful of fruit and syrup. He swung the spoon to the sundae and let the cherry slide slowly onto the dollop of whipped cream atop the center of the ice cream. He moved the dish along the counter half the distance to Mickey, where they could both look at it from two points of view.

Mickey did not know what he should do. He felt dumbfounded. *Look at the size if that thing. I guess he means it for me. Won'er why he went to all that trouble?*

Arthur Weinstein spoke softly. "I think it's the best one I ever made. Certainly it's the largest—*and* fanciest." He eased the dish toward Mickey. "Enjoy it. All last week, Mickey, after I started feeling better, *getting* better, I thought how nice it would be to make a nice thing like this for you."

"Gee—Mr. Weinstein, I don' know—if I can eat all—"

Arthur Weinstein interrupted Mickey's stammering: "In fact—this one is simple compared with all the really fancy ones I dreamed up. Ach—if you could see some of them—this long—this high—with twice as much. I don't have a plate here large enough to hold what I was making up in my head." He slid the dish farther, until it was in front of Mickey, then reached for a long-handled spoon. "Is it all right if I help a little?" He scooped up a small amount of chocolate ice cream. "I will take some of this kind, if I may. That'll be better. A young man your age shouldn't have too much chocolate. It's not good for your skin—your complexion. But, take the cherry. It's yours."

Mickey smiled, slicing a large chunk of ice cream from the center of the mound, sliding it through whipped cream, butterscotch sauce, and chocolate syrup, savoring all the rich tastes, letting the concoction melt and blend in his mouth before swallowing in small portions.

Mr. Weinstein walked from behind the counter. "I will sit here, Mickey—this stool—to your left. This way I won't bump your elbow."

Mickey had just put a heaping spoonful in his mouth. He wanted to speak, but worried that the ice cream might spill out. And it was too cold to swallow. Already his teeth ached. He grunted affirmatively, looking up at the druggist, nodding *yes* to him, twisting to face him more, sliding the sundae to place it between them.

The man and the boy were fortunate no customers entered for a while to disturb their ice cream sharing, to interrupt their quiet words and smiles. For ten minutes they welcomed each other back.

19

*W*hat a wonderful man!

I wouldn't have lasted as long at that drugstore as I did if it hadn't been for him. I wouldn't have put up with Morton Weinstein's crap if my Mr. Weinstein didn't make things worthwhile.

Good man. GREAT man!

If it hadn't been for Arthur Weinstein—

20

Mickey only took money from the cash register when Morton Weinstein worked alone. Then, he rationalized, it simply was to compensate for fewer delivery trips, less tip money, more work inside the drugstore. *Doin' damn chores!—fer nuthin'!*

Then what he filched was only one coin, maybe two, depending on his frame of mind, level of anger, desire for vengeance. He persuaded himself that only coins should be taken. Bills were too dangerous. They would, he felt, be more liable to be missed. And if it got too easy to get dollars from the drawer he might be tempted to heist a fiver. Maybe a ten someday. Worst of all, because of getting that greedy, if he got caught, he would surely lose his job. He wouldn't see his Mr. Weinstein anymore.

But one afternoon the huge, ancient, fancy ornamentally-embellished, gold-color-painted cash register was in perfect working order again.

The repairman was gathering his tools as Mickey passed the register and Morton Weinstein to hang his jacket in the back room. The druggist kept banging down heavily on the *No Sale* key to make the cash drawer spring open forcefully, thumping solidly into his bulging midsection. Each time the drawer flew open a single clear bell tone sounded prominently. He kept on vigorously shoving the drawer shut—opening—shoving—closing—opening—slamming shut—time and time again, thudding into his large abdomen with each opening.

Mickey watched coins and bills repeatedly appear and disappear to the clamor of banging key depressions, signal bells, violent slams. Morton Weinstein's face was contorted into a scowling, grimly smiling mask; his bald head glistened with a film of sweat as he pounded the repaired machine and his stomach absorbed the impact of each forceful drawer opening. Mickey frowned, watching him from the back room doorway. *That sonofabitch! He's ugly. He REALLY is ugly!*

"I don't know," said the repairman, Ed Wisneski, "if you ought to be doin' that, mister. It just got fixed, don't you know." Morton Weinstein growled something unintelligible, forcing the *No Sale* key down again.

The repairer shook his head slowly, side to side. "I might have to do another repair job, you keep that up. And you can bet it'll go on the bill too, mister." The druggist snarled.

"I'm making damned sure the damned thing is repaired right, Wisneski"— PUNCH—SLAM—"if I have to pay damn good money"—PUNCH—

SLAM—"to fix something that probably isn't worth the trouble!" PUNCH—
SLAM.

Ed Wisneski put the last of his tools in the large black leather tool bag. "You're
not treatin' that thing right, mister, I'm tellin' you. That's a fine piece of
equipment. They don't make 'em like that anymore." Still kneeling, he closed the
tool bag, securing it with a short belt across the top. "But that don't mean you
should mishandle it. It's sturdy all right—meant to last a long time—but you ain't
supposed to do things like that to it." He stood up, tugging up the heavy bag, put
on his work-soiled cap, and pulled a sheet of paper from his shirt pocket. "Here's
my bill, Mr. Wein—this is what you owe me, Weinstein."

The druggist snatched it. "Seven-fifty? Just for what you did?—that little?"

"That's it. Parts and labor—one part was hard to find—that's what took me
so much time before I could get here before this—and my half hour to fix it. It's
all fair enough."

"Hah!—I should make such good money in this place." The druggist
forcefully drove down the *No Sale* key, springing the drawer open, standing to one
side to let it extend its full distance, jerking to a noisy stop, coins bouncing about
in their slots. He took money from the drawer, handing it to the repairman
without looking at him. He slammed the drawer shut. "Make sure you mark this
bill paid!" Ed Wisneski set the tool bag on the floor, digging a pencil stub from
this shirt pocket. He wrote PAID in oversized block letters on the bill and scrawled
his name and the date, smiling at the druggist's fitfulness, then hoisted the bag a
second time. "Weinstein—your machine is FIXED! I come back again—even if all
I do is get in your front door—you pay again!" He lumbered along an aisle, feeling
sure that Morton Weinstein was glaring at his back, but not caring. He had done
his work, and done it right.

Mickey's scheme to compensate for lost tip money collapsed. But he mentally
shrugged it off after his disappointment at first. His cash cache was steadily
increasing; he had added a fifth Prince Albert can to the oilcloth bundle; and he
spent practically none of his secret funds, except for an occasional candy bar to be
nibbled. And his father regularly gave him his twenty-five cent allowance each
Saturday night if he was not away driving cab or on Sunday morning if he had
driven on a late shift. *But now I got no way of gettin' even with that fatso sonofabitch
for workin' for nothin'.*

Arthur Weinstein's time he spent in the drugstore increased as he regained
vitality. Toward the end of his first week back, Mickey noticed that Morton
Weinstein spent less time at work. Thursday he left at five p.m. On Friday he put
on his topcoat at four-thirty and strolled out without a word. *Betcha he's gettin' even
with my Mr. Weinstein!* Mickey was sure, the more he thought about, that his
nemesis was being spiteful; that he was deliberately taunting his older brother; that
by leaving early—Mickey pictured Morton Weinstein scheming—he was simply
feeling that he was only making up for two long weeks he had put in alone. *The
slob always tries to get even with everybody—for anythin'. Don' matter to him his*

brother was sick. He coulda died with that pneumonia. Maybe he almost did die—an'
Fatso never told me. But think he cares?

On Saturday Arthur Weinstein worked alone. Mickey asked about the brother
but Mr. Weinstein only said he had something else to do, adding, after a pause,
"He might be in this afternoon, after lunchtime—maybe." But he did not sound
angry to Mickey. *If he's as suspicious of Fatso as I am, he sure don' ever show it.*

Mickey looked for tasks at the soda fountain, but everything was in place. The
floor was too clean to be swept again. The newspapers and magazines and comic
books up front were neatly arranged. He walked the aisles to see if shelf contents
were in order. He groaned softly in mild disappointment when he realized there
was nothing he could do for his Mr. Weinstein. Then the druggist placed a large
paper bag next to the cash register. "This should keep you busy for about two
hours. Then we'll clean up a little in the back room before lunch. And after, I'll
have a little more for you to do in the neighborhood—just a few places to go
before you are off for the rest of the day. I want you to go out early today. You *must*
play sometime, you know."

For the next three weeks Mickey experienced unusual happiness. It took a
couple days before he was aware that each day he was feeling pleasures to which
he was unaccustomed. Everything seemed fun. It was a rare period. He did not
have a worried or angry thought, not a single complaint. His world became a
different place; bright and cool and warm and wonderful and exciting and happy.
School was interesting. He breezed through homework, starting it cheerfully,
completing it without frustration. He received compliments when called on by
teachers to stand and speak. Red-penciled grades of B+ and better appeared on
returned quizzes and marking-period tests. In the third week the principal, Mrs.
Mulligan, whose scary-looking face looked like the rough surface of a pineapple,
stopped Mickey in a hall as he was leaving for the drugstore. "Miss Benson tells
me you are doing magnificently lately. I've seen your latest grades, and it's nice to
see they're getting better." She bent forward and patted him on a shoulder. Mickey
felt embarrassed. He had never heard her say nice things before. She went on,
smiling: "I always knew you had the abilities to be a superior student, if you just
put your mind to it."

She patted his head. He smiled at her gentle touch, astonished at her delicacy,
recalling the time he had felt her quickness and strength with a thin, springy
wooden ruler across his knuckles when she had substituted for a teacher and
caught him in horseplay with a friend. "It's nice that you have learned to be a good
boy—and a good student."

Mrs. Mulligan, the last time he had been sent to her main floor office weeks
earlier, had told him it was her second and final warning that he pay greater
attention in the classroom, that he stop whispering with others, stop throwing
things, that he do better on quizzes and in recitations and at the blackboard. "I
want you to know here and now that your next appearance in my office will be
with one of your parents at your side!—trying to get you back into school again!—
after suspension!"

But now that seemed so long ago to Mickey. Even sibling differences with his sister melted away. His father's moods seemed to brighten. And the irascible Morton Weinstein subsided into less storminess. Mickey thought he scowled less, that his voice had changed, that it was not as harsh.

On the third Saturday of the three-week period Mickey got curious. Later, because of it, he wished he was dead. If it had not been for Morton Weinstein— if he had not left the drugstore—

21

"Listen up *again*, some of you people—I see not everybody's paying attention to what I have to say."

The room gradually, but quickly, became quiet. *I must be one of the ones he's talking about. I didn't hear him say anything before this—so busy thinking about the Weinstein brothers.*

The figure in the doorway held a clipboard almost at eye level, peering over it into the room of faces looking toward him. *Funny how that makes him look. Reminds me of the way that Morton Weinstein used to look peeking out that back room window.*

"Everybody whose last name begins with A through F, get your things together and come into this other room. The next step takes place in here, for all of you. But it all takes time, so you'll have to wait your turn." An audible, soft groan swept through the audience.

Well, I'm not in the first group. It's funny how that guy reminded me of the fat-stuff Weinstein brother.

But maybe it's not so strange. I've been thinking about that drugstore job—and about maybe if he hadn't left the store when he did—

22

Morton Weinstein left the drugstore at noon, going far downtown to see his and Arthur's lawyer. Earlier, Mickey had eavesdropped on the brothers' conversation in the back room, learning that Arthur would tend to the store while the younger brother would spend the afternoon with the lawyer, then visiting a midtown druggist whose owner wanted to retire. Morton Weinstein was the most happily excited Mickey had seen him, animatedly talking, almost babbling at some points, about plans for a second drugstore; one he would manage while Arthur would stay here. The thought of Morton Weinstein being somewhere else all the time gave Mickey a sudden feeling of pleasure. Standing to the side of the doorway, he soundlessly applauded in surprised glee.

Arthur kept reminding his unexpectedly enthusiastic brother to be cautious, to be careful not to get them in over their heads. Morton waved a hand at him each time, a don't-worry-about-it gesture. "I'll see to it that I get someplace—that *we* get some place that will be good for us. The times are getting better already—we can see that every week from our books—and they'll get better yet. I want to be ready—I want *us* to be ready—and I will be!" He walked along an aisle to the front of the store, tugging on his overcoat. "I will get us what should be ours. Be sure, Arthur." The door slammed behind him.

Arthur Weinstein said, "Yes, I will, dear. Everything's on the list. And whatever cooking needs to be done, I will help you with it. But right now, you need rest. I don't want you getting any sicker. I will be home by seven. Good-bye—and rest." He slowly put the ear piece on the wall phone hook, looking glumly at Mickey. "She's starting to feel better now. But she always rushes. She always wants to go back to doing everything again too soon. For a few days she kept feeling worse with her cold. She didn't rest enough—insisting she do her housework—that she *liked* doing it—that it made her feel better. She was feeling fine, she said. And what happens? Two days in bed, that's what happens. That wonderful woman wants always to do too much." He shook his head slowly, side to side, a worry frown on his forehead.

"And now she wants to do the shopping. Just out of bed this morning and she wants to go out—" he sighed. "The fresh air would be all right, but the shopping? Carrying groceries? Even the little she wanted?" Mickey stood quietly, letting Arthur speak his concern.

The man's face brightened. "But I have you to tend the store for me, Mickey. So I will get our things for her—and when I'm back, I'll make us each a small ice cream soda—just a small one so we don't spoil our appetites for our suppers."

It was four-thirty, and Arthur, list in hand, left the drugstore, saying he would be back in no more than twenty minutes. "Mickey—it will be all right for you to make change from the register for whatever customers want from the front of the store."

Mickey was stunned by the permitted access to the money. He could barely utter yes when asked if he knew how to operate the keys. "For two prescriptions that are ready and that people want to pick up themselves—I keep the delivery prescriptions in the back room—just get their names and check them with the bag label. Then have each customer check the label on their bottle, just so they will be sure for themselves. But if either of them wants to talk to me about something about their medicine, just tell them to wait, or to come back. It's up to them." Mickey felt excited by the trust.

"And customers for the soda fountain? You must know how to make things there as well as I do, I'm sure. You've watched me often enough. So you can take care of that too, don't you think?" Mickey grinned, keeping his lips together, worried that he might appear too eager, that Mr. Weinstein might change his mind.

"Of course, Mickey," Arthur said, smiling, winking, "you won't be making things for them like I do for us, will you? That's my special treat for *you*—for *us*."

He was gone. Mickey was so enraptured that he did not remember seeing him leave; only suddenly aware that he was alone.

For the second time Mickey felt pride, the kind that rises from achievement. He felt pleasure spreading over him. The store took on new proportions as he imagined it now as his. Mickey himself took on new dimensions in his own mind as he examined everything for which he had been given responsibility.

He pictured quitting school and being in the store every day—working with his Mr. Weinstein; with the other brother out of the way, working in the downtown drugstore, out of sight—*and damn well outta mind, especially!*

I'll take care of everythin' in the front and Mr. Weinstein will only have to make prescriptions and we'll both make sodas and sundaes and real good ones too and talk with the customers and with each other and put the radio back on the counter to have music in the whole store again and hire a kid to make deliveries and PAY him for helpin' around the store once in a while if he felt like doin' it at all because me and Mr. Weinstein could really keep this place lookin' good all the time with no trouble at all and then Mr. Weinstein and me can be partners when I get older and our drugstore got bigger and better and I'll say yes when he and Mrs. Weinstein ask me to live in their big house in the country with them and the two of us—just me and Mr. Weinstein— will drive back and forth every day in our own fancy big car and the fatso brother with his ugly face and mean eyes and big thick black mustache that hides his mouth will be gone and won' come back ever again and we'll all be happy again without him growlin' and fightin' with everybody and slammin' and bangin' things and makin' me work for nothin' in the store all the time and hidin' his fuckin' money that I'll bet my Mr.

Weinstein don' even know about or else he'd see that the fat sonofabitch took it all outta that damn cigar box 'stead o' hidin' it away like that!

So his mind wandered as he wandered through the aisles, touching this and that at shelves here and there, straightening magazines, spinning alternate swivel-stool tops in opposite directions along the length of the soda fountain, working from front to rear, making certain the cash register drawer was fully closed, staring at the cabinet door below the counter area where Morton Weinstein worked in the back room.

He musta jus' had that money in there only that one day to keep it safe 'til he could get it to the bank.

Mickey squatted by the door, still staring at it, vacillating between forgetting about what he had seen before and reassuring himself that hidden money was now safely in a bank.

It ain' none o' my business, I guess—'cept—if I'm gonna be Mr. Weinstein's partner someday I oughta know what's goin' on.

He rocked back and forth on his heels. *Shit!* He snatched the door open.

Everything in the dim cabinet looked the same, as well as he could remember. A few round cans, several bottles, what appeared to be the same cigar boxes as before, behind everything else, stacked one on another in two columns. Mickey studied it all carefully. *These four bottles in front, to the left—the smallest one second from the right—three cans, all the same kind o' scrubbin' powder—one big bottle behind the middle can—two stacks of cigar boxes, one four high, the other five high, back of the big bottle, against the right side wall. Yep, everythin's the same as before!*

Mickey quickly, calmly took each bottle and can from the cabinet, putting them on the floor, in the relative positions they had been in the cabinet. He slid the two columns of boxes forward. *There's the one I want!* He clumsily lifted four boxes off the one he was certain had earlier held the hidden money, hands shaking, his heart starting to race now, losing his calmness. Moments ago, when he had only been *thinking* about what he would do, his nerves were steady, remembering how smoothly and calmly he had infiltrated his father's room, searched through his wallet. Starting to remove things from the cabinet he had worked easily. But now, inches to go, his body tensed, mind tumbling, head aching.

The top box of the second stack slid toward him, nearly falling off when the column, pulled too far and too roughly, became unbalanced on the front edge of the cabinet. Mickey had forgotten about the recess below the cabinet. He clutched the tipping box by the top, centering it safely, lifting the upper boxes, reaching the one with the suspected treasure. He worked intently at prying up the cover, using fingers to tug up a corner of the top, then inching a fingertip into the gap he had made, concentrating intently, careful not to mar the wood or further damage the remainder of the already broken paper seal, working the fingertip to the center of the cover where a brad held the box firmly shut. Tipping the box enough to see better, he could see the gap widening, could see more of the brad's length. He gulped an extra swallow of air in a deep breath, then held it in anticipation of seeing the money again—more than he could imagine. The cover resisted Mickey's efforts but his two hands firmly held onto the box and the cover as he smiled slightly at the thought of seeing the tightly coiled slim cylinders. *That's if I'm right an' the money is still in this box.*

A sudden sound seemed deafening, so intensely was Mickey concentrating on caution. The jangling bell, tripped by the opening front door, this time did not have its sound mingled with other ordinary store noises. Mickey's excited heart thumped more quickly with the startling sound.

He jumped upright, panic-stricken, bumping his head on the counter edge. The clamorous bell sounded ominously vigorous, as though Morton Weinstein had charged headlong into the store in his reckless manner.

Oh, God!—don' let it be Fatso! He'll kill me! His eyes started to water from the pain of the bruise on his head as he stared dumbly at the things he had moved out of the cabinet onto the floor, sure he would not get them back into place in the cabinet before Morton Weinstein charged through the doorway into the back room. *Don' even let it be my Mr. Weinstein!—please!* He stared at the box in his hands. His bowels loosened. He felt warm moistness between his buttocks, wetting his skin, staining his underwear. He could smell foulness.

"Hello—

"Somebody—anybody." The voice was muffled, insistent, unfamiliar. Mickey spun around to face the partition window, feeling pain of the slight cut on his head with that sudden twisting.

"Hey, in here—everything all right?" the voice called loudly. It was a man's voice though Mickey did not recognize it as anyone he knew. A huge relief swept over him; at least it was not one of brothers. The boy stepped up onto an sturdy inverted wooden crate to look into the front of the store, the box Morton Weinstein used sometimes to raise himself to see better, and be seen better.

Mickey recognized the caller as one of the many salesmen who regularly stopped at the store. "Oh, it's you, Mickey. I was worried for a minute. You know, when nobody answered. I had to call a couple of times. Then I started getting nervous, thinking something might be wrong."

"It's OK," Mickey said. "I was just in here lookin' for a Band-Aid to put on my head." He touched the wound, looking at the blood on his fingertips. "I banged it and got a cut—but it ain' bad. I'm awright." Mickey smelled his foul odor more keenly, wondering if the salesman smelled it too, even if he was in the other room, on the other side of the window. The wetness and stickiness on the back of his legs was annoying. He imagined how terrible his underwear must look, how disgusting. He felt anger rising.

"I'll be back in an hour or so, tell Mr. Weinstein," the salesman said when Mickey explained the druggist's absence. As the front door closed behind the man, Mickey knelt carefully on the floor by the open cabinet, trying to keep the knickers fabric from pressing against the back of his legs and emphasizing the spilling of his bowels into his clothing. His rump and legs felt more uncomfortable; his odor was stronger, worse. But he steadfastly started closing the cigar box cover and pressing the brad back into place. *I gotta get the hell outta here!*

Jeez!—and I hafta clean up this place first! He wanted to rush getting rid of everything there in front of him, get it all back inside the cabinet, and in the right places too, get it out of sight. Forget about it.

But I awready got this far, didn' I? Only need another couple o' seconds to know fer sure. Maybe I'm wrong. He lifted the lid.

That fat bastard IS hiding this! Why else he's got it in here like this? In a cigar box—stuck inside there—in the back—behind everythin'—under everythin'.

Is he hidin' it from my Mr. Weinstein? Why would he do that? The fatso sonofabitch!

Mickey's sense of urgency was swept away by anger. Any thought of being abruptly discovered left him. From the front right corner of the box he pulled out the slimmest roll of bills, tugged off the rubber band, and counted the twenty-dollar corner numerals. *Thirteen! Three more'n the las' time! Thirteen times twenty. Think!*

C'mon, THINK! Jesus kee-ryste!—two hunnert and—sixty bucks! He stared at the money in his hand, stared at the large clustered ends of other rolled bills in the box.

Fatso's cheatin' somebody!—hidin' all this!

Mickey became entranced with the money, oblivious to his sheer panic of moments earlier. *I swear—I'm gonna tell my Mr. Weinstein about this!—I'll say I foun' it by accident. I'll fix Fatso!*

But what am I gonna say I was doin' way back in the friggin' cabinet? He pulled another roll of bills part way up, thicker, bigger round, a large 20 in the corner.

He'd hafta believe his brother first—before me—if Fatso said I was tryin' to steal their money. 'Less I could make it look like I was a hero.

I could hide all o' this in the back yard with the rest o' what I got—tell everybody I was hit in the head and robbed—and I awready got the cut—wouldn' hafta fake that part. That's it!

But then I'd hafta take everythin' in the cash register besides—and smash a lotta things to show what a fight I had with the robber—with two of 'em!

But breakin' things and stealin' from the register would hurt my Mr. Weinstein. He don' deserve that.

The hell with it!

He tamped the second roll of bills back into place, then rolled the cylinder of twenties in his hand tightly again, replacing the elastic band, pressing the small tube down into the right front corner of the cigar box, in the exact location he had found it.

I oughta just take off with this whole fuckin' box of the fat bastard's money anyway! He'll never catch up with me!

He remembered the G-Men he had seen in movies and read about in mystery magazines. *I'll bet I wouldn' be able to find anyplace they couldn' find me—and they'd do it easy, too! I'd hafta go to school anyplace I went cuz a kid my size and my age would be asked why I never went to school and the next thing I'd be asked a lotta friggin' questions and right after that police would be talkin' to me and then they'd call*

in the G-Men because the cops couldn' make me talk and the G-Men were a lot smarter
and they'd find out in five minutes all about the money and I'd be off to jail in no
time—knowin' those guys!

Frig it!

Impetuously, he pulled up one roll after another, looking at corner numbers,
finding one with a big 5 on it. He snatched off the rubber band, slightly undid the
thick roll, riffled the bill edges until he reached about the middle, and steadily
jerked out a bill with little tugs. He put the bill between his teeth to hold it, and
tensely twisted the bills back into a tight cylinder again, taking three turns with
the elastic, as he had carefully noted it had been done before, and jammed the
cylinder down into its place in the box.

Mickey stuffed the five-dollar-bill into a knickers pocket, then hurriedly put
the boxes and bottles back into storage, repositioned exactly as they had been. He
eased the cabinet door closed, calmly, smiling confidently. He suddenly became
aware that he had lost track of time. He now had no idea how long Mr. Weinstein
had been gone and started moving more quickly to straighten the area. He used a
wet paper towel to wipe the floor where there were traces of dust, carefully drying
the water mark. He rushed into the cramped toilet cubicle, stripped off his
knickers and boxer shorts underwear, and held the soiled shorts under running
water. They were not as filthy as he thought they might be, but his sense of smell
had been right. He grimaced and breathed through his mouth when he first took
the knickers and shorts off. He hurriedly used wads of toilet paper to clean his
soiled skin, then swabbed his groin and buttocks with wet hands. The water was
barely tepid and Mickey wiggled about to ward off the coolness as he washed
himself. He quickly got to rinsing his underwear, finally twisting and squeezing
the shorts, wringing out as much moisture as he could. He shivered as he
reluctantly pulled on the damp underwear. The inside of the dark-brown corduroy
knickers were cleaner than expected, but he wiped the insides lightly with a damp
paper towel because he was certain he detected a tinge of foulness. He felt better
as soon as he had roughly pulled on the knickers and buttoned the fly. He flushed
the toilet twice, though the second time was unnecessary, and made a final quick,
but close, examination of the floor and counter area.

Mickey had no idea of how much time had elapsed. But he did know he was
now safe, still the only one in the store. He chided himself for the risky thing he
had done, thinking how lucky it was that no other customers had interrupted,
especially that his Mr. Weinstein had not appeared. He wondered how soon he
would be back, deciding to at least look busy when he did return. He treated
himself to a tall glass of Coca-Cola with crushed ice floating in it, periodically
sipping it through a straw as he aimlessly polished the soda fountain counter. Then
he wandered about the front of the store, looking after things, looking industrious
for Mr. Weinstein.

I guess I was pretty slick, though—wasn' I? Did everything beautifully—even
though I got so scared for a second there that I shit my pants a little.

He'll never miss that five bucks—the fat prick!

23

But—man, oh man—that next Monday—that was the worst day of my life!—up to then, anyway.

How old was I? Thirteen, was it? It must have been thirteen. It was when I was at the school where Mrs. Mulligan was principal—Public School 89, was it? Well, anyway, it was P.S. something or other.

And my old man—that look on his face!

24

Mickey's father stood at the foot of the school's outside steps, scowling. The boy thought he seemed to be trembling, watching his son's every movement with an intensity Mickey dreaded. He had seen the same visage before, when he was being thrashed. Mickey could not think of what could be wrong at school to make his father wait for him like this.

His father spoke immediately, his voice tremulous. Mickey was familiar with the quavering voice of anger when his father was trying to control himself, as the man said, "I'm staying with you until I learn what this is all about, damn it!—and you'd better damn well not be guilty or they can do what they want with you!

Mickey's nervousness tumbled into fright. "But I ain' done—I *haven'* done nothin' wrong—*anythin'* wrong. My marks are good. I showed 'em to you—yesterday—an' the end o' last week, too. Miss Benson said she was gonna—going to—send you a note saying how good I've been doin' all last month and this month." His father's scowl did not change.

"And Mrs. Mulligan said she would tell you, too."

"Don't give me none of that innocent stuff! Get going!" His father waved an arm away from the school, pointing down the street.

Mickey felt thunderstruck. *Oh, shit!—he means the drugstore!* He heard, fuzzily, "I'll see that things are straightened out!"

Mickey was bewildered, then his stomach felt queasy as they walked quickly to the drugstore. He tried thinking what was wrong. *How can I be in trouble?* When his racing mind caused him to dawdle, he felt firm pushes at his shoulders, his father propelling him along.

It can't be the cash register. I ain't taken nothin' from it for a long time—and Mr. Weinstein SAID I could make change—I had his permission!

Bet HE don' know we're comin' cuz I'll bet only Fatso himself got my old man to do this—the fat fucker is doin' this on his own—that's what it is!

It can't be the boxes! I put everythin' so exactly back in place even Sherlock Holmes couldn' tell I ever was inside the box—or even in the cabinet!

Won'er if the ol' man found out I was makin' more tips than I gave him. But how could he? Maybe he's seen me stashin' away money in the back yard. Yeah—maybe that's it! He never said nothin' 'bout the drugstore. Yeah—that's it, all right! Boy, I better come up with a good story for holdin' out on him. Here's where I get the shit whacked outta me again!

At a street corner Mickey expected them to cross to the opposite sidewalk, to the side of the street where their apartment building was, to head to the backyard cache— *Maybe he seen one time when I was hidin' money in the cans*—but his father steered him straight ahead. They kept up their quick pace, past their building entrance. Mickey's anxiety worsened. He was now sure they were going to the drugstore.

It can't be the work in the store. I do everythin' I'm supposed to do. Mr. Weinstein will tell the ol' man how good I am and how he lets me watch the store—and make change for the customers—and make sodas sometimes—an' cuz I do everythin' good an' don't make trouble an' don't sass the fatso sonofabitch even when he's a pain in the ass an' makes me work for nothin' while he's makin' deliveries or makes customers come in themselves while I do everythin' around the place cuz he don' even wash a friggin'—

Mickey was stunned when he saw his Mr. Weinstein working at the soda fountain, dolefully taking a glass from a woman just rising from her stool. He did not respond to Mickey's frantic telepathic appeal he tried to deliver with a long, intense, emotion-charged look. Mickey wanted to call out to him, a casual, cheerful greeting, as if nothing was out of the ordinary. But he did not say anything. He could not. Everything was *not* ordinary. *Things ain' right here! Somethin's up! Jeez!* Mickey knew he was in for trouble. *But what?—why?*

He and his father stood in the front of the store, near the long row of swivel stools, his father looking about, only glancing at Arthur Weinstein behind the fountain.

Morton Weinstein came from behind the cash register and strode hastily along the aisle between the soda fountain and a long, six-foot-high stack of shelves, glaring at the boy, pushing him aside as he turned and went to the front door, locking it. Mickey felt himself pushed along the aisle to the rear of the store. He stumbled, then ran along the aisle when he was slammed in the back of his head with a blow that felt like the heel of a hand. *Why's the fuckin' door locked? It's early— too early! They never closed this soon before!*

"Into the back room—into the back room!" Morton Weinstein said loudly and angrily. Mickey felt another thump to the back of his head by his father. In the back room his father and Morton Weinstein towered over him, the druggist yelling, "I know what you've been up to—and I'll prove it!" Mickey cowered but was momentarily lifted bodily by the back of his shirt collar. "Stand up straight!" his father hissed in his ear, keeping a tight grip on the collar. The boy gasped for breath.

Mickey was frantic. His mind pounded, struggling for what it might be that the druggist had discovered that infuriated him. *I ain' snitched nothin' from the drawer—since I can't remember when!* He desperately wanted to have his Mr. Weinstein nearby.

The voice in his consciousness was a low rumble: "—neither—just that if I didn't get you over here in a hurry he'd let the police take care of matters. Weinstein called me this afternoon—I was taking my nap after lunch and the super banged on the door 'til I got up and had to go out in the hallway to find out on the phone that you're in some kind of trouble. What is it this *damn* time?" His father shook him by a shoulder. "What've you been up to *now*?"

Morton Weinstein railed at the father about the boy's upbringing—being lazy—not doing what he knew he always had to do—always complaining—being slow doing work in the store, being slow making deliveries. Mickey trembled as he listened to the man's growling. The druggist pounded a meaty fist on the work counter, then again. He moved a step to kick at a waste basket in a corner by the toilet, crossing the small room to kick the cabinet doors under the counter.

"Mr. Weinstein—you got me up out of sleep to get me here—and I've got to drive a cab all night starting at six. You know what I do for a living. So what's this all about?—or I'm leaving. I didn't need to come here for you to tell me you think he's lazy! Don't threaten me with police just because *you* think he's lazy. That's wasting my time! Your brother says he works hard—and does everything good."

The druggist snorted. "Hah—him! He thinks the boy is wonderful. But that brother of mine—always got his head in the clouds—thinks *everybody's* nice—*being* nice to everybody. Never worries, that's him. If it was up to him he'd give this store away!"

Mickey bobbed about in his father's unrelenting grip, sometime almost dangling as his father pushed and pulled him about like a rag doll, pushing the boy in quick, short jabs toward the druggist and pulling him back, shaking Mickey side to side a couple times as the druggist glared and ranted.

"He's a thief!" Morton Weinstein hissed. "A no-good, stealing little brat!—and lazy too—like I said. Now this!—stealing!—damn stealing!" Mickey bounced and swayed like a marionette as his father twirled him about to stare into his son's eyes.

The druggist's voice raised to a higher pitch, getting hoarse-sounding. He tugged vigorously at the boy's shoulder from behind, trying to turn him around again in the father's powerful grip. "Look at the kid's face," he growled. His fingers hurt Mickey as he squeezed and half-turned the boy about. "That'll show you! See? I'm right, ain't I?"

Mickey's mind dizzied from the combining mental fright approaching terror and the physical rattling. The tight grip on the back of his shirt cinched the collar at his throat, tightening into his throat, strangulating. Raspy coughing for gulps of air made his throat burn. His eyes unfocused as the physical roughness continued, battered by his body being jerkily twisted about, pulled one way by his father, clawed by the druggist. The raging Weinstein brother let go of the boy, then doubled over toward him, his face a dozen inches from the boy's, poking a stubby finger into the bony plate of Mickey's thin chest. He vainly struggled away from the thumping, probing, accusing finger.

Morton Weinstein clamped a hand onto Mickey's shoulder, roughly turning him to face where his other hand jabbed the air, index finger pointing toward the cabinet door Mickey had entered. "Thief! No-good damned thief!—robber!—crook!—liar!"

Mickey's fuzzy eyesight relayed the poking finger images to his brain. *Shit! How'd he find out?* He fought back tears, with an awful sense of impending doom. He remembered being so calculating, so painstaking, so exact, so clever. The druggist hurled Mickey aside, only his father's grip keeping him from becoming a heap on the floor. Mickey bit the inside of his cheeks and lips to keep his chin from quivering.

He wanted to curl in a ball in a dark corner, to hide in the deepest part of the cabinet. He wanted to run. He tensed against hammering blows he expected from his father. Memories flashed: THUD!—for being late for supper; WHACK!—for a school marking-period D; pounding slaps on his rump for joyously and adroitly daubing liquid black polish to the soles—besides properly doing the *uppers*—of a pair of his father's new shoes in need of their first polishing. Holding the two shoes together in a hand and extending an arm full length, he turned the gleaming shoes one way, then another, satisfied with their appearance. But his eyes caught the tan color of the leather sole and the scuffing of one evening's wear. They looked nowhere as good as the tops of the shoes. He uncapped the polish bottle again and quickly painted the offending surfaces, to please his father with that extra bit of attention.

The druggist's voice became an unintelligible, thunderous din to Mickey. Pushing at the boy again, he got on his fleshy knees, digging into the cabinet, wildly strewing bottles and cans on the floor behind him. On all fours, he poked his flabby bulk into the cabinet, ridiculously bobbing his broad buttocks up and down and side to side, struggling in the confined space, gradually working his upper body out into the open again.

Mickey's jerky swaying had stopped, though still trapped in an unyielding grasp. The shirt collar was still tight. He kept struggling for breath. His father curiously watched Morton Weinstein moving about on his hands and knees, muttering oaths, grumbling angrily. One by one, puffing and sweating, he pulled two columns of cigar boxes from the cabinet, lifting each carefully from inside, slowly placing it on the floor, one column five-high, the second six boxes tall, stacked inches from the first pile. He struggled to his feet and stood triumphantly, clothing rumpled, balding head glistening with perspiration.

Mickey heard his father's angry voice. "What the hell is all this? Don't be so damn mysterious!"

The druggist peered menacingly down at Mickey, then leaned slowly forward at the waist, his beefy hands clasping his legs above the knees. For a moment he just held that pose, thrusting his face at Mickey's. "Go ahead," he said, in a low voice. "Go ahead—tell him." Then he shouted. "Tell him why we're all in this room! Hurry up—tell him!—tell him!" Mickey shuddered, turning his face away, eyes tightly shut in fear, trying to avoid Morton Weinstein's hot, strong breath and the torrent of angry words.

In sudden quiet, he could hear his Mr. Weinstein speaking. Mickey opened his eyes and saw the older brother standing in the doorway. "Please, Morton—and you too, sir—please don't be so rough. He's only a boy—a child, Morton. You are terrifying him. Please calm down."

Morton Weinstein stayed in his hunched posture, only turning his head slightly to his brother, keeping his eyes on Mickey in a scowling stare. *"I'm* handling this, Arthur. I will show you I was right!—that *I* know what goes on—

how this kid thinks!" He poked Mickey's chest with a fat fist, forcefully, hurting him. Each time the boy tried to pull back, he felt himself pushed forward, the shirt collar pinching his neck, his throat closing.

"The dust—you little monster. That's how I know—thief! Want to rob me, eh?—little robber." He thumped Mickey's chest again, this time with a fist. With his left hand he reached to his side and shifted the top cigar box on the column of six, being careful not to touch the top of the box. He then lifted it by an upper and lower corner, slowly passing it before Mickey's face. "Think you're smarter than me, huh? See what I'm showing? See the top of this box? Know what this means? *I* do!" Mickey was puzzled. His mind struggled to understand what Morton Weinstein was doing.

The druggist put the box on the work counter, then clumsily unstacked the same column on the floor, standing straight to hold a six-inch-square wooden cigar box in fingertips of both hands, extending it toward Mickey's father for a moment, then firmly clasping it against his paunch. With intense deliberation, he tugged at the edge of the cover, pulling the brad loose, slowly lifting the cover. The father's eyes widened.

The box lowered into Mickey's vision. There was the money he had seen before. There were the short, thick cigars, the rolled cylinders of currency. *He don' KNOW I took nothin'! How could he know for sure?* The druggist slammed the box onto the counter.

Mickey trembled as he heard him speak, almost as if in answer to his thought—explaining how he had carefully blended talcum powder and dust he had collected from things stored on upper shelves in the back room, using the dust to darken the talcum to make it look like actual dust, then put his concoction into a rubber syringe and gently wafted a thin film of his special dust mixture onto the tops of the two columns of boxes of cigars. "I always kept the same two boxes on top—those two had stale cigars in them—the fresher ones were always in the other boxes, except this box, too—but it was always kept in the same place. And it was always my job to take new cigars from this cool, dark storage place and add to the stock in the cigar case out front. Arthur—he doesn't like smoking, especially cigars—so he left that up to me. So I'm glad I went to all this trouble. I knew I'd be right. I *knew* I'd catch the kid. HE'S why I did it! I *knew* I shouldn't trust him!"

Mickey's mind raged. *How come you didn' trust me? You didn' even know me!*

"And if that brother of mine doesn't take care of things, then *I'll* see that everything's done right! Be sure of that!"

What a lotta crap that is!—done right—what crap!

"Can't trust none of these kids these days—and if it was up to me he wouldn't have got this job in the first place, you can bet on that. No kid would have got such a good job making such good money for after-school work—and I was right about this kid working—"

Mickey mentally snickered, despite his anguish. *Woikin'—'stead o' workin'— here he goes again—can't even talk right—he must come from Brooklyn!*

"—wouldn't even wash a glass without being told to—a hundred times!"

Arthur Weinstein spoke quietly, stepping toward his brother. "Morton? You have money in a *cigar box?* Why keep money like that?" He lifted the box lid, frowning at what he saw. "In with *cigars?* Why keep cigars hidden? Why keep *money* hidden?"

Morton glared at his older brother. "I just kept it handy in case—we might need cash suddenly—to maybe—say, pay for deliveries from the warehouse." Arthur looked at him curiously.

Mickey thought the answer was silly. *You didn' need that much money—you liar!* He wanted to yell at him that there was always enough money in the cash drawer to pay for anything!—that he had often seen Morton Weinstein pay out a lot of money from the register for goods left by many deliverymen—never heard him tell anybody he would have to go into the back room for extra money. But Mickey did not yell out in defense. *I can't let him know I watched the register—that I was always watchin' him!* Mickey was thankful that the pushing had stopped, but he wished the grip at his neck would loosen. Each time he wriggled to ease it the tension increased, making him cough and sputter.

"Tell me about the money, Morton," Arthur said. Mickey thought his voice was stronger.

"Well, it was like this—the first time I noticed the dust was disturbed," the younger brother said, "I had to count the money—the emergency money—but it was all right. It matched the record in my wallet. And do you know how much time it took for me to do that? It was a great waste of my time! And it turns out it was all this kid's fault!

You prick! You're keepin' score on how much you hide!

Arthur said, *"Emergency* money?"

Morton ignored his brother. "So I just thought maybe I was clumsy pulling out the boxes that time."

What the hell you takin' 'em out for? Gonna hide some more money? Steal it from the store?—from my Mr. Weinstein?

"I figured I must have brushed it off myself. But the *second* time! That time when I checked the boxes almost all the dust was gone—and five dollars was missing! That was the *second* time I had to count that money!—because of him!" The grip at Mickey's neck tightened. His face started getting purple.

"Now what do we do with you?" the fat druggist shrieked as he thrust his face at Mickey, then glared at the boy's father. "Hah?—and you, mister—what are *you* going to do with him? He's *your* son. This is what he has learned? You let him be a thief?"

Mickey felt himself lifted, his feet clear of the floor. One of his flailing legs caught the edge of the open door, barking his shin. His ribs slammed into the work counter. His head swam, dizzied from the sickening wrenching. Distantly sounding, it seemed, his father's voice was shouting at him, raging. He heard varying tones and pitches and explosiveness. Words were muffled, dulled by the pain in his head. It felt ready to burst from pain and pressure. Fingers of one hand clawed at the strangulating collar twisting tightly in a punishing grip. Mickey's other hand reached out, waving aimlessly, fending off objects seen fuzzily, flashing in and out of his view in his gyrations. His eyes hurt, a reddish veil seeming to be drawn shut before them. His whimpers of fear escalated to apprehensive low-pitched shrieks of terror, anticipating slaps and punches. "You hear me?" The question pierced Mickey's desperation. The pressure round his neck seemed less. "Or I'll thrash you good, you hear? *Then* we'll send you off to reform school!"

Mickey's terror peaked. Fear-stricken nerves and muscles lost control of involuntary body functions. Warm urine trickled only briefly before flooding down his legs, soaking his clothing. His bowels loosened, diarrhea-like fecal matter oozing from his body, then rushing out in a short spasm. He shivered uncontrollably, collapsing limply.

"See!" his father shouted, "—you know you're guilty—pissing in your pants like that!" Mickey was shaken roughly and pulled upright. "Stand up, I said! Stand straight!" Mickey's legs seemed to him to have no strength. "And you stink! What'd you do? Crap in your drawers too?"

Mickey wobbled, legs weak, feeling numb all over his body. He clasped fingers of both hands together tightly at the back of his head, pressing palms hard against his skull, a barrier against blows, pressing elbows against each other, shielding his face. He felt himself pushed away violently, feet doing quick, short jig-steps trying to keep balanced. He sank to one knee, between his father and Morton Weinstein, struggling to not fall. The two of them looked at each other, glowering, seeing Mickey's reactions as admissions of guilt, as proof, as justification of their inquisition, feeling satisfaction—as had witch-hunters, nodding righteously at the plight of a sputtering captive bound to a chair on the end of a long pole dipped into a pond, testing for witchery.

Half kneeling, half squatting on the floor, waste-soaked, foul-smelling clothing sticking uncomfortably to his skin, Mickey trembled. Sobbing, he heard the angry accuser talking to his father, deliberating what should be done in the next few minutes, how best he should be punished, agreeing to call the police, turning him over to them—right away! Morton Weinstein pressed; his father condoned.

REFORM SCHOOL!

Horrifying stories—true, rumored, untrue—which was which?—from friends and others on the streets, at school—flashed like strokes of lightning in Mickey's fear-crazed mind. Two kids he knew had died at one place. Their smiling alive faces flashed in his brain, then instantly contorted into frightful masks. He remembered another one—a kid from a gang two neighborhoods away. *Awful what happened to him where he was! Then to a crazy house!* Mickey whined softly, burying his chin against his chest, head still embraced, shielded. He hiccupped, triggered by a gasp for air. The spasms went on, mixed with gulping breaths. No more bravado. More afraid than any time before. He pressed his arms more tightly against his ears, muffling angry words and sounds. *I wanna die!*

He was lifted slowly, hands tugging at him from behind, hooked under his armpits. He felt himself turned around, pressed against a body, arms encircling his shoulders. A voice talked quietly above his head. Mickey's mind and breathing jerked convulsively. *My Mr. Weinstein! Oh, God—thank you!—thank you!* Mickey's breathlessness eased, his breathing slowed. Soft, warm, strong fingers probed the boy's tightly positioned defending arms and clasped fingers, then pressed against his cheeks, stroking one part of his face, then another. His crying became tears of relief. Anguish slipped further away with each soothing, alternating light and strong pressure and stroke at the back of his neck, with each pat and rub at his shoulder blades.

"—hired him. He's my responsibility. And I will not tolerate threats of police and reformatories for a five-dollar-bill. Nobody *knows* if any stealing was done— except this boy here." Arthur Weinstein held the boy more snugly. He put up a silencing hand when his brother interrupted.

"I have twice trusted this boy with the store, Morton. And I never once felt I had to worry about money in the register. Now I find out it's you I have to wonder about—keeping money in cigar boxes?—in a dark corner? *Hiding* it?"

Morton Weinstein sputtered gutturally, hemming and hawing, spitting out disconnected words. Arthur stretched an arm at him, palm toward his brother's face. But Morton persisted. His voice rose to shrillness, repeating things already said. Arthur slammed his palm onto the counter, grimacing in pain for an instant. "Morton—I will not have your intimidation any longer!

"You are not to say a word!

"I will no longer be subservient! That's what I've become—because I *let* you do things here, knowing you enjoyed being in charge. You are smart. You've done good for this store—but it was in the beginning—mostly when you first started years ago, then for the next two, three years. I felt lucky having the top graduate in your pharmacology class working with me."

When his brother started to interrupt again, Arthur held a palm high, toward him. "Not a word, Morton," he said quietly.

"I'm not sure if I like the idea of another store for us, Morton—but I will let you go ahead with it—maybe.

"Remember—Poppa left the drugstore to me—because he was from the old school—the old country—everything to the eldest son. I don't know if that is the way things ought to be done, but, nonetheless, that's how it was—and how it *is,* in our case. But he told me to use wisdom, to be generous, to be fair. That's why I saw to it that we have been partners, from the first month after your graduation.

"I respect your ambition. I want you to get what you want. Your good wife deserves that you stay ambitious. Frieda has worked hard for the two of you, and she's been patient—as I have been.

"Morton—certainly every one of us has faults. One of mine, I believe now, is that I've too often overlooked yours here in the store."

Mickey's trembling and heaving for breath slowed as he pressed close to his Mr. Weinstein. His head hurt less. Morton Weinstein stared into the front of the store, looking out through the partition window. Mickey glanced at his father, saw him leaning against the counter, arms interlocked across his chest, looking back and forth between the brothers. *He's gonna let Fatso call the police? Gonna help send me to reform school?*

"Listen, Morton—you can be a *good* man. You've become greedy, not just ambitious. Your irritability never stops. You are harmful to people. Not just here in this place. Now Ruth and I see it with Frieda when we visit, even at the dinner table. And that is terrible—grousing and growling about everything under the sun while eating." Morton Weinstein's neck reddened, but he kept staring into the front of the store. His fingers curled into fists on the counter.

Arthur's speaking was less tremulous. "Your voice is filled with ugliness when you talk to people. In a better neighborhood—if that's what *you* want to call one where people have more money—you would drive people away. They would not be regular customers. You are absolutely ungracious to people around here who make it possible for us to earn a living in times like these."

Morton Weinstein did not interrupt, not looking away from the store front, waiting for his brother to stop speaking, then said fiercely, "He deliberately stole that money. He had to go to a damn lot of trouble to get to a box I protected so carefully! He deserves reformatory! It won't be my fault if he gets away with stealing!"

Arthur's voice stayed steady. His words almost escaped Mickey, now calm, breathing easily, ashamed of his odor, embarrassed by soiled clothing, embarrassed by his tears.

"I will not," Arthur said, "let a life be ruined for a five dollar bill!—a five dollar bill that should not have been hidden in the first place! And only one of us here in this room knows if that trifling amount really was stolen. You do not have any real proof of what you claim. The boy's father has no proof. He knows only what you have told him.

"Morton—I do not, for the life of me, understand all that money being in a cigar box—put away like some thief would do—hidden away!

"Morton—carefully listen! Think with your head, your businessman's head—not with your angry heart.

"Call the police—I will not work in this store. I will end this partnership. I will sell my share. Then your problems will begin in seriousness. You will find the ugliness and bad temper you seem so badly to want—for which I wish I knew the reason." His brother's neck reddened again. His knuckles whitened as he mightily clenched both fists.

"I say what I say carefully, Morton." Arthur's voice started to tremble again. "As a promise—not an empty threat. If you thought it was only a threat, it would change nothing. It is time that I do what needs to be done! I didn't have the will before. I kept waiting."

Mickey felt pulling at his shoulders. "Son," his Mr. Weinstein said, the boy looking up gratefully at the word, "you wait outside for your father."

Walking awkwardly, Mickey moved listlessly through an aisle, disgusted by the feel of his wet legs and cold-feeling knickers rasping his skin, sickened by the underwear soiled with slimy bowel wastes. He retched at his own smell.

Outside, the coldness of his legs seemed greater, worsened by the cool breeze off the Hudson River. But he felt a sudden flush of warmth. *I'm free! No reformatory! Yippee! I made it! My Mr. Weinstein's wonderful!*

A moment later, Morton Weinstein stood in the front doorway of the drugstore as Mickey was roughly pushed by his father to start their walk home. In low, raging tones the druggist hissed at Mickey. "I promise that you won't work around here again. I will go to every store in this neighborhood—no—even farther! I will go from store to store for a dozen blocks north and south and as far east and west as I can go to tell what happened! And I will tell every customer you made deliveries to the same story so they can shame you when they see you anywhere! You will not escape because my brother was a fool!"

Mickey did not see the Weinstein brothers again. He cried days later when he realized he might not again see the nicest man he had known. For days he wanted to die, to avoid his father's ceaseless condemnation—in front of Margaret; as a preliminary to seeing that he got busy with homework; as a preface to ordering that his chores get done with; at the supper meal. Mickey had not received the beating he had anticipated once his father got him alone. That puzzled him. Thrashings had often been prompted by far less severe behavior. But the stream of oral punishment seemed incessant.

Mercifully, Margaret did not taunt him. One night she stood by his bed, speaking softly so their father would not hear, consoling Mickey, trying to still his sobbing.

After school, one day, reluctantly at first, then compulsively driven, he wandered to the drugstore. He peered between taped-on garish sale posters, hoping for a sight of Arthur Weinstein, vainly looking for him at the soda fountain, ready to run if he saw Morton Weinstein. For two weeks Mickey agonized over the despair he had caused the gentle brother. He wanted sorely to see him, to look into his eyes, to show he understood the risk the man had taken—*I didn' mean to hurt ya, Mr. Weinstein! I didn'—honest!*—to show his own torment, to see that by now his Mr. Weinstein had not condemned him, too.

Days later his father announced, "We're moving!" Mickey cried himself to sleep that night. He slept fitfully. He had bad dreams. He overslept, after angrily shutting off the clamoring alarm. His father furiously awakened him when he returned from his night of cab-driving, after first rousing Margaret. She was at the kitchenette table, in her nightdress, eating corn flakes and milk as Mickey ran tearfully into the bathroom. They were both late for school.

On the Sunday they were to leave the neighborhood, while his father was gone for an hour or so to borrow a pickup truck for the moving trip, Mickey suddenly remembered his backyard cache. He left Margaret to pack the last few things, to add another carton to the crowded front room. He ran down the front steps, turning right, waving at his sister watching him curiously from a window. He trotted hurriedly for a block east, wanting to confuse his sister if she leaned out the window to watch where he went.

Anticipating his wealth, he quickly circled the block. Approaching the alley to his building's backyard, he could not see Margaret looking out the window, searching for him. He walked more slowly, suddenly thinking of his Mr. Weinstein.

He walked past the alley, back up the front steps, tears burning his eyes, pursing his lips, then letting them break into a slight smile; leaving his treasure of five Prince Albert cans to perhaps be found by someone.

25

I sure lost a lot when I lost my Mr. Weinstein.

I'm just lucky I didn't get the shit whaled out of me when I got home that day! I wonder why not? The old man did whack the hell out of me for a lot less than stealing money.

Well—at least once I had to count my blessings for escaping a good licking—that's for sure.

Let me see—what happened after that?

26

Mickey put his hand up high without hesitation when the teacher asked who wanted to be in the school play.

"My boys' home room has the largest number in it—enough to fill all the roles—and I'm one of the directors of the play. Mrs. Fein is the other director and her girls' home room will provide the actresses needed. I coach the boys for all the Act One practices for Scene One with just boys in it, and Mrs. Fein does the same with girls for Scene Two, with only girls in it. Then the last two weeks we all practice together for the big Act Two. It only has one scene, and that's when we have boys and girls together.

Even as he raised his hand, he wondered why he had done it so quickly. *I ain' no actor! I ain' ever done no actin'.*

When young Mrs. Smythe had earlier started the home room class period by explaining about the annual school play, he had thought of Cary Grant in that part of one of the three British troopers serving in India, in *Gunga Din,* his favorite movie. He remembered how many times he and other kids had cheered him and Douglas Fairbanks, Jr., and big, tough-looking Victor McLaglen as they swashbuckled through their barracks and fort compound, through village streets, as they leaped about on rooftops gallantly, cheerfully, easily, battling and defeating howling Thuggee native rebels. The five times he had seen the film, and all the many other adventures he had seen on Saturday mornings on screens in noisy movie houses packed with great numbers of boys and girls, on hooky-playing afternoons, and in after-darkness forays through side doors from theater alleys and upper-floor fire escapes, these all stimulated his recent recurring thoughts of how great, how exciting it must be to be a movie star, an *actor.* He kept his hand up as Mrs. Smythe made her selections.

"I have one role left," she finally said, looking Mickey in the eyes, "and I think you would do just fine. I wasn't certain at first, but I can see things now that— makeup and costumes can do a lot. You'll look wonderful." She smiled at Mickey.

When he learned the role in which she thought he would do well, he was repulsed. Then he thought quickly: *Heck, it is a way to be an actor—an' I won' be the only one—an' it's somethin' to do—someone different to be. It ain' everybody can be an actor. Go ahead! Do it!* The teacher asked, "Will you do it? Do you *want* the part?"

"Yes, Mrs. Smythe."

She said he would be Johnny Wheeler, who would become Gloria. And she selected Simon Roth to be Harold, who would become Paula. Eleven other roommates would be other preparatory school boys, some in bit parts, others in several supporting roles, and there would be two major roles.

Mrs. Smythe, standing behind her desk, raised both arms high, signaling for quiet, for attention to be paid to her. "This is a very funny play, boys. It's a comedy about young men at a private preparatory school—and, incidentally, so you'll feel better, they are young men about your own ages—and these young men are to attend an intraschool dance to be held at a private school for girls about ten or so miles from their own school."

Several boys groaned in displeasure. One said, "Gee whiz, Mrs. Smythe—do we have to do somethin' like that? Can't we do a mystery? Or somethin' else, maybe? Anythin' besides one that means a lotta girls in it?"

She did not answer, holding up a hand for silence, smiling slightly, amused at the reaction she had expected. She continued, as though uninterrupted. "The play takes place in two acts. The first one has two scenes leading up to the second act. There will be a ten-minute intermission, then the second act is in one long scene, about what goes on at the dance." There were more low groans.

"Now this dance has been an annual social occasion arranged by the headmaster and headmistress of each school for many years—a traditional event, to help teach young girls and boys about social amenities—how to properly act with others. But—for the most recent years tension increased at each dance because of growing snobbery with new classes from year to year."

"Yeah," an anonymous voice mumbled, "bet we know who's to blame, too—the dames, right?" Mrs. Smythe smiled again.

"For many years, for both schools, the dance was a looked-forward-to event, but with the snobbery there was boredom at the dance, then reluctance by the boys to even go. Many girls felt the same way. But parents, especially mothers, remembering their days at the schools, eagerly planned their child's participation. And they had their eyes to the future for their boys and girls, seeing good marriages, important families."

A boy hooted, "Whoopee!" then gave out a sharp tongue-and-lips raspberry.

"Behave!" Mrs. Smythe said, patiently.

"So," she went on, "the dance this comedy is about is what happens when the boys decide to embarrass the girls—they say it's to get even. They want to make up for the stories they heard about what took place at the last two dances. They want to avenge the snubs of many of last year's girls who wouldn't dance with most of the boys."

Glancing about the room, Mrs. Smythe sensed she had to speed her synopsis. Boys were looking through the windows to outside. Some slouched, to make their disinterest obvious to the teacher. One was whittling a pencil point with a pocket knife.

"The play's author has contrived that two boys will bring their quote-*sisters*-unquote to the dance at the Crestwood School for Young Ladies. And the authorities of each school give in to pleas of the boys' dance committee that the visiting quote-*sisters*-unquote—Paula and Gloria—be allowed to attend the dance rather than having to each stay at home alone while their quote-*brothers*-unquote were off dancing for an entire evening.

"Now then—can't you see what's going to take place? All the funny things that can happen in such a situation?" The faces she saw were blank, uncomprehending, not even one with a puzzled look.

She sighed and went on, trying to stir enthusiasm in her home room class. "The plan of the boys is to all pay attention to the quote-sisters-unquote of their schoolmates, and generally ignore the Crestwood girls. That's their scheme to inflict humiliation to repay the snooty girls at last year's dance. What happens in Act Two is more involved than I've explained and there are a lot of funny lines and funny scenes. And it's not until just before the play's close that the quote-*sisters*-unquote end their masquerades and show themselves to be boys from the school. I'm sure you will all love it once we get into rehearsals and you get into the spirit of things."

Mickey's and Simon's roles were the most important of all the assignments, Mickey quickly learned. He had second thoughts about having volunteered—first, not wanting to play the part of a girl; secondly, woefully doubting that he could memorize so many lines, remember so many things to do, *how* to do them. Worst, he was disappointed that he was chosen so late in Mrs. Smythe's selections— almost last. *Then* to be a *girl!*

He made wistful pleas to Mrs. Smythe, then an angry one, for some other role, anything—a *shorter* part!—he was sure he could not learn such a big part, he cajoled; such an important one—and Mrs. Smythe would look bad—and all really because of *him,* he coaxed. And he did not want that to happen to her, he wheedled.

Mrs. Smythe smiled, patient throughout his oration. Then she insisted it was Johnny Wheeler/Gloria or nothing. "Except for Simon, I think you're better suited to be Gloria than anyone else in the home room. They're all too large, meaning too bulky, too chunky, and I want the girls to be slimmer types. Or they're too tall. Or they're just too clumsy. You and Simon are better, believe me. You'll do nicely *because* you're smaller."

Dammit!—somebody else sayin' I'm little!

Mickey sat quietly, thoughtfully, staring at the floor. Mrs. Smythe watched him expectantly.

"Simon's not making the fuss you are. And you *did* raise your hand on your own. And your hand *was* one of the first ones raised." Mickey shrugged his shoulders, staring at his clasped fingers, plinking thumbnails against each other.

"I s'pose I could play a girl—'cept all those guys'll laugh at us all the time."

Mrs. Smythe spoke promptly, softly. "And you can't take any kidding, can you?" As Mickey looked up from his fingers into her eyes, she made herself frown, as though her feelings were hurt, as if she was very puzzled. Mickey decided on one last plea. "Yeah, but you don't know these guys. The ones here in the home room are bad enough—but those in the rest of the school—when they find out—"

Mrs. Smythe's expression did not change. "I'm sorry you don't—won't—"

All I gotta do is watch Margaret. She's almost thirteen, just like that Gloria. I'd just hafta do things the way she does—an' the way all her girlfriends do 'em. When I hafta be a pain-in-the-ass-Gloria I'll just think of Margaret—do things just like pain-in-the-ass-Maggie. For once she'll be useful! "I'll do it! OK, OK!"

At that point Mickey did not wholly comprehend his and Simon's roles—shy, pretty, demure, slender young girls, with the cleverness of smartening thirteen-year-olds, cleverness that did not have to be taught, cleverness that came naturally; with budding breasts and other changes in figures; still with the uncertainness of females undergoing early experiences with lipstick, powder, rouge, and eyepencil, with biology, with boys.

Simon had not made a single objection to Mrs. Smythe's choice of a role for him. But Mickey was not surprised. *I always thought o' him as a sorta sissy anyway.* Simon was not adept at playing stickball during recess—maybe a passable hitter and fielder, but not that great. *I'm a lot better'n he is, any day—that's fer goddam sure! They let him play sometimes if he asks to—but he can't hit a spaldeen fer nothin'! I play more'n he does—and they ASK me to play!*

Simon did not want anyone to call him the nickname Si, or any other nickname either. He said his mother wanted him called Simon; and besides, he said, he liked that name himself. But guys called him Si anyway, and he answered to it, without making a fuss.

He was good-looking, extraordinarily so, even pretty; dark hair, thick and wavy. His eyes were so dark brown that they appeared to be black, and they were set far back into his head. Eyelashes were black, long, and thick. Eyebrows were full, black, gracefully arching above the deepset large eyes. His nose was small. His skin was smooth, unlike the complexion of nearly all other boys, afflicted with acne and crusty flakes of healing blemishes.

The more Mickey saw of Simon's girlishly attractive face, the more he was conscious of and embarrassed by his own telltale facial marks, additionally scarred by impetigo. He knew he would be compared harshly to Simon in their roles. Each time he self-consciously examined his face in a mirror, the pit on his right cheek seemed to deepen and widen; the raggedly misshapen scar above the outside corner of his right eye seemed to spread from day to day. He felt terrible. Mickey agonized that, in no time, the entire right side of his face would be disfigured. Every day he tried to avoid looking in mirrors. In the school's lavatory, before and after urinating, he busied himself with the buttons of his fly to keep from glancing at himself in a mirror, afraid he might be fascinatedly drawn close to the glass for a minute examination. He took to avoiding his close-up reflection even in window panes and store windows, shunning mirrors at home and at friends' homes.

Mickey mulled over Mrs. Smythe's choice of him for a girl, mystified. *I got pimples and blackheads and those damn scars that are still red-lookin' an' I'm small an' I'm skinny. Why the hell did she take me?*

The two boys borrowed clothes from their sisters. Simon's sister—Rebecca, nearly two years older than he—cooperated with him excitedly and spent a lot of time with her brother, looking at this item and that item, comparing it with something else in her wardrobe, she modeling it, he trying it on, talking about colors, she explaining makeup. Unembarrassed, she showed him how to stuff tissue paper into the brassiere he would use—the way she used to, she said, when she was thirteen trying to look fifteen or sixteen. Simon later carefully explained tissue-stuffing to Mickey, who asked "Whadda they wanna do that for?" Simon simply smiled and said he would learn all about that later sometime somehow and that he would then understand. Rebecca showed Simon how to sit and walk and bend to pick something up from the floor and other things she had been taught and had learned herself.

"And the two most important things," she added, smiling, fidgeting with excitement and anticipation, "I'll show you how to act with boys. That's first. Second, I'll show you how to make the girls at that school dance really angry with you. You'll be so good as what's-her-name that you'll be the star of the show!"

Simon reacted to her coaching with intelligence and aplomb, absorbing Rebecca's guidance in the manner a professional actor would. Mickey was another matter. He asked Mrs. Smythe what he would need for clothing, and came close to refusing to go ahead with the role when she soon afterward matter-of-factly gave him a written list. "A brassiere?" he argued. "Even underpants and a slip? I gotta wear her underpants? What for? A dress is bad enough!"

"It's the way I want it done. I want you two to *be* girls when you're on stage—not just boys wearing girls' dresses. I want the audience to believe that each of you is a girl! The audience will not know beforehand that you two—you and Simon—are not really girls until a surprise ending closing out Act Two. That's why I want the audience to *believe*—to *know*—that you and Simon are *girls*."

Mickey only told his father and sister that he was in a school play, that he would have a lot of rehearsing. "It's s'posed to be a comedy about some rich-kid boys goin' to some dance at some rich-girls' school or someplace like that and that the play wasn' anythin' special but just somethin' I hadda do 'cause all the other guys in my home room are in it cuz the teacher said everybody hasta participate by actin' a part or bein' a stagehand or somethin' else to do with the play an' I figgered I might jus' as well try to do good in it 'cause there wouldn' be any kids around the neighborhood bein' as they were all doin' somethin' with the play anyways an' it would keep me busy after school when I wasn' doin' homework."

To answer his father's perfunctory question, Mickey said, "Nah—I dunno when it's gonna be—going to be—playing—except it's in a few weeks—five or six I guess. I know we practice during the week after classes and every Saturday morning nine o'clock to twelve. I'll let you know when the date of the play is. I only know right now that it's on a Friday night sometime. I hope you're both there." He hoped his father would be driving his cab nights then, that his sister would think *I don't want to go see his dumb old play!* He hoped they would both forget about the play, except remember that it accounted for why they saw less of him sometimes. He hoped they would each be too interested or involved in what they did themselves.

Stealthily, hastily, when Margaret was not home, he searched the bureau drawers and the small closet in her room, finding one each of the list items. He dangled the small brassiere by a shoulder strap on a hooked forefinger, staring at it with an interest he had not had before. "Looks small to me," he said aloud, laughing, thinking of lingerie photographs he had seen before, paying no real attention to them at the time.

But he did not dare take one of her two pairs of shoes for the play. Her play-shoes were too abused-looking, and the black patent leather Sunday School shoes were out of the question. *She ain' got enough shoes that I could snitch a pair without 'em bein' missed.* But Simon's sister came to the rescue when Mickey told his difficulty to Mrs. Smythe.

Beginning rehearsals were read from scripts and Mrs. Smythe experimented with moving her young actors about on the gymnasium floor as if it were the auditorium stage. She explained to Mr. Pagani, anticipating his usual grumpiness, that the gym was better in early practices because she could more easily move among the boys on the floor trying this or that movement or position. And, she added firmly, she had the principal's permission. And, the locker room was next to the gym when some of the boys needed to change into costumes in the next week or so.

Mrs. Smythe artfully guided the boisterous, often inattentive boys through repeated trials of line-reading, memorization, speaking properly and projecting, responding to cues, sternly reminding them about *not* looking into the audience so that later, when on a stage, they would not try to find someone they knew. She worked hard at getting them to look at each other when speaking lines required eye contact between two actors.

"You must make eye contact with whomever you're speaking, if the lines call for it—and you must be *serious!* And I already know that most of you will try to make someone laugh when they say their lines. That's been going on forever in the theater, even with grownups. I know actors and I know young boys, so I'll have none of that! I do have a sense of humor, though you might not think so—and funny things do happen now and then—but be serious." Behind her back, she crossed her fingers, hoping for good luck with her plea.

Mrs. Smythe had Mickey and Simon dress for their girl roles long before any of the boys had to appear dressed for their prep school parts. She maintained her insistence to Mickey that he and Simon would both more quickly get better at being Gloria and Paula by dressing the parts early on. "You're being very troublesome, still. I don't really like to make comparisons, but you don't hear Simon complaining, do you?"

Wearing makeup embarrassed Mickey, but the wig made him feel more mortified than the makeup, even more than the girl's clothing. It was long blonde hair, with tight, dangling curls reaching to his shoulders. Simon's was short–haired brunette, with bangs covering the forehead. Mrs. Smythe o-o-hed and a-a-hed and h-m-med as she fit the wigs and studied her handiwork and how the boys looked as girls. She combed and shaped the long blonde tresses, soothing Mickey. "You'll look quite good. Besides—blondes have more fun. Mickey grunted.

Wonder how she knows that? She's got brown hair!

At the start, the two boys transformed themselves to girls in the locker room with all the other boys. Their companions were quick to begin with whistles, lustful-sounding groans, hoots, and catcalls. When Mickey and Simon stripped their school clothing, Mickey stayed naked only long enough to hastily pull off his too-large boxer shorts and quickly yank on the lightweight and seemingly too-small panties of his sister's, keeping his back to others in the locker area. Then he awkwardly donned the small brassiere, with coaching from Simon, and hesitantly stuffed the small cups with wads of thin paper peeled from a full roll of toilet paper. Simon had to urge Mickey to keep adding paper each time Mickey thought he had done enough. "You've got to look like a real girl, understand? Keep stuffing." Mickey went about his task in a furious hurry, but Simon worked unhurriedly, languidly, seemingly indifferent to eyes. The mild jibes and jeers became a din of shouts and profanities and obscenities.

"Hey—looka them tits!"

"How 'bout a date sometime, honey?"

"You know how to fuck? Wanna? Huh? Let's!"

"Oh—I feel like jerkin' off! Wanna do it for me? Honey? You sweet thing, you!"

Somebody pinched Mickey on a buttock, then he felt a hand reach from behind, then a second, and a third, as he raised his arms to let the dress slide down from over his head, wriggling hurriedly, trying to cover himself quickly, all the hands grappling the paper-packed brassiere. Fingers nearly succeeded at unclasping the backstrap before Mickey pulled away. Yanking the dress down by the hem just above his knees, he glanced at Simon, surprised that no one was bothering him, no one was clutching at him; seeing, with a longer look, that Simon merely ignored remarks to him, that he seemed amused by Mickey's tribulations. "C'mon, Simon—let's get outta here—'way from these jerks!" Simon winked at him and smiled slightly as Mrs. Smythe's insistent door-banging and sharp commands from the hallway, succeeded, to a small degree, in quieting the boys. A moment later, when stoop-shouldered, gray-haired Mr. Pagani entered, waving his long-handled feather duster high, the noise quickly died. No one in the school could recall ever seeing Mr. Pagani without the duster in a hand and he was known for unhesitating disciplining use of the wood handle, thick feathers tightly clenched in fingers. Mr. Pagani had long ago learned one way to command respect from schoolboys.

Mrs. Smythe, again anticipating, had persuaded Mr. Pagani to match his locker room clean-up times with her after-school rehearsals. The second rehearsal went easier for Mickey. Mrs. Smythe, without making reference to the noisy goings-on two days before, had the boys-playing-boys keep practicing lines and stage movements while she sent Mickey and Simon ahead from the home room to the locker room to get into costume.

"And, you two—I want complete costumes. No shortcuts, do you hear? No telling me you did everything you were supposed to, I mean. I'll be checking both of you for completeness." Mickey glared at her. *She must mean me, I'll bet! Sissy Simon don' mind doin' this stuff!* Mickey was certain of his speculation when he saw the intensity in Mrs. Smythe's eyes. He seethed inwardly, but acquiesced, fully regaling himself as she wanted.

As the rehearsals went on the boys did get into the spirit Mrs. Smythe had predicted. And they soon found things to amuse them other than harassing Mickey/Johnny/Gloria and Simon/Harold/Paula. But Mrs. Smythe nonetheless continued to have those two go to the locker room some ten minutes or so before the others, and Mr. Pagani was always on hand, sweeping, cleaning, polishing, feather duster firmly gripped in a hand.

Mrs. Fein's group of young actresses appearing for the first joint practice of Act Two was a great relief to Mickey. *Now these guys'll have somebody else to give a hard time to 'stead o' me an' Simon!* The flirtatiousness and foolishness the two teachers expected were evident from the first moment, and each teacher, with patience and understanding, with a mixture of joviality and occasional seeming anger, kept tight reins on their charges.

With boys trying to show girls they could do better at acting than the girls, and the girls doing the same with the boys, the rehearsals went far better than the directors had thought they would. Their excitement grew, as did the boys' and girls' enthusiasm. The girls delighted in Simon's sister-coached portrayals, and said to Mickey that he wasn' *that bad*—and that, in fact, sometimes he was pretty good, too.

In the sixth week there were two opening-curtain-to-closing-curtain rehearsals, on Monday and Tuesday, with only Mickey and Simon in costume. Mrs. Smythe and Mrs. Fein sat in the darkened auditorium watching the first practice on the school stage, thankful for all the time spent moving people about on the gymnasium floor. Mistakes in positioning or movements were simply called from the darkness to someone on stage. "Keep right on going with your words, this time. Just remember to fix the mistake the next time through. OK, let's keep going on."

At the Tuesday closing curtain, the directors told the cast they had Wednesday off, and they had to put off saying things about the dress rehearsal Thursday and the performance on Friday until the raucous cheering subsided. The teachers finally had to go up on stage to get the attention of someone specific to briefly instruct on a point about the dress rehearsal.

Mickey rushed through getting changed into street clothing. Simon was talkative about the rehearsal just done, how much he was enjoying acting, how funny the play was. Mickey interrupted him. "C'mon, Si—Simon. Let's get goin' if we're gonna meet the others at the Neapolitan. You were so good tonight, I'm buyin' you whatever you want."

Simon sat on the locker room bench, his dress draped over the seat beside him, the brassiere on the dress, the brown wig on the bench on the other side of him. The towel used to wipe and scrub makeup from his face was draped over his lap. "Why don't you wait around a little bit until I get ready. I'm sorry I was talking so much."

"Naw," Mickey said, "you always take too long. I'll see you over there."

On Thursday, except for the home room sessions, the actors and actresses were not good students in the various classrooms to which they moved, one subject after another. The dress rehearsal was on their minds. The boys got to the locker room earlier than usual. Mr. Pagani got there early, too, though he first spent some time in Mrs. Fein's home classroom, tacking a thin canvas curtain in place over the window in the upper section of the entrance door, then installing a temporary chain lock on the inside. Mrs. Fein had the principal's permission to make her area a girls' dressing room for two evenings, as long as the room was restored to order for Monday morning classes.

The young thespians, in their separate dressing rooms, fidgeted and chattered excitedly, knowing there was only one last time to say lines properly, to get prompting and coaching from the two directors, to move about on stage without colliding into someone or something without tripping or falling. Now there would be changes of clothing between scenes and acts. This was the last practice for the stagehands, too. Mrs. Smythe and Mrs. Fein had taught them well and were confident that set changes would be made quietly and efficiently on show night.

In a music practice room next to the locker room, Mrs. Smythe and another teacher, Miss Kleinschmidt, spread and patted makeup on boys' faces. Accompanied by joshing and jeering among the boys, they drew defining, darkening lines on light-colored eyebrows needing emphasis. Lips were painted, eyes colored with mascara. They combed unruly hair. They made certain that hands were washed and fingernails cleaned. Ties were checked to be the right color for a suit. The two women fussed over each boy in turn, surrogate mothers. In the locker room, the last to have makeup applied, Mickey and Simon dressed as girls from the skin out once again, free of heckling.

When their turns for makeup came, all the other boys were sent to the auditorium, told to sit about and relax, or practice lines, or do whatever they wanted, as long as they behaved. "Be sure you don't make nuisances of yourselves with the girls there!"

The teachers kept Mickey and Simon for last, wanting to give them the most attention. Mrs. Smythe, with greater experience, worked on Mickey. "I'm afraid you'll need more work, young man. There are some things I'll have to fix. Now, Simon—he's a little luckier than you are and doesn't need much. Miss Kleinschmidt can take care of him easily."

Seated in a folding chair, Mickey squirmed as Mrs. Smythe fastened a barber's apron around his neck, carefully spreading it to cover the dress, tucking it under the wig tresses. She pulled wig hair back from his face, fussing and fretting as she daubed, patted, and smoothed creams and pastes on his cheeks, jowls, temples, nose, forehead, chin, and neck. She darkened and thickened pale, wispy eyelashes with mascara. She scrubbed dark pencil-coloring into his platinum blonde eyebrows, at the same time creating a feminine arch. Mickey's back was turned to Simon and Miss Kleinschmidt, unable to see how his friend's appearance was changing. When Mickey did not have his eyelids tightly squeezed together against Mrs. Smythe's rubbing, patting, and poking, he could only glare at a chalk-powdered blackboard for distraction.

"There now," Mrs. Smythe said, making slight adjustments to wig curls, stepping back, smiling down at him. "Want to see what you look like?" She reached to a table at her side, lifting a large, oval hand mirror, aiming the reflecting glass at his face.

Mickey could not believe he was the one reflected, peering timorously back at him—a passably pretty girl, he thought. After a moment he slowly said, "Not bad, Mrs. Smythe—not bad." He pondered the image. "Nope, not that bad." He kept studying the surprising image, turning his head to one side, to the other. He straightened in the chair, then leaned forward to bring the two faces closer together. The image had no disfiguring impetigo crater three quarters of an inch from the nose. He turned his head slightly left. The girl visage's temple was clear; no shallow, ragged, reddish-tinged impetigo blemish. He slumped back against the chair back, squinting, staring harder at the mirror face, trying to eliminate seeing the mirror rim, trying to mildly blur the image, to make it appear to be at a greater distance. He hunched toward the mirror again, pursing lips, smiling widely, turning head side to side. He arched brown eyebrows, slightly at first, then more so. He glowered, creasing his brow, fluttering eyelashes, trying to imitate what he had seen his sister and other girls do. He pouted. He brought a hand to the tresses, in the manner of his sister in her self-examinations, touching the curls and waves surrounding the girl-in-the-mirror-face.

He looked up at the expectant Mrs. Smythe's eyes, sensing that he was blushing under the makeup, hoping she could not see any trace of it. "It's OK—it's good—what you just did. I'd go out with someone lookin' like that—if I was to go out someplace with a girl—'cept I don' do stuff like that. I mean—uh—uh—you know what I mean?" The teacher smiled, nodding understanding, amused by Mickey's acceptance of a standard for going out with a girl. Mickey smiled, too, satisfied.

He turned to Simon to see his transfiguration, and found him peering back at him. Mrs. Smythe had been right. It had not taken Miss Kleinschmidt long to make her subject into a facially stunning Paula. Simon looked as though he had no pancake makeup or powder on his skin. Miss Kleinschmidt had applied only a bit of red coloring to his finely shaped full lips, and had been sparing with rouge on his unblemished complexion. She did only enough to compensate for stage lighting. Mickey was surprised how little needed to be done to make Simon really good-looking—*Nope, not just good-lookin'—pretty!—wow!—really pretty.* Sitting slumped in his chair, looking intently at Simon, Mickey remembered that several times he had thought the other boy looked more like a girl than he did a boy. *Even his build is more like a girl's!* More than once Mickey had thought Simon was prettier than Margaret, even prettier than Simon's own sister, Rebecca.

Simon smiled confidently at Mickey, who mustered only a hesitant half-smile in return. He felt flustered, and it annoyed him that Simon seemed so sure of himself. Mrs. Smythe interrupted their mutual examinations by having Mickey stand, taking the makeup apron from his neck, fussing over him with final primping. Miss Kleinschmidt had Simon stand, turn round in one direction, then another, posing in several positions.

Satisfied with their handiwork, the teachers shooed them into the hallway, then began funneling the girls into the music room. Their excited chattering lowered in pitch and volume as they stared at the two boys' expert external metamorphosis. Low, teasing whistles sounded, mixed with snickering and giggling. In a moment, once all the girls were inside the makeup room, the boys were forgotten.

Suddenly alone in the quiet corridor, they pondered what to do next to while away time until a quarter of the way into the second act when they would appear on stage. They agreed that they did not want to face the coarseness of their schoolmates. Mickey said he did not think he would be able to control anger. Simon suggested that they move to the stairs at the distant end of the corridor where they could sit on the landing between this floor and the next one up. There would not be any hecklers to bother them—no one would see them if they sat on the steps that twisted in the opposite direction up from the landing. "We could go over our lines one last time, Mickey, with no one anywhere near us."

It was dim on the landing, twenty steps up from the hallway, the only light coming up from the first floor below, and it was quiet. On the next flight of steps upward, sitting side by side, Mickey felt awkward in his feminine clothing. The silk form-fitting underpants felt peculiar, pinching in more than one place, restraining, not like the comfortable loose under drawers he always wore, looking like the shorts boxers wore. The clasp at the back of the brassiere dug into his backbone.

Simon broke the silence by saying Mickey's lines that began the roles of Gloria and Paula. Mickey was again impressed by Simon's skill with memorizing lines easily and perfectly. He had already learned that Simon knew all the lines for both of them soon after practice started. Mickey had tested him several times—during rehearsals, at lunchtimes, in hallways when changing classrooms—by asking random questions about how lines should be said, or asking Simon to give him cues to practice passages.

They took turns cuing each other with the lines of various boys' roles so they could recite their own parts. Mickey agreed with Simon that they should not put any emphasis into saying their lines for fear that sounds would give away their darkened, quiet place to anyone lingering in the corridor. They kept softly calling out lines in turn. No one disturbed them, though they could hear noisy voices of girls finished with their turn in the makeup room and of boys who restlessly left the auditorium and chose to flirt with or annoy the girls. Their giggles and laughter and taunting were garbled and echoed off the tile-lined corridor walls and terrazzo floor.

As Mickey said lines and his eyes became accustomed to dimness, he occasionally glanced at Simon, marveling at his transformation. The other boy sat relaxed, a perfect Paula. He gave cues promptly when Mickey faltered, whispering the lines surely, speaking and acting as though he had always been an actor, always been Paula. Simon showed none of the awkwardness that Mickey felt.

At the end of saying lines, Mickey turned his head to peer at Simon again, still fascinated. Simon was looking at him. "Simon, I can't get over how you look like that gal you're s'posed to be. You really look great! I wish I—"

"You are," Simon interrupted. "Are what?" Mickey said.

"Pretty."

"Pretty?" Mickey was puzzled.

"Uh, huh. You make a nice Gloria."

Mickey felt his face tingle with warmth, then feel hot. *What am I blushin' about?* He was embarrassed, certain that Simon was only trying to make him feel better, trying to get him to relax, to do well in about a half hour when they would be on stage.

"Yeah, you're very pretty," Simon repeated. Mickey looked away, his eyes searching for something on which to concentrate, to make himself not feel so nervous. *I oughta be feelin' better'n this after so much practice—so long wearin' these clothes!*

"I like you better than all those others down there." Simon gestured to the sounds coming from the corridor down the stairs. "You're not noisy like them." His voice lowered to more of a whisper.

"You're not so raucous, or vulgar. You're not as coarse."

Mickey wondered what *raucous* meant. He had never heard the word before. "Yeah, sure I am," Mickey said, eyes focused on the landing below them. "You just don' get to see me when I ain't aroun' doin' this actin' stuff." Mickey smelled the perfume that Mrs. Smythe, in her final primping touch, had lightly sprayed above their heads, letting it settle on their wigs and shoulders. Simon had moved closer to him, leaning back, an elbow on the edge of the next higher step, other arm resting along the edge, extended toward Mickey. With those fingers he tapped Mickey on the shoulder.

"I see you more than you think I do." He shifted his position again, slightly closer. Mickey sat more erect, pressing against the wall, trying to escape the light touch of Simon's leg against his.

He said, "Let's do our lines some more, Si—Simon. You're good—an' I wish I was that good. But I need a lot more practice, I'll tell ya!" Simon did not answer.

They sat quietly, Mickey feeling more nervous with each moment and at a loss as to what to say or do.

Simon sat up straight, leaning closer to Mickey. Mickey felt a pressure against his back where it pressed against the stair edge. Then he felt a sensation just above his knee. He was sweating under his makeup, he could tell that. Fingers dug mildly into his back, then he recognized the sensation above his knee when a soft touch became a clenching grip. A new awareness came over him. *Oh, shit!* A tingling started in his groin. Simon was speaking quietly in his ear, but Mickey's mind was agitated, tumbling thoughts about, unable to understand the other boy's words. *God!*

He wanted to get up from his stair seat, to stand straight, but could not. He seemed to have no strength. *Goddam!* Simon's arm at his back had moved up, crossing from one shoulder to the other. Mickey realized he was being held in a hug. *Jesus!* Simon kept talking, his voice down to a low whisper, his breath giving Mickey a strange sensation in his ear. His loins tingled more strongly. *What the fuck's he doin'?* Simon's other hand loosened its tight grip and slowly slid along the inside of Mickey's thigh as he brought his legs together firmly, then squeezed them tightly. He felt fingers dig slightly into a shoulder as Simon talked more quickly, still softly, his lips brushing Mickey's ear, words still unintelligible to his confused mind. The arm at his shoulder squeezed, tugging at him, gently, firmly. Mickey's whole body flushed, then he felt he was in a raging fire. He squeezed his eyelids shut tightly, rebelling against a new-found agony.

He was suddenly aware that his penis was starting to swell and elongate. *Shit! Shit! SHIT!* He made a large fist of his own two hands, pressing it into his groin, trying to defeat the enlargement, pressing his legs together more tightly. Simon's hand moved quickly along the thigh, fingers probing insistently, prying beneath the determined fist. Mickey felt Simon's lips press lightly against his neck, then felt his tongue flicking against the flesh, lightly, then with increasing pressure, moving forward to Mickey's throat, kissing it firmly, flicking his tongue more rapidly, against tightened neck muscles. Mickey's fearful trembling increased. His penis was beginning to hurt as the silk cloth restricted its growth. The stiffened flesh was actually bending under the strain of trying to be free of the fabric. He pressed his thighs together forcefully, pushing his double-fist down, trying to pin his organ between his legs. But his engorged penis became steadily stiffer, striving to spring upward. Simon's fingers suddenly discovered the bulge in the smooth underclothing. His hand at Mickey's shoulder clenched it sharply, making Mickey grunt in slight pain. The hand yanked him backward. The stair edge pressed a painful furrow across his back.

Mickey's squirming kept Simon's fingers from working under the elastic edging of the underpants. But Mickey was suddenly afraid of the other boy. He forgot he had thought of him as a sissy. Simon seemed possessed of a strength with which Mickey could not contend, that was hurting him. He suddenly realized he was afraid of Simon at this moment.

It was quiet. Simon was not saying anything and he had pulled back from Mickey. Mickey opened his eyes as Simon wriggled, changing his position. Mickey could hear his own breathing. It sounded deafening suddenly. He was afraid he would start gasping, that he would cry out at Simon, that others in the echo-chamber corridor only twenty steps down would hear and come investigating. He could not have them be discovered! He held his breath as long as he could before slowly, desperately letting air slip out as quietly as possible.

He glared at Simon, twisted about into a new seated position. He seemed to be peering into Mickey's lap and his fingers still insistently poked under the big fist. He brought his arm from behind Mickey, pressing the forearm harshly across Mickey's chest, pressing his back harder against the stair edge, sharpening the pain. Mickey's eyes started to water and burn. The forearm, pressing firmly, slid down. Mickey felt pressure against his solar plexus—where he had once been pounded by a fist and had plunged into semiconsciousness—pressure hard across his ribs, forcing his torso further back. He kept his fingers clenched into a single fist, but could not keep it protectively over his groin. Simon's probing hand forcefully pushed the fist upward. Mickey's strength ebbed abruptly. He cried, but made no noise. Sensing the lessened resistance, Simon's forcefulness diminished. Mickey felt relieved.

He turned his head to the wall as a painful pressure built across his forehead. His back hurt from being harshly bent. His ribs hurt. Simon's fingers kept probing the elastic of the underclothing leg opening. Mickey's penis still hurt from straining against the snug silk material until his organ lay against his lower abdomen. Suddenly Simon's hand pushed strongly and fingers slipped upward beneath tearing elastic.

With the whole hand inside the smooth undergarment, the damaged elastic was completely broken and the silk fabric expanded easily. Probing fingertips fondled soft pubic hairs, then moved to the base of the twitching organ. With quick movements, some of them painful, the warm fingers gripped the entire swollen penis and firmly turned it to point downward, slipping the hand and penis from under the useless elastic.

Both were now free of confining silk fabric. Mickey shuddered in anguish. His mind screamed. *Dammit!—dammit—help—somebody—please!* The hand gripped his penis more tightly as he squirmed. He felt pain across his back again as he was pressed backward again, more vigorously this time. Simon's strength seemed limitless. *What if somebody sees us?* Flashes of bursting colors like exploding fireworks seared his brain with panic. He wriggled harder against Simon's effort but felt peculiarly powerless to fight him off.

Simon's pressuring hand stroked his penis in long, slow movements, gradually easing the foreskin back. The tip of Mickey's penis quickly became slippery with fluid seeping from within. He thought how much the strange hand felt like his own when he did to himself what Simon was doing. His panic subsided. He squirmed less. The stair edge burrowing into his back did not bother him as much now. Simon seemed to be easing his pressure. The bursting, hurting colors diminished, then were gone.

Simon's hand moved more quickly. Mickey's head fell slowly back, gently resting against a step. He felt better, panic receding like a wave quickly moving back from a rushing assault. He felt pleasant. He did not want to resist. Time drifted. Mickey's tightly entwined fingers relaxed its fist, then almost separated as both hands rested on his abdomen. An ecstasy began. Then it was different.

The feeling was not exactly the same. *That's not—somethin's—oh, God!* He lifted his head, feeling light-headed—*Damn—I'm dizzy—Jesus!*—looking for

Simon, seeing only the top of his head in the dimness. The other boy's head was over Mickey's groin. Mickey abruptly realized that Simon's lips had softly encircled the end of his rigid penis, that Simon's head was moving in quick up and down strokes.

Much as it will with a cat—so it can spring high and far instantly when startled from a purring slumber—energy within Mickey coiled and uncoiled. An overpowering panic surged through him. With an explosive burst, he forced Simon up and away, shoving furiously at his head, sending him hurtling backward onto the landing. He fell against a side wall, struggling for balance, but lost it and tumbled forward, going end over end and sideways, rolling down the twenty steps with increasing speed. Simon's arms flailed about, hands groping for something to grab to stop his momentum. He grunted several times, struggling to keep them from becoming yells or screams. Mickey frantically got to his feet, reaching for Simon, trying to keep him from falling, but he could only move to the edge of the landing and stare at the tumbling figure. Simon rolled to a heap at the foot of the stairs. In the light of the corridor, Mickey could see Simon's stunned, fearful expression staring at him.

Mickey fumbled under his dress, pushing his flaccid penis under the silk panty, tugging down at the torn elastic, trying to reshape the garment. He was filled with sudden rage as he rearranged the dress back down at his knees.

"You no-good fuckin' bastard! You're—"

Simon shushed him, telling him not to be so loud.

Mickey waved a hand angrily at him. "You're a fuckin'—"

"I didn't mean anything! I thought—I just thought—shush!—please!"

Mickey tried to make sense of what Simon had done. *In all the pictures I ever seen only women were doin' that—kissin' each other down there—an' I seen some of men kissin' women there too—an' doin' that other stuff—layin' on top o' them—I dunno what for—but what HE jus' done? Jesus!* He could hear footsteps running in the corridor and voices calling. Simon shushed him again. "Please!"

Mickey growled at him, "Fuck you—you—you're a sonofabitch besides bein' a bastard—that's whatcha are! I heard about guys—but it was always bullshit to me—" The sounds of running feet and voices were closer.

"Please—just tell them I fell while we were rehearsing—that I tripped!"

Mickey felt strangely triumphant, superior. "You—you—" Simon's face showed anguish that Mickey had never seen before on anyone he had ever known. "You—*cocksucker!*" As quickly as it was said, he felt ashamed of his forceful accusation. Simon's face creased with greater anxiety. "I liked you," he said, pleading.

"*Fuck* you, Simon—" Simon glanced quickly over a shoulder, stared at Mickey again, and moved up two steps, then two more. "Mickey, they're coming. Why can't—" Mickey uttered the same profanity, then again, his voice lowering as sounds in the hallway grew louder. He quivered with fear and anger.

Mrs. Smythe was among the runners who appeared at the foot of the stairs, and she demanded to know what the noise between the two boys was all about. "And

I'm not sure I would have liked the language, young man," she said angrily, looking intently at Mickey. "I didn't hear it plainly, but it didn't sound at all like anything proper!" Mickey saw that Simon was staring hard at him, and thought his eyes seemed to be watering. Simon closed his eyes and clenched his lips between his teeth, creating a thin line across his face. The teacher started up the stairs.

"I'm sorry, Mrs. Smythe," Mickey muttered, shrugging one shoulder. Behind her, boys and girls were peering up the stairwell. "We was just horsin' around and Si just fell down when he was running' up the stairs yellin' that he was gonna punch me for sayin' some things about him playin' a girl, that's all." He watched Simon's eyes open as Mrs. Smythe reached him. His face was still toward Mickey but he did not look him in the eyes. His gaze went left over Mickey's shoulder, far into the distance. He thought Simon smiled, but he wasn't certain.

"Well, then, "Mrs. Smythe said, putting her hands on Simon's shoulders from behind, "it doesn't seem to me you really can say much yourself. After all, you're also acting the part of a girl, if you'll remember—if you'll take a look at yourself standing there." She turned to face the boys below who were starting to heckle from there, quieting them. To Mickey she said, "Why would you pick on Simon? You're not envious of how well he's doing his Paula, are you? You should be ashamed, if you are." Mickey's quivering ended, but he was annoyed with the teacher. *Sonofabitchin' Simon did all this an' I'm the one gettin' picked on!*

Mrs. Smythe shepherded everyone to backstage for the start of the dress rehearsal. Mickey, staying to the rear as the group moved, watched Simon's back as he walked along the corridor with Mrs. Smythe's arm about his shoulder, expecting him to drop back to say thanks, hoping he would not, hoping he would.

The rehearsal went well for Mrs. Smythe and Mrs. Fein. They sat quietly in the darkened auditorium as the cast performed far better than expected, neither coach making any comment when someone on stage faltered with lines or when some matter of acting business went differently than it should have. They were pleased with the cast as players helped one another through a difficult moment. The two directors were pleased with the skill at improvisation shown as the play went on. The women excitedly applauded when the final curtain closed, rushing onto the stage to effusively congratulate their young actors and actresses, taking time here and there to give encouragement where needed, to coach how something should be better done. Boys thumped boys on arms and shoulders and backs; girls hugged themselves and one another and cried and giggled.

For Mickey, afterward, the rehearsal was as though it had not taken place. His mind seemed blank. Sitting alone in the quiet locker room, he was certain he had disgraced himself. He slumped on the bench, trying to remember specific things about what he had just been through, worried about what he might have done as Johnny/Gloria, mentally preparing what he would say about his failure after weeks of practice, dreading the next night's performance. He wondered if there was some other exit from the locker room and the school. He did not want anyone to see him, to talk to him, to himself have to talk to anyone. He wanted to hit something.

Then he remembered Simon on stage. Suddenly, clearly, Paula spoke, looking Gloria directly in the eyes each time needed. Mickey looked for even flickering embarrassment, but Simon was Paula, right through the moment the two boys pulled off their feminine wigs on stage to deride the Crestwood girls. Just as suddenly, there in the locker room, the image of Paula was gone. There was no Simon, either.

Mickey recalled Simon standing on the stairs, again seeing his fearful expression, hearing him say, "I liked you." *He liked me? Then why'd he—?* Mickey wondered how he would react if he saw Simon at the Neapolitan. *Maybe I shouldn' go. Naw—I'll jus' stay away from wherever he is in there. Why the heck should I be the one to stay away from the place? Maybe HE won' show up.*

Thumping sounded in the locker room. Mickey, startled, looked about anxiously, listening. Someone was vigorously knocking on the entrance door, then he heard it squeak open. "Hello-o-o in here." Mrs. Smythe called again, louder, "Anyone here? Simon?" Mickey sat up abruptly, looking at himself to see how he was dressed, looking to see if he had his pants on if she appeared. He stood up, fastening his belt, hurriedly tugging on his shirt.

"Naw, he ain't here, Mrs. Smythe. It's jus' me. I'm jus' finishin' changin'." *That's funny! Where'd he go to change? He sure didn' go out the street lookin' like that!*

"I dunno where he went." *But maybe after what happened—maybe he did go out lookin' like a girl—bein' in a hurry to get outta here! Who'd know the difference out on the street. Hell, it's dark outside already. I wonder how far away he lives?*

"You two were wonderful," Mrs. Smythe said, still out of sight. Her voice echoed in the empty space. "And *you* don't have a thing to worry about. Little things here and there could have been different, but nothing was serious enough to really have to change anything. You were just fine, Mickey. And you will be fine tomorrow night, you'll see."

Shit!—I don' even remember the thing! That realization absorbed Mickey so that he forgot about the teacher's presence. *How come I can't remember somethin' I jus' did?*

Mrs. Smythe's voice echoed louder. "You tell Simon the same thing for me if you see him before I do, will you? Mickey? Good night—Mickey."

"'Night, Mrs.—" The locker room door sounded loudly as she pulled it closed sharply to let him know she had gone.

Simon was absent during the home room period that started the next school day. Their other classes differed so Mickey looked for him in the corridors, curious about how Simon would react when he saw him, curious about how he himself would react to Simon, hoping to see him before being seen, wondering what would happen. But he did not see Simon any time Friday.

Mickey felt he was lucky. Neither his father or sister would be in the audience. He was relieved when each, at separate times when he off-handedly asked, said they could not make it, both saying they had forgotten being told earlier. His father grumbled, "You should have reminded me sooner. I already have something to do. I can't change things now—not this late!" Mickey was disappointed, then annoyed, that after all this time his father had not even asked what the play was about, or what his role was.

Margaret snickered. "Why do I want to go see a bunch of dumb boys in a dumb old play? And you don't know anything about acting anyway!"

Good!—then I'm gonna throw away those things of yours! He felt satisfied. *You'll look forever for 'em—I'll show ya!* Then he was disappointed again. She, too, had never asked him about the play, or about his part. *But I'll bet you prob'ly don' even know your things are gone!—but I hope you do!*

Mickey arrived for costuming as late as he thought he possibly could, wanting only enough time available to get dressed quickly and have Mrs. Smythe put on makeup. He wanted to be the last one for her to work on instead of one of the first as she usually mandated. Anything to avoid Simon. And he was successful. He did not care that Mrs. Smythe worked roughly, grumbling about his tardiness, about all the trouble it made for her—with all she had to do. He shrugged his shoulders. "I couldn' help bein' late, Mrs. Smythe. I hadda to do chores an' things at home— an' some homework—or I'da been in a lotta trouble. You don' know my old man—my father."

Mickey waited nervously in the wings, staying there throughout the first act. He knew he would not be pestered there by anyone. He kept going over his lines, feeling he was going to have as much trouble on stage as he was in the darkness. He had not yet seen Simon, or Mrs. Smythe either. He thought she surely would be fluttering about everywhere, checking everything, encouraging everyone. Listening to onstage lines and audience laughter Mickey slowly felt better. The performance seemed to be going well. Then he felt worse, his worry growing again. *What do I do if he don' show up?* Nearly soundless bustling went on about him, someone coming offstage, someone going onstage, noiseless shuffling behind him as others got ready. *Jesus!—don' forget your darn first line!* He turned to look deep into the backstage area. *Oh, boy—I'm gonna be in trouble! Even Mrs. Smythe ain' aroun' anywhere!*

Mickey moved to stand near a back wall when the intermission began, to be out of the way of stagehands making set changes. His own enthusiasm rose when he heard cast members and backstage people excitedly whispering about how well the play was going, about how much the audience was enjoying the show.

As cast members went on stage behind the curtain for the start of Act Two, Mickey moved forward again to the wings. Looking over his shoulder, he saw Mrs. Smythe leading Simon along through shadows and people, gently nudging others aside to make way until reaching Mickey's side. Simon looked intently at the teacher as she whispered to him, then he stared out at the onstage action, listening to lines being said there, mouthing the words of the speakers, even as they were saying them. Mickey watched him closely, marveling at the other boy's memorizing ability.

After the first few seconds onstage, Mickey felt good and did well performing Johnny/Gloria. As he said his lines, nearly perfectly, and moved about the stage, almost flawlessly, he felt a growing excitement at how well he was doing, at how much he was enjoying his own acting and the performances of classmates. Not until a point where they were to look at each other did Simon's eyes meet his. Mickey had been dreading the moment.

Simon performed Harold/Paula with perfection. He appeared to see only Gloria, oblivious to Mickey. With the first curtain call, performers making their bows, listening to loud, vigorous applauding, Simon stood at some distance from Mickey as they stepped forward, wigs in hand, from the wide line of cast members and were cheered and whistled at. And he stood farther away when Mrs. Smythe hustled them back to the stage for a second appearance, this time of only Gloria and Paula, still with wigs in hand.

After the final curtain call, backstage was a bedlam of hoots and hollers and laughter and yells of relief. Mrs. Smythe and Mrs. Fein let go their tight reins but Mr. Pagani, feather duster in hand, patrolled the boys' locker room diligently, shushing, grumbling to himself, urging the actors to hurry and change and leave so he and his two helpers could clean up everywhere and go home themselves. Mickey did not see Simon throughout the hustle-bustle. He wondered where Simon changed his clothes—or if he did at all.

Simon was not at the Neapolitan when Mickey arrived late, hesitant again about encountering Simon, as he had been after the dress rehearsal the night before. Simon did not appear at any time during the boisterous get-together of young actors and actresses.

Nor was Simon in the home room Monday morning, or in any other class. After several days, boys in the home room session that began each school day now asked Mickey if he knew where Simon was. At first Mickey wondered if the questions were asked in some needling manner, looking for any sign of coarseness or suggestiveness, worried that Simon might have said something to someone. "Nope," he would answer, or say, "Naw, I don' know either," or simply shrug a shoulder and quickly get busy with something.

Mickey thought of asking Mrs. Smythe about Simon at the start of his second week of absence, but decided against it. At the end of that week he learned from someone during a lunch period in the cafeteria that Simon and his family had moved to California.

27

W-h-o-o-o!—*what a guy that Simon turned out to be! And what a hell of a way to find out something like that—what that—that—that stuff about a queer was—things we all used to hear about from other kids. We all used to just laugh every time anybody said the word queer. None of us knew for sure what the hell we were talking about— or why we laughed. I wish there was someone I could have asked about things like that.*

I don't know what I'd do if I ran into something like that again—what with where I'm going. Turn in his ass?

Uh, huh—you bet! But—well—hell, he was a nice enough guy otherwise—a smart SOB—and a damn good actor, too. He sure fooled me about a lot of things. Anyway, something like that probably won't happen again—at least not to me.

A voice bellowed, overriding his thoughts. "GEE THROUGH JAY! Let's get with it! Gee—aitch—eye—jay! That's all for now, so let's get going!"

Huh? Oh—that's the next bunch—G through J. He looked at his watch. Getting closer—but at this rate I've still got a lot of time.

Let me see—my luck held out—going through that thing with Simon.

It sure did hold out—through everything. My butt saved from going to reform school—finding out what—queer?—OK, queer—what queer really meant—finding out the hard way! And that city—what a hell of a place to grow up—and on your own, too.

28

The oblong-shaped borough in which Mickey lived was generally a crisscrossed regular pattern of straight streets and avenues. It also had random long and short thoroughfares that angled sharply or just a little bit across the regular pattern. Along one river bank, here and there, the roadway for motor traffic—everybody called it a parkway—wriggled and drifted slightly, fitting minor contour changes.

In the lower section of the borough, which was an island, angling streets and avenues were more numerous, and the entire pattern was more tightly compressed, containing dense sections of numbered and named enormously tall buildings that caused dark shadows when the sun was not straight above. Several miles north, the narrow upper portion of the borough had a looser pattern of thoroughfares, many of the blocks not so rigidly rectangular, often with curving, angling shapes. However, there were still buildings that poked stiffly up into the air, though not as high as downtown. The borough teemed with people. Hundreds and hundreds of thousands lived there. More came in each day to work, to do business, to visit others or go shopping, for recreation, for excitement, to forage. A place to work, for most people residing in the borough, was nowhere close to a place to live. Going to and from work meant time-consuming travel, easily becoming boring and sometimes troublesome, but unavoidable, making people hurried and fractious.

Towering buildings set on deep footings drilled in thick rock created narrow canyons through which people on foot and in cars and trolleys and buses moved in fixed and irregular flow patterns.

Subway trains roared noisily underground, their sounds and smells and heat vented up into the streets through large, coarse grates in the sidewalks. Elevated trains roared and clattered noisily above many crowded streets. High, thick-diameter steel columns supporting miles of steel tracks created a challenging, deadly maze for impatient, rushing, aggressive, belligerent motor vehicle drivers, creating a nerve-jarring adventure for cautious or timid drivers. Parked vehicles, pushcart vendors, passenger buses, rattling and bell-clanging trolleys, and darting children and adults sent cars and trucks weaving in and out of inside and outside traffic lanes, dashing around El columns. Tempers always seemed taut. Indifference to everything seemed to be the customary mood.

High in the air, dark trestles filtered sunlight, breaking brightness into shadows and darkness, further confusing motorists and pedestrians. Accidents were commonplace.

A ten-year-old girl darted from between two vegetable vendors' high-wheeled pushcarts and was tripped by a corner of a cobblestone block that stuck up less than an inch above the uneven road surface and she was crushed by the huge front tire of a huge, dirty, fully-loaded coal truck before the staring, grimacing, horrified driver could do anything to change what was to momentarily happen to the small girl and him. Bystanders said it happened so quickly she never uttered a sound, that she never saw the truck, that she died without knowing even an instant beforehand that she was about to be killed.

After Mickey wriggled through the crowd of adults, seeing the bright red blood squeezed from the slight body made him retch. It made a wide stain all about her and marred the truck's front tire. Mickey wanted to run.

He silently raged at all the grown people standing, looking, talking. No one made a move toward the girl, to see if anything could be done for her, to help her. Only the grimy truck driver got attention, sitting on the ground near her, slumped against the splotched front tire, forehead resting on forearms bridging his knees.

Understanding had not reached Mickey's mind that nothing could be done. *Why don' somebody even look at her up close? Maybe she's—* He had seen other forms sprawled on streets, but more distantly. And there had always been people milling about them, doing different things, until they were covered with sheets or pieces of clothing, at least over their faces. Things had looked neater those times. He stared angrily at a chubby, short man just inside the edge of the crowd past the front of the truck. *How can that sonofabitch stand there like that, eatin' that friggin' apple?*

He stared at the small rag-doll remains, splayed in the slowly spreading, darkening redness between massive front and rear wheels. Her face did not show pain. *Why don' nobody cover her up?* He wanted to pull off his shirt and put it over her face, but he turned away, pushing through people crowding closer, getting free of them, breaking into an aimless run.

He ran and ran, slowing as he began breathing harder, as his head ached from pounding feet hard on asphalt streets and concrete sidewalks; then trotting, not wanting to walk yet, not until he was farther away. He glanced into store windows as he flashed by them, looking for images to replace those of the peaceful face and destroyed body; changing glances to longer looks as he moved slower, then more slowly.

Something caught his eye—a display of model trains. *Wow—look at them!* But they were not moving along the tracks. After only a few seconds visions of the accident again swam through his mind as he tried to concentrate on the big Lionel locomotive. He got himself moving, reluctantly walking away from the store window, struggling to not envision the girl's light-colored hair and pale skin with a bluish tinge to it.

Two street corners away, after a slow walk, eyes searching everywhere for real things to replace his mental images, Mickey saw a pretzel vendor pushing a decrepit cart with a big crooked wheel on one side, a smaller wheel on the other side. *How the heck does he steer the thing?* Mickey dug into a pocket and spent one of his last two nickels for a salted soft pretzel, thinly spreading a daub of mustard over the top surface clustered with large salt crystals. He looked to see where he was, how far he was from his own neighborhood, then walked slowly toward home, thinking how tangy the mustard tasted.

29

*H*ell *of a place—that city! Never saw anything like it since.*

Maybe I'll get back there someday—when I'm all done with this.

Boy!—the things that happen there—the things that happened to just ME! It's a wonder that I made it this far!

30

Hooky was better than going to school, to Mickey's mind. But school was a must, he understood that, or there could be trouble if the school system ultimately revealed excessive absence and sent out a truant officer. His father's anger the first time Mickey had been caught playing hooky turned to rage and got him a painful thrashing the second time. But today Mickey decided for hooky. He had not been caught at it for nearly two months and had not been absent for illness for more than two weeks, and then it had been only for half a day.

I think I'll go on some kinda adventure today—jus' get on the subway an' go where it goes—see wha' happens. He paid no attention to how far from his neighborhood he had walked when he randomly chose a subway entrance and went down a tile-lined stairwell from street level for a ride someplace in the labyrinthine subway system.

He dug a coin from a pocket, dropped it in the turnstile slot, then slowly, steadily pushed at the bulky wood crosspiece, amusing himself with trying to feel when it would click past a certain point so it could no longer be freely moved backward again. He felt the locking action take place, then pushed himself through the turnstile more quickly until the crosspiece disappeared into the housing and another arm of the four-piece unit swung out of the housing and locked into place behind him. *There—just like a regular customer. I paid my way this time!*

He did not care where he was going. *Anyplace is good enough for me!* He was surprised to find he was alone on the center platform of the two-way express-stop station. Nor could he see any waiting travelers on the local-stop platforms on either outer platform on each side of the tunnel. He meandered to the far end of the long platform, near where the first car would halt. In the dark distance past the opposite end of the long lighted platform he could hear the low rumbling of an oncoming train, then he could see faint light coming from round a bend three hundred feet away. Being the only person in the great openness of the station with its wide center and narrower side platforms gave him an eerie sensation. *Boy—it sure does feel spooky down here—jus' me here—in all this—jeez!*

The train noisily rattled and rolled from the tunnel darkness and the front of the first car screeched to a halt close to where Mickey had guessed it would stop. He could barely make out the standing figure of the train operator through the grimy glass of his small, dark cubicle. Entering the first car through the front door,

Mickey glanced at the other end. It was empty, and being alone in the smaller area made him feel better than he had in the vastness of the station. It was late enough on the weekday morning that most people had reached work already. Kids traveling from one neighborhood or borough to a school somewhere else were already in class, too.

He stood peering ahead through the front-end connecting door six to eight feet ahead of him, looking into the tunnel darkness, balancing himself during the jerky start from the station and into the unlighted tunnel. He did not hold on to a vertical pole or overhead strap or seatback grip. *Anybody* could do that, but not everybody could smoothly keep balance when older rattletrap cars started moving. Mickey smiled when the rough start was done and the train settled into a clattering roll. He mentally added another hands-off start to his string of successes, trying to recall what number he had reached.

He moved forward and slid into a forward-facing two-passenger seat, the first one back, opposite the door to the train operator's compartment, staring hard at a torn, dirty advertising poster on a metal wall ahead of him, not seeing the poster, thinking of what he could do when he got someplace. *Won'er where I'll wind up?*

Directly behind him, there was another row of the same style seat on each side of the car, then sliding doors on each car side, then long center-facing seats on each side of the wide aisle, extending to a second set of sliding doors at the middle sides of the car. Farther past them, other long side seats faced the aisle. A third set of sliding side doors were at the rear of the car, then two sets of forward-facing two-passenger seats on each side. Vertical hand-hold poles, bolted to the floor and ceiling, were widely spaced the length of the compartment. Worn leather straps, closely spaced, dangled and swayed from long ceiling rails that extended from end to end on each side of the car's center. Several bare ceiling light bulbs were burned out; others were broken, jagged edges protruding from sockets. Cigarette stubs, candy bar wrappers, and newspaper sections littered the floor.

Mickey's eyes focused on the torn, dirty color poster three feet ahead. Most of a woman's face in the large faded photograph was ripped away, but her nose and mouth and chin still showed. Above her mouth someone had drawn a large crayon-scrawled mustache, thick in the center, from nose above to lips below, sprawling left and right, quickly getting thinner as it spread past her cheeks and ears, then swirling upward and inward in tightening eccentric circles. Below the debasing adornment, her pink-lipped smile showed white teeth, tinged with subway grime, words in a nearby balloon proclaiming the teeth to have been made white because of a miraculous-acting toothpaste. Mickey momentarily, disdainfully stuck out his tongue at the half-face and turned to look at whatever might appear through the greasy side window at his left.

The subway car jerked and swayed through the long dark tunnel between stations. Interior lights flickered when there were small gaps in the power line—the third rail—paralleling the worn train tracks.

Mickey was not certain when he got the feeling someone was looking at him. Then he oddly felt that the someone was not merely *looking*. He sensed, with a peculiar prickly, tingling feeling at the back of his neck, that it was a stare. *Who is it?*

He shifted position uneasily, leaning into a corner formed by the seat and the window. He felt twitchy inside. He slowly swung a leg up onto the seat, turning more sideways, pressing his back against the window and car side. He stretched an arm casually along the handrail at the top of the seat back, lazily tapping fingers on the rail. He studied the small horizontal advertising posters on the opposite side of the car, above the windows, close to the ceiling, extending the length of the car. He tried to look casual, pursing his lips, softly whistling, keeping time by tapping fingers. He looked at one overhead poster after another, working to the rear of the car.

The express train rattled and swerved through the long, dark underground route, charging ferociously into and through a lighted local station, hurtling along on its deafening high-speed run. Mickey tried to distract himself by peering out an opposite window as the train roared by waiting people on the platform. Men and women were statue-like silhouettes against yellowed tile walls, reading folded newspapers, holding shopping bags and bundles, tightly gripping small children startled by the noisy string of cars. Mickey saw the figures strobiscopically through closely spaced black columns separating tracks.

Too soon, the diorama was left behind. Sensitivity to being watched overcame Mickey again. *Somebody's in this fuckin' car!*

His stomach felt more fidgety, and neck hairs rose more. He wanted desperately to appear unconcerned about anything, to look indifferent. Loud, clashing train sounds seemed less noisy as his mind whirled with concern over what he was sensing. He let his head loll to one side, onto his shoulder, and closed his eyes, to give the appearance of dozing, to let a suspected occupant see his eyes closed. *This is dumb! I ain' seen nobody else here. What am I doin' this for?* He let his arm hang loosely behind the seat and sway with train movements. He made slits of his eyelids and peered intently throughout the car. *Nothin'! Nobody's here!*

Then he saw movement at the far end, behind the last seat on the right. A small dark-colored ball rose slowly from behind the seat. It looked brown.

Focusing fuzzily on the object through slitted eyelids, Mickey felt growing fear. Whatever it was now looked fully round, perched on the seat back, definitely brown—in fact, two shades of brown, the upper part darker. *I don' like this shit!* He opened his eyelids more to sharpen the far image. Just below the dividing line of the two browns, two white marks grew.

Mickey's dangling hand tightened into a fist, stirred by nervousness. *That's a head! It's a colored kid! Those white things are his eyes!* He did not move, stricken with anxiety. His mind raced faster, remembering things he had heard—terrible things—frightening.

A dark-brown wool knit stocking cap was pulled down snugly over ears on the head leaning on the handrail. The skin of the head was a lighter brown, enough lighter to be noticeable to Mickey at a distance. Eye whites were accentuated by the dark colors.

He remembered the Johnson boy, that he was nothing like the terrible things about colored kids that Mickey had heard from other kids in the several neighborhoods in which he had lived the past few years. He gripped the seatback railing tightly, then let it go when he thought his tense grip might be obvious to the watcher.

Mickey wished there was another car in front, that this one was not the first in the train. *Then I wouldn' have nothin' to worry about. I could just get up, jump through this door between the cars and hold it shut from the other side if he comes after me.*

He told himself there was nothing to worry about. *So what if there's somebody else in this car? What does that mean? Jus' another kid playin' hooky too.*

Maybe we could do somethin' together.

Yeah, sure—go someplace with a colored kid—that's trouble fer sure!

He turned his face more away from the brown head perched on the seat back, but only enough to still be able to peer sideways, to keep alert to whatever the head grew into. His mind started developing full-blown worry about what was next, what he ought to do.

I can' tell how big he is. Maybe I'm bigger'n him. I could get tough with him if he starts somethin'. Oh, shit, I'm too little an' not strong enough to get tough with anybody—dammit!

Nah!—this guy wouldn' do nothin' anyway until the train was gettin' ready to stop. That way he could get out a door quick if he wanted to. Mickey's eyes strained to keep a sideways focus on the head.

If there was another car in front of us there might be somebody to help me. They wouldn' have to do nothin'—I wouldn' say nothin' about this guy—jus' sorta hang aroun' whoever's there—and this colored kid would stay away—maybe even take off somewhere else.

C'mon—stop fuckin' around! There ain' no other car!

Mickey considered banging on the train operator's compartment. Maybe he would help. "But *why?*" he knew the man would say. "There's no trouble!" *An' it would be jus' my luck he'd be colored himself—then I'll really be in trouble!*

How long before the next stop? I'll get outta the door before he can get to me, that's what I'll do.

Mickey paid closer attention to the watcher through slitted eyelids, moving his head slightly as though he was looking at the overhead advertising posters. The colored kid had sat up straight. Mickey guessed him to be about his own age, but he thought he looked skinnier.

Shit!—he knows I see him!

Mickey stood up, trying to appear indifferent, moving two steps to stand close to the sliding connecting door at the car front. He circled both hands about his eyes to keep out light from inside the car as he stood swaying to the car movements, peering ahead into the dark tunnel, edges of his hands pressed against the grimy, thick, wire-reinforced glass.

He pulled one hand edge back from the pane, far enough to examine the cloudy image of the car interior behind him on the door glass. The figure at the far end was standing. Then the silhouette moved into the aisle. *Damn!*

Lights glimmered in the darkness ahead. *Good, good! It's the station!* Brakes began squealing the train to slowness, the stop still some distance ahead. The silhouette in the reflection was more definable, now more forward, past the far end doors, closer to Mickey.

The train operator applied insistent pressure to the brakes, pressing hard against the control handle on the top of his console, cursing worn brakes, worn wheels, worn tracks. Looking ahead, to the left, Mickey could see the long center platform rapidly come into sight. It was deserted. So were the southbound and northbound local-stop platforms on each outer side beyond closely set steel support columns. Mickey recognized the station as one of several on the subway line where passengers could go to another level to get a train traveling to some other part of the city. He cursed his luck that for a second time in only a few minutes he encountered deserted platforms. He wanted people about so he could make himself disappear from the silhouette in the grimy reflection.

Mickey kept an eye on the reflected figure, apprehensive, expecting some sudden action by the colored boy when the train stopped and in the few seconds before the sliding doors opened. But the colored boy now was seated on a long side-wall seat on the left side of the car, just past the center door. The train bumped and jerked to a halt, swaying between the platform and blackened support columns. Mixed with screeching, clanging metal sounds were whooshes and gasps of pumping air brakes tightening, releasing, tightening, releasing brake shoes on hot wheels. Even as the car slid and vibrated to a standstill, the train operator actuated the door control, swooshing them open for the length of the train, some snapping apart quickly, others opening slowly. Some mechanisms were older than others, or in better condition.

Mickey spun about, darting for the open door two seats past him, leaping onto the platform, veering so sharply that he lost balance and stumbled, banging one foot against the other. In a worried glance he had seen the other boy bolt from his seat, charging for the opening mid-car door.

There was a short reprieve for Mickey. The mid-car double doors opened only partially, not wide enough for the colored boy to get through. He collided with the two vertical rubber door bumpers with a hard grunt, struggling with both sides, trying to squeeze through the narrow opening, growling oaths at the malfunctioning doors. Mickey put out a hand instinctively against his stumbling fall, regaining balance, sharply aware of a burning sensation on the heel of the hand where it had scraped on rough cement. He did not know the other boy struggled with doors.

Mickey saw stairs going upward far down the platform as he recovered from tripping. He scrambled toward them. On legs long for his height, he churned quickly in desperate movements to escape. Fear gripped him; squeezing lungs, binding muscles into knots, cramping joints, banging inside his skull, stabbing his brain. He could feel tears burning dry eyeballs. He gulped air. *Get your fuckin' ass outta here!* He ran harder. *Get away from the nigger sonofabitch!* His breathing seemed to thunder in his head. Huh-huh-huh-huh-huh-huh-huh-huh-huh-huh. *C'mon—c'mon—get up them fuckin' stairs!*

He ran faster, lungs aching, up the long flight of steps two at a time to a broad landing, wanting to stop to get his breath, but instead lunging clumsily up another long set of steps. He could not hear sounds of a pursuer in the din of train doors swooshing shut and the noisy, rough start. Scrambling madly upward, Mickey twisted to look over his shoulder. *Oh, shit! Here he comes!* The other boy's outstretched arm and widespread clawing fingers were only two to three feet from Mickey's back.

Mickey's gasping, gulping breathing hurt more. His feet missed treads he was trying to take two at a time. He lost ground. The other boy was taller, with longer legs. Mickey's hands and knuckles banged and scraped on cement steps and the metal of the center support railings. He saw red wetness on fingers and backs of his clawing hands, but he did not feel pain. He had a sudden thought to stop running and frantically climbing steps. A giant signboard flashed on in his mind. Huge red letters flashed and pulsated—STOP!—QUIT!—QUIT! QUIT! For an instant he wanted to let whatever might happen simply happen, to not have to panic anymore, not have to struggle anymore. Instead, the letters disappeared in a brilliant yellow flash and he started taking some steps three at a time. But his legs could not move out and up easily to cover the new demand. He only stumbled more. Suddenly he could not hear train sounds, only muffled thuds and slapping of pounding feet. A frantic glance over his shoulder showed the assailant had dropped back. He seemed to be off-balance. Mickey horrifyingly realized the chaser's broken stride was caused by him keeping an arm stretched ahead of him, his hand striking at space between them, slashing.

The other boy was not using both arms to pump himself evenly up the stairs. In that glance and in an instant of understanding Mickey recognized something. A new burst of energy suffused him, opening his tightened throat and gasping lungs, letting him take bigger gulps of air, strengthening his legs. He bounded three steps at a time easily.

Seconds of time seemed sliced into millionths, separate slithering pictures, agonizingly long moments. Mind images snapped into focus, horrifying imaginings of what could happen.

The *something* Mickey recognized was a curving, long blade of a finger knife; a blade of sharp, hard metal that extended from a thick, broad ring worn on a middle finger, poking up from the back side of a hand, a knife used to cut apart the thick cords of bulky, heavy bundles of newspapers. Close to where the finger joined the broad part of the hand, the hooked blade arched up from below the knuckle of a fist. In use, a worker would swing a bundle of newspapers with one hand to a working location by its tie-up cords, holding the cords up from the top paper as the bundle was positioned, aiming a tight fist bearing the deadly protruding knife at the heavy twine binding. A practiced worker could, with grace and deftness of a skilled sword handler, precisely hook the sharp blade on the inside of the curved metal in under a thick cord of twisted jute, combining lifting and slicing motions to cleanly sever tough strands. Mickey had seen Mr. Schwartz use such a knife in such a manner many times in his variety store when newspapers were delivered to him.

Mickey felt a tug in the center of his back, felt his coat being pulled. He arched his back inward, away from the pursuer, fingers clawing at steps as he tripped and stumbled. Another burst of new energy and effort carried him to the top of the stairs. Suddenly he felt free of any restraint and in a leap soared onto the large passenger platform on the upper train level. Waiting passengers were startled as he drove into their midst, scrambling through the barrier they were. One yelled an oath at him; others cried out in surprised fear as he shoved, knocking away packages and under-arm folded newspapers. He charged through another knot of people, then ran toward where he was sure turnstiles would be at the far end of the platform, staying close to the dingy tiled wall to keep from being pushed down onto the tracks by the pursuer.

The noise of the angry people diminished quickly. Mickey could only hear echoing thuds of pounding feet. But the sound was different, more frightening. He could only hear what he thought were his own running steps. He worried that the pursuer was running leisurely behind, trotting easily, step-for-step footfalls synchronized into sounds matching Mickey's rushing gait. Keeping his frantic pace, Mickey glanced awkwardly over a shoulder. He could only see the cluster of angry people staring after him. He slowed to a walk, then stopped, first bracing himself against the yellowed tiles with an arm, finally leaning his back against the wall. He peered at the adults, expecting to see the colored boy emerge threateningly.

Mickey sidled to the edge of the platform, peering the length of the sunken tracks, wondering if the other boy was trying to conceal his advance by skulking along the rails. Mickey heard no sounds of an approaching train, so he kneeled on the rough cement and carefully leaned out over the tracks, looking if the colored boy was moving along under cover of the overhanging lip of the platform. Mickey cautiously guarded against a quick grab from ambush.

The bastard nigger's gone! He ain' here nowhere!

Where the hell did he go?

I'll bet he's behin' them people! I gotta get outta here! I can' get another train from this station that's goin' the same direction. He could just get on it with me an' I'd be in the same trouble—only this time he'd be mad!—madder!

He could still be back of some post along the edge of the platform. He could still be watchin' me right now!

Mickey walked to the turnstiles, watching over his shoulder. He banged his body and hands hard against the thick wood crossarm, charging into the entrance area, darting past the attendant's cubicle, running up steps two at a time, into fresher, chillier air and bright daylight. He darted into a deepset store entrance as a hiding place, pressing close to a plate glass show window, carefully watching for the colored boy, hoping he could outrun him again if he appeared, if he saw Mickey. Mickey calmed until he thought: *Might as well get on with what I was gonna do.* He set out to walk several blocks to another local station.

Meandering in search of the next subway entrance, he thought about the fear and experience he had just had, congratulating himself on his running ability, on his courage in examining the tracks and under the platform lip for the colored boy. He could almost again feel the tug at his back. *Shit!—that S-O-B must have—*

He stopped, undoing the half dozen large bone buttons on the front of the cloth overcoat. Wriggling out of the sleeves, he turned the coat to its back, examining. A gash almost six inches long, cleanly cut along most of its length, parted the fabric close to the seam, starting just below the base of his shoulderblade area, changing to a wide, ragged tear as he had twisted and arched his back in terror. He stared at the damage, his face twisting into signs of anguish. *Aw— shit!—my friggin' coat's ruined!*

Shit!—shit!

I better figger out some story to save my ass if the ol' man sees this.

That FUCKIN' nigger!

Feeling the chilly air in spite of his anger, Mickey put on the coat again, thinking of what he could do about its condition. It was the only one he had that was warm enough for the season. He kept walking south, watching for the familiar metal rail fencing of a subway entrance. By the time he reached it, he had sorted through simple and complex plans to keep both his father and sister from discovering the damage, and if that failed, to explain it well enough to avoid physical punishment. *Maybe I could repair it myself good enough so he wouldn' notice. Maybe Margaret—maybe she could fix it for me—if she knows how—if she's home—if she won' snitch on me. Nah—she don' know nothin' 'bout sewin'!*

Halfway down the entrance steps Mickey changed his mind about continuing his trip south. *I think I'd be better off more close to home. Then I can get goin' on somethin' to fix this friggin' coat. I gotta think o' somethin' real quick!* He waited for a northbound express that would take him to where he could change to a local that stopped at a station in his neighborhood.

There were more than eighty blocks northward to home. He was sure he would have his problem solved by then. *It hadda be!* When he reached his neighborhood station several blocks from home, his legs seemed to weigh tons as he trudged up stairs to the street level. He started the long walk, through a shopping district along an avenue. Extensive shopping areas thinned and became interspersed with old brownstone buildings and newer apartment blocks. Within a few northbound blocks, the neighborhood was almost completely residential with a small store here and there, sometimes clustered in pairs or threes. Mickey walked unhurriedly along his route, paying little attention to the neighborhood character as it changed. He thought of confrontation with his father over something, he rationalized, that was not his fault. He had not yet given a single thought to explaining his absence from school and his presence on the subway during school hours. *This goddam overcoat! He'll whip my ass cuz o' the tear. Don' make no difference to him how it happened!* At the beginning of his worrisome trek home, he studied trappings of display windows in storefront after storefront. He gawked at lurid posters in a movie theater lobby. He counted taxis heading south. He watched nervously for any colored boy who might be his assailant, who had somehow discovered his quarry again. He watched for any other colored boy who might be a new threat. But he reminded himself that he had never seen a colored kid in this neighborhood. They just never came here. He looked for girls about his own age, only to look at them. But every distraction was shunted aside by increasing urgency to devise answers to his father. Periodically, he calculated the number of blocks remaining before reaching his basement railroad apartment.

When he turned the corner onto his street, he desperately made up his mind to conceal the coat among other clothes. *Aw—geez, no! That's dumb! It's the only thing you got to wear for this kinda weather! The red lumberjacket's too heavy!* Eighty blocks of traveling time had not produced a worthwhile solution that would satisfy Mickey.

Heck—I'll jus' make sure he don' get to see it, tha's all. Then out of all the befuddled, complex reasoning, Mickey had a sudden clear solution. *An' if he does, I'll jus' say I forgot to tell him I found it like that in the coat room after classes.*

Yeah—that's it! I'll tell him some kid musta done it by accident and didn' say nothin' an' I forgot to tell ya. I wasn' in a fight or nothin'—or horseplayin' aroun'—honest I wasn't!

If Margaret saw it first, he would tell her the same thing—and tell her not to snitch! And maybe get her to sew the tear if she could. He was sure his father would get suspicious if he started wearing the red-plaid lumberjacket this soon, not being that cold enough yet.

No one was home as he searched the long hallway and small rooms off it, carrying his carefully folded topcoat. He called his sister's name as he walked the chilly dimness, but she did not answer. She was not sleeping in her room, nor had she left a note telling her whereabouts. *Jus' like her! An' I'll be the one to catch hell if the ol' man gets home early an' I can' say where she is!*

He looked into his father's room, peering to read the clock on the straight-back chair by his bed. *Three-oh-five! Geez—it took me almost two hours to get here after that run-in!*

Mickey realized he was hungry. He had not had lunch; nothing to eat since breakfast—a small glass of milk, a bowl of cold cereal. He rummaged in the icebox, barely cool, finding a thin package of sandwich meat and a small dish of crusted-over baked beans. He combined them between dried slices of whole wheat bread smeared with soft butter about to turn rancid, washing gluttonous bites down his throat with the last of the warm milk.

He flipped the latch of the ice compartment. *Sure enough—it's empty! That's why the meat and the beans tasted like they did. Somethin' else I'm gonna catch hell about, I'll bet. It ain' my fault the iceman came when no one was home!*

His stomach was full. The headache was gone. He was tired. He slouched in a decrepit, sagging overstuffed chair in the front room, thinking about his problem. In moments, physical and emotional exhaustion overwhelmed him. He fell asleep.

He said nothing about the coat to Margaret when her arrival noises awakened him, and was studying school books when his father walked in a half hour or so later. Nonchalance and quiet were easy at mealtime in another half hour. He only had to comply with his father's edict that children do not talk at the table unless spoken to by a grown-up. His father did not say one word during supper.

While his father read a newspaper in the decrepit, sagging overstuffed chair, alternately dozing, Margaret was busy in her tiny room barely large enough for her metal folding bed. Mickey listened to a succession of radio adventure serials, read more of a Richard Halliburton travel adventure book, then went to sleep on the folding army cot in the room he shared with his father; leaving him asleep in the front room, knowing better than to disturb him in slumber.

Mickey's fears about the outcome of the day did not materialize, and he successfully kept the torn coat from being discovered. The next day he persuaded Mrs. Engleman on the third floor to repair the coat almost as good as new and to keep it as their secret.

31

*W*ell—*that thing the kid had wasn't a regular knife, but he sure would have done a number on me with it just the same—and I was sure on the wrong end of it, too. Like being on the wrong end of a gun—the hole always looks a lot bigger than it really is.*

Running up those stairs! I don't think I'll ever forget that—especially seeing that thing on his hand—knowing what it was—what it could do.

Scared? Having such a big slash in the coat was scary enough. It could have been worse!—a lot worse! I hate to think what that ring thing could have done to my face.

Well, those are the kinds of things that happen when you move around alone in a big city—especially being such a young kid—and being small—and a featherweight besides.

But—I got lucky again that time. One more time. Like a cat, I guess. Let me see—how many did that leave me out of nine?

32

When the leader asked if it was right that Freddy had said Mickey wanted to be in the club, Mickey answered, "I sure do."

The leader glared at him. "You jus' can' *say* you wanna be a member and tha's all there is to it!" Mickey felt awkward, sitting in the chair, wondering if he really wanted to go through with all this. It was starting to seem different than he had thought it would be. *What the hell is growlin' at me like that for?*

Freddy hurriedly led Mickey through an alley between buildings; over a half dozen fences four to five feet high that were boundaries for tenement backyards; up back stairs of one of the aged buildings; up three flights of inside stairs; out a backyard window onto a fire escape; down the fire escape; through another backyard window from a fire escape landing on a first floor and through a long dark hallway to the front of the building; diagonally across a street to a corner building; through a dim hallway onto another first floor fire escape landing, down those steps, through several more backyards, clambering over low fences again, scaling higher ones, dropping several feet to the ground. Every time Mickey asked where they were going, Freddy shushed him, extended a hand back toward him and waved him to be quiet. The puzzling journey ended in the basement storage room of a building two blocks from where they had started. Mickey wondered why the trip was made to seem confusing when he knew exactly which building he was in and on which street.

Freddy nudged Mickey from behind, moving him into the middle of the dimly lighted, musty smelling room, whispering, "Sit in the chair, Mick—and don' say nothin'." A figure moved from the dimness at one side of the room. Freddy leaned forward toward Mickey and quietly spoke. "Hey, Mick, this is the club leader—Tony Minelli." Later Freddy told Mickey that his first name was Antonio, "—but you better only call him *Tony*—an' for Christ's sake, don' ever let him hear you call him a guinea or a ginzo or a wop—cuz he'll kill ya!"

As Mickey entered the gloomy cellar room, his eyes made a quick sweeping glance; he saw several figures in the shadows along right and left walls, four standing, two seated on boxes. Mickey had seen most of them, older boys, at one time or another throughout the widespread neighborhood, but did not know all their names. Two of them had reputations as mean, tough kids.

Tony extended no welcome, no handshake. He glowered and the darkness and meager overhead lighting made his face look harshly distorted. He softly growled his first warning to Mickey in a low voice, then smoothed his voice. "It's easy *now* to say you want in wit' us—cuz you don't have no idea what it takes. You know what? You don' look like much to me. But I guess since Freddy brought ya here there's some things we maybe could use you for.

"But there's things you gotta do first—an' you know what I think? You look like you'd be scared shitless when the time comes. Fuck it up—jus' one o' the things—and that's all for you bein' a member. Got that?"

Tony walked from side to side past Mickey as he talked menacingly. Mickey was uncomfortable in the old straightback chair. It seemed it might collapse if he made any movements. He could feel a buttock pushing through the torn seat-caning.

A little above his head, a light dangled from the ceiling, forming a small illuminated area around the chair, the aura limited by the slope-sided metal shade. The light was from a small bulb, not throwing heat on him, even as close as it was. Now it was the only light in the large cellar room. With a hand wave, Tony had signaled other pull-cord lights to be turned off. A weak light at each side of the room disappeared. Legs and sneakers moved away, backing into darkness.

Stillness. Quiet.

From one side, Mickey heard Tony's voice, lowered in tone, menacing. "One thing we really don' like is somebody from some gang tryin' to get inta our club." The voice moved to behind him. Close. "We don't like fuckin' spies! Got that?"

Don' turn aroun'! He might sock ya! Just sit!

"The members of this club stick together," Tony snapped loudly, from behind, close to Mickey's ear. Then in the other ear, in a much softer voice: "We always have and we always will!"

The sharp voice shifted from one side of Mickey's head to the other, sometimes at a short distance, sometimes directly into an ear, sometimes loudly, harshly, other times softer. "Nobody better fuck wit' us. We don' go lookin' for trouble, but nobody's gonna fuck wit' any of our people—or they're fuckin' well gonna get it stuck up their ass! Got that part?"

Mickey's neck and shoulders were tight, tensed to ward off a blow. He turned his ear away from the now raspy voice, his mind whirling for an answer, for something to say to break off the snarling. He blurted, "I got it—but—I mean, you don' hafta worry about—"

"Shut the fuck up! If I wanna know somethin' I'll ask ya!

"Nobody's sayin' you're a friggin' spy. If you were you wouldn' be sittin' here— an' I wouldn' be talkin' to ya." Unintelligible, quietly spoken words sounded from spectators in the darkness. Tony said, "We know what we needa know—that *I* needa know! I just wanted to take a good look at ya myself—close up! So you jus' listen! Got that?"

Mickey thought of movies with hoodlums and gangster leaders grilled and shoved and punched by tough-talking police detectives, and got angry. But he did want to join with others of the neighborhood. He was tired of going it alone; it was not safe. He was tired of nothing to do, no one with whom to do things, no real adventures. He glared into the blackness, looking for the leader. *I ain't no friggin' gangster! You can' talk ta me like that!* He sat still, trying not to appear curious, now that his eyes were adjusted to the gloom, wondering about other boys positioned along the dark cellar's walls. He did not want the leader to think he was rattled by the harangue and by the forbidding eeriness of the setting.

Freddy had warned him. "Don' be nosy when we get where we're goin'! You ain't s'posed ta know who's gonna be there, so don't make it look like you're tryin' to find out."

For nearly a minute Mickey sat on the chair in the cone of weak light, waiting for the leader to growl again. *They must be his feet I hear movin' around.* Fidgeting mentally, Mickey tried to sit comfortably on the unstable chair. His back was beginning to hurt from slouching. He wondered why Freddy was so secretive about the club, about who was in it, what the members did as a club.

"Go 'head—get outta here," the leader said, somewhere behind him, at a distance. "We'll let ya know." Mickey rose slowly, stepping to one side to avoid bumping into the overhead light. Freddy materialized beside him, gripping Mickey's arm, turning him about, then nudging him into the shadows. Mickey could see the outline of a door frame and as he and Freddy reached it, the light behind him was turned off. Freddy gave him a slight shove and whispered, "G'wan, Mick—get on outta here. Jus' go straight a little ways an' up the stairs. Go back to your street, or go home—someplace—but don' hang aroun' outside o' this place. Hear me?" Mickey heard him move off, then he was alone in the darkness.

Two days went by before Mickey saw Freddy again. The first day Mickey played hooky from school. The second day he went to school with a note that he had laboriously typewritten on his father's secondhand portable machine, followed by carefully forging his father's signature with a fountain pen, tracing the signature by holding the note paper on top of a short letter his father had written but never mailed—and that Mickey had retrieved from a wastebasket—and holding both papers tightly against an apartment window through which sunlight streamed. As he had started tracing he congratulated himself. *I'm gettin' pretty good at this. It must be at least the tenth time already!*

But Freddy said nothing each time Mickey saw him near enough for words. He acted as though there had never been a cellar examination. Mickey was angry at the club, angry at Freddy for not being the friend he thought he should be—confiding whether Mickey had passed. *The hell with 'em! Who needs 'em?*

The next day, at lunch in the grade school cafeteria, Freddy told Mickey that his initiation would start that afternoon after school was over at three o'clock.

Freddy led Mickey through the same alley as three days earlier, but this time not trying to create a baffling maze, instead following a direct path to the same cellar room. The leader extended no welcome. He stood rigidly before the candidate, arms intertwined tightly across his chest, standing two inches or more taller than Mickey. When he spoke, he did not snarl or growl, but menace and challenge were in his tone.

"To be in this club ya gotta prove you're as good as anybody else in it, as tough as anybody else in it! So—what we're gonna do is play follow-the-leader. Freddy's your pal, so we're gonna let him go first. You're in the middle of the line when we start out.

"Alls ya do is what everybody in front of ya does. Got that?" Mickey was nervous, but said he was ready.

"Good. Jus' remember, each time a guy who's the leader does something, everybody else in line does the same thing. When everybody's done it an' we're ready for another test the guy who did it first goes to the back of the line and the next guy moves up to start it off again. It's easy! Got that?"

The band of boys dispersed in the shadows of the cellar pulled together in the center as the leader designated the line order. They started from the dingy storeroom, filing through a narrow interior corridor, up stairs into the backyard. Freddy led the quiet file to a six-foot-high wood-plank fence. He clambered up it and stood precariously on the horizontal two-by-four crossbrace a few inches below the fence top, his back to the group. He stepped up higher to balance atop the vertical fence boards, and in another second leaped ahead, to the opposite side of the barrier, falling out of sight. Tony Minelli quickly scrambled easily atop the fence, briefly mimicking Freddy's balancing pose before disappearing on the other side. Joey, someone Mickey had not seen before, was next, followed by Hunky, the Hungarian kid. Mickey only knew Hunky was from Pennsylvania and his father was a coal miner until he died because of something wrong with his lungs. In quick succession two boys Mickey did not know also scrambled easily onto the fence then leaped down on the other side, the last boy jumping upward first and twisting half about to face Mickey as he fell out of sight. He widened his eyes and grotesquely crossed them, stuck out his tongue, and rapidly waggled his hands as he disappeared.

Mickey had to struggle to reach the top of the fence. He had never been strong. He had quick reflexes and could run fast, but he did not have a lot of muscle power. He could move with extraordinary agility to dodge pursuers in a fast-paced round of tag in a schoolyard or out on the streets. He could run stickball bases faster than most other players, but he could not do a lot of pushups or chinups.

Get up!—Get up! Don' louse up the first thing tried! Cloth at his knee was snagged on a nail as he threw a leg up over the fence. He worked awkwardly, hands scraping the rough lumber, a foot finally blindly finding the horizontal two-by-four, fiercely struggling to keep balanced, first in a crouched position, weakly pushing himself erect, finally teetering atop the rough-sawed boards. He was stunned by what he saw on the other side of the fence.

There was a swath of cement closely paralleling the fence, a walkway. The four who had gone before stood in a semicircle at the far edge of the walk, looking up at him.

Tony poked a finger toward the walk several times, pointing out the target. "Not on the grass, kid. Got that?"

In the first moment on top of the fence, teetering, struggling for balance, staring at the cement that seemed far below, Mickey had almost instantly calculated how hard he would have to shove off from the fence to hurdle the walk, to land on the damp, spongy earth and scrubby grass. But Tony Minelli's pointing finger took away that option.

Mickey lost his balance and fell clumsily to the pavement. One foot, then the other, smashed angularly onto the cement. He struggled to let no involuntary sound escape him other than a low grunt. He started to keel over but got his balance despite shooting pains in both feet, both ankles. *Shit! I hope I didn' break nothin'!* His temper flared as he felt burning sensations. *These bastards didn' land on this cement!*

He tried to appear nonchalant as he moved without letting himself limp round an end of the semicircle of boys to take a place to watch the last three fence-jumpers do their turns, half-expecting small congratulations for his first success. But he was ignored. Tony Minelli yelled, "Okay, you guys over there—c'mon aroun' the end insteada over the top. We gotta hurry up an' get movin'. Got a lot to do."

Mickey stared at the back of the leader's head, getting angry again as he watched the three remaining boys come through a fence gate twenty feet to his left. He wanted to speak out—*Hey, wait a minute—ginzo!—ya said we all hadda do the same—an' now ya let those guys off without climbin' or jumpin'.*

The leader turned to face Mickey. "You ready, kid?" Without Mickey's answer, he said, "Let's go, you guys!" The file formed a second time, Tony Minelli leading, Freddy trailing.

The leader's task was easier for Mickey. It was not as physically demanding, but more nerve was needed. Tony Minelli led the file to a backyard fire escape and, while others watched, tugged down the ground floor pull-down ladder, scrambled up the two dozen rungs, then ran up a flight of metal stairs to the second-floor landing. He clambered agilely atop the narrow band of metal that capped the slender vertical rods of the fire escape structure. Nearly twenty feet in the air, he balanced himself on the cap railing, then walked along it. Moving slowly for ten feet, he kept his arms extended to his sides, countering losses of balance, delicately keeping his body and weight critically positioned. His fingers inscribed invisible patterns in the air. He looked to have the grace and skill of a ballet dancer, the smooth agility of a gymnast, as he glided the length of the inch-wide rail. At the far end he leaped lightly down to the slotted landing and leaned over the railing, waving the others up to the second floor.

Joey did not have the leader's easy grace, nor did Hunky. Mickey was even less graceful. He was quick and agile at ground level, but he had never been tested on anything as high as what he now faced. Standing hesitantly on the railing, nervously gripping a handy part of the skeletal structure, inborn acrophobia nearly overcame determination to pass the test with flying colors. His memory suddenly dredged up a past warning—*Don' look down! Look straight ahead! Don' even look up!* In that instant he could not connect the words to who had once said them or what he had been doing that brought on the stern advice. But he made himself look down anyway, frightened that a step might be misplaced. He looked only as far as the narrow rail he had to walk, intensely focusing on it. The treacherous path along the rust-scaled rail was not easily walked, but Mickey was successful, fighting off erratic sensations of lightheadedness. His stomach stopped its fitful churning after he jumped heavily onto the second floor landing, safely away from the yawning backyard.

Mickey's anger rose again when the five who followed him with their balancing-act walks only went two to three feet along the rail before jumping onto the landing. Tony Minelli did not berate any of them.

"Okay, Joey—your turn," Tony said. "Whatcha gonna make us do?" Joey waved a beckoning arm, going down the metal stairs to the ground floor landing. The others followed, forming about him as he leaned over the long outside railing, peering at the ground. In a quick movement, he grasped the top rail with both hands close together, then vaulted over the railing, dropping about eight feet to a patch of overturned soft earth. He fell vertically, arms held tightly against his sides. To Mickey, he seemed to land lightly, effortlessly. Joey quickly raised his arms above his shoulders, spread wide apart, like a circus performer who acknowledges audience applause, then stepped aside to make way for Hunky, who immediately followed over the rail. Mickey watched with widened eyes as Hunky repeated Joey's landing pose, though not so gracefully. Then, casting aside any thought of still-sore ankles and feet, Mickey vaulted the railing in the style of Joey and Hunky. He took the landing impact more on one foot than the other, feeling sharp pain in the left ankle, teetering forward, stretching arms wide, fingers of each hand spread wide, palms to the soil. He did not want them to touch the ground, dreading disqualification. He struggled for balance, picturing dirt smudges on his knees. *C'mon, c'mon!—Up!—UP!—not the knees!—not the knees!* He stood straight, reaching his arms upward, spreading them wide, smiling.

He moved out of the patch of soft soil to turn and stand with the others, looking at those still on the fire escape. *Okay so far. But it sure looks like these guys knew aheada time what they'd be doin'! Minelli made ME land purposely on the cement back there! But they ain't kiddin' me none. THEY jumped onto the dirt instead, I'll betcha—and the last ones didn' even jump at all!*

The three boys on the fire escape went over the rail in quick succession, without hesitation, and landed easily. They moved so surely and quickly that the last jumper nearly landed on the boy scrambling to get out of his way. Mickey envied the way they did the task so easily. *Pretty quick I'm gonna be a leader. What the hell can I do that these guys won' think is too easy?*

It was Hunky's turn to lead the way. Mickey and the six others followed in a closely spaced file, up the ground floor ladder of the same fire escape, then up four flights of metal steps to a short ladder mounted on the wall of the building, a ladder leading to the rooftop, and onto the tarred, gravel-covered surface. Hunky paraded the line of boys on a meandering route about the roof, over a low wall dividing the two buildings and to the next rooftop, through a maze of drying sheets, shirts, and underwear hanging on several long parallel clotheslines, crossing another low wall onto another roof, finally onto the roof of a corner building, then directly to the eighteen-inch-high, foot-wide cement-capped barrier that served as minor protection at the roof edge against some fifty feet of space to the backyard ground below. He twisted about to see that everyone was together, then turned back to face the edge again. For a moment he contemplated the chipped cement capping the low wall. Hands at his sides formed fists. Hunky slowly swung them back and forth several times, then bent his knees—Mickey thought he was about to do a deep knee bend—and sprang upward and outward, landing atop the cement. He jerked balled hands about, then the fists uncurled and the fingers stretched and flexed, and he settled into waving his hands, randomly up and down, backward and forward, balancing himself. Standing still and erect, head up, he seemed to be looking straight ahead. Seconds later, both feet together, he hopped backward, landing heavily on the graveled surface. Mickey thought Hunky's shoulders slumped. "Get goin', kid!" Hunky ordered, not turning round, his voice husky. Then he twisted to face the group. Mickey's anxiety worsened when he saw how pale Hunky's face was. "C'mon, you—let's go, kid! Move it!" he said, voice still hoarse.

Mickey imagined the yawning space past the roof edge, what things might look like if he looked down, what might happen to him there on that edge. He felt knots in his stomach, felt woozy. *Shit!—Oh, shit! Wha' do I do now?* Hunky took a step toward him, saying, "Can't—huh?"

Mickey wanted to look behind him to see if Tony Minelli agreed with the risky ledge hop. *He'll think Hunky's right—that I can't—that son of a bitch!* He stepped around Hunky, moving to within inches of the parapet. He took as deep a breath as he could without revealing he had. He did not want his shoulders to move or make the sound of ravenously gulping air. He balled his hands tightly, closing his eyes, praying, gently swinging his arms backward. *I'll do it on five!*

Arms forward—*One!*—and back; forward a little more this time—*Two!*, back and forth a bit quicker—*Three!* Mickey felt as if he was trembling hard enough to shake apart. *I wanna puke! Two more to go!* Arms back again. His fingers hurt, so tightly clenched. If he had not been a nail-biter, fingernails would be digging into his palms. *Four!* He opened his eyes, staring straight ahead, avoiding looking at the spot onto which he had to jump. Across two small back-to-back yards he saw the rear of the opposite tenement building. His eyes flicked left and right nervously. Rising above roofs, sprouting from the dividing lines of the backyards, the tops of skinny clothesline poles were a thin forest of dark, separate crisscrossed vertical rods, some tipping at awkward-looking angles, a jumbled pattern against growing evening dusk. He made a hard, extra-vigorous arm-pumping motion with each arm, in unison.

FIVE!

He bent, lowering his torso almost to his knees, tightening thigh muscles. He held his breath and pulled in stomach muscles, so much so his abdomen hurt. His eyes snapped down to focus precisely on the narrow width of cement that he had to jump up onto—and then not lose his balance. *Oh, God!*

Do it—you dumb asshole!

Fuck it!—GO!

He threw his arms forward against an invisible restraint, swinging them up with all the force he could muster, thrusting his torso upright. Strength surged through his thighs as he pushed his feet sharply against the roof. He moaned, desperately trying to keep any sound from being heard by his judges.

Arms flailed the air; eyes riveted their stare to the crumbly cement capping; upper body tilted forward perilously, then jerked backward, arms stretching behind, groping for safety.

Mickey's feet landed evenly on the capping, spread slightly apart. Pressure against the soles triggered a burst of air from his straining lungs. He grunted loudly.

Something caught his eyes in the void below his feet. Fully balanced on the narrow ledge, standing nearly erect, hands unclenching from aching fists into widely spread fingers, he stared down. *Fuckin' Hunky! These no-good bastards!*

A rusted top-floor fire escape landing, extending almost four feet away from the side of the building, with an area of several feet to either side of his perch, with a high railing on three sides of the landing, was just below, no more than four or five feet down. *You sonsabitches!*

He was standing on the narrow slab four feet safely above the fire escape landing. Below the level of his feet was a short ladder from below the roof edge to the slotted metal landing. The usual hand railing that curved up and over a parapet was missing from this short ladder between the landing and the roof. *These guys musta been real lucky to find this setup. Now they use it jus' to scare the shit outta new guys in the club!* He seethed with anger. His dread had been wasted—no terrifying fatal fall and terrible death. Ugliness flashed in his mind as he pictured thudding onto a cement walk with a sickening sound, his body bursting at several places, spraying and splashing blood everywhere, his skull smashed, every bone breaking, pieces of bone spewing about through ruptured skin. He had really only faced a harrowing tumble onto the fire escape structure. Thoughts of a terrible death sickened him momentarily, but he realized he was being watched closely. He thrust the agonies aside. *I'll show 'em!*

Mickey turned slowly, confident, smiling, looking down, his eyes sweeping the arc of boys watching him—hoping his great sense of relief did not show; happy that he had met their most difficult challenge. He hoped he had made it appear easy to Tony Minelli. But every nerve felt as if it was jumping and jangling about. He worried about how he looked to the leader. Blood pumped noisily through his head. There was pressure against eardrums. There was thumping, vibrating, reverberating and crackles, pings, and ringing in his skull. His stomach dilated and contracted; his heart pounded his ribs. He wanted to vomit, but he did not. He glanced at his fingertips, agonizing that tremors might disqualify him. But nothing gave him away. He stepped down casually onto the roof, moving to one side of the group, becoming an observer of the others who quickly and listlessly went through their turns. None provided the dramatic flair Hunky had shown for Mickey's benefit. Mickey now fully realized that each club incumbent, in turn, had contributed to the scheme of initiation terror.

Tony Minelli moved out of the semicircle, turning to stand with his back to the low parapet, moving to face Mickey. "It's your turn, little guy. Now you're the leader."

Mickey was annoyed that some of the others had not done each feat as he had been made to do, Tony Minelli excusing them. He looked up at the leader, steadily, trying to avoid showing anger. "Tha's okay with me. I just gotta figure out somethin' to do—that *everybody's* gonna do."

Tony frowned. He snarled, "Hey, kid—listen! I got your *everybody* RIGHT HERE!" He poked the air vigorously with his forefinger, pointing at his crotch. *"Right here!"* Mickey tensed.

"I decide things aroun' here! Got that?

"An' here's what I decided *for* you. You ain't gonna have to think up nothin' to do. I got my mind all made up!"

Mickey waited, uncertain, wondering. "The guys here thought up somethin'—and I okayed it." The leader's frown changed to a leering smile. It made him look evil. Tony Minelli looked at others behind Mickey, eyes slowly sweeping from one side to the other, then back to Mickey. Mickey was tempted to look at the faces behind him. Instead, he stubbornly returned Tony's challenging stare. *I wish I could see myself. I hope I look tough to him!* The leader's leer turned to a malevolent grin.

He brought his right hand up slowly, curling four fingers into the palm, thumb extended, using the thumb to point back over his shoulder. His grin widened, even white teeth contrasting brightly with his olive skin. His eyelids narrowed. He kept slowly moving his hand back and forth, thumb softly jabbing the air behind him. Mickey was mystified. *What am I s'posed to do?*

Tony turned his back to Mickey. The group was still close to the edge of the roof. Dusk was swarming over the city. The leader moved nearer the edge, pointing at something ahead of him. Mickey could not make out the leader's target. There was nothing in front of him but the building roofs two narrow backyards away and clothesline poles poking into the air several feet above the rooftops. Tony stepped to the parapet, putting a foot on the cement cap, standing dramatically still, in an erect theatrical pose, pointing. Only a few feet from Mickey, the leader's form was becoming a solid silhouette because of the dusk. *Dammit! I can't tell what he wants me to do!*

The only thing Mickey could make out at all nearby was the top of a badly split pole teetering toward his roof, five or six feet away. It was one of the thick, round poles—many of them more than fifty feet high, almost as high as the rooftops, some even higher—put in place in small backyards to serve as attachment points for clothesline hooks and large pulleys. The pole at which Mickey stared rose ten feet or so above the roof parapet and had greatly warped with age, after seasons of heat and cold, searing sunlight, steamy summer months, howling wintry winds that had driven sharp sleet into the split wood surface, to later melt and soak fibers inside, more deep inside each winter season. Occasional thick layers of ice over successive years had bent the upper section into a long warped shape, a pronounced long curve high on the pole, tipping the upper twenty or so feet.

Clothesline—two from many windows, hooks anchored deeply in brickwork at either side of a frame—stretched to the pole at every floor. Incessant tugging of hundreds of pounds of wet fabric and lines sagged and strained by waving, flapping, bed linen, shirts, underwear, stockings, dresses, and every imaginable other item for many years forced the drying, weakened wood to yield toward the building, tipping sharply near the rooftop.

Tony Minelli faced Mickey. "You better get to it quick. We'll be outta daylight pretty soon. Got that?' Mickey frowned, staring at the leader. "Get to what? I can't tell what you want me to do."

"It's easy—real easy." Minelli kept smiling.

"Alls you gotta do is jump onto the top of that pole there and climb down to the ground—then wait there for the rest of us." He said it simply, quickly, clapping his hands together sharply several times. "Let's go, you guys—get a move on! Get lined up behin' this guy." Mickey was stunned. He stood staring at the leader. Minelli still smiled. "Hey, kid—when we're all in the backyard, we'll finish up with the las' two things the other guys still behind you gotta do. Then we'll be all done. Okay?" He walked past Mickey, who had nothing now to look at but the spindly pole top.

Go fuck yourself—an' you guys, too! He wanted to spin about, yell at them, stalk angrily away, defy them, be superior, ignore the foolish assignment. He looked unbelievably at the pole tip. *How can he say that's ALL I gotta do? That thing is a million feet in the air!—an' way out from the roof! Is he shittin' me?*

He felt his shoulder nudged. Tony Minelli hissed in his ear. "Wastin' time, sonny! *My* time! An' ever'body else's time!" Mickey wanted to turn and scream them all out of sight. *Oh, God—what am I gonna do?*

For several seconds he was overwhelmed by the same terrifying thoughts that bedeviled him getting ready to leap onto the parapet moments earlier. In a snap judgment he decided that leaping into a darkening sky across what seemed to be a vast space at a difficult target perilously high in the air wasn't worth doing. *For what? Jus' to get in some dumb fuckin' club? Who needs 'em?* Now the thoughts were more suffocating, the vision worse: Missing the slender, distant pole; flailing through the upper darkness into lower blackness; hurtling at increasing speed; seeing things flash by, out of reach; futilely screaming away the certainty; arms stiffly pushing away the widening strip of walkway he knew would finish him. He felt the agonizing split-second of incredible total body pain of smashing impact on cement that would spray his blood on the pavement, grass, and dirt, that would break and pulverize bones inside him. He squeezed his eyes shut, suppressing a yell of rage and fear. He bit his lower lip, felt his face contort. He pushed back sobs.

Someone in the shadowy group called out. "Whatcha waitin' on?" Tony Minelli reached forward, poking Mickey lightly on a shoulder. Mickey's ears were ringing. Again he felt an urge to vomit. The leader moved closer. He used a shoulder to nudge Mickey's shoulder. "Whadda ya say, kid?"

Mickey surged with an explosive burst of anger and energy. He flailed his arms savagely, to throw off Tony Minelli's insistent nudging. He could hear the leader grunt as Mickey's elbow drove into his middle, slamming air from his lungs. *Take that!—fucker!*

Mickey charged blindly forward, enraged, bent on escaping his tormentors, determined to pass the terrible test. His legs churned across the short distance to the parapet. He felt as though his feet were trapped for step after step in the thin layer of sun-softened tar spread over the roof surface as waterproofing. He stumbled, regaining stride, one leg stretching eagerly forward as he leaped ahead, landing one-legged on the cement cap, kicking the other leg forward to keep up the running motion, lurching his whole body forward and up, feet wide apart, as far as they would go, arms spread-eagled. He never took his eyes from the silhouette of the slender pole tipped toward him, dimly separate from the dark sky.

He launched himself defiantly, wordlessly, spirits suddenly soaring; conscious of quick whooshing of air from his lungs, tightening his diaphragm, straining his stomach muscles.

His chest slammed into the pole, his cheek scraping across the coarse, split grain. One knee slammed along the pole, sending excruciating jolts up and down the full limb as both legs went to each side of the pole. Instinctively, both thin legs circled the rough wood, feet crossing at the ankles. He pulled tight and tighter with his arms, striving to clutch each opposite shoulder with a hand. He closed his eyes. He relaxed, letting out short whimpers of relief.

The others behind him were clapping, hooting, whistling, calling out praise. Mickey felt himself slipping down. The rotting top section of the pole was waving about from the force of his contact, sporadically straining against the line attachments to the building. He clutched the pole tighter, head sagging against it. He pulled his face back quickly when he felt burning sensations where his cheek grazed the coarse wood surface. In exhaustion and relief, taking a moment to gather his thoughts, he dropped his chin onto his encircling arm, grunting in anguish when his ragged tongue touched teeth. A side of the tongue had been crushed between clenching teeth as the side of his face slammed into the pole. Everything hurt; chest, tongue, arms, face, back, legs, *everything!* His head pulsated. With his eyes still closed, he could see himself making the awful leap. *You dumb bastard! You stupid—you shithead!*

Strength seeped into his muscles. Arm by arm, leg by leg, he loosened his clawing grips on himself and the pole. He looked over his shoulder, back across the space. It looked even wider than it had from the rooftop. The watchers blended into a single, large, lumpy dark form in the failing daylight. Suddenly Mickey remembered he was the leader, that he had to get out of the way of the others. He stretched a foot down, feeling for the top long, rusted metal spike, the first step down in the climb to safety. One spike after another, he worked his way down through the maze of hooks, pulleys, and lines spaced along the length of the high backyard mast.

He smiled with the feel of soft, yielding mixture of earth and grass cushioning his feet when he leaped down from his one-legged stance on the last spike. He glanced at the narrow strip of cement pavement. *Fuck you, sidewalk! You didn' get me! I beat you instead!*

Mickey looked expectantly up at the roof edge. Any second the next candidate in the follow-the-leader test would soar from the roof to the pole. Mickey, relieved, gratified, hoped the next boy and the others would be as afraid as he had been, and be as lucky. He dreaded the thought of seeing a dark form of someone who had unskillfully and unluckily missed the pole rushing down at him, dreaded hearing a terrified scream. As dark as it was getting, he was sure that the third jumper would be leaping soon after number two started to climbing down the spike steps. They would all have to hurry if the last two challenges by new leaders were to be done. *But after THIS thing, I got nothin' to worry 'bout. What could be tougher?* Mickey smiled broadly. *I'm gonna be a club member!—an' I'll be in the gang!*

His smile faded. Glowering up into the gloom, head tipped far back, spine arched sharply, he watched for number two to hurdle the space. He was distracted by movement at the edge of the roof, to the left of from where he had jumped. Something moved on the parapet, near the fire escape. Then he heard dull, clunking sounds. A figure moved down the roof ladder, followed by another silhouette, then another, another. He lost count when the figures moving over the edge blended into one mass. The dull sounds got louder, feet thumping and pounding down the steps and across landings. *Everybody up there's comin' down the goddam fire escape!*

You sonsabitches!

Astonished, Mickey was surrounded by dark figures, some patting him on the back and shoulders, saying how great he had done. Tony Minelli moved through the figures, close enough that Mickey could see his serious face. In a moment the leader smiled slightly. "You got balls, kid! Big balls!" Mickey wanted to punch him in the smiling mouth.

"Let me tell ya, kid. The others wanted to do the same thing—but—well, gettin' dark like it is—I figgered they couldn' see good enough—too dangerous—an' I gotta protect my people—now it's getting so late—unnerstand?"

You lyin' prick! Mickey's hands balled into tight fists.

"Yeah—sure—Tony—sure. I unnerstand." Mickey's throat was so tight as he answered that it pained. Tony Minelli's words angered him. With one quick flash of insight Mickey concluded that not one of them had intended to make the leap; that he had been led to the parapet with the expectation he would back away from it and from the challenge. Mickey wondered what made him surprisingly vault so recklessly from the roof. Then he sensed that if he had collapsed under psychological terror up there, he knew he would have faced two dreaded consequences—membership with constant reminder of failure or rejection or distorted details of cowardice spread luridly about the neighborhood.

He sensed more. Not only the rooftop test had been rigged against him. The follow-the-leader sequence flashed through his mind. He visualized that it all been carefully orchestrated beforehand; each event, each moment appearing spontaneous, for his benefit.

"But, kid,"—Tony Minelli's words seemed just so much jabbering to Mickey now—"ya sure did a helluva job up there." Mickey clenched his fists tighter.

"Ya done a lot to show ya deserve to be in the club. Havin' balls enough to do that jump was the convincer with me, I'll tell ya!" Mickey clenched and unclenched his fists several times. *I wish I had the balls to paste ya one! It's a good thing for you that I ain' bigger and stronger!*

Mickey began to feel pride in what he had done to prove himself—what none of those with him had dared. He looked for Tony Minelli's eyes in the deep shadowiness, glaring, trying to make out his face more clearly. *He's bigger'n me—an' stronger—but so what? Shit, he didn' make the friggin' jump! Neither did these other bastards!*

Tony Minelli patted Mickey's shoulder, turned, walked away. The others followed without a word to Mickey, walking across the small backyard to an alley leading to the street. They disappeared in darkness on entering the narrow opening.

33

I have to say—I guess anyone would have to say—that was one of my nine lives. Hell, if cats can have nine lives, why can't people? We need them just as much!

That damn pole jump!—and other things that kept happening—sure make me happy there were at least nine lives, in my case anyway.

34

The club, as Tony Minelli insisted it be called, was a gang, like other gangs in neighborhoods in every borough. Each came into being to meet the needs of youths to have strength, will, courage—greater than a boy alone could realize. Gangs flourished according to the leadership of the titular head.

A gang had territory, jealously guarded. A peer stranger was regarded as a trespasser, looked at suspiciously; treated roughly if suspected of being a marauder rather than a straying wanderer unaware of invisible boundaries.

Alone, a boy learned less of street life and survival than was needed. Alone, a boy was less inclined to defy authority—adult, police, or gang. A boy wandering alone was an outsider, often catcalled, pestered, intimidated. Moving about with a friend sometimes eased tribulation, but many times, in many locales, even a twosome was treated as an individual.

Gang characteristics varied. Some were passive, individuals grouped for common defense, struggling to maintain passivity, to simply enjoy collective privilege of being friends, hoping trouble could be avoided. Others roved near and far, satisfying urges for adventure and power, searching for gratification through daring, bravado, defiance, belligerence. Gangs changed from passive to aggressive to belligerent as the mixture of personalities shifted, as forces outside the gang influenced its existence. Boredom or revenge occasionally took gangs beyond their territories.

In a predominantly ethnic or racial quarter two or more gangs often coexisted, ruling limited areas. They quarreled with one another when territories bordered, and they squabbled among themselves in their own sections—Italians opposing Italians in Little Italy, Irish against Irish, Negroes versus Negroes in Harlem, Germans against Germans in Yorkville, Chinese vis-à-vis Chinese in Chinatown, Spanish confronting other Spanish-speaking in their various clusters. Many gangs had absolutely limited ethnic or racial membership, but occasionally gangs banded together temporarily, staunchly joining under brief treaties to repel aggressors daring to expand control. Outside of districts composed of a dominant nationality or race, gangs were mixed, ruling heterogeneous neighborhoods.

Harlem was the most fearsome territory. Its geographic area, the number of inhabitants, their often ferocious appearance and often odd costuming, its aura of mystery, all of these provided ample intimidation. Rampant rumors of fights, knifings, razor slashings, and savage mutilations reinforced outsiders' worries. Only gangs with sufficient motivation—blinding infuriation, sworn vengeance— dared impingement of Harlem.

A school week went by after Mickey's backyard initiation. He heard nothing from the club or Freddy. He thought that was peculiar. Always before, on a casual basis, he and Freddy had joked together in class and consorted outside of school. Now Freddy always seemed busy with books and papers in the classroom or too occupied with others after classes or in the schoolyard. When Mickey did talk with Freddy for only ten to fifteen seconds each time twice during the week he was told to take it easy, that he would hear soon enough. No club member was visible anywhere in the neighborhood during those long days either. Mickey felt shunned. He was sure his disdain for the initiators while they stood at the base of the clothesline pole was plain to them despite the near darkness.

Mickey went to school the first two days, played hooky the next day, went to school on Thursday. On the last day, just before lunch, he begged off the rest of the day at the school nurse's office, eyes reddened and face flushed by poking a finger down his throat outside her hallway door.

In the start-of-the-day home room period, Freddy had been Tony Minelli's messenger again, quietly and quickly telling Mickey to meet him after school, this time at the front stoop of a designated building number on a designated street. Mickey felt relieved, certain he had been accepted. He smiled after Freddy moved away to his own seat. *Why else another meetin' with the leader? If I flunked Freddy woulda jus' tol' me right here that I did. Hot dog! I made it!* He imagined himself wearing the green and red windbreaker jacket with large white felt block letters HR CLUB emblazoned on the back. *I'm gonna be a Hell Raiser!*

Mickey was punctual for the meeting with Freddy and Freddy was late again. Mickey began to believe that this, too, was part of the HR Club technique— making him fidget by having Freddy intentionally be late. He wondered if every new candidate had to go through the same routine. Looking along the street, to the west, toward the Hudson, Mickey could see the sky was darkening along the horizon. The sun was about thirty degrees above the rocky cliffs rising from the wide river.

Freddy led Mickey on a straightforward route to the familiar basement room, the setting of the first inquisition. The hanging light above the rickety chair was on. No other light illuminated the musty, foul-smelling area. Freddy disappeared after telling Mickey to sit in the chair.

The next several minutes alone in the chair under the yellowish light changed Mickey's mood from a state of eager curiosity to anxious restlessness. He could barely hear voices from the cellar perimeter, and the weak light did not shed light much more than an arm's length from Mickey. *Christ! Whatta lotta bullshit this is to hafta go through!* He was startled from his worry and reverie when Tony Minelli suddenly materialized, almost jumping from the shadows to stand in front of him. The leader beckoned, turning away sharply and moving to the basement door.

Mickey snapped to his feet and followed through a short, dark corridor, up a flight of stairs, through a hallway on the first floor, out the front door, down a dozen stone steps to the sidewalk. No one else from the basement followed them.

Without looking back, Tony Minelli strode off to the right. Mickey hurried, keeping pace, to the side and a quarter-step behind. They quickly traversed the long east-west block of look-alike brownstone and brick tenement building fronts on both sides of the street. Crossing the wide avenue, the leader kept a quick pace, Mickey working harder to keep close throughout the next long block. At the next busy avenue, Tony Minelli stepped into a corner doorway of a boarded-front store, motioning Mickey in beside him. Mickey was befuddled with all these goings-on, annoyed with what he thought were now pure shenanigans. *Fer cryin' out loud! More bullshit!*

The leader pointed across the broad thoroughfare as a northbound subway express train clattered, whooshed, and roared overhead along the elevated open-air track. Ahead, to where Tony pointed, Mickey could see the remainder of the long street extending east toward the park. On the other side of the avenue, small groups of Negro men and youths congregated, standing about, clustered along the curb, sitting on stoops, standing in doorways, circling light poles that had been turned on by a master switch somewhere in the city as Tony and Mickey entered their doorway observation post. It was a few minutes after sunset and street lighting appeared all over the boroughs to ward off street darkness.

A dozen train cars hurtled along the El track. Before the last crashing sounds faded, Tony was explaining that Mickey had only one last thing left to do to be in the HR Club. Mickey listened intently, looking at the leader incredulously. He spoke angrily. "You *really* mean I *gotta* do more? After all I already wen' through? Hey, wait a minute—there shouldn' be nothin' left fer me to do!"

Tony smiled slightly. "Ya got it wrong again, kid. *I* decide—not you."

Mickey hesitated, thinking he should simply walk away. The leader's voice was low. "Hey, it's up to you, kid. Do it or don' do it. I don' care. *We* don' care. There's plenty o' others who wanna be in with us. We can take ya or leave ya. So now *you* take it or leave it!"

Mickey leaned out the doorway, looking left and right, along his side of the street, examining the sidewalk as far as he could see, not knowing what to look for that could be another test. He studied the other side of the avenue, through the shadows cast by the elevated train structure, searching far left and right along that sidewalk. *What the hell can this bastard wan' me ta do?* Mickey was apprehensive; an even greater impulse to walk away building within him.

Why does this guy always pick this time o' day for this kinda crap? Won'er if there's others from the club hidden somewhere ready to do somethin' to me—jus' to scare the shit outta me some more? What the hell's goin' on with these guys?

Tony was speaking again. Mickey turned to look at him. The leader was pointing across the street. "There's all ya gotta do." Mickey looked where he was pointing. "Walk from here to the stone wall at the park—an' that's it. But make sure ya *walk!*—that ya don' run it! We'll be watchin' from both ends."

Is he shittin' me? From here to the park? This time o' day? It'll be dark quick. I'll get killed goin' through there! A white kid? Now? So late?

"Take it or leave it, buster!" Tony prodded.

I won' make it halfway through that fuckin' block! Jesus, I jus' missed killin' myself las' week! Am I s'posed to be lucky twice in a row?

"We'll have somebody at the other end to watch ya go over the wall. After ya do you'll be on your own. Jus' go on home from there. We'll get in touch with ya later."

Mickey did not trust him. *They won' have nobody at the other end!*

"Runnin' outta daylight, kid! Ya easy got enough time left fer a nice walk fer yaself, but ya shouldn' be fartin' aroun' here right now makin' up yer mind." Mickey's stomach tightened. He felt like vomiting, like going away, back to his rooms, just to go do something simple like read comic books, even do homework.

"I figger you oughta make the walk in five or six minutes. Remember—walk! No runnin'! It ain't that far ta go. You'll have plenty o' time to get back home quick."

Mickey tightened his shoulders. *I've gone this goddam far. Fuck it! I can run fast if I don' like it in there.* He started slowly from the doorway, cutting diagonally across the intersection to the far sidewalk corner. He could see from the doorway that there were no colored people there. He looked back along the long blocks from where he and Tony Minelli had started. Darkness was pressing down the low band of daylight on the horizon showing between distant buildings. *I can't do this! I shouldn' do this!*

Looking back, he could not see Tony Minelli in the doorway. He had stepped deeper into its shadows or had gone. Mickey could not be sure which. He turned his back to the sliver of sunlight to the west, glared toward the far park wall he could not see, took a large breath, and stepped off. He tipped his head down, looking at the sidewalk, keeping eyes focused fifteen or so feet ahead, shutting out everything else from his attention.

Heads turned as he walked east. On his side of the street men lounged on building steps, drinking beer in glasses or cups, poured from small tin pails filled at a nearby tavern; some drank from the pails. Mickey's plan was to distract himself from what was at hand. He thought only about the stone wall ahead. He would look at the ground, not stare at anyone, not look into eyes like those he had seen in the subway car not too long ago, not let himself see dark faces. He would be casual, not nervous. *Nobody'll bother me. I ain't doin' nothin'!* The thought of an ostrich protecting itself with its head buried in sand did not occur to him.

On the opposite sidewalk, thirty seconds into the long distance he had to cover, a small knot of colored youths, of several hues, about Mickey's age, watched his progress into their territory. Mickey sensed their attention, shrugging it off as the group receded behind the limit of peripheral vision to his left. Mickey raised his head, forcing his vision straight ahead, staring at where the wall would appear.

He lengthened his stride and hurried his pace, drifting closer to the curb, glancing minimally left and right without moving his head, plotting a course around individuals and groups standing about.

Stickball players in the street's deep shadows slowed play as Mickey approached. Other kids, across the street and ahead, looked sternly at him. Bigger kids on his path glowered as he passed closely. Intrepidly, he strode toward the park. Gray daylight turned a deeper color. His head ached across the brow. His heart thumped vigorously, the pulse pounding in his ears. He approached the quarter-mark to his goal. He heard indecipherable low yells from across the street and decided, with hope, that they were not meant for him, each just a call from one kid over there to some other neighbor kid over on this side of the street. Words were muttered in the small groups of boys as Mickey went by. Men said nothing, only the youths. Mickey's eyes flicked left and right, up to the lower-level windows. Dark faces watched his progress.

A bottle crashed on the sidewalk twenty feet ahead, splintering apart explosively. Shards of glass flew in every direction. Beer foamed on the cement, splayed about in a splashed pattern, looking like an amoebae seen under a microscope.

Jerking nervously at the flat, sharp blast of the breaking bottle, Mickey encouraged himself with unspoken words. Resolutely, he kept his pace. He wanted to turn, to see if he was followed, certain he heard walking sounds, some seeming more like shuffling. But he thought that might show fear. He glanced across the street again. A heavyset boy walked step-for-step with Mickey, as though mocking him. In a second floor window above that boy, a dark hulking form waved a fist in the air. Behind the heavyset boy others moved to join him, two or three keeping step, as though in a dancer's chorus line, others ambling in a loose-jointed, arm-swinging, jerky, uncoordinated-looking gait. As he neared the halfway mark, Mickey saw two cars parked on his side of the street, one behind the other, still some distance away. He worried that someone might be lurking behind the cars, or between them, out of sight.

The younger men of those sitting on building steps with friends, drinking beer, some swigging liquor from small bottles wrapped in brown paper bags, moved down the steps, standing close to the sidewalk curb, sullenly eyeing the skinny blond white boy.

Something from behind struck Mickey heavily on the left shoulder, ricocheting ahead, past his cheek, arching upward, curving slowly downward, thudding dully onto the sidewalk. A small head of lettuce, leaves fluttering loose as the coarse cement tore at it, rolling to a slow stop ahead. An empty milk bottle—he saw it in a glance, inches above the asphalt road surface, just before it hit—smashed in as many pieces as the beer bottle moments before. A battered, small metal child's toy dropped from an upper window clattered and rolled noisily on the sidewalk several feet ahead, balancing momentarily on the sidewalk edge, clanking onto a sewer grate, rolling into the curb opening and dropping to be swept away in an underground flood of moving waste.

"Whatcha doin' here, whitey?" Mickey could not tell from where the voice came, not even whether it was from behind or ahead, or to either side. He glanced at a tall, lean figure sitting on stone steps ahead and saw him pull with a hand at something in his other hand, then extend a fist in the air toward Mickey, but seeming to pay no mind to the boy. The fist rolled and twisted, down and around, up, back and forth, inscribing invisible lines in the dusk. Now closer, Mickey could see a long, thin knife blade swishing in the air. The knife-wielder seemingly ignored Mickey. He was carving the evening air into thick chunks, thin slices, swirls and convoluted shapes, poking lightly, shaping, jabbing harshly, sculpting an invisible form into a different form.

Another low voice sounded, different than the other. "Hey, muhfuggah!

"Hey, you—muhfuggah!"

Mickey crowded the curb so closely that he stumbled into the street. He hopped back onto the sidewalk, walking along the edge of the curbing, eyes down again, moving quickly. He crossed the first two fingers of his left hand, then added to his wish for good luck by crossing the other two. A small, flat fruit crate landed on one of its corners to his left, in the street, cracking apart, splinters of wood breaking off. Mickey's heart pounded faster. He took longer, faster steps. Across the street, the heavyset boy's group still kept pace. Mickey's breathing turned to panting. He saw a torn-sneaker-covered foot poke between his legs from behind. The foot twisted, catching Mickey's shin. He hurtled forward, stretching his arms to break the fall, tipping to one side, landing on his left elbow. He rolled clumsily off the sidewalk into the gutter. Sharp, crooked blocks of cobblestone—asphalt paving cover had long since worn away along most of the entire street—dug into his spine as he thudded onto his back, still rolling, bumping onto his right shoulder. His head rocked back, first striking the curbing, then an exposed cobblestone. He yelled with the sudden sharp pain. The funny bone in his right elbow struck stone, sending excruciating, numbing pangs the length of his forearm into the fingers. Panic-stricken, he scrambled to his feet, frightened, disoriented. *Which way's the goddam park?* A bottle hit the back of his leg; a hard object struck the nape of his neck.

He started a slow run toward the park, splashing through water puddles in the street, slipping and sliding on bits of garbage and trash. Running so near the curb, he stumbled into it several times and moved more to the center of the roadway, away from forbidding figures forming barriers on the sidewalk. To his left, across the street, the ominous group still kept pace, two boys moving onto the asphalt and cobblestones, moving around parked cars on their side of the street as they trotted. In the fast-settling darkness, Mickey could see glimpses of the low wall of the park ahead of him, sight of it appearing in gaps in speeding two-way traffic along the wide avenue, Central Park West.

He gulped air ravenously, increasing running quickness, pumping arms and legs frantically. With a burst of speed, he out-distanced the heavyset boy's pack. Things hurled from windows and stoops on each side of the street landed all about him, some glancing off head and body and limbs. But fear numbed the impacts.

Pounding in his ears muffled hoots and hollers in the air. Bombardment stimulated successive bursts of energy and speed. Anxiety and agility helped him leave adversaries behind.

Mickey stayed running along the road edge. Ahead, on his side of the sidewalk, boys, youths, and young men drifted from stoops onto the walk, standing alone or joining others, forming pairs, enlarging groups—a scattered pattern of barriers. Nearing the two parked cars on his right as he ran in the street, he felt he might be safer being close to them, forgetting that moments earlier he worried about lurkers behind them. Now he saw them as two helpful obstructions keeping anyone from getting to him. He glanced over his left shoulder, checking the distance to the heavyset boy's pack across the street. The leader had fallen behind, his follower charging ahead, but Mickey was still safely in the lead. Looking ahead toward the wall, a dark figure flashed from behind the rear of the second car, then jerked back out of sight, as Mickey rushed pell-mell past the first car. The figure had thrown a broken, spindly framed wooden chair into the path of Mickey's headlong run. It bounced and rolled, but Mickey had time to lift his legs sharply up, springing high to dodge the splintering piece of furniture.

Mickey thudded heavily onto the pavement from his high-bounding leap, feeling a sharp pain in his left ankle. He stumbled in his ungainly landing, regaining balance, charging ahead even harder for the park wall. Over the wall he would be safe in the bushes and trees.

He burst from the street recklessly, barely looking to either side for oncoming cars, running full ahead in the form of a racer crossing a finish line—straining, arms stretched high, head back, chest arched, reaching for an unseen tape, feeling the success of having finished a magnificent race, exhilarating in the victory. *I made it!*

Without breaking stride, he darted across the north-south avenue. Car horns blared as he ran between opposing double lines of moving traffic, making quick decisions about which car was going to make what move, bent on touching his target, that low thick wall of hewn stone blocks, bent on reaching the safety of the park.

He gasped for air as he stood at the wall for three or four seconds, oblivious to whether he was still pursued. He joyously slapped the top of the wall with palms of both hands, doing it several times with exaggerated motions for the benefit of watchers Tony Minelli said he had assigned to verify the completed challenge.

Suddenly he remembered the heavyset boy. He turned around, anxious. A dark figure stood at the corner on the other side of the traffic, speaking to the knot of boys with him, pointing at Mickey, arm fully extended, fingers poking the air. Three slender boys moved out of the group, starting toward the wall, slowly weaving through heavier traffic in both directions. Mickey vaulted over the stone wall, dropping lightly onto the grass, wincing at the slight pain in his left ankle, mustering strength and speed for another run, worried that the hurt ankle would slow him too much.

Desperation, long legs, and second wind combined to surpass the efforts of his pursuers. Mickey's panic diminished slightly with each backward glance showing he was easily keeping a safe distance ahead. He slowed his sprinting to maintain the distance and to conserve energy, but carefully watched behind, worried that one of the chasers might have his own explosion of energy and close the gap, maybe even catch him. He ran through bushes and thinly wooded sections, trying to befuddle the hastily following runners; crossing expanses of cropped grass field and knolls; crossing a network of paved walks. The pursuers were relentless, but Mickey had greater determination.

At the eastern boundary wall of Central Park, higher than the first wall on the west side, he leaped up for the top of the barrier, clawing fingers scraping the rough stone, throwing a leg over the top. Rolling over the wall, he could see two colored kids closing in on him. Mickey darted through two-way traffic toward the cover of buildings, again confusing and alarming unsuspecting drivers, dashed between two parked cars, and made a fast right turn to head south toward the corner, planning to turn into a cross street and disappear among people walking there or into a doorway somewhere. He grinned, excited and relieved, at what he was afraid might only be an apparition, but the sight was real. At the nearby corner, a blue-coated, helmeted police officer, white face standing out in the dusk, sat astride a big dark-hued horse, facing north, had just quickly turned his attention to learning what was causing blaring horns and squealing brakes and had seen a small figure reach the sidewalk and start loping toward him. At the sight of the police officer, Mickey slowed to walking. The horseman glowered down at Mickey as he sauntered past the horse. The officer wagged a cautioning finger when Mickey turned round at a building corner to appraise his situation, then shifted on his horse to watch traffic.

Mickey squatted until he could peer beneath the horse's belly and see the park wall. Two silhouettes rose rapidly above the parapet and leaped to the sidewalk. Mickey could not see faces, and he felt smug, knowing he was well concealed beyond moving cars and the mounted policeman on the large horse, and in near darkness. The silhouettes lingered, walking a few paces north and south a couple times, searching the maze of traffic and headlight beams stabbing the dusk. Mickey, staying close to buildings, quickly walked south along Central Park East instead of turning the corner and seeking a hiding place. He had to figure out a route home. He discarded the notion of going back through the park; he had heard too many tales and read too many newspaper stories about its dangers at night.

In minutes he found an entrance to a local-stop subway station, a type with no attendant required, with no waiting passengers that he could see. Scraping along on his back, he wriggled through the low space at the bottom of a high vertical framework of intermeshing fixed and revolving horizontal bars designed to keep anyone from passing through until a coin or token dropped in a slot released the locking mechanism.

Mickey traveled a long way south to a station where he could take a free crosstown shuttle west, then boarded a northbound express that took him three local-stop stations beyond where he had infiltrated the subway system. He walked south to home, striding rapidly, staying in the brightness of storefronts and street lights, pleased that many people were out on the avenue. He could have a safe trip home, concealed in the movement of others.

It was nighttime when he finished the subway odyssey that had taken about forty-five minutes. He was worried about what mollifying explanation he could give about getting home later than he should, past supper time. But his father had left a note saying he was visiting someone, and there was no word about his sister's absence.

Eating a cold sandwich, listening to a radio serial, Mickey mulled over what had happened, what might happen the next day; certain that he would be a Hell Raiser—*especially now!* Remembering skepticism after other tests, he wondered how many other club members had made the same initiation journey through that long street. He tried to picture Freddy doing the same thing—*or even Hunky—or one of the others I don' know the name of.*

He wondered if anyone from the club had seen his defiant, victorious slaps on the west park wall.

35

*F*unny how those guys planned all those screwy things for me to do—just to get into their damn gang—and not doing any of the really tough things themselves. I'd still bet nobody else in that bunch ever had to walk through that colored section—ANY time of the day, let alone right before dark! Not even Tony Minelli! What kind of leader was he?

And Minelli always calling it a club—making everybody else say club instead of gang.

36

Mickey got his onetime eager wish. He became a Hell Raiser, though a reluctant, disillusioned new member of the club—the gang—a near unwilling inductee because he did not know how to reject the membership. He could not think of a good reason not to agree the second time Freddy, still the emissary, told him to appear before Tony Minelli to take the club oath. During one night's sleep after not hearing anything from Freddy or anyone else for almost a week after getting to the park, Mickey was surprised to find himself awake, realizing that his mind was racing with thoughts about ways to stay out of Tony Minelli's group of boys. He tried pushing the ideas out of his mind so he could get back to sleep. *What am I thinkin' 'bout things like this for? I wanna be in the gang. I wen' through too much crap not to. I deserve it!*

The first time Mickey had been told to be at the cellar—to arrive on his own at a certain time—instead of feeling excitement and anticipation, he fabricated a dentist's appointment: "Freddy, I can' help it! I can' get out of it or my old man will tan my hide. I mean it! My butt'll be sore fer a week! He tol' me three times awreddy that he had saved money for too long so he could get my teeth worked on! *Shit,* Freddy—I don' wanna go to no goddam dentist. Ya oughta know that!"

He kept the cellar appointment the second time he was told to appear, worried more about retaliation for spurning the new order than about not being in the HR Club. Freddy had told him, "Boy, was Minelli pissed! Ya shoulda seen his face! Ya better make it next time, I'm tellin' ya—or I dunno what!" Mickey now detested Tony Minelli and disliked most of the others. His anger did not diminish over several days. He fumed each time he remembered the backyard events, the frightening traverse to the park wall and beyond.

Nonetheless, when Tony Minelli handed him a large paper bag and Mickey pulled out the red and green, waist-length, long-sleeved windbreaker jacket, he felt better. He relaxed. He held the jacket up, dangling from his fingers, turning it several times, looking at both sides. Large, white felt block letters proclaimed HR CLUB. Mickey's name was in small white letters on the left breast panel. *Now* it was worth the seven dollars and sixty-five cents he had had to scrape together on short notice and give to Freddy a week earlier. More fuel had been added to the fire of his anger when Freddy had walked by his classroom desk and put a note on his desk, without saying a word. Mickey got more annoyed each school day when

Freddy continually ignored him. He had heard nothing from the gang after the last initiation escapade until Freddy gave him the scrawled note:

Give me $7.65 as quick as you can.
I got to have it in two days.
Don't ask me why. Tell you later.

The added measure of mysteriousness in things having to do with the gang annoyed Mickey once more. For two days he sold things to kids at school for dimes and quarters and after school he prowled a wide area of the neighborhood for deposit bottles, adding those proceeds to four crumpled dollar bills he had cached at home in a Richard Halliburton book about adventures in foreign lands. *Yep—it's sure worth it!*

"But, kid," Tony Minelli cautioned, "We don' wear these aroun' the neighborhood here—jus' when we go off somewhere else—maybe two or three of us at a time—maybe more. But we don' want no people in the neighborhood thinkin' we got some kinda *gang* aroun' here. If we did, then every time somethin' happened then we'd be the ones catchin' hell—from them— an' from cops."

Mickey acquiesced to calling the Hell Raisers a club instead of a gang, but he considered it just more fakery. The word *gang*, to Mickey, sounded more powerful, more cohesive, more right. There were no written rules. He had vaguely expected something like the mimeographed pages he had seen for Aunt Ellen's weekly book club, or in the booklet for his father's Moose Lodge. The HR Club had no bylaws, no officers, no avowed purpose, no regular meetings, no quorum requirement, no membership roster. Word of mouth, sometimes spread quickly, brought members together if Tony Minelli had special reasons.

In a short time Mickey's fury subsided. Passing the demanding initiation tests became a source of pride. His leap across space to a thin, trembling pole brought him congratulations from HR Club members who had not been there, saying they wished they could have been so they could have seen it. *Sure ya do! But I'll bet none o' ya woulda done it! Jus' like none o' the ones who were there didn' do it!* At least membership let him pass time at street corners that were casual meeting places— hangouts—in HR Club territory.

The Hell Raisers rarely lived up to the bravura name. Members often taunted one another with jeers and noisiness throughout the neighborhood, usually in poorly organized stickball games, or in slapdash horseplay, generally merely being nuisances. Occasionally there was testing of the gang's pecking order, usually with nothing changing. When restlessness got more or less unbearable, they traveled subway routes, exploring, avoiding troublesome engagements if opposition seemed stronger, if they might be humiliated.

Hooky-players gravitated to first one neighborhood meeting place, then another, perhaps another, until a small nucleus might form. After-school formations happened the same way. Late-morning Saturday gatherings formed more slowly, after sleepyheads were finally roused by annoyed parents.

As members in groups ranged farther beyond their territory—restless or bored or feeling brave—they occasionally vocally sparred with smaller bands. But they were always careful. Even sullen, challenging loners or pairs might be sentries posted as enticements, to pull roamers into an ambush. As a rule, the farther from home, the more careful HR Club members were. But sometimes, if instinct or opposing numbers let them believe they had strength, their aggressiveness mounted. If Tony Minelli led an excursion, rambunctiousness often became belligerence. But there were more pleasant times than troubles.

Riverside Park was a long, narrow open space between the wide river and tall buildings backed by taller buildings; a thin swath of greenery extending from the middle of the island north, almost to the towering George Washington suspension bridge crossing westward to the neighboring state. The park was a roaming ground, touching different classes of neighborhood. It was an amphitheater for planned or spontaneous contests with peers—for scrub football and pick-up baseball, for far-ranging games of tag; for challenging, but sporting, follow-the-leader tests; for rough, but usually not mean-spirited, episodes of king-of-the-mountain at a big, smooth rock, high and burnished enough to make defense easy and assault difficult. "Riverside's for fun," a club member told him.

The quiet, slow-moving river was another arena when there were calm times and peaceful moods, when they moved and played easily. Members congregated among the large boulders strewn densely along the river's earthen bank, huge, craggy stones put down to prevent erosion. They dove into the murky water from the highest rock found. They chased one another among the rough boulders. They playfully shoved emerging companions back into the water. They dared the wide river and downstream current, heading for the distant opposite shore, trying to outdistance those claiming to be the *best* swimmers. No member ever drowned, but more than one was well scared, some mightily, though never admitting to it. They wandered to where long wood piers jutted far from the shoreline. Throughout a day, particularly at high tide, men and women, mostly elderly, mostly from the old country, fished for eels with droplines from the sides and the end of a pier. The boys liked the piers because a headlong run could be made, building speed to make a high leap, waving arms wildly, kicking legs crazily, scribing an arc in the air, plummeting, yelling and screaming, plunging into dark water dotted with oily smears. If a jumper streamlined for a smooth, effortless, painless entry into the water, members booed and catcalled, insulting the diver for lack of daring. A favorite running assault on the river surface was the cannonball—curling into a ball, as large as possible, pulling into the round shape at the peak of the launch, knees pulled up, loosely encircled by arms, head pressed to knees, plunging into the water—WHUMP! A skillful leaper could send up a large circular spray, or by slamming into the water at an angle, a fancier, fan-shaped, curving water form. Loud cheers honored the noisiest cannonballs, or sprays that were the best-looking, or the highest, or the widest. Half-hearted efforts were soundly booed.

Eel fishers grumbled and yelled at the antics, but HR Club members defied them with taunts and jeers and profanities, darting away from slow-moving, awkward pursuers who threatened to kick their little asses.

Sturdy pilings—thick, round, driven deeply into the river silt—along pier sides and at corners, provided height for true dives, for better, more admirable movements with semblance of athletic skill. Some pilings were high enough for a jackknife, a half-twist, a forward somersault.

Swimming in the river meant a bath or shower had to be taken to wash away the grime and oily film of an industrial waterway rife with river craft and ocean-going ships, a river carrying sewage seaward. A lesson quickly learned was to swim with a closed mouth to avoid bits of feces. Sometimes they would swim with a short length of stick or tree limb in a hand, striving to be the first to snag a "white eel" to hold aloft triumphantly, with a victory yell and howling laughter, claiming whatever had been bet beforehand. *White eel*—a discarded condom floating on the river surface, undulating in the current as it drifted to the harbor and the sea.

Painted horses rattling along up-and-down wavy metal tracks of a convoluted steeplechase in a huge Luna Park building at sprawling Coney Island in Brooklyn gave them another outlet for rambunctiousness; to be the cowboys they read of and saw in movies. Then they would saunter through the grounds, sporting their colorful jackets, eyeing girls, eyeing other youths wearing their own jackets.

Or they would desecrate the Riverside Park tomb of the Civil War general Ulysses S. Grant and his wife by scrambling over whatever was accessible on the outside of the structure, not out of maliciousness, only in search of challenge. Farther south was a more satisfying challenge—greater heights could be reached, a greater distance could be seen. There they could more easily scale the lower part of the towering white stone monument dedicated to soldiers and sailors, able to get as high as the base of the great, high round columns ringing the memorial.

Across the river, the high, crumbling faces of cliffs were assaulted many times at many places north and south of the massive George Washington bridge. The bridge itself was always worth something, at least for walking and running along when boredom left time to be filled. One afternoon, alone, Mickey walked slowly across to New Jersey and back to Manhattan because he felt like he wanted to see the magnificent view without anyone else being with him. On his long, idling walk back to his neighborhood, with words like *neat* and *swell* and *great* slipping in and out of his mind as he thought about the round trip bridge stroll, he promised himself he would walk back and forth across the bridge again sometime.

In the high, musty halls of the Museum of Natural History, the gang members were subdued, behaving well, intimidated by the environment. They were awed by towering skeletons of prehistoric creatures; astonished at the enormousness of a reconstructed whale suspended from a cavernous room's ceiling by frail-looking wires, joking grossly about what they would look like if the huge replica crashed down on them. After Mickey's first visit to the museum, he made other solitary trips, curious about dioramas and reconstructions and displays others in the HR Club had rushed past. He roamed quiet, shadowed halls and spacious rooms, restudying life-size Eskimo and American Indian displays; staring at models of the half-naked ancient men, women, and children, dressed in animal skins, living in wilderness settings, carrying on family life. He peered closely at relics of past centuries, cultures, races, and nations. He was amazed at exquisite taxidermy that preserved native and exotic animals. In the great buildings, he immersed himself in the result of efforts and skills of people dedicated to preserving history for understanding and appreciation. He did not profoundly comprehend his feelings and satisfaction, but enjoyment each visit was sufficient to guide him back.

Being a Hell Raiser, for Mickey, was a better way for learning to deal with day-to-day street life. Personal risk was less; and he had others from whom to draw knowledge and experiences, for learning people's ways. Members provided strength, courage—real and foolish, companionship, friendship, care. But continuing became more difficult for Mickey. It seemed that tension at gatherings was increasing. There were more quiet talks between Tony Minelli and individuals and small groups than there used to be. The leader's rule became more belligerent. There were fewer jaunts purely in search of dispelling boredom. Physically weaker and less aggressive members were intimidated more often. It became bullying. Conflict between aggressive members became more noticeable—and more worrisome to Mickey and others. In the cellar meeting place there was almost a fight between Hunky and a member Mickey did not know well, somebody new to the gang. He had only seen him twice recently and did not remember his name— *Iggy, Ziggy, Nicky, something like that.* Mickey had wondered about *his* initiation— *Why wasn' I part of making a new member?* Tony quickly jumped between their pushing and shoving and shushed their angry yells. Mickey had just come into the room and could not hear their words. A few minutes later he heard a whispered rumor there was going to be *real* trouble—and one of these days soon, too! But no one would say what *real* trouble was.

37

The room stirred again when a different voice than earlier boomed, "Next group—K—L—M—just those three. Pick up your stuff from in here and form in this other room, through this door. Snap to it."

Oh boy, they haven't got to me yet, darn it! Wish things would speed up. I'm getting tired just sitting here. I have to get up and stretch or my back will never get straight again.

Voices grumbled. Chairs scraped. Feet shuffled.

There's a better looking chair. At least it's got a cushion on it!

Sound level in the room lowered. Dozers returned to catnapping.

It's sure been a long time since I've thought so much about things I've been through. I guess I can say I've been really lucky—and mean it!

38

Mickey took part in two minor forays out of the neighborhood. Each time it was one of Tony Minelli's lieutenants who gave Mickey his assignment, but after each event it was the leader who said he did a good job, making Mickey curious. He did not know what he had done that was so good.

His task each time kept him on the fringe of the activity for which the HR Club—jackets worn—roamed from its territory. Finally getting to wear a gang jacket going afield pleased and excited Mickey. But each time he was frustrated and disappointed by orders to remove the reversible jacket and turn it inside so the black side showed and the red and green colors and white lettering would not be visible while he was posted as a lookout.

Once posted at a major street intersection, the second time assigned to a first-floor doorway at the top of a dozen stone steps, he twice angrily felt relegated to unimportance as grim gang members left him. "Watch out fer guys lookin' suspicious!—'specially maybe wearin' gang jackets—or jus' serious-*lookin'* bunches o' guys—even only two or three stickin' together—headin' to where we're headin'."

All the time the others were gone, Mickey intensely scanned as far as he could see, worried that he might miss something important; dreading that his failure would mean failure for whatever it was that gang members had set out to do. At each station, lonesome in a few minutes, grousing about his assignment, he ultimately persuaded himself that he would do the same thing with any newest gang member if he were the leader. It was a smart thing to do until more was learned about the guy. *Someday soon I'll be goin' on ahead—like those guys now out there somewhere—an' another new guy will be doin' this kinda stuff—bein' at the bottom o' the totem pole.* Mickey had recently heard the totem pole expression used by someone on a radio show and wondered what it meant. Now he was learning.

The raiders took only about a quarter hour for each sortie, returning unscathed, laughing, signaling Mickey to fall in with them as they left an area. Trailing, he listened to disjointed chatter about the exploit, unable to determine exactly what had taken place wherever it was the others had been. He thought it was smart not to be too inquisitive. The leader or the others might be annoyed if he started prying. He came to suspect that whatever they had done was generously embellished, for their own benefit, and later for the adulation of members back in the neighborhood.

Three weeks after the second incursion—again a short time before sunset—
Freddy sought out Mickey. "There's a really important meetin' goin' on an' Tony's
orderin' everybody to be there—quick!—or else!"

Mickey had been loafing about outside Mr. and Mrs. Feldman's candy and
newspaper store, hoping that one of them might come outside and ask him to go
to the newspaper distribution to pick up their daily bundle of papers for their
outside news stand. Ten minutes before Freddy found him, old Mr. Feldman
brushed past Mickey and turned down the boy's offer to do the chore, mumbling,
"Nah, nah—I'll do it myself. Mein Gott, I certainly need the exercise," *certainly*
said as *soitenly.*

Mickey later wished he had stayed out of Freddy's sight or had paid more
attention to Freddy's agitated state or come up with a good, quick alibi to justify
not answering the sudden call. But, spotted by Freddy and not having an excuse,
he trotted alongside the excited boy, who would tell him nothing specific but
either kept grimly silent for a couple minutes at a time or suddenly jibber-jabbered
for ten to twenty seconds at a time.

In the basement, never used as a casual meeting point, more than twenty boys
sat on old chairs and a decrepit sofa and on overturned and upended fruit and
vegetable crates. The sofa was a new item in the cellar room's furnishing and
apparently, to Mickey, the assortment of crates had been brought in recently as
seating places for this large gathering. Two boys sat on a large, thin mattress on the
floor, bent along its length to create both floor and wall cushioning.

It was the largest attendance of HR Club members yet. Mickey had not seen
seven of the boys before, but they wore gang jackets. Remembering the edict about
no jackets in the neighborhood made this get-together seem sinister to Mickey. He
felt uneasy.

Talk in the musty room was in soft tones. In the light of a single dim bulb in
the dangling metal shade, Mickey could barely distinguish figures along the walls
and in corners. He casually counted again, slowly. *Uh, huh—twenty is what I get,
countin' me. But it don' look like Tony's here yet.* Mickey sat quietly with Freddy,
waiting with increasing edginess. *I really don' like this. These guys here are too quiet.
An' Freddy's more nervous than I ever seen him.*

Tony Minelli often seemed to simply materialize. Mickey was abruptly aware
the leader was sitting on a bentwood chair—the same one Mickey occupied at their
first meeting. In one glance past the area under the light nothing had been there,
and seconds later, in another slow sweeping look about, there was Tony seated
under the light. Mickey suddenly realized, with that appearance, that, oddly, he had
never seen Tony Minelli *approach* a group. That puzzled Mickey. He recalled that
many times if he looked about a group he was in, the leader might not be there, or
even nearby. But in an eye-blink Tony would be part of the group, listening or
making a point, or commanding attention merely by the force of his presence.

The soft talk stopped, abruptly. Suddenly it was just still.

The leader looked steadily at Mickey's companion. "Don' worry about us
getting' the crap knocked outta us, Freddy. We'll be ready for 'em, pal. You know

we been gettin' set for somethin' like this. You been helpin' me get stuff stashed away." Looking about the room, Mickey saw several boys staring at the floor. Another one sat hunched forward on his crate, elbows on knees, chin in hands, eyes closed. Toward a corner, sitting cross-legged on the lumpy mattress, a blond boy scowled and stared at the ceiling.

Freddy leaned to Mickey and his words overrode what the leader was saying. "I guess he means it. An' I guess we gotta do what's comin' or it's the end o' the HR Club.

"I don' get it,' Mickey said.

Freddy shook his head slightly, slowly, side to side, resigned. "Jus' stick with me out there on the street—an' hope everythin' gets quieted down—nothin' happens. I'll give ya a hand if I can.

"But if I *ain'* aroun' an' you see somebody you don' know, lay the sonofabitch out before *you* get laid out. You know—the Golden Rule!"

That befuddled Mickey. "The Golden Rule? That's 'Do unto others as you would have them do unto you.'"

Freddy whispered again. "No, no, kid—Golden Rule *Two!* "Do unto others *before* they do unto you!"

Oh, Jesus! We're all gonna be in a friggin' fight? Oh, shit!—I ain' never been in a real fight—'cept for that redheaded kid a couple o' years ago at school recess—an' that was mostly jus' pushin' an' shovin' an' some rasslin' aroun' on the ground—an' it was over real quick!

Tony Minelli's sudden loud voice broke up their talking. "Get whatever you wanna use an' get up on the street an' spread out! You guys who been members longer know what to do. You new guys buddy-up with one o' them who's been aroun' for a while. He'll show ya what to do—how things go. Hunky, you an' Joey start gettin' stuff an' passin' it out."

Hunky used a large key to open the huge lock at the front edge of a large wooden storage bin along a wall. Mickey had noticed the container before, a bulky rectangular form with long carrying handles projecting at front and back of the box on each end, a tool box just like those used at building construction sites. He had thought it belonged to the building owner and never gave the box a second look. Hunky lifted the slanted, heavy lid, propping it against the wall, and bent over to reach into the deep compartment. As others clustered about, he lifted out short pieces of two-by-two lumber, two stubby baseball bats, lengths of heavy toilet pull-chain—interlocked small pieces of folded angular metal loops—tied tightly together at one end to form several loose strands about eighteen inches long. Last, he pulled out a dozen or more doubled heavy woolen knee-length stockings, one stocking inside the other, each improvised weapon with one large or several smaller pieces of stone in the toe—many of the pieces fist-sized, all of them many-angled, sharp-edged, sharp-cornered trap rock, the kind used in laying down a solid base for roadway construction. The weapons cache was quickly distributed. In the eerie shadows, silent, intense members brandished cudgels menacingly; furiously flailed the gloom with swooshing stranded chains; whirled long rock-laden stockings. Others only held them or kept them next to where they sat. The leader ordered silence as the practice of some got more vigorous, more vocal. "We don' wan' people livin' in this buildin' or anyone else in the neighborhood comin' down here or callin' the cops because of a racket we're makin'!"

Those with lumber and bats thrust at and parried one another or invisible opponents. They clubbed handy targets, splintering old furniture into uselessness, smashing slotted fruit and vegetable crates. Those with chains danced about, slicing air, slashing at grimy stone walls, leaving ragged swaths of abraded brick and cement. Stocking-swingers, holding a long fabric tube by an open end, created blurs of motion, whirling missiles through angular planes, cutting the air like a huge circular saw blade. With quick aim a sudden target was solidly smashed by the spinning projectile. Close-quarter movements were practiced, smashing at any random target.

Tony Minelli left the cellar, followed in straggling order by several of the boys. After a few moments, he called impatiently from the street, angry at the slowness of those still behind. His summons was passed in low tones into the hallway, down the cellar steps, through the basement maze. Veterans prodded lingerers along.

Daylight was fading. On the sidewalk, Tony Minelli shunted armed members to various points in several directions, lookouts far left and right at street corners, others concealed in doorways, some in below-ground areaways on both sides of the length of the street. Others were posted to stone steps at scattered building entrances, with the assignment of feigning casualness—just hanging around.

Freddy was not going to be of help to Mickey. The leader sent him to the right, to be a half dozen buildings away, a casual step-sitter. Freddy argued it would be better if he "could kinda of stick with Mickey, it bein' his first time out an' all for this kinda thing."

"Hey, Freddy—I tol' *him* once awready—an' *you* oughta fuckin' well know it by now—*I* decide—who goes where an' who does what! Now get your ass movin'—both o' ya!"

Mickey and someone he did not know were assigned to a building a short distance west on the long block, to sit at the top of the steps, to be two boys talking, to be lookouts. They were to use their higher vantage point to watch for outpost signals from the far end of the street, at the intersection where marauders would enter HR Club territory.

This time Mickey did not feel unimportant. He and the other boy—when they got to the steps he said his name was Aaron—were two buildings away from Tony Minelli's location in a high doorway to their right, across the street—his command post, positioned to look down in every direction, to see the flow of events. Mickey and Aaron had the job of being sure word was quickly passed to Tony, whose last instructions were intense: "Let me know things quick—damn quick! Things that you see—things that people tell ya to let me know. I need to know what's goin' on all the time. Got it? An' hey—I picked you guys myself! You're OK!

"Then when things get hot in the street, start kickin' ass! Show them bastards they ain't such mean fuckers! Tear their fuckin' MF patches right offa their fuckin' fancy jackets! I'll give half a buck for each patch!" He ran across the street, disappearing into his command post doorway.

He was gone only a moment when Mickey realized they did not know what signals would tell them when the MF Club was beginning its assault. He darted to the command post and was back in less than a minute with the answer—a waving yellow bandanna in a second floor building hallway window across the street when recognition was made at either end of the street. "Last couple o' times out wit' us, kid," Tony Minelli said, "you were out on the edge o' things. But this time, you'll be up close, believe me. I hadda put other guys out there as far as I could get 'em who know a lot o' the MF guys by sight, in case any o' them assholes try sneakin' in. But bein' close will be okay for ya. I think you got balls, kid, after seein' the things you already done."

There was nothing to do but wait in the deepening dusk. Anxiety caused Mickey's throat to hurt when he swallowed. He wanted to urinate. His lower abdomen pained as bowels cramped. He wondered if Aaron felt the same, but the other boy did not seem nervous or worried. Mickey bit at one fingernail after another, futilely—they had long since been nibbled to the quick before he became a gang member. He wondered aloud to Aaron if they would be able to see a waving bandanna because there was not much daylight left, but Aaron did not answer. Tony Minelli had told Mickey the bandanna-wavers were up high to keep from being seen by the raiders as they moved into the street. Mickey leaned forward slowly, looking to the west, squinting into the street shadows below the fringe of sunlight on the river cliffs. He looked past Aaron, to the east, to the brighter area, painted by the setting sun, wondering who was doing the same job near the east intersection. *Boy—do I hafta piss!* He looked west again, and east again.

Oh, Jesus! How long has that thing been wavin'?

He punched Aaron on the shoulder. "You better get to Tony quick—I mean goddam quick!—I mean fuckin' quick!" As Aaron jumped down steps two and three at a time, Mickey started after him, stopping halfway down. *Where the hell am I goin'? I don' even know what I'm gonna do! Fer Chrissake—I got nothin' in my hands. I got no weapon!*

To be sure he had seen the slow up-and-down waving motion he looked again at the upper window on the east corner where a signaler had been stationed. The bandanna could not be seen. He looked left to the west corner, then across to where Aaron had disappeared into the command post. The entire street was still. He could see no one. It was too dusky to even spot members sitting on steps. *I won'er if I really did see that bandanna?* He moved back up to the landing at the head of the steps for better vantage. He searched back and forth between the opposite street corners. *What the hell is goin' on?*

In the rapidly diminishing daylight Mickey felt like a prisoner waiting for execution, with nothing to do but wait, hopelessly staring at a gallows.

Light came on in a lamp pole at the curb in front of the house next door. Others flickered on, fixtures high on widely spaced metal poles the length of the street, glimmering pale yellow, barely relieving last daylight grayness. From the east, where Mickey was sure he had seen the bandanna signal, a figure at a slow run moved through the street shadows and pools of lamp light, and turned and took steps two at a time up into the command post.

Members who had been sitting on steps at random buildings on both sides of the street to the west drifted nearer Mickey. Those poised in doorways with unlocked doors opened them and slipped inside dark vestibules, peering intently from deeper ambush. Drifters took new positions closer to the command post. Mickey looked along the street in the opposite direction, to the east. *Damn! Every time I look away, somethin' happens!* A large cluster of figures moved toward him in the dusky light far to the right. *God, I wish Aaron would get back here!*

Massed dark-clad figures flowed along the road surface, skirting the few cars parked on each side. Clusters of two and three shapes paralleled the main body, moving on both sidewalks. Mickey could not see any activity at Tony Minelli's doorway, though the advancing unit was halfway to the command post. He anxiously looked west again, but that end of the street was inactive.

Peering through narrow door openings, the lookouts kept their posts, ready to close in from behind on MF Club members if any of them came in from this other direction.

In the large group, individuals were becoming discernible in the quickly brightening street lighting. Mickey was fascinated by the steady, unhurried movement of the mass. *Closer—closer. Nobody looks afraid—at least not from where I'm at.*

No one seemed in charge of the force. As it moved from shadowiness between street lights into brightness as the group neared each street lamp, and as they got closer to Mickey's position, he saw that individuals resembled members of the HR Club—young, different Caucasian hues, different shapes and sized, seeming intense, scowling, looking mean, wearing jackets—silk-looking fabric, brightly colored, shimmering with movement. Mickey strained but he could not see any weapons.

They strode slowly, stopping close to the block's midway point, short of Tony Minelli's doorway, as if prearranged; as if the leader's location was precisely known.

In number the MF Club seemed to match the HR Club. Mickey hoped they matched each other in *every* respect. But Tony Minelli's and Freddy's warnings were klaxons in his mind— *They live up to their name—they're mean fuckers.*

Mickey had expected a prompt confrontation between two leaders, even thinking Tony Minelli would move out into the street and halt the MF Club much before advancing as far as it had. Nearly thirty seconds that seemed like thirty minutes passed without anything happening. Those on the edge of the MF Club shifted to face outward, along the whole perimeter of the group. Those who had moved separately along two sidewalks turned toward HR Club members sitting on steps.

Mickey studied the quiet, block-long setting, getting more nervous about Aaron's absence, about his own now unsatisfactory position, so close to the center, close to the command post, near the ominous-looking group, certain he must be visible, that he had been made a target. He worried more when he tested the door behind him. It was locked.

Tony Minelli sauntered confidently down the stone steps from his dark hallway; Hunky, Joey, and two others were one and two paces behind and to each side, but Aaron did not trail them. Mickey felt worse about being alone, feeling trapped in the shallow doorway, escape only remotely possible. He would have to smash the thick glass in the upper door section to get away. It would be dangerous to do. There would not be enough time to clear away jagged glass along the edges of the upper half door section if he had to scramble through the opening.

With Tony Minelli present, standing six feet from the leading edge of the MF Club group, nearby step-sitters rose, some to lean against metal or thick stone banisters, still trying to look casual. From both street ends, corner sentries moved toward the center, gathering stair-loungers and those loitering in doorways. Mickey worried about what seemed to him to be the leader's error in getting so close to the big group so quickly. *He won' stand a chance if those guys decide to move on him!—neither will the others! They'll all be goners!*

The leader's act did not seem to be the right thing to do. It was a big risk. Mickey remembered the only risk he had seen Tony Minelli take was to leap from a six-foot-high fence. *But onto dirt, not cement! I'd still bet on that!*

With sudden clarity he remembered his first test for membership. *That damn dirt looked like it was just dug up!—all loose an' soft! That cheatin' bastard! It was all dug fresh? Jus' special for him an' his buddies, I'll bet!*

He thought about the walk on the second floor fire escape. *More fakin'! Never had his fingers more 'n' an inch from some part of that thing—so he could reach for somethin' safe quick, without even tryin'!*

He thought over story-swapping with others. He recollected that anyone telling about Tony Minelli's heroics had heard it from someone else, who heard it from somebody somewhere: "Joey tol' me"; "I got it from Hunky"; "Patsy an' Eddy said Chuckie said so."

But him standin' out there like that now—up against that bunch—only four guys backin' him—I dunno! Looks stupid to me—'less he's got somethin' worked out already.

Mickey could not hear voices, but Tony Minelli appeared to be speaking. He had taken a step forward, gesticulating, poking the air with a finger, aiming it at the group he faced. Then he stood arms akimbo, feet spread, chin jutting, hunched slightly forward, head thrust at the opposition.

The large group spread slowly left and right at its front edge. A stubby figure, shorter than Tony Minelli, took a slow step from the crowd. Detached by distance and height, as though a spectator in a large arena, Mickey watched small movements, posturing and gesturings by two opposing figures; perceptible shifts of the throng for better position; heads turning, to locate opponents, to find escapes.

Mickey had never seen anyone stand before Tony Minelli and not be humble, or cower to some degree. But the stubby figure did not give one sign of intimidation. Rather, he took a half-step forward. Tony Minelli gesticulated vigorously again, shifting weight from one leg to the other, a hand cupping his crotch, moving the hand about vigorously, trusting his pelvis at the stubby figure, thrusting a shoulder forward, then the other shoulder. The opponent took another step ahead, directly at Tony Minelli.

Mickey was enthralled by the choreography, all seeming to become more remote with each second. He was becoming reluctantly excited by the mystery of this first-time experience. He shivered with tension.

My God—I can't believe I'm here!

This is terrible!

He closed his eyes, until he was suddenly startled.

He did not see the start of the melee. There had only been one loud, sharp shout in the street, then guttural sounds, grunts, gasps, indecipherable yells.

Mickey could not see Tony Minelli or Hunky or Joey or the other two. There was no individuality; only a dark mass that swirled and spread through the street lighting and the gloom, creating thin lines of runners from street corners and stoops and doorways and areaways, streaming toward the mass. Gyrating, rolling, wrestling, tumbling figures, reinforced by runners, thickened the dark mass, now resembling an ink-releasing octopus with writhing tentacles.

Mickey focused his mind and vision on what was happening below him, retreating into his shadowed, shallow entrance, pressing hard against the wood and glass door. The street mass vibrated with flailing chains, slashing cudgels, whirling stockings, swinging kicks, and poking, clubbing fists. Attackers and defenders in both groups thrust and clawed and grappled. Two fingers in Hunky's right hand were painfully dislocated in a brawling tumble. His brief scream briefly rose above other sounds. Many arms pumped up and down, and spun round and round, driving, parrying. Someone's lower leg bone was so quickly shattered that no pain was felt for several seconds. Standing, kneeling, and prostrate figures were all targets. Gang members struck their own kind in split-second mistaken actions. Joey's left forearm was broken when someone jumped on it when he was down. Attackers pursued dodging evaders. Blood gushed and seeped. Tony Minelli and the other leader, warning others away, hurt each other quickly and seriously.

Figures broke into the open, pairing off, performing separate dances of viciousness. To Mickey, in his detached lofty site, the frantic octopus had turned into a large, dark, pulsating irregularly shaped planet with tiny moons floating and whirling about each other a brief a brief distance from its surface.

All the outpost sentries had drawn in except Mickey. He stayed in his dark corner, appalled by the rage on the pavements. Sporadic, unintelligible oaths emanated from the fierce action. The pitch of anger and pain cries intensified, bringing shouts from building windows to stop it, and loud threats to call the police. Quickly lengthening shadows dissolved into smothering darkness.

A stumbling figure broke from the dark mass, staggering to the foot of the steps below Mickey. Another figure, brandishing something over its head, charged after the weaving stumbler.

The first figure sprawled forward on the stone steps, weakly crawling upward, collapsing before getting halfway up the flight. For seconds he laid still as his pursuer vaulted to him, then the collapsed boy struggled to his hands and knees, looking up at Mickey.

Aaron's shadowed face was visible in the street lighting. It was covered with blood on one side. Mickey could not see the right eye in the red wetness gushing from a wide tear across Aaron's forehead. Large drops fell from an eyebrow and from the tip of his nose. Aaron tried vainly to wipe blood from the flooded eye with a hand, but awkward fumbling smeared streaks across the unbloodied side of his face. Kneeling, he put his red-streaked hands out, palms up, imploring. Mickey was certain he heard Aaron sobbing.

The pursuer did not see Mickey in the dark sanctuary. As he started up the steps, intent on Aaron, he drew back his upraised arm farther, his swarthy face contorted by a massive rage. His fury peaked at the sight of his victim's vulnerable position, his supplicating pose, back turned to the attacker.

Like a tennis player's powerful, serve, the assailant's rough two-by-two piece of lumber scribed an arc, from behind the attacker's back, high over his head, accelerating, moving with blurring speed. His tightening grip squeezed the sharp corners of the wood into his palm and fingers.

Mickey reacted. He had no second thought. There was simply movement in response—like an involuntary knee-jerk to a tapping stimulus at a sensitive leg joint.

He leaped from the doorway, taking one launching step on the broad landing at the top of the stairs. His feet were slightly spread apart as he sailed downward through the short space, torso bent forward, arms spread-eagled, balancing his flight. His feet thudded into the assailant's chest and feet. The two of them thumped heavily down the steps onto the sidewalk, rolling about clumsily, struggling to get upright. Mickey, vision hazy, got to his feet first.

Stunned and disoriented, Aaron's attacker staggered, rising on wobbly legs, facing away from Mickey, still clutching his deadly piece of lumber. Hulking, his eyes searched, quickly looking left and right, body jerking and twitching, hopping completely about, snarling at the sight of Aaron and Mickey.

Mickey saw the two-by-two suddenly lift and start coming at his head. He ducked under the arm, squealing sharply in fear. He took short bent-over steps left, clawing at the areaway railing to keep from falling. The attacker lost his balance, spinning sideways, completely missing his target. Mickey clutched the railing, leaning sideways against it, exhausted, glancing left and right, then into the sunken areaway, then staring in anguish at the confused club-wielder. He thought about vaulting the railing and dropping the short distance onto the cement of the small courtyard.

I'll be trapped. He'll block the steps up! He'll kill me with that thing! He realized that the metal gate to the vestibule below would probably be locked! Even if it was open, he could only get *behind* it, try to hold it shut against the bigger boy's strength. Then he would have to call for help from guys in his gang. *They'll never hear me! This guy'll kill me for sure!*

Coming out of his spinning stumble, seeing Mickey again, the aggressor raised the club high, pulling it behind his head, clutching it with both hands. With the snorting roar of a huge enraged animal he bounded forward. Mickey dodged awkwardly, feet slipping as the club came down mightily. His knee touched the sidewalk. The other leg sprawled outward. He crooked an arm over the railing, struggling to get to his feet, at the same time scrambling away from the arc of the club.

The rushing MF Club member stumbled over Mickey's outstretched, thrashing leg. The attacker's plunging arms, fingers tightly interlaced in a double fist on the piece of lumber, had nothing to push against to ward off falling. Momentum propelled him forward. He fell onto the railing at his waist, toppling ahead. Mickey, still hanging by a bent arm draped over the same railing, other hand on the pavement for support, watched the other boy's leg scissors the air, trying to kick feet back down to the sidewalk—futilely. He went over the railing into a looping plunge. The deep, snorting roar became a desperate, fearful, rising shriek.

Through slender metal uprights, Mickey glimpsed the upside-down face, starkly shadowed by railing bars and street light, contorted in fright, mouth wide as he shrieked. The piece of lumber, still tightly gripped, brought far forward in the headlong dive, was now, for a second's fraction, pointing toward Mickey, clutched in the falling boy's fist, directly at his chest. Curiously not letting go the club to use hands and arms to break the fall, the inverted figure instead thrust the weapon upward at Mickey's head. The lumber poked through the railing, the tip flailing inches from Mickey's frightened eyes.

The upside-down face was gone; the stick clattered to the sidewalk next to Mickey. He heard a crunching, sickening thunk, a dull grunt.

Oh God!

Mickey's stomach and throat pulsated so vigorously he thought he was going to vomit. Acrid, bilious fluid burned in his throat and upper chest. He pulled himself upright and stared down into the small, dim areaway space.

The assailant was askew on his back, head lolled to one side, face toward Mickey, eyes closed, blood leaking from his nostrils. One arm was bent to an abnormal angle, the hand under his shoulderblade. The other hand twitched, rose and fell, rose and fell again, beseeching.

Mickey looked up at a movement on the building steps. Aaron was peering over the stone railing, wiping at his red-smeared face. Flowing blood had brightly stained his HR Club jacket and dully discolored his dark shirt.

Noise had stopped. As if startled by a thunderclap, Mickey realized his back was unprotected. *Oh, shit!—any o' his buddies in that bunch out there see what I done?* He jerked his head around, terrified he would see the act of someone smashing at him. Then he turned about completely, slowly, tensely. The street was quiet, nearly empty of people, heavily shrouded in dusk. The last of the entangled, combative crowd melted away, moving toward each avenue east and west. Lone and paired fighters moved slowly, couples supporting each other against pain and injuries. Hell Raisers sat on building steps in poses of fatigue, dejection, frustration. The end seemed abrupt to Mickey. He looked up at windows across the street. Lights were on but shades were pulled down. He thought he could see the outline of watching figures in some windows that did not have lights on. *I better get outta here! Somebody musta called the cops!* He listened for sirens but it was still quiet.

The boy in the pit groaned. Mickey did not know what to do about him. He did not know what to do about anything, looking at Aaron for a helpful sign. Aaron steadied himself by resting his forearms on the slanted stone railing of the steps. Blood flowing from his forehead wound had slowed to dribbling slowly down his face. He stood leaning forward, staring down into the areaway at the attacker.

He spit vehemently at the prostrate boy, muttered a garbled oath, and spit again, spraying drops of blood and saliva broadly. He wiped blood from his face, carefully scraping upward from his chin, across the cheek to the eye. He snapped that hand down sharply, flinging the gathered blood and sweat at the boy sprawled on the cement. It struck his face in a splashy pattern, but he did not react. Aaron stood stiffly erect, arched his back to relieve stiffness, then turned slowly and walked down the steps, turning right, toward the broad avenue, walking east with a trace of unsteadiness.

Where's he goin'?

Aaron walked without a look back, weaving with faltering steps. Mickey called out loudly, facing Aaron's back, "Hey, what am I s'posed to do with this guy?" Aaron paid no attention to the worried yell.

Mickey called out to HR Club members scattered on building steps. Some glanced up, but no one moved. He looked for Tony Minelli. Mickey was stunned by Aaron simply walking away without a word, that Aaron so quickly and absolutely detached himself from those horrifying moments, that he did not even seem the least concerned about his companions, that he did not make an effort to find any of them, to give help if it was needed. *He mighta been killed if I hadn' jumped that guy! An' now he walks away without sayin' nothin'!—not even sayin' thanks!—not one goddam word for savin' his ass!—maybe savin' him from bein' dead!* Mickey was puzzled.

His association with the HR Club ended at that moment. In the next few seconds he had flashing memories of fun-filled, spirited, playful adventure—good times for him, the best he had ever had. Boredom had been dispelled by those times. He knew he had benefited from unity and strength, that he had gotten strength. He had relished the close presence of many gang members; most of them, at least. He had enjoyed the dares and minor risks. But the stupidity of what had just been done in the street aggravated his irritations. It overwhelmed him, frightening and sickening him.

Without another look at Aaron's assailant, now *his* own victim, Mickey leaped away from the areaway, going in the opposite direction from Aaron, trotting for several yards before slowing to a painful, limping walk. At the distant west corner he slowed more, turned left and walked several blocks south toward his street, going home. Twice he stopped to inspect himself in the glass of lighted store windows. At a parked car, he examined his face in a small rearview side mirror. He was relieved to see no marks or traces of anyone else's blood splashed on him.

His father was home, though he had left a note in the morning saying he might be late, dozing in a chair, with an open newspaper spread across his chest and lap, and Margaret was cooking hamburger meat for supper. She looked at him as he passed to the bathroom, but did not say anything.

He was home almost on time to eat; he was unbloodied; clothes were not torn; trembling had subsided. *Boy—lucky this time!—again!*

Mickey successfully avoided Freddy the next day at school, and for the next days, and then for three more weeks. He kept to himself, ready for a reason for Freddy, or for anyone else in the gang, why he could not attend a meeting, or any other gathering, no matter how informal. He carefully, from a distance, scouted every usual assembly point to avoid meeting another HR Club member. He stayed home more often after school, keeping window shades down. He entered and left the family's basement rooms through a back door of their building, skulking watchfully through a long backyard route to a street.

In schoolrooms, Freddy went about his activities as though Mickey did not exist. To Mickey, Freddy had changed. *Not jus' with me—with everybody!* Mickey looked at Freddy's back, two rows over, three seats ahead. *Always sittin' slouched over anymore. No more jokin' with everybody—no gabbin' all the time. An' now when he walks he looks like he's hurtin'.*

It was as though the HR Club had dissolved into nothingness. Mickey's recent times now seemed a hazy, episodic dream, flashing vignettes, becoming murky quickly, murkier with each remembrance, with remembrances further apart.

Mickey did not understood how the dissolution could be so abrupt, so clean. He never learned the reason for the viciousness of that late afternoon. He did not see Aaron again. He never learned what became of the boy who had toppled into the areaway.

39

That kid could have split Aaron's head open as easily as hacking through a watermelon.

Mine too!

And me stumbling—at just that right second. Lucky again!

And suppose that kid got killed because of falling into that areaway? I would have had something to do with it.

What makes things happen to get to such a point?

40

Weeks after Mickey's family had moved to another Spartan basement apartment in a new, distant neighborhood, he came home early from visiting a new acquaintance. After half an hour or so the boy's mother said her son had to study, but she would make them each something to eat before Mickey left, and she put together thick meatloaf sandwiches. She wrapped another one in waxed paper for Mickey to take along as she watched him ravenously devour his at the kitchen table. He intended to take it home for supper but ate it as he walked slowly along to his new address.

His father was storming throughout the small rooms. Mickey started backing out the entrance when he sensed the rage as he started into the cellar flat, but he was seen and ordered inside. He worried that he had been caught at one of his lies about a school absence. His father stood facing him, pounding a fist into a palm. Mickey watched him tremble with rage. He was madder than usual. Anger usually only showed in his eyes at the beginning of the anger, piercing brief looks, piercing stares, eyebrows pinched down into vees to the bridge of his nose; skin rippling at the sides of his face as teeth clenched where bones flexed at each side of his jaw.

"You know what *she* did?"

"She?"

"Margaret's gone!"

"I don' know what ya mean. I don' know where she went. I can't help it. She never tells me what she's gonna do or where she's gonna go—even though ya tol' her to always tell me."

"*Gone!* Don't you understand that word?"

Gone where? How?

What for?

Mickey said, trying not to yell back, "Sure I do—but I still don'—you mean jus' like *that?*" He thought for a moment, then spoke more quietly. "She's not here now? An' from *now on?* You mean *gone* gone? She ran away?"

"Your *mother! She* took her away—while I was working! All she left me was this damn note! Six goddam words!" He crushed the small piece of paper into a ball in a fist and jammed it into his shirt pocket.

His father stormed about the room again, picking up things, slamming them down. He punched walls, slashed fists at furniture, hurled books and magazines and newspapers. Mickey stayed wary, ready to dodge anything indiscriminately thrown. He was relieved his truancy had not been discovered; wanting to be elsewhere before he became a target of the rampage.

Still raging, the man snatched up his short leather jacket and cabdriver's cap and rushed out the door. In the quiet, Mickey leaned against a wall. *How come she took her away after all this time? I won'er what the note said?*

Mickey suddenly felt embarrassed, because it seemed to him that a great relief had settled on him, relaxing him. But then he quickly thought he should not feel that way. He thought he should feel bad that his sister would not be in their home from now on. *But, hey—now I don' have to be responsible for her no more! An' I won' be gettin' in Dutch an' gettin' lickin's for things she did—an' for things she did that were her fault an' not mine!* He felt a lump in his throat when he swallowed.

Geez—I'm gonna miss her anyway—I guess—even if she was a nuisance a lotta times—even if I did get my ass whipped a few times cuz of her.

My mother, huh?

Ain' seen her since that funeral—must be two or three years—for her father. They all said he was my grandfather.

I wonder what she looks like?

I don' remember.

I don' know what my mother looks like.

41

I *still don't know what really happened that day—how everything went. If Margaret knew anything beforehand, she sure didn't let on. Or I was too busy—maybe too dumb—probably—to notice it.*

But it was that changing schools that kept me busy enough.

42

Hooky from high school, as often as he wished, after a brief time at the new school, was easy for Mickey. It was far simpler than doing the same thing in grammar school.

There, the greatest problem had been dodging truant officers. They were like sheriffs and marshals and bounty hunters in pursuit of outlaws in movie badlands, dark saloons, and ghost towns. Each school day they prowled streets, playgrounds, alleys, and condemned tenement buildings in search of incorrigibles.

In mid-June Mickey learned that in the fall he was to attend a high school in another borough; a long, tedious trip by underground and elevated subway trains. He wondered if he would run into another colored kid again—or guys from some roaming gang. *But, hell—I can' spen' all my time worryin' 'bout stuff like that. Prob'ly never happen again—keep my nose clean—keep on the look-out, tha's all.*

When he first complained about the school assignment, his father only muttered that now carfare would be needed. When Mickey muttered and grumbled about time and distance and getting up earlier and getting home later and having to make lunch, his father wagged a thick index finger. "Stop your yapping, your complaining! You don't have to *walk* miles to and from school like I did. Now *quit it!*"

The city became sweltering. With Margaret gone, his father was home even less. Mickey's time was more his own, to fill as he wished. Whenever he asked what time to be home for supper, the answer invariably was a variation of "It doesn't matter. You'd better figure on fixing something to eat for yourself. I don't know how late I'll have to work. I might have to do a little overtime—maybe even a double shift. Who knows? Not having a telephone here, I can't call and let you know anything."

The new neighborhood did not have many boys his age. And he seldom saw them; they were busy with family activities. The families seemed different. Something else seemed different, too. Mickey investigated diligently, finally persuading himself there was no gang.

Mickey drifted aimlessly with the summer. He slept late, shrugging off sunlight sifting through windowshades and creeping round their edges, making sharp patterns in his room. He read pulp magazine mysteries. He walked the long, high, beautifully shaped George Washington bridge across the wide, placid Hudson River many times. On a day made intensely brilliant by sun uncluttered by clouds or usual city haze, on his first trip alone across the span, fascinated by the sparkling river, he peered over the railing, idly leaning forward, head far past the rail, hands in his jacket pocket. The sensation startled him. His eyes had a pulsating feeling, searching for focus. Everything in his mind started moving, turning and twisting, building to faster and faster rotations, spinning to gray blurriness. He jerked his hands from the jacket pockets, clutching the rail fearfully. Then he felt safely back on the walkway, no longer lifted up and over the shoulder-high barrier. With those quick movements he learned thereafter to touch the railing first, even lightly, to preserve a sense of safeness.

On one round-trip, late evening walk on the bridge it was fog-shrouded, giving the walk a mysterious, stimulating appeal. Weak light from widely spaced overhead walkway lights made small pools of pale yellow on the long promenade. A mist-like rain filtered through the fog as Mickey wandered, bored, restless, wanting *something* to happen to liven the uneventful, long day. Then he saw a tall, slender figure materialize, approaching slowly, moving more slowly than Mickey, appearing to be in deep concentration; in a moment, closer, suddenly recognizable as Sherlock Holmes, in double-billed cap and long, flowing, caped overcoat, hands in pockets, paying no attention to Mickey, but strolling alone on the soft marshy ground of an English moor, trying to solve a baffling mystery, piecing together extraordinarily difficult clues unfathomable to anyone else. Mickey became concerned by two other figures barely visible past Mr. Holmes in the murky fog, walking shoulder to shoulder, keeping a steady distance behind the detective. The lone, tall figure strolled past Mickey, not seeming to notice him, and the two huddled figures went by, also ignoring the boy. The smaller person seemed to be a woman to Mickey, though the figure wore a bulky topcoat against the cool dampness and the head was covered by a large, oversized cap, of the sort his father wore while driving his cab. Mickey worried about the situation, about the detective's safety, considering that two mysterious figures seemed to be tailing him. Should he go after the detective? Warn him he was being followed? A hound baying in the distance worsened Mickey's anxiety. A noisily approaching car's headlights brightened the fog, making it appear yellowish. The yellow quickly got brighter and the car sped by at too high a speed for such limited visibility, lights on high beam, brilliantly reflected back at the driver, briefly washing Mickey's area in brightness. Looking in Mr. Holmes' direction, he could barely see his back and the two figures seemed to have moved closer to him. The quick flash of automobile lighting receded into the fog and the trio was in gloom again. A mournful horn sounded below the bridge, warning of a river peril. Mickey watched the car's tail lights become less red, paler, quickly gone; he wanted to shout to Sherlock Holmes.

Suddenly Mickey was alone again, realizing that the only reality had been the speeding car. *I sure wish I could be somewhere besides here—doin' this kinda stuff—only imaginin' things.*

The World's Fair was a wondrous exploration. A long interborough subway ride brought him to the spacious grounds of Flushing Meadows in Queens. The trip was miles long, but roaming the vast area was gratifying. His mind absorbed everything he saw, soaking up details by scores, continuously searching for more, standing long moments viewing whatever piqued his curiosity or interest.

Several times he leaned back in a large, comfortably cushioned high-back seat for a lengthy ride in semidarkness through the large Futurama constructed by General Motors. A series of connected upholstered chair-like seats, with high partitions at each side, joined together at either side, formed an articulated train of seats that followed a convoluted route along an undulating irregular perimeter of a diorama—the future of the 1960s. The seats were individual compartments, each facing inward toward a great miniaturized panorama, letting an occupant be alone with thoughts on what was shown below as if seen from a high-flying airplane. *Wow-e-e-e! Jus' like that kid I saw in the movie las' week—flyin' all over India on a magic flyin' carpet on all kinds o' adventures.*

The line of chairs moved slowly, perspective changing, twisting into slow turns; rising to a heaven's view of a sprawling city surrounded by spacious open lands; lowering gently for closer looks at city features in a soon-to-be future world: "Much of it now being constructed," said a man's mellow voice, "—to be a reality in many of our lives, certainly for young visitors with us today."

Each seat had speakers built into high upholstered wings at both sides, through which a man's soft, smooth, almost hypnotic voice narrated facts and predictions, extolling the miracle depicted; "So close in time," the voice kept repeating now and then.

Mickey's favorite diversion on the grounds was the gigantic cigarette-making machine in the Lucky Strike building. It was spellbinding with all its automatic workings. He had never seen anything like it. The awesome, intricate, enormous device was tended by a few workers located singly along the fabricating route, seeming to be unimportant to the process, standing about, waiting, ready to restock the machine's needs as components were steadily used, waiting to fix minor mechanical flaws that rarely occurred.

The huge assembly used myriad components fed into the machine by only a few coverall-uniformed workers at a starting point at one end of a long, narrow building. The components were then sorted, collated, pushed, pulled, lifted, turned, rotated up and down and about, an amazing number of functions taking place along a clanking, whirring, buzzing, thumping route, one that twisted through turns of every angle, rising, rolling back over its path in the opposite direction a few inches higher, or a foot higher, even higher, falling down short and long distances, but not freely, not like a roller coaster, controlled, going down measuredly, held in tracks, moving precisely and quickly and regularly to another function.

Great quantities were fed into the great machine: Bulky wads of shredded tobacco; rolls of thin, fragile, white cigarette paper and clear cellophane and shiny tinfoil; green-and-red-printed package paper, stacks of green-and-red-printed thin carton cardboard—to be shaped into single cigarettes shaped into twenty-cigarette packages manipulated by mechanical fingers and claws into ten-pack units slid into cartons and in turn slid into simultaneously forming cartons closed and sealed and grabbed by larger metal hands moved by arms and claws, filling large corrugated cases. The cases, too, were manipulated by mechanical claws and arms and rams that stacked two layers of cases onto precise, automatically positioned pallets that were then nudged onto a motorized roller conveyor. Pallet after pallet disappeared through a wall opening into a storage room. Mickey walked back and forth along the spectator promenade the length of the huge device, stopping to read explanation posters or dwelling on some intricacy of the machine until taken with another of its magical workings, then another.

The Futurama was fascinating and Mickey made the inspiring ride four times on separate visits. However, the enormous, complex Lucky Strike machine that worked seemingly flawlessly was more awesome to him. He spent far more time studying the machine than taking rides to contemplate the future. It was a mystery to him that people were able to construct such an imposing *thing*, a *machine*, one that could do so much, without making a mistake, doing everything automatically, with only one tending person here and there along the marvelously complex noisy route. On later visits to the World's Fair, he would return to see the machine at work; bending, leaning, peering, watching, peeking, staring at some enthralling process segment or just some small step, even a particular movement.

That Futurama is nice—it's fun. But all that stuff's in the future. But this thing! It ain' in the future—it's here right now—in front o' me. It's a miracle!

Summer days were park days, too: Riverside Park, Central Park. To go to either was easy to do—just walk a few blocks from where he lived. There was plenty of time to himself, so he would do that most often. No subway ride. No colored kid— or other troubles. And simple wanderings were satisfying. No money was needed, unless for a soda or an Italian ice, or for real ice cream; then he would swipe deposit bottles from hall closets and areaways. Most of the time he would just wander; something might happen. He watched squirrels scamper; watched warily for what might be troublesome. He did a lot of thinking and wishing. He planned adventures for someday. He visualized the world he read about in geography books. He schemed how to get to places in those books, so that a long time from now he would not just have to remember words and photographs and wishes.

Mickey always watched for prowling groups of boys, straying from their territories, using the parks for mischief; lately they had been used as arenas for settling differences between groups. The neutral ground kept police away from their own neighborhood, leaving the boys unharassed, leaving streets and buildings tranquil for residents, keeping them from calling the cops for every little thing, real or imagined.

In Central Park, Mickey wandered worn, long, meandering footpaths, skimpy trails, paved walks, grassy knolls. He slept sprawled on a meadow where sheep used to graze way back when. As a mood struck him, he lazily walked or eagerly trotted the irregularly shaped perimeter of the main reservoir. Looking through the high chain link fence, the water was inviting, but he knew there were too many eyes watching for trespassers. The zoo was fascinating, where he could see more than cats and dogs and mice and rats.

He fashioned lumber and tree wood into awkwardly designed, roughly made sailing craft, resembling rafts or scows or an ark rather than sleek vessels, joining adults and children at a park lake sailing every size and shape of genuine model boat of careful construction and obvious value. Oh, to have one of those, he thought often. He thought what a great surprise it would be to receive such a boat as a gift, even to receive a kit from which he could do nearly every bit of handcrafting himself. He did have a birthday coming at the end of the month. *Even if I only had the kit I'd have plenty o' time left to have it ready to use this summer before gettin' back to school. But the ol' man is always sayin' I oughta be studyin' an' readin' books 'stead o' makin' models an' lookin' at comics.*

If he had money he would pay for one or two rides on the carousel, always astride an up-and-down jumper, not one of the immobile prancers or standing horses bound forever to the platform. Sometimes he would succeed in snatching a brass ring as he whirled by the long wooden ringholder, an extended arm on a pole near the ticket booth, each ring worth a free ride.

Mickey spent part of one hot sunny afternoon with a boy he met at the merry-go-round—Jerry. They trusted each other quickly and laughed and joked. They had a long game of catch with an old, gray, dirty, smooth tennis ball the boy had, a ball surprisingly lively for its appearance. Resting after their vigorousness, sitting in shade on a slanted embankment, Jerry said, "I've got somethin' we can do—if you wanna."

"Yeah? Wha's that?"

Jerry leaned to Mickey. "I can show ya a place in the park for somethin' really great!"

"What makes it great?"

"I could tell ya, but it's better if I don'. In fact, I won'! It's somethin' you really hafta find out about for yerself. It's better that way. You game?" He nudged Mickey's arm. "You'll get a kick outta it."

Mickey was puzzled why Jerry wouldn't explain, or even give a better hint. "The only thing I'll tell ya right now is there's a good chance to maybe see the best sights you've ever seen. It's hot enough. If we're lucky, you won' be sorry." In three or four minutes they reached the edge of one of the park's lakes. Jerry pointed to a long, wide, arching footbridge, made of wood, crossing a strait of the lake. "In another couple o' minutes you'll see what I mean."

They worked their way through clustered bushes along the shoreline, edging to the bridge footings. The substructure was built far stronger than it needed to be, a complex framework of thick square wood beams with chamfered edges. It looked as if it could withstand raging floods, not at all likely with the park's relatively shallow, placid waters.

Jerry led Mickey through the network of supports and bracing into the deep shadows beneath the walkway. Mystified, still curious, Mickey let himself be drawn to the center of the bridge. Strong sunlight slanted into the hideaway, pouring from overhead through openings between wide walkway planking extending a couple inches beyond the bridge's metal guard rails along each side, planks laid down long ago. Some planks shrank more than others and the gaps varied in width. Thick and thin swaths of sunlight painted black and white patterns in the two boys' maze. Slightly past bridge center, Jerry motioned Mickey forward to him. Finger to lips, he cautioned for quiet, hurrying Mickey with faster hand movements. He whispered, "Now alls we hafta do is wait." Mickey squirmed for a comfortable position within the angular framework. *What the hell are we waitin' for?*

Every couple minutes Jerry would warily move to the side of the bridge structure and ease out of the framework to hang precariously out over the water, clinging to some part of the bridge, looking up, looking for something on the bridge itself.

After several searches, Jerry pulled back quickly, signaling Mickey for quiet, signaling as though to get ready, twice soundlessly mouthing those two words vigorously to Mickey. Footsteps sounded overhead; slow, scraping, shuffling noises. More than one person, Mickey mentally calculated. He could hear low voices. *What's goin' on up on the bridge? What the hell are we s'posed to do down here?*

Mickey could define that there were two people stopped above, a man and a woman. Their voices sounded young, though he still could not understand words. He pressed up, putting his head closer to the plank openings, turning an ear up, straining for words, then looked back to Jerry to ask him a question.

The boy was peering up between planks. Mickey stared at him, dumbfounded. Jerry's positioning looked awkward, precarious, as though he might fall any second; head tipped back, forehead against rough wood, arms braced where he could find support, legs contorted.

Suddenly Jerry turned his head, grinning at Mickey. He pointed upward excitedly, the index finger of his other hand pressed tightly against his lips, jabbing the air with the upraised finger, then at Mickey, up at the bridge again, then signaling Mickey to move to him. Mickey edged closer. Jerry tugged his arm vigorously, still with a finger to his lips. He untwisted himself from the framework, eyes on Mickey every possible moment, shifting from one hand to the other to brace himself, to keep a finger to his lips. Mickey brushed closely by the other boy, contorting his arms and legs as Jerry had done to prop himself, nervously pressing hands and feet against things that felt solid. He arched his back, tipped his head back awkwardly; uncomfortably, painfully, twisting it this way and that so he could peer up evenly through spaces between planks, first with one eye, then the other, also trying to use both eyes.

He made out a man's figure, first through one opening, then through adjacent gaps. The figure leaned his back against the bridge rail, alternately gazing overhead into the sky, then staring at the horizon. "No, no," Jerry whispered in Mickey's ear, "not through there!"

What the hell's so important 'bout doin' this?—tha' we gotta be so secret? Mickey shifted to another narrower opening, then to a third, at least an inch wide. The patchwork of light and dark beneath the bridge befuddled his eyes. His neck hurt. The coarse wood dug into his forehead. He concentrated on seeing what it might be that made Jerry so insistent. *What in hell am I lookin' for?*

His astonishment grew with comprehension. The girl on the bridge faced opposite the young man, looking out over the lake, leaning forward, resting her forearms on the waist-high railing. She wore a loose-fitting, light-colored, thin summer dress that billowed easily in the hot breeze. Her feet were comfortably apart, spaced carefully to keep her high heels from poking into the slots in the weather-worn planking—one foot on either side of the opening through which Mickey peered so intently.

Brilliant sunlight filtered through the flimsy material gathered loosely about her waist and floating widely about her calves. In the interior soft golden light her slim legs angled up from her widely spread feet. Mickey's eyes widened. The girl's limbs converged to where they were separated by a narrow swath of dark yellow curly hair that extended up toward her belly, spreading into a short, broad triangle.

W-o-w—what a strange view to have of someone!

He almost shouted his surprise, biting his tongue in determination, remembering the young man up there with her. He felt the sensation that had been becoming more troublesome for him during the past weeks. *Christ!—I'm gettin' a hard-on!* It had been a long time since Buddy and Patty. Mickey felt a sudden revulsion. *Does this here Jerry kid have a sister he treats like Buddy did Patty?*

Mickey's fascination continued. He felt elated at this sudden intrusion without detection; this peculiar pleasure. *This ain't nothin' like pictures!*

Looking at friends' ragged-edge, crinkled small photographs of women having men do to them what the friends said was fuckin' had made his groin flush with heat, made blood pump into his penis, twitching its smallness into fullness. None of the friends could explain why the men and women would let pictures be taken of them without clothes on, or why they would let pictures be made as they did that fuckin'. He thought it strange a man would let a photograph be made showing him kissing a woman's privates, putting his tongue between skin folds he held apart with fingers. *An' her havin' so much hair there. Don' look at all like Patty did. She was only all smooth in the same place. Won'er what that must be like for him?*

Other friends' photos flashed into his mind as he stared up, holding his breath, afraid his breathing would be heard. One image exploded vividly into his consciousness. A nude woman knelt bent forward on a bed, buttocks resting on her feet, facing the camera. A naked man sprawled the length of the bed, on his back, both arms crossed under his head, facing the camera, smiling. His long, thick penis was erect, the woman clasping both sets of her fingers round it, hands resting in his thick groin hair, her lips nearly engulfing the large tip. Her wide, joyful eyes also looked at the camera. The image made Mickey moan softly. In his mind he screamed at himself to be quiet. A dark-eyed face flashed in his brain as rapid, shifting out-of-focus, in-focus images. *Oh, God—Simon!*

He was suddenly ashamed of the times he had awakened at night with wet, sticky underwear, his penis leaking; of times he had groped through bed coverings and underclothing to his stiffened penis, gripping it tighter and tighter, steadily pulling back the foreskin as he slowly stroked his small hand about the small shaft, steadily desensitizing the usually protected flesh of the tip, increasing to firmer, quicker, then finally frantic movements, agonizingly forcing ejaculation, agonizing over the exquisite relief.

He could not take his eyes from the plank opening. The girl shifted her weight from one leg to the other, then in a moment, back to the other leg, then started swaying her hips, almost imperceptibly, unconsciously. Her gentle sideward movements added motion to his flashing mental images. The curious viewing angle stimulated him. His excited mind raced, then started tumbling. It seemed incredible to him to be in this place, doing what he was doing. It astonished him that he was able, with such ease, to stare for so long at the most secret of secrets. His erection became painful, constricted by bunched clothing, by the hunched spying position.

He felt light-headed. An awesome guilt swept over him. Fear shook his body. *If that guy catches me I'm all done for! He'll kill me!*

However, the quiet voices above him made him feel he was still safe. He did not want to lose the tantalizing sight, but the discomfort in his crotch worsened. He squirmed about, contorting his crotch area. His left leg tingled with the sensation of going to sleep, like an arm would when he bumped his funny bone. His foot was already numb. Jerry tugged at his arm, whispering hoarsely, "Lemme get back there!" But Mickey still did not want to relinquish the cramped hiding spot. He ignored the digging fingers, then pushed them away. The girl's long legs, her secret place, her buttocks, were irresistible. Mickey groaned again at the pain in his penis, at the excruciating pain in his testicles.

He yanked his arm from Jerry's clenching, digging fingers pressing violently into both his arms. He wanted to escape the boy and the bridge. He struck angrily at Jerry, then started clambering away, toward the side opposite the couple above, intensely wanting to be out of the bridge underpinning. Jerry punched at his back. Mickey spun about, infuriated, smashing a fist into the boy's face and blood spurted from Jerry's nose. The boy toppled back with a surprised yell, slipped and stumbled on a crossbrace, then arched backward into open space, away from the bridge, in an ungraceful, flailing, back somersault into the lake. Water splashed in high, wide foamy plumes. The girl screamed in a short gasp, terror-stricken by the tumbling thing that explosively erupted from beneath her as she stared down at the water.

Mickey scrambled frantically through the long framework, struggling for the shore. The man on the bridge cursed loudly at Jerry, thrashing in the water, flopping toward the bridge, reaching for solidness, legs pedaling, feet feeling for bottom, trying to keep his chin up. The girl screamed again, longer.

Mickey scraped a shinbone savagely when he missed a foot-thrust at a brace, but he did not feel the pain. He lightly bumped and harshly banged his head several times. He leaped from the framework to bushes crowding the shoreline, splashing through water over his ankles, worried that the young man would hear the splashing and charge after him. He scrambled more vigorously, more clumsily. Mud gripped his feet and he could hear gulping, sucking sounds as he desperately pulled up a captive foot with each step. He was certain the young man had to be watching him, that he could not be missing his noisiness.

When hidden in tall shrubs on the steep embankment, Mickey realized the young man had not seen him, that he did not know there were two Peeping Toms. He watched the confused Jerry paddle first on one heading for solid ground, paralleling the bridge, then splash in the opposite direction, repeatedly glancing up at the bridge walkway. The young man kept abreast of Jerry, patiently waiting for the bedraggled boy to make it to shore.

Serves the sonofabitch right!

Jerry was shouting: "Please, mister—" His words were sputtering as he rose and fell in the lake, gasping, spitting water. "Let me outta here! I wasn' doin' nothing'! Hey—"

Mickey turned and pushed through the dense shrubbery, puffing, hurrying until the noisy scene faded. At a distant place on the lake edge, he sat on a rock and sloshed his sneakers, still on his feet, in water until the half-dried mud was gone. His mind replayed the image of the blonde girl, and his body disturbingly reacted again. He felt his face flush, and made himself think of other things. From then, during that afternoon, and on other days, too, the same thoughts, at unusual times, stimulated and embarrassed him.

In the middle of that summer vacation, he turned fifteen.

43

Damn!—seemed like I had trouble every time I turned around—even when I was trying to do things right.

Seemed like damned if I did, damned if I didn't.

And I wasn't even in high school yet. But I had all that time to kill on vacation.

44

Mickey strove to keep out of trouble the rest of the summer. He wanted nothing disturbing to somehow get back to his father. He saw little of his parent, who worked long, erratic hours, or spent time with friends. Mickey would often find a scrawled note by his father at home saying he would be away for a night, visiting Aunt Ellen. Mickey, the first time that summer he read such a note, remembered he had not seen her for months; not any time during the two last neighborhood moves; in fact, he had not even heard her name mentioned. *I wonder why I don' go on any of the visits? Maybe it's too far away. Nah—I gone long ways with him before to other places. Maybe she's not feelin' good.*

Well—at least the old man gets to see her. Maybe tha's what's keepin' him in a better mood every time he goes to see her. At least he's not botherin' with me too much— not even at all.

As much as possible, as much as he could endure, Mickey avoided boys who were strangers. *Some sonofabitch like Jerry ain' gonna get me into somethin' like that again!*

He kept to himself to skip trouble. Wandering his own new neighborhood and nearby other ones, he played occasional stickball games in the streets; and checkers or tag or touch football or softball at a Park Department playground. But he would not let himself be persuaded by newfound acquaintances to do something they hinted, or even promised, would be defiant, riskier, more exciting, more adventuresome. Because of reluctance he would not explain, he became less sought after for participation—"He's a scaredy-cat"; "He ain' got enough balls"; or "He ain' got *no* balls." He stopped pilfering bottles from areaway vestibules and hallway closets in search of pocket money. It was simpler—no fear of being caught stealing—to cull bottles from garbage cans in backyards and at street curbs. He did not want to work in another small store where temptation would prove too much.

I ain' gonna find another Mr. Weinstein! I know that!

Searching for coins through subway grates filled time, too. It was better than poking through smelly, slimy garbage, and often produced more money. The best hunting grounds were in midtown, where hundreds of pedestrians an hour passed along each city block. Equipment was simple; a thick, heavy hardware store metal nut tied at the end of a long piece of strong wrapping twine—and chewing gum. It all fit easily into a pocket. All he had to do was peer down into a large shadowy subway ventilation opening covered by large rectangular metal grates with grids of rectangular openings and look for accidentally dropped coins.

A search began with a long subway ride. Nearing whichever station he had decided on, preparation of the gum started. Two to three sticks of regular chewing gum were chewed into a soft, wet wad, using just the right amount of spit—or a large lump of bubble gum was sometimes used. On the street, walking slowly, chomping the gum steadily, keeping the mass in his mouth at the right consistency, he started a money search, strolling through the stream of pedestrians, examining ventilator grates—singles, groups of twos and threes—looking for certain constructions in the ventilator openings, those with horizontal shaft turns just a few feet below the ground surface, creating a spacious ledge, a collecting place for things of every type that would fit through the grate openings. Air flow usually swept paper and other light objects away from the ledges and brighter coins could usually be easily seen. It was just a matter of diligence and patience for Mickey to gather up enough coins to get him through a day of small pleasures.

When he spotted a coin, he stuck a piece of gum to a side face of the nut, pressing sticky material into the threaded hole for positive contact, to keep the gum from separating from the metal at a crucial moment. Squatting on the grate, unmindful of walkers, Mickey carefully lowered the pick-up device through the grate opening, sighting down the string to align the weighted gum above a coin. Occasionally he would retrieve the nut and line and lower it through a different opening because the angle was askew. Everything done correctly, a coin adhered easily to the gum. To be certain, he lightly bounced the string and nut, tapping the coin on the cement below before lifting, just to make sure the coin was securely attached. The mined treasure was brought to the surface and stuffed in a pocket. The next mining attempt only required blowing or wiping dirt off the gum, or sometimes re-chewing it, adding spit for the right degree of stickiness.

Many explorations brought in small amounts, but Mickey did not mind. *It's honest—no trouble this way.* Then he learned of delivering bundled newspapers.

City newspaper printing plants clattered day and night to spew out an endless flow of morning, afternoon, and evening editions to satisfy reading wants of the city's readers. When the evening edition was printed and bundled in early afternoon, trucks were loaded and driven to hundreds of drop-off points about the city, in all boroughs, tossed by handlers from tarpaulin-covered stakebody trucks. Drivers knew where the delivery stops were, and handlers riding the back knew how many regular count and short-count bundles should be left at each place. Every afternoon trucks of several publications crisscrossed the boroughs, often reaching a stop at about the same time as two or three or four competitors' vehicles.

One drop-off point was eight blocks from Mickey's home street. Drivers jockeyed to get as close to it as possible. If they could not completely weave through cars, truck, hand pushcarts, and El columns, a handler had to work doubly hard—bundles first dropped into the street from the tailgate, then laboriously lugged the remaining distance, ten, fifteen, or twenty or so feet. The air would fill with sounds of beeping and blaring horns, angry threats, shrill whistling as a cop worked to clear traffic; with jeers, catcalls, gleeful insulting and laughter of boys who would later carry or cart off bundles to places throughout several neighborhoods.

The boys were hired at so much money a bundle to deliver papers with a newsdealer's name on it from the drop-off point to ubiquitous tiny candy and novelty shops and to little grocery markets and to drugstores and news stands. The delivery boys would gather as much as two hours early before delivery time. It had not taken kids long to make their pick-up sites into social meeting places.

When Mr. Schwartz asked Mickey, in Jewish-accented and city-accented words, if he wanted to make a dime for each of two regular bundles of ten papers and a nickel for a bundle of five papers—"Don' be vorried, sonny, dey are not t'ick, heffy newspapers for a boy your little size. Dey von' be hahd to carry," he said—Mickey quickly agreed. He needed something to do, and could use such easy money; and he had heard the guys always had a good time at the corner. It was a major intersection of the wide thoroughfare under the El and a four-lane east-west transverse street, the same width of the broad north-south avenues. The site was splendid for rambunctious boys. They gathered along two wide sidewalks that were ninety degrees to each other, fronting two sides of a large combination pharmacy and variety store. Wide store doors were set back far from the sidewalk corner and angled widely between street and avenue, creating a large expanse in front of the series of connected doorway entrances. The open pavement, the doorways, the parked cars, weaving traffic, and thick El columns were all part of a large arena for energetic play, for challenges, for being nuisances.

Every afternoon an assortment of handmade orange-crate scooters and battered bicycles littered the corner itself and both the avenue and the street sidewalks, scattered aimlessly, leaning along sides of the store or against cars and trucks or left carelessly sprawled on the sidewalk, looking like wounded animals. Two large wagons with high wood-slat sides added to the clutter of transport, belonging to two boys each with several large bundles to pick up, and equally little attention was paid to where they were left untended, blocking people's paths. Grumbling pedestrians were forced to maneuver through an area that looked as if it had been storm-struck.

The beginning of each afternoon was quiet, slow-paced. Small groups built, and small talk varied—about outwitting teachers and school authorities, telling the latest jokes, relating shrewd escapes from drudgeries and chores of home, comparing movies and movie stars, most of them men, gangsters and heroes alike; trading tales of hooky escapades, planning for days ahead, talking about girls. But as more boys closed in on the corner, the scene grew noisier, activities more boisterous. Tag games were common. Block-long sidewalk races made adults furious, forced to dodge careering ungainly wood-crate scooters driven by fierce charioteers, howling loudly, to scare people out of the way and to keep themselves pumped up emotionally. Unyielding determination and reckless abandon in contests left splintered hulks and remnants along the course. But damaged scooters were easily repaired for the next day's rendezvous. Every boy had an extra one or two two-compartment crates put aside at home, in a cellar or a backyard or on a fire escape, if a whole new body was needed, or one could be pulled apart for replacement braces. And crossbar-handle lumber was held in reserve as spares, too. Front and rear roller skate trucks seemed indestructible and only had to be bolted back in place if they worked loose.

No matter how often a passersby or someone from the store bellowed at a boy or at small groups, or at a large clan, no heed was paid. Only the sight of an approaching police officer tempered the boys' mood. The cop understood restlessness and fun-seeking. He meandered through the score or so of boys, seeming indifferent to them, aware of their studied poses, seemingly busy with quiet conversations or with well behaved pastimes. Occasionally, as a reminder of his presence and authority, he would give a quiet warning about a carelessly strewn scooter or wagon, or a bicycle parked too close to the store's doors. His route and departure were followed attentively by the boys, giving him a full block of distance along his beat before rebuilding the next round of activity and crescendo of sound. The officer knew that would happen when he walked an acceptable distance, but it did not bother him. There would not be any real trouble; he could not recall when there had been anything needing official action. He enjoyed creating the truce between the grownups and the kids, and doing it in this manner made him feel he did his job the right way—the first thing to do was keep the peace.

There was an unmistakable rule at the corner. A newcomer learned it quickly. Mickey had it told to him firmly shortly after his arrival at the corner on his first assignment from Mr. Schwartz's hole-in-the-wall smoke shop and newsstand—no troubles were allowed to be fought over at the corner. It was astonishing to Mickey to later see flaring arguments quickly smothered by everyone nearby. Any disturbance was quietly quelled by as many boys as were needed. He asked why fights did not take place. "That's how it is—and always was. An' it's gonna stay that way!"

The spirit of the corner was a rarity to Mickey. Tensions were diligently eased to harmlessness. Anger and ferocity were not allowed to disrupt the meeting place. That time of day was a relief to each boy there. A curious, welcome peer truce pervaded that small bit of the constantly stirring city. However, there was thriving competition. Stories and jokes were tried to be outdone. Games commenced—pitching pennies from a curb against a wall; hectic rounds of tag, resulting in yelling pedestrians and screeching brakes and blaring horns; light poles were shinnied, racing for fastest times, up, down, and round trip. Any standing object was leap-frogged. Ride-the-pony contests were hearty, noisy, hooting-and-hollering struggles demanding the most efforts for soothing ruffled feathers, for quieting exploding tempers. There was one other contest—severe, only occasionally done. It was reserved to resolve an unusually intense personal competition, or as an ultimate personal dare. Only a few had found nerve to sneak a ride on the back of a bus traveling the long block to the park. Sneaking a second ride on a bus back-end as a means of returning to the corner was doubly impressive, and unquestionably settled whatever matter brought on by a thrown gauntlet. With even a perilous ride in one direction, satisfactorily witnessed, an issue was settled, calm was restored—another corner rule.

Ride-the-pony—simply devised, physical, forceful, strenuous, aggressive, invigorating, energizing, painful, challenging, exhausting, rewarding. When the corner group became large enough—at least three to make a pony, four and five were better—a contest invariably got started. "Hey! We got enough. Whose in for pony?"

Raucous, amiable arguments started over balance in strength, agility, and determination. As many as eight players made customary full teams, with no replacements allowed during a match—one team, decided by luck of a draw, to start as the pony—a form between a building wall and a curb, blocking a sidewalk, making pedestrians scurry round it and into the street to make their way—the other team to be the riders. Boys who did not play cheered on their favorites.

A pony formed with a player's back solidly braced against a building, back straight, feet several inches from the wall, legs slightly bent, spaced widely enough laterally for solid footing. The second team member doubled over forward, feet also widely spaced, placing his head between the anchorman's legs, jamming his shoulders tightly against the anchor's thighs, pushing his neck up into the vee of his teammate's crotch. He encircled his arms securely about the thighs and the anchor's hands gripped the head-down player's armpits from above. Numbers one and two formed the head and neck of the pony.

A third player became part of the pony by contorting into position as number two had, head deep between the legs of the boy ahead, shoulders thrust tightly against the back of his thighs, to start forming the pony's body. The fourth and fifth and other pony team members did the same. An ideal pony had a physically strong neck and back, and a smart, quick-minded head, watching along the back to the rump, the head being a signal-caller, quick with instructions to players by name once the struggle between pony and riders began.

Opponents, equal in number, whether a full team of eight or if fewer, were riders! The undesirable, fretful task of being a referee was thrust on some hapless boy who had not been selected as a member of either team.

A rider took a furiously fast, bounding, running start, from ten feet behind the pony, from out in the street. Rider teams congregated out in the street, usually encircling an El column, intimidating drivers with their shifting mass, resulting in horn tooting and beeping and blaring that added to an afternoon traffic din. A charging, yelling or screaming rider leap-frogged as high and strongly as possible, soaring over the rump, trying to land as hard as possible on the pony's back to break a connection between pony members, then immediately surging further ahead by skootching forward every way possible, legs dangling on either side, using fingers recklessly to make grips and pull himself along, working his torso up and down and moving hips and splayed thighs vigorously forward to get as close to the neck and head as he could. With every warning shout from the pony head, body members stiffened and gripped legs tightly against a rider's crunching landing, shouting muffled encouragement to one another. At the head's warning yell, or feeling impact, the pony was allowed to momentarily sway side to side to keep the rider from clambering forward, struggling for arm-encircling contact with a rider ahead. A rider would try to force himself between coupled pony members, rupturing the connection without his own feet touching the ground. If pony-player grips failed from lack of strength or sudden or no longer endurable pain, and the pony came apart, that ride was over. The pony lost, riders won a point. If a leaping rider was unstable, unable to maintain a grip or balance with legs or arms or hands on the momentarily bucking bronco and fell to the pavement, or if a rider's foot touched the ground, the ride was done. The pony won, riders lost.

There were constant and usually frantic differences over whether a rider's foot touched pavement or a pony connection had really been broken. The rule was that a referee could not quit his assignment and he quickly became harried and frazzled, and rooting onlookers added to the confusion and noise.

The real test was when all riders were in place. Closely watched by the head-player, and calling a sharp command at the instant the last rider landed heavily into place, the pony twisted and pitched wildly. Individual pony-players either responded by name to curt, frantic shouted orders from the head or reacted to what they sensed had to be done at their point in the formation to toss off a hand-clawing rider trying to hook ankles at the pony's underside.

Riders grabbed at anything—with two exceptions; eyes and ears were forbidden, under threat of expulsion from corner activities—to remain with the pony, veering at reckless angles atop the pony to counteract yawing, bucking, swaying pony gyrations. Clothing and flesh were clamped, torn at, clawed, scraped, and stretched.

The pony bucked so high that feet of pony-members lifted from the pavement. The articulated line writhed so desperately that mingled pony and rider bodies often came perilously close to crashing down. Victories had to be clearly won, decided by the referee. In many contests a tie was declared when entangled bodies collapsed in a heap, laughing, cursing, gasping, grunting, moaning with pleasure or pain. Long, loud vocal differences that seemed they might turn physical were pulled up short with a draw ordered by team leaders. With a draw, teams continued their roles.

After each team gained a point, roles were switched; riders became the pony, the pony split apart to become riders. Another struggle began until two points won the day for a team. Time, injuries, exhaustion, and loss of intensity usually prevented another three-point match. Sometimes if full eight-player teams could not be initially formed, another smaller pony game might later be started when several more boys gathered at the corner.

Mickey garnered scrapes, pulled muscles, bruises, pains, and pleasures, pleased with the unvicious roughness, the growing strength he felt, his own sense of victory with his team's wins.

In three weeks Mickey felt accepted—*I think I'm in OK wit' these guys. I'm gettin' along pretty good with most of 'em.* During the last part of summer he had a sense of always having been a part of life there for two to three hours or more five times a week. He laughed easily, told jokes well. He worked hard at and quietly suffered the rigors and pain of being a struggling bronco-busting rider or part of a writhing, battling pony. As others did, he boasted about his bluish and yellowish and purplish body discolorations as they accumulated. One afternoon he was kidded mercilessly about his smallness and being a lightweight by two boys who only outmatched him slightly, but they had seniority on the corner, so Mickey complained to no one else. In a short time he thought some of their joshings were more intense, more challenging. He worried what was behind it, wondered if he was right about such worrying.

Mickey felt strange sensations on some days when he joined goings-on near the pharmacy doors. One time his neck tingled in the back. Once he swore that neck hairs rose. But he busied himself quickly each time he felt nervousness or uncertainty, distracting himself with something physical rather than getting drawn into talk.

One gloomy afternoon there were no games when Mickey arrived, just a knot of boys along one wall of the building, a dozen feet from the doors, around the corner from the usual avenue side of the meeting area. In minutes Mickey was being kidded, then needled by Blackie and Chet, the two annoyers who had started pestering him a few days before. Then he was asked point blank if he was ever going to snitch a ride on a bus.

He felt desperation. He thought about simply saying he did not *feel* like doing it—had not given it much thought—besides, it was not such a big thing to do— he could do it if he *felt* like it, but did not see much reason to—but he kept quiet, staring back at faces that stared at him.

From the circle of boys words babbled at him. "There's plenty o' time before the trucks show up!"; "Mosta the guys are gonna be late—so there ain' enough of us to make up sides fer anythin'"; "Hey, kid—you stan' aroun' watchin' other guys when they're makin' their run—an' you kid with 'em when it's over. Now how 'bout you?"

The circle, spewing words in low tones, slowly shifted from the wall, sidling across the sidewalk, to the curb, easing Mickey, in the middle, along with it, with deliberate timing. The small group's sounds were covered by the wheezing and squealing of a long green bus coming to a halt. As it rolled by, Mickey, in a quick glance, saw only a few seated passengers. The driver was a hulking figure who appeared to be much too large for his seat.

The circle of boys crowded the curb at the rear of the bus, shielding Mickey from the driver's view in his tall, narrow right-side mirror outside the front door. The circle tightened, then opened, shunting Mickey into the street. Faces in the cluster smiled and laughed. Someone muttered, "Better hurry up an' get ready, kiddo!"

Mickey pleaded that his sneaker soles were too smooth to be any good. The boys were quiet, staring, some frowning. The driver took his foot off the airbrake pedal. The sharp hissing swoosh accented the demanding looks of the boys. Mickey made a scrambling leap for the back of the slowly moving bus.

His right hand flew up to grab a small side reflector fastened to the curved corner, squeezing it tightly. One foot slapped against a narrow, down-sloping shelf across the bottom of the bus, a foot above the ground, as his left hand clawed at the rear window rubber molding. With these weak connections to the machine, he hopped on his other foot along the asphalt, trying to improve grips to pull himself onto a safe position out of the driver's sight. The bus swerved from the curb, centrifugal force working at Mickey's body, harshly, tugging, almost making him lose his grip and footing. He started to panic but remembered his peers watching. He could hear encouraging yells as he clambered to stay with the bus, growling and roaring into traffic, rushing faster and faster.

The bus charged into its straightaway route, accelerating more, only narrow space between it and parked cars, rumbling headlong to the next broad road, the west drive bordering Central Park. The engine clattered and roared inches from Mickey, on the other side of a diamond-grate partition against which he tightly pressed, pushing to be part of the bus, to get into its skin, struggling to keep from smashing into blurry black pavement.

The back end of the bus vibrated frighteningly. The acrid stench of swirling exhaust fumes was sickening. Thin spots of oil spattered on the improvised footrest kept the worn rubber soles of his sneakers from gripping firmly. Mickey was in an ungainly position, clinging in fright that was growing to terror, trying to be unseen by the driver in either an exterior sideview mirror or the inside wide overhead rearview mirror at the front of the bus. He bent at the waist awkwardly, discomfort and pain increasing, buttocks stuck out, pressing his torso sideways as much as he could against the bus body; shifting weight tentatively from one tiring leg to the other tiring leg; forcing one sliding foot after the other back up the shaking, slippery angled shelf. He screamed aloud: "Hang on!—hang!—Jesus!—don' get yaself killed, ya shithead!"

Oh God—let me make it!

He stretched to the right, moving his head to the bus corner, peering ahead along the bus's side to see how much longer his ride would last. The rushing wind watered his eyes; road dirt pestered his face. He jerked his head back, squeezing eyelids shuts, more afraid. He clung tenaciously as the bus whooshed past a score or more of parked cars.

Jesus!—oh, God—please!—help me hang on!

The leviathan rumbled east, jerking and surging as the driver manipulated brake and accelerator pedals erratically in his duel with drivers and jaywalking pedestrians. Mickey agonized with each jolt and swerve. One specially forceful forward surge made it feel as though the footrest had been snapped from under his sneakers, as a magician snaps a tablecloth from beneath a dinner setting. But only one foot trailed in the air. Then the other one slid slowly, fractionally, down the smooth ramp. Fingers hooked onto the rear window ached from cramps. Hands and arms tensed, straining to support increasing weight as his legs failed. The trailing foot bumped along the asphalt. The bouncing created more drag and harsh, punishing force. He lost strength in the leg still on the bus. It slid off the incline as he struggled futilely, as he screamed.

His toes scraped along the rough street surface. Bent, clawing fingers on the window molding could no longer withstand yanks and cramps. Mickey lost that grip, crying out in anguish, yelling loudly aloud at the sudden pain in his right shoulder socket as he dangled by his stretched arm from the corner reflector. His feet bounced unrhythmically on the pavement.

He sensed the bus slowing; straining weakly to pull himself up to where he could scramble along in a semblance of running, to get balance well enough to let go entirely, to run safely, to mercifully stop struggling. His body twisted left and right as he kept his death grip on the reflector, dangling from the reflector, like a wobbling fish lure being trolled. He scratched left-hand fingers blindly at the bus, grasping for anything to grip. He pictured being terribly broken, like a collapsed, disjointed, sprawling marionette. He shrieked in terror at the split-second image of his head bursting open, sounding like a dropped watermelon spraying its watery liquid and black seeds in every direction. He saw his head thumping, bouncing, and coming apart, splattering brains and blood everywhere, streaking the black road.

Hard braking and a sharp turn toward the curb tore Mickey loose from his fragile union with the bus. In the next ten to twelve feet, he slammed hard onto the pavement, bouncing and tumbling, struggling to keep his head pulled in, chin tucked to chest, his body scraping the oily, coarse asphalt, straining to wrap arms about his head and keep them there. He saw a flailing arm slam a parked car.

His legs jerked about in the air, smacked the ground, bounced, kicked aimlessly, were still. He lay on his right side, staring at gray exhaust fumes spewing from the bus several feet away. His right shoulder felt like it was on fire. People were shouting. Those who had run reached him as he sat up slowly and groped at himself with numb fingers, touching the painful shoulder. Thin sleeves of his sweater and shirt had been torn through on one arm. Skin on the back of a hand was abraded into a large, moist, burning wound. People stood in a circle talking at him or with one another, some yelling. Three times he was asked if he was all right. Hazily, he could see a gray uniform looming over his head. It was shouting, cursing, waving a fist. A woman reached out to Mickey, but he pulled away.

His nose hurt. Blood streamed from it, leaking into his mouth, dripping down his chin onto his shirt. People asked unintelligible questions. His ears were ringing. Cheeks and chin burned. They were scraped raw. He could not recall hitting his nose but it hurt. The bridge was swelling, tender to touch.

Mickey staggered to his feet, waving off reaching hands. He tested himself, shifting weight slowly from leg to leg, touching knees and elbows, head, ribs, arms. Nothing seemed broken, only numb or sore, and there were a lot of scrapes on his skin. The hubbub slackened. He pushed through the ring of adults, heading away from the big, angry bus driver threatening to whip the shit out of him, if he could get his hands on him, who would see that he got arrested, too! Mickey wriggled away from his big hands and slipped through people extending hands to help him and ran across the street at a slow trot, shutting out high-pitched obscenities yelled by the driver.

Across the street and a quarter block from fading yells, he touched himself again in a few places. *Jesus Christ!—I coulda been killed!*

What a fuckin' dummy!

Blood still trickled from his nose. Now his lips were burning from cuts, blood seeping from them, too. His nose was swollen worse. He could not breathe through nostrils, instead gulping air through his mouth, drooling and spraying blood with each gasp. He pulled a wadded, soiled handkerchief from a back pocket—*Shit! My pants are all torn, too!*—wiping his chin and lips, pressing the cloth hard against his nose, sopping up blood, trying to stop the seepage.

He limped toward the drop-off corner, planning explanations of his appearance, determined to quit the limp when he arrived. He had not heard of anyone else falling off a bus before. What would they say? *Screw 'em! I'll jus' say a car cut at me jus' when I hopped off at the end and it clipped me an' knocked me down—an' almost' ran me over, it did—but I was too quick for it!—rolled right outta the way—quick as ya please—yep!*

Shock kept pain from washing over him quickly. He moved faster toward the corner, an exhilaration filling him. *I DONE the damn ride!—without even a chance to get ready—no right kinda sneakers—no wipin' off where I hadda stand—nothin'!—no chance to think about it—no chance to get my mind made up!*

Whoopee!

He tallied his injuries, thinking again that he could have been hurt worse, even killed, because of what happened in only a few seconds. He wondered about death. Comprehending it was difficult, troublesome. His rooftop leap to a clothesline pole flashed in his mind. *What a fuckin' stupid thing tha' was—such an easy way to get myself killed!—an' hidin' on that subway track, with all that 'lectricity and maybe a train squashin' me good jus' cuz I was tryin' to get away from that colored kid.*

He tried to shake off thoughts of death, but it kept plaguing him. *Does anyone ever talk about it? I never even heard my ol' man ever say nothin' 'bout it. He musta known somebody who died. I won'er why he never said nothin' to me or Margaret about dyin'? An' none o' the kids I knew ever said nothin' either.*

He only knew what *looked* terrible. *Like that girl at tha' coal truck! Part o' her hadda be flat after bein' under that big wheel—with that full load o' coal on—flatter'n a pancake! Jesus! What tha' musta been like for whoever got her outta there!*

But her face looked all right—like she was sleepin'—'cep' for the red puddle under her cheek. An' that colored man covered with the sheet all spotted with red bein' carried out on the stretcher from the buildin' to the ambulance. People said he was dead, what with his face bein' covered with the sheet—an' his brown ankles stickin' out from under. Wonder if his face looked like he was sleepin'?—or like he was scared?—like I seen in movies.

The last Mickey had seen the colored man before being on the stretcher was from about a half block away, from a hiding place in a first-floor vestibule just behind a sawhorse-and-clothesline police cordon keeping back curious spectators. A distant small dark dot atop a white shirt darted back and forth in an open fourth floor window, sending out aimless bright bursts of color and sharp-sounding poppings and ricochet whinings at police on the street and in windows opposite his own. The police chipped away the brickwork on all sides of the colored man's window in puffs of reddish dust, sniping at him with rifles and revolvers.

That was Mickey's limited knowledge of death. Bloodless shootings in western and gangster movies or the disappearance of someone struck by space-gun rays seemed harmless, even glamorous, not ugly, not final.

A roar built behind Mickey, a bus shifting gears, changing speeds, accelerating noisily from the park end of the long street. He glanced over a shoulder, saw the bus charging, overtaking two slow-moving cars. The first car, just passing Mickey, at the three-quarter mark to the newspaper corner, had a nervous-looking middle-aged woman driving hesitantly. Her car straddled the double white center line dividing the four traffic lanes. Opposing drivers honked and blared horns, but she did not budge from where she felt safe, away from parked cars on her side of the street. Mickey had a sudden idea.

He broke into a fast run, glancing back to locate the bus. The two cars and the bus had progressed, the rear of the decelerating bus abreast of Mickey when he darted between two parked cars. His timing was perfect. He gained on the slowing bus in only two or three seconds. It squealed to a halt at the corner opposite the pharmacy. In the bus's last few feet of slow movement, Mickey leaped onto the back end at the right corner, into perfect position for snitching a ride. In three to four seconds, and at almost the same moment as he saw boys who had goaded him come into sight, he lightly hopped from the bus to the pavement. They applauded and cheered as he flamboyantly lunged toward them between moving vehicles traveling in two directions.

Praise and questions flew as he told his lie of being hit by the car when he reached the park and a long, harrowing, painful ride all the way back on a return, westbound bus. For an hour he was the hero of the corner, urged to retell the escapade to new groups as more boys appeared. Mickey did not need to elaborate the first bus ride, but the return was generously embellished with suspense, danger, strength, endurance, and determination. Then the delivery trucks started arriving.

By then Mickey had washed in the pharmacy's men's room. He took off the shirt and thin sweater and rinsed bloody spots on them under cold water to get rid of the stains. He shivered putting each on again, but he knew they would be dry and unnoticeable by the time he got home, sleeves pulled up high on his arms to hide fabric rips and tears. He worried more about the bruises and scrapes on his face and his swollen nose. He was betting it was broken again. The bridge hurt when he touched it, and he still could not breathe through the nostrils. It felt the same as that other time, playing catcher in a pickup baseball game during a boys' club outing at Bear Mountain up the river.

He had lunged far left to grab at a wild pitch that floated behind a batter—but the eager, unskilled hitter swung clumsily at the bad throw. That swing was nearly completed behind his back when the whirling heavy end of the bat smashed into Mickey's face, his eyes on the erratically sailing ball dropping in an arc behind the batter, his mitt aiming to intercept the ball.

Blinding flashes of color exploded like fireworks in split-second changing eruptions. Mickey heard a crunching sound in his head. He heard a short, grunting, hoarse yell that ended quickly, but did not know it was his own cry. The explosions were gone suddenly. Instead there was what seemed only an instant of blackness, diffusing into grayness, steadily lightening, first at the edges. Great separate aches in his head throbbed; continuous high-pitched ringing sounds accented a god-awful pain. The deep gray turned the color of thin fog, then the fog dissipated. He realized he was sprawled on his back, frowning at the sky. Slowly he opened his eyes and moved them a little from side to side. People's faces came into focus. Beyond them, he could see green trees poking up, sticking into the sky.

But now it was different, here at the street corner. There had been no unconsciousness, but the pain, constant for minutes at a time, was as bothersome as before—and there were the same lingering buzzing and ringing in his head as last summer. It hurt to just barely touch his swollen nose, testing its condition. *The fuckin' thing is sure enough broken again all right! Jesus H. Christ!*

The three bundles labeled Schwartz eventually were accessible in the sorting. Mickey needed help to hoist them onto a shoulder. He was stiffening from the physical battering, and it hurt to bend down and stand straight and lift arms and walk and grasp things and turn his head in any direction, even lift it up and press it down. He started on the eight-block walk north, worried that he would not have stamina for the distance. The bundles seemed to get heavier with each block traveled. He was staggering by the time he was only halfway to Mr. Schwartz's store. He dropped the bundles heavily to the pavement, gasping. He thought about telling Mr. Schwartz that his papers had not been delivered, but in two or three seconds discarded that notion. He rested several minutes, papers carelessly piled at his feet. He could not think of anything even he himself deemed believable.

He got the help of a man passing by who easily lifted the bundles onto Mickey's shoulder. The boy plodded north, feeling miserable about his lot at the moment and about his lot in general, annoyed because he felt pain and stiffness; but on this part of the trip he wobbled less than before. Half a block from the newsstand he crossed the avenue, going under the El, heading directly for Mr. Schwartz, an old, heavy figure hunched in his doorway, peering south, wondering why Mickey was late again.

There was a gap in the traffic in both directions, in the two lanes beneath the El and in near and far lanes outside the columns. His split-second evaluation was *that* was the moment to dart to the store, to show Mr. Schwartz he really was eager, that being late was not his fault. He started trotting to the far curb, breaking into a stumbling run when unseen car horns tooted and blared angrily. Then it became a headlong, careering dash, aiming for Mr. Schwartz, who was startled by the sudden warning blasts and stared wide-eyed at Mickey's foolhardiness.

Mickey tripped, missing his footing at the curb, desperately clutching at the three bundles flying away from his shoulder like planes peeling away from a tight flying formation. Hands clawing air, striking out, stretching for the papers, were useless in his tumbling fall. He cried out sharply at new pain when his scraped shoulder slid across the sidewalk. In seconds, every earlier wound was pummeled in the two rolls he took, stopping at Mr. Schwartz's feet.

He could no longer restrain tears. There was no need. No peer was present to see him. He felt extraordinary humiliation, sprawled clumsily, Mr. Schwartz glowering down at him. Mickey raged at himself, damning inability to do things right. He was afraid.

Jesus!—I'm scared shitless! Wait'll I get caught at home lookin' like this!

Mr. Schwartz tugged at him, lifting up, gasping, softly saying Jewish words. He held Mickey closely, saying in English that it was all right to cry, speaking Yiddish again, consoling with more English, using calming words of whichever language seemed best to him, stilling Mickey's trembling. Only Aunt Ellen had held him like this before, after his trouble at the Weinsteins' drugstore.

Mr. Schwartz, jerking nervously, as Mickey sat hunched on the sidewalk, dragged a newspaper bundle across the cement, clenching painfully at the heavy manila cord knotted at the top. Mickey felt ashamed, watching him. Mr. Schwartz's face, above his scraggly beard and mustache, was red. He seemed in pain. He held a hand to his chest as he pulled the bundle in short strokes. Mickey grew angrier with himself—*he* was always the one who carried bundles inside, who heaved them onto a counter, cut cords, spread newspapers along the countertop, tidied up by throwing cords in a wastebasket.

Mr. Schwartz shouldn' be doin' that! It's my job—what am I bein' paid for, goddam it! He's too old for this kinda stuff! Mickey struggled to his feet, making awkward movements, looking like a crippled animal. He gently tugged the bundle away from Mr. Schwartz, jerked it up off the pavement, swinging and lifting it to just inside the door, dropping it lightly it onto the cigar case top, then doing the same with the other bundles. He snipped cords with shears, spread the papers tidily along the thick glass top, carefully put the cords in the trash box, and ran from the store without stopping for his money, usually paid each day.

The two-block walk home seemed longer than usual to Mickey. He dawdled along the way, betting with himself no one would be at the tenement apartment; planning what to say about his facial appearance and the condition of his clothes if someone was there. He was lucky again and won his bet. No one was home. A scrawled note said his father had stopped by for a sandwich after delivering a fare over on Riverside Drive and he would be working until eight o'clock, maybe later.

Mickey washed his wounds, carefully this time, using soap and warm water. He lightly smeared painless mercurochrome on facial marks, but agonized through slow painting of the large shoulder scrape with dark brown, searing iodine. He suffered equally while daubing iodine on other tender marks that would be concealed by clothing, clenching his jaws, softly grunting, groaning, and whimpering with strokes of the slim glass rod applicator. He bandaged the shoulder injury, then buried the shirt and sweater at the bottom of the trash can in the backyard.

From the time his father reached home, Mickey sat or moved about with his head down or with the most marked side of his face turned away or covered by a seemingly casual hand. He had worked at making the bright red mercurochrome marks fade to light pink with soap and water, but the scrapes were beginning to scab over. The marks were darkening, easy to see, and his father did.

He was skeptical about Mickey's answers. "That story had better be right, hear? Because I'm checking with Schwartz. I don't see how you could get that many marks on your face from tripping over a curb."

Mickey was not much of a hero at the corner the next afternoon. Everyone was involved with usual activities, none of which interested him. His mind was absorbed with what Mr. Schwartz would tell his father, what would happen after that. He was too weary to play or root for anyone, but a night's rest and sleeping late in the morning boosted his strength so he had no trouble hoisting Mr. Schwartz's bundles and carrying them eight blocks.

Mr. Schwartz said his father had stopped by. "So I tol' him jus' vaht I seen awreddy,"—Mickey groaned, anticipating his father's anger—"an' vaht a good boy you vahs, t'inking 'bout de papers an' 'bout me instead of youself—puttin' dem all inside even so you was hoit.

"Of course, now daht I t'ink 'bout it, I guess didn' t'ink to tell him daht ya vahs so reckless—runnin' careless like daht 'cross de street an' trew all those movin' cahs like ya did."

The next afternoon his father was unexpectedly home when Mickey, before going to see Mr. Schwartz and then to the newspaper corner, stopped by in midafternoon to leave some comic books a friend had lent him. In the center of the front room was a small, well worn, faded-red four-wheeled child's wagon, pull-handle resting on the floor.

"If you're going to be so clumsy,"—his father snapped, "from now on I want you using this wagon to cart Mr. Schwartz's papers! I'm not taking any chances you'll fall again—and tear clothes next time." Mickey stared at the wagon.

"Clothes are hard to get these days! Money doesn't grow on trees, damn it!" Mickey sighed. "I know this thing will be useful—and you'll see how much easier your job will be for you."

Mickey said, "Excuse me. I hafta go to the bathroom before I leave." He was stunned. *I can' show up at the corner with that dinky-lookin' thing! It ain' no way as sharp as those neat big ones a couple o' guys down there got. This lousy li'l' thing for a lousy small bunch o' papers anybody could carry with one hand! I'll be laughed at every time!*

The handle was too short for Mickey to use without bending down, and then it was uncomfortable. So his father tied a length of doubled clothesline to the metal handle as an extension, forming a loop handle.

A block from the newspaper corner, after dejectedly walking head down, towing the rattling wagon, one wheel making a clunk-sound each time a long flat spot rolled across the pavement, Mickey solved his dilemma. He hid the wagon behind garbage cans in an alley between buildings. And he worked up an excuse for his father if it was gone when he got back: A gang of tough kids stole it, yanking it right out of his hands as he started to battle them. He had worried about getting his clothes torn, so he let them have it—but at least they let him keep the papers.

Each afternoon, at the corner, he hoisted Mr. Schwartz's bundles to a shoulder and left at an energetic pace. A block north, across the avenue, he transferred the small bundles to the rickety wagon. From this point, he really did not mind using the cart; it did make work easier. And if his father ever asked Mr. Schwartz about Mickey hauling the papers as he ought to be, the old man could answer honestly. *Pretty damn smart, ain' I?*

After his last afternoon at the corner Mickey was disappointed he would not be lugging Mr. Schwartz's papers anymore. He would miss the pocket money; his father had let him keep half of it. He explained to the storekeeper that he would not be getting back into his neighborhood from the distant high school until after the time he was usually reaching Mr. Schwartz's store with newspapers. Mr. Schwartz had frowned when Mickey told him two days before, then sighed, "Vell, t'ings go on, don' dey?"

Mickey sat halfway up the stone steps of his building. *Tha' kid who tol' me 'bout the papers was right. I did have a helluva good time mos' days—an' I was a hero to those guys for a little bit.*

45

*H*ero, hell!

But still lucky!

At least lucky enough to be sitting here—waiting for God knows what after getting out of this place.

He randomly and briefly focused attention at places about the room, looking at other occupants, wondering what they were thinking, what they were feeling.

I wonder if any of them grew up like I did?—doing those kinds of things—lousy things—going like hell using up my nine lives—and only once in a while having some plus thing along with all the minuses.

Always moving around in the city, living in one apartment after another, that was a minus—and never staying anywhere very long—not long enough to make any real friends—and starting high school in a place a long way off sure was a minus.

But Sing Lee was a plus—and so was that How Chin peddler friend of his—and so were Mrs. Kelsey, with her Martin and David.

46

Mickey made his first trip to the new school on the Tuesday after the Labor Day holiday, detesting the journey even as he made it, detesting the school without having been in it, or even seen it, or even been anywhere near it. It meant getting up a lot earlier, followed quickly with a long walk to a subway station that was farther than to his former school building. The ride was long, noisy, and monotonous. The long string of cars was sparsely occupied; adults here and there throughout, absorbed in reading, or heads lolling in rhythm with car movements; few boys or girls his age, usually lone travelers, preferring to be alone, he strongly sensed, or sitting in pairs, to feel secure, close to each other, talking in low voices, ignoring anyone else.

When the local subway went south two stops to an express stop, Mickey got off and changed to a northbound express that switched onto tracks going to another borough. There the subway left its burrow to become an elevated train rattling deafeningly between block after block of apartment buildings and stores, then tenements and factories and warehouses, then taller apartment buildings— less congested residential neighborhoods with wider streets, with greenery.

The new school seemed overwhelming. It was the largest in physical size that he had attended, and had the most students. Four grades—freshman, sophomore, junior, and senior—hundreds of teen-aged children—converged on its building each day, swarming hall mazes, clambering stairways, cramming classrooms and lunchrooms.

In a short time Mickey sensed a society in the gray buildings similar to the HR Club. Each grade disdained the one below it, the freshman class burdened with the combined snobbishness and arrogance of three other grades still essentially their peers, still children. Within each grade cliques prevailed. Nationalities, religions, and races clashed, too. The new, higher level of school environment quickly seemed to be little different from what Mickey thought had been left in the past when he stared up at the massive, solid-looking stone edifice for the first time. It was difficult to make friends. Everyone seemed suspicious. Mickey was suspicious, wary of Buddy Caseys, Tony Minellis, and Jerrys.

In a month he wanted to quit high school, but knew it was impossible. However, he gradually learned hooky was easy at the big school. There were only two truant officers. An occasional day's absence, pleading illness, was perfunctorily accepted on a student's say-so. Two days out of school needed a parental excuse note. But Mickey resolved that vexation—cleverly, he thought.

He composed a brief, plausible explanation, first writing a handwritten note slowly, thoughtfully, following a prototype he had made by copying a genuine excuse note his father had written during the last grade-school term. Mickey had been surprised when that teacher had looked at the note and handed it back to him rather then keeping it on file. He started to put it in a waste basket near the teacher's desk, then refolded it and put it between pages of a schoolbook. In a flash he had a glimmer of an idea that such a note might one day be useful. Several months later he schemed its use.

Here and there he drew a line through a word, putting in another, making certain the message still sounded adult, using words his father used when talking. Next, he laboriously tapped key after key of his father's secondhand office typewriter to slowly produce the excuse. At the bottom, from the secretly stored last term's note, he carefully traced his father's scrawled, hen-scratching signature, holding two sheets of paper tightly against a sun-brightened window pane. When the error-free note, bearing what looked to be a genuine signature in ink, was readily accepted by the teacher, and kept, and when nothing adverse about the note happened after a week, Mickey was sure he had successfully resolved another matter of getting by in his existence.

His first report card had passing grades, good deportment, and attendance was marked only at three days absent, two of them covered by one forged note. The six-week report card was given to students to take home for parental review and signature. Mickey had kept his in pages of a book in a stack in his room for three days when the teacher reminded the class that the cards were due back in two more days. He had been unconcerned when he prepared the note, but now he was worried about the absences tallied on the card.

"I know," the teacher said, "some of you *wish* you didn't need them looked at and signed, but they will *have* to be one of these days. So you might as well get it over with!"

I been tryin' to dream up somethin' 'bout that two-day thing I signed his name to a couple o' weeks ago—but what do I say to the ol' man if he asks about it—an' sure as shit he will!—damn! On the morning the card was due back, he pressed it to a window pane, on top of the note with his father's signature. *This is twice now this ol' note has come in handy!* The light coming through the paper and the card was weak, but sufficient. *The ol' man won' get aroun' to askin' 'bout a report card anyway. I'll worry 'bout that later.* At the start of school the next day he confidently put the card on the teacher's desk.

Life became more bearable for Mickey as hooky became simpler in late autumn. Then one evening his father told Mickey he had arranged an after-school job for him with a Chinese laundry owner, a man named Sing Lee, and the laundry was in the front basement of a building several blocks away. It was a short distance but the broad avenue he would cross was one border of an affluent neighborhood extending three blocks west and down the hill to the wide Hudson River.

Sing Lee's hand laundry was in a predominantly upper middle class Jewish neighborhood in the west side middle seventies and Mickey's father had delivered Sing Lee by cab to the Chinese man's darkened store late one night. His father had first driven tourists to Chinatown and all four had just left the cab when Sing Lee, slightly drunk and excited over a good night at gambling with friends, flagged him. Worried about a long subway trip with pockets full of winnings, Sing Lee happily wanted to pay for security. Driver and passenger was each surprised at the coincidence of living several blocks apart uptown, and Mickey's part-time job came about because of Sing Lee's talk of increasing workload, his need to get completed work delivered, to get soiled material picked up.

Mickey's father and Sing Lee agreed Mickey could spend two hours a day with the laundry owner each of five days after school, plus each Saturday morning until noon, but sometimes until about three o'clock in the afternoon just before holidays when he was extra busy. Sing Lee would pay the boy fifty cents a week and said Mickey would keep all the tips he earned from customers, but Mickey was disgruntled when his father sternly instructed him to turn over all money. But he made no protest. He knew, in time, he would work out some plan to keep a share—*jus' like at the Weinsteins' drugstore.*

Mickey was apprehensive. *Oh, no!—the guy's a Chink! What does a Chinaman do besides work in restaurants? Wha's there to runnin' a laundry? How much work could there be for a kid like me? There won' be any real tips—not like the drugstore!*

The laundry was in a storefront, the only one in the long block. It had steam-covered six-foot-by-six-foot plate glass window with a large, bold, broadly curved red-letter sign reading SING LEE; below it, tucked horizontally into the arc of the owner's name there was a straight line in smaller bold letters: Hand Laundry. The store interior was long and narrow, once a basement railroad apartment and converted to a store by installing a large plate glass window overlooking the sidewalk. The store was cluttered, smelling of ironed starch, humid with steam from two large washing machines in each of two small rooms and a small cylindrical sleeve press and a big, corner-filling mangle press in two larger rooms. Farther into the flat was a tiny bedroom and an adjacent small hallway alcove with a double hot-plate on a counter and a wall cabinet containing a few cups, glasses, dishes, and tray of eating utensils.

Mickey entered the store hesitantly, a step behind his father, seeing no one inside. His father approached the high, wide counter extending across the room, putting a hand out and tapping the small bell on the counter three times. Suddenly Mickey was startled by a broad, flat face popping up from behind the counter, impatient with bell-ringing, looking to see who had opened the creaky door. The face seemed more light brown than the true yellow Mickey had anticipated. It remained completely expressionless as Mickey's father introduced the boy and man to each other. Sing Lee was small, not much taller than Mickey, and wiry-looking. He seemed to have no fat on him. Veins stood out on his hands and arms. Neck muscle cords and veins were so prominent they looked as if they might burst. Dark eyes peered intently through slitted, slanted eyelids. Sing Lee was the image of every Oriental Mickey recalled seeing in the movies. It made him nervous. The Chinaman, unblinking, stared at Mickey as his father recounted the boy's chores and other terms of the job Mickey would start the next afternoon. Then with a sudden broad grin, exposing large, even yellowed teeth—a grin Mickey realized was sincere and friendly—he extended a thin, bony arm and strong bony fingers across the counter to welcome the boy. Mickey started working for Sing Lee the next afternoon.

The storeowner spoke better English than Mickey had expected, soft, lilting, rising and lowering tones. But he was not fluent and had difficulty with some sounds and words and had many peculiar pronunciations. However, they communicated easily, often with laughter over his expressions and Mickey's confusion trying to understand. The work was easy. Delivery bundles were often bulky, but everything was lightweight. Customers were in a four-square-block area of six-, seven-, and eight-story apartment buildings, each with an automatic elevator. Occasionally he lugged one or more bulging pillowcases stuffed with soiled clothing and bed linen from customers back to Sing Lee to be redone. The lugging was clumsy, heavier, tiring work, but when a customer saved time and effort, Mickey got a more generous tip than for only making a delivery.

Exploring the neighborhood excited Mickey. In one backyard, returning from a delivery through a newly discovered shortcut, he found a loose, large rock in a stone-and-brick foundation wall. Idly chipping away the little remaining deteriorated mortar, he easily pulled out the block of stone, exposing a squarish opening. *What a perfect hidin' place for somethin'—maybe a school book—maybe two. Stan' 'em up on edge an' the rock would stick out only an inch, maybe even less.*

In the second week Sing Lee asked Mickey to do him a favor. He had been so busy working that he had had no time to go to the butcher shop for meat for his supper meal after closing the laundry. "You go bootcha two brock up heer and down one brock." Mickey had become accustomed to his old-country-Chinese difficulty in pronouncing the letters *l* and *r*—something he learned from B-movies with Oriental characters—and knew the man meant *hill* for *heer* and *block* instead of *brock*. "You buy me one-kwahtuh-poun' frung stick—no maw." He extended five one dollar bills to Mickey. "Here, you take maw money than you need."

The butcher looked puzzled. "Frung stick? I don't carry anything like that. What kind of meat is it? Beef? Pork? Poultry maybe?"

Empty-handed, Mickey returned to the store and dutifully reported to Sing Lee, who said, "No frung stick I no bereeve! He have much frung stick! I buy flum him two, thlee time a week!"

"Well," Mickey said, "I'll jus' go back an' ask him again. Maybe I didn' order right. Frung stick, right?"

"Frung stick!—frung stick! He know. I buy him because he awra time"—Mickey knew he meant *all the time*—"have flesh meat. He know I have—uh—spesh–ee–ar"—Mickey knew he meant *special*—"way to cook. We tawk of it many time."

Mickey reiterated his order to the butcher. "You're s'posed to have a lot of it all the time. The one I'm gettin' it for said so. He said you got it in the big refrigerator behind ya there, and in the meat counter here in the front, too."

The butcher motioned Mickey to one end of the long refrigerated showcase. "Now you follow me along on your side, looking in the front there, and I'll go along this side. Now—here's what I've got."

In unison they moved to the other end of the case, the butcher itemizing each white enamel tray's content. "And everything in the walk-in freezer is out here in this case. See? *No frung stick!*"

Frustrated again, Mickey trudged to the laundry. The Chinese man rolled his eyes to the ceiling, pressing hands together in prayer fashion at his chest, uttering a string of foreign words Mickey was sure were oaths more than prayer. "I go myserf but too busy. Things in wash must come out now!" Pointing to the side of his torso, he said, "Frung stick!—frung stick! Many time buy flum him! You tell bootcha man that!—is wha' I buy awra time!"

Mickey rushed off again, breathlessly explaining and gesturing to the butcher, pointing at his own body as Sing Lee had pointed at his. "The darned Chinaman says he always gets it from you!"

The butcher laughed loudly. "Well now, why didn't you say it was for the Chinese customer? I *do* have what he wants." The meat cut name he explained was not anything Mickey had ever heard. "All I know for names," he told the butcher, "is hamburger—we get a lotta that at home—an' I know 'bout steaks an' pork chops—but not a lotta *those* at our house—an' bacon—ham—liver—ugh!"

The butcher weighed and wrapped a small piece of meat, taking money and giving change. "Don't worry, this is what Mr. Lee always buys. Too bad you didn't say Mr. Lee right away. I would have known what you wanted—saved you a lot of trouble."

Mickey felt uncertain when he laid the small package and change before Sing Lee, hesitantly explaining that it might not be right but the butcher insisted he take it. The laundryman opened the paper wrapping, looked at the meat, looked at Mickey, smiling. "Ah—*frung stick!*"

Mickey relaxed. "But the butcher said it's *flank steak.*" Sing Lee looked at Mickey. "Yes—is light. Is what I say—frung stick."

There was an Irish family—the Kelseys—in the midst of many Jewish residents. They lived in a large ground-floor apartment in a building diagonally across from Sing Lee's, slightly up the hill. The older of the two boys was Mickey's age, the other a year younger. He met them when Mrs. Kelsey invited him in and introduced her sons while she searched for money to pay for the bundles Mickey delivered. The only other children in the small neighborhood, scattered throughout many buildings, were younger, only seven or eight.

The three boys talked uncomfortably because of being strangers, but they became friendly after a few more deliveries. Mickey never saw Martin or his younger brother, Daniel, outside their apartment. They said they weren't allowed to play in the streets. The friendship grew slowly, limited by Mickey's deliveries and pickups. After a few deliveries, Mrs. Kelsey would call them from school homework to chat with Mickey while she went after money or did last-minute gathering of things to be laundered. He wanted to call them Marty and Danny—or by any nickname they said—but Martin cautioned him both their mother and father did not want to hear anything but their given names.

The Kelseys had a lot of laundry done by Sing Lee, enough that Mickey delivered twice a week, often three times. Mrs. Kelsey once confided, as she counted out payment, "I abhor doing washing and ironing! Dusting and using a floorsweeper doesn't bother me—and now that I have a fine Hoover vacuum cleaner that Mr. Kelsey had delivered a few weeks ago, it's quite easy, takes no time at all—but those things are only once-a-week tasks. Now, washing and ironing— that's another matter. I had so much of them growing up as the oldest girl in my family in Boston, I hope I never have to do another lick of either again. With a family of two boys in school and the father a downtown businessman, we have a lot of both needing to be done. You already know that, don't you—being here so many times a week."

Mickey looked forward to Kelsey deliveries, even refusing tips sometimes, but Mrs. Kelsey always insisted he take the money. For Mickey, it was quite enough that he regularly had boys his age with whom he could talk in a quiet setting, without maliciousness, without coarseness, without toughness and tension and brutality and fear; boys he liked who showed him books, games, balsa-wood flying models they had built and were building, and showed him vacation snapshots; boys who were like Walter Cartwright.

Then Mrs. Kelsey, one cold afternoon when he told her Sing Lee said he did not have to be back for half an hour, sat him at the kitchen table with Martin and Daniel. She served them freshly baked, chewy Irish oatmeal cookies and tall glasses of warm milk. He gorged himself, but acted politely doing it. His belly distended. He stared at it. This must look awful. *Bet I look like tha' fat ugly Mr. Weinstein!* His consumption did not escape Mrs. Kelsey.

Another time, Mrs. Kelsey, looking up from her seat at the kitchen table, said, "You must know, but I'd like to say it, my Martin and Daniel like you very much." Mickey felt his face grow warm. "Because of that, sometime very soon, we would like you to have a supper with us—all of us—Mr. Kelsey, too." Mickey wondered what he was like. He had not seen him yet, because he often stayed late in his downtown office. The offer excited Mickey, anticipating a wonderful meal made in that marvelous kitchen from which emanated such delicious aromas each time Mrs. Kelsey opened the hall door.

Mrs. Kelsey was much like his Mr. Weinstein, and weeks passed enjoyably because of her. Hooky became less appealing and satisfying. Martin and Daniel were good students, and the three of them talked about the differences between the private Catholic school they attended and Mickey's huge public high school. Their willingness and eagerness to study and learn was quickly apparent on

Mickey's second visit and each time after that. The three compared studies and homework. Mickey felt encouraged; challenged, but not in a fierce way.

The two boys, like their mother in many ways, were also like their father, Mickey decided after joining the family supper in their large dining room. Mickey had nervously asked Sing Lee to leave work two days later at five o'clock instead of the usual six p.m. closing, explaining the supper invitation. "Oh yes," Sing Lee said. "It okay. The lady come in long time ago and say you a good boy. Last week she tell me soon she want you eat with them when the mister there. You go. It very important in China when invited to special meal." Mickey was amused by Sing Lee's earnest approval of his request, expressed in his slightly sing-song manner and unusual pronunciations of words beginning with *l* and *r*.

Mr. Kelsey was quiet, not the boisterous Irishman had Mickey imagined from movies and remembered from neighborhoods where he had lived; not at all what he expected. The man was slender, and tall—appearing so even when he sat—and he spoke with a slight Irish brogue from parental upbringing, further tinged with a pronounced Boston dialect. He smiled occasionally, but was mostly serious in mien and talk. However, Mickey liked him. The food was the most delicious Mickey had eaten since Mrs. Cartwright's place, and as generously served. Mickey wondered how the two other boys were able to stay so slim. *Must take after their father*—and he remembered all his table manners.

As Mrs. Kelsey was much like his Mr. Weinstein, Sing Lee was too. Soon after Mickey started working for him, they had come to like each other well, able to joke about their differences—age, nationality, customs, or whatever amused them. Mickey was inquisitive about people who seemed so strange to him. Sing Lee thoroughly enjoyed explaining Chinese customs, religions, beliefs, their many holidays; telling stories of his China boyhood and of many brothers and sisters, and of home, a city so far away. Mickey was fascinated. He only knew of China and the Far East from well thumbed geography and history books, and some movie travelogues. He had long been intrigued, in his city wanderings, by the compact, exotic, densely populated, mysterious, fearsome section known as Chinatown, only a few miles south of where he lived. He had been at its edges often, but dreaded impinging the narrow, twisting, busy, unkempt streets he could see along for only a short distance, looking exactly as shown in books and magazines and movies.

One time, in the fall of the year before, on a day of hooky and idle time-killing and exploration, he walked a street of what he had been told was the unofficial border of Little Italy and Chinatown. He felt nervous at the sight of so many Oriental foreigners, but forced himself to appear relaxed, to be oblivious to all those Chinese people on the opposite sidewalk as he strolled casually past storefronts. *There's plen'y o' my own people on this side o' the street. I got nothin' to worry 'bout!* But he knew he was not really in Chinatown itself, only on a border street. Though not immediately conscious of them, there were as many Orientals moving along and standing about on his side of the street as there were Caucasians.

On that first perimeter excursion he looked for *mysterious* Orientals, the ones he was sure were only recently arrived from the Far East. At one point he was emboldened by realizing there were as many white adults across the street as there were old and young Chinese, and those white people were standing about, moving, and gazing into window fronts, appearing unconcerned. He crossed the street to that side and strolled slowly, window-shopping.

At a corner he peered along a shadowed, narrow, teeming street, crookedly turning in another direction halfway down the block. He was certain that people who looked his way had menace in their eyes—*sinister* eyes, he decided—threatening him to stay out. He was more suspicious when he saw two men in ankle-length dresses, hair tightly braided into waist-long ropes dangling down their backs. They suddenly left a building twenty feet away, darting in short, shuffling steps toward him through milling Orientals, all of them—he was certain—suddenly facing Mickey, staring meanly, menacing. The two men seemed to be gliding with deliberation toward *him,* but they suddenly veered away, crossing the street, entering a doorway, disappearing. He was sure they were tong warriors, sure they were hired killers, concealing small and terrible razor-sharp axes in voluminous sleeves. He had seen the same characters in movies, read of their murderous exploits in mystery fiction magazines.

But with a new confidence born of brief association with Sing Lee, Mickey knew he could now be safe in Chinatown, even if there were many murderous tong members hereabout. *Mr. Lee's a real Chinaman!—a Chink!—born right in China! I wouldn' have nothin' to worry 'bout, I know that—if I was down here wit' him—I could go a whole half dozen blocks inside Chinatown—no, I could go—we could go a lot farther inside—not just here on the edge like this.*

Mickey shyly asked Sing Lee if he could sometime go with him on one of his once-a-month visits with friends in Chinatown, promising that he would be no trouble, that he could take care of himself. The man seemed reluctant. The boy mildly pestered him. Sing Lee acquiesced, and Mickey's father agreed to the trip. "It'll be good for you—to see, to listen, to experience."

Mickey was not disappointed with the visit that started just after noon on a Saturday. Sing Lee always went on his periodic visit after he closed his store as usual at three p.m. But for this time, he made a large hand-printed notice on a shirt-stiffener cardboard and on Friday put it prominently in the front window, above his name—

CLOSED SATURDAY AFTERNOON!
IMPORTANT!!!—FAMILY!!
SORRY!!!

The sign was pressed tightly against the window glass, edges securely taped to keep out steam moisture that would make inked letters run.

Mickey was amused and pleased with the prospect of his newest adventure, off to a forbidding place where thousands of Chinese lived; so mysterious that no other western boy, he was sure, had ever been there before. And he was to be guided and protected by someone he was sure was a respected and powerful figure of Chinatown.

Sing Lee—laundryman, not a powerful lord—was content with his people, quietly introducing Mickey to men and women, who usually spoke their own language only, then leaving the boy to his own resources while he rapidly conversed with friends and talked his curious, unintelligible language, as he ate strange-looking soups, noisily biting into vegetables Mickey had never seen, hungrily devouring strange food concoctions. He persuaded Mickey to taste, to sip, to bite, to chew, smiling at the boy's uncertainty that turned to pleasure, coaching as Mickey struggled with chopsticks.

As they strolled the crowded, busy streets of the foreign community, Sing Lee told Mickey to roam nearby stores at times when he wanted to linger for short periods with friends, explaining with his mixed-up *l* and *r* letters, "You weer be aw-light heah wire I busy with flends. I have say to many aw-leddy that you ah *my* flend so you can know they weer be yaw flend too." As Sing Lee visited many merchants Mickey heard no English, but he was too excited and interested by everything to be bored. He happily explored store windows and interiors as Sing Lee progressed through several blocks. He watched cooks make all sorts of meals, ladle soups into bowls, and precisely and effortlessly cut up cooked chickens and meat chops and large slabs of ribs into small slabs with incredible speed using fast-moving cleavers and razor sharp knives. He looked at and carefully touched countless objects he had never seen before, awed by the incredible detail of miniature carvings, by the needlework of decorated clothing. The scope of new discoveries seemed endless.

In the following days he worked harder to show he was grateful for Sing Lee's attention. *Seems like the least I could do to pay him back.*

The Kelsey brothers said—when Mickey told them of his excursion—they wished they could do the things he was able to do so easily. They wished they could be like him, they added. Mickey scoffed. "You guys gotta be jokin'—what with all *this!*—what with everythin' you two got!" But Martin and Daniel were earnest in their envy. Martin repeated they wished they could be like him, and Daniel silently nodded agreement.

The brothers invited Mickey to a small Halloween party at their apartment attended by a half dozen boys and girls from their school. He was intoxicated by the frivolity. It was the first party he had attended in his life. And the day after Thanksgiving he gorged himself in the Kelsey's kitchen with the remainders of the family's large holiday turkey, chestnut stuffing, tart cranberry sauce made with the whole berries in it, not just the canned jelly type he was used to and liked so much but rarely had, and an assortment of pies with ice cream and whipped cream. The feast surpassed the small roasted, stuffed chicken his father, after working the early holiday morning, had brought home from a delicatessen at two o'clock in the afternoon for them to wordlessly nibble at while it was still warm, on a depressing Thursday that did not seem like a holiday to either of them. At five o'clock his father woke from napping in a chair, washed his face and hands in the bathroom, put on his short leather jacket, and left the apartment, saying, "I'll be back!"

Damp, cold daylight-short days of December alerted Mickey that Christmas was close. He wondered about presents, wishing he might be given a game or a model airplane kit. *Boy, I wish he'd get me somethin' besides a book again. Always pickin' out some serious thing—so I can learn somethin', he says—or I'll bet it's gonna be clothes again—or shoes—nothin' jus' for fun.*

Mickey's covert cache of tip money covered the cost of any rubber band-powered, balsa-wood flying model kit he wanted, but could not work on at home. Martin's gift of a duplicate kit his father had bought him had absorbed Mickey for a brief time in his small room, but he put it away angrily when his father groused, "Make better use of your time—dammit—studying! Your grades can stand improvement—a *lot* of improvement!"

His father's work days were longer during the extended holiday shopping season. He was often irritable at home, and sometimes in a stormy mood, getting there late after leaving early in the morning, usually when it was just getting light. Sometimes his father woke him as he was leaving, but most times he was already gone when the clamor of Mickey's loud alarm tore at his unconsciousness. When his father got home it would be after many hours of traversing teeming slushy city streets blanketed with grimy snow grayed with city dirt, angered by impatient, harried, angry passengers and pedestrians, shoppers rushing everywhere. *I'll bet he's like this cuz Margaret ain' here! He's gettin' worse every day!*

Mickey saw less of the Kelseys, busy as they were with shopping, parties, visiting relatives. Each afternoon was more depressing for him than the one before. It was worst when there was no answer to the Kelsey doorbell. He would leave neatly wrapped bundles of fresh laundry stacked next to the door, trudging away more disconsolate than he had been.

His dismal moods were dispelled by an unusual announcement: "For the two weeks before Christmas," his father said, "you can keep the money Mr. Lee pays you. Keep the tips, too. That's so you can go shopping on your own. Maybe you want to get something for Mr. Lee—even though he's not Christian. He knows what Christmas is for us folks. And there's Aunt Ellen, definitely.

"And I'll mail whatever you want to send off to your sister. Make sure you get her something. And I guess you like that customer of yours—Mrs. Kelly—or whatever her name is—sounded to me like Kelly—the one with the cookies—with the two boys you keep telling me about."

Mickey was nervous about making a gift list. For two days he did not, only thinking about it, worried his father might change his mind for some reason, deciding he finally could safely make plans. A right thing to get Margaret was the most puzzling, vexing choice. He began to think about her, remembering happy and angry times. *What's it like for her now? There with her mother—my mother, too. Geez—I don' even know what my mother looks like anymore—it's been so long since I seen her. Might jus' as well say I never had a mother. I only know other kids' old ladies! I won'er if I should get my ol' lady somethin' for Christmas?*

But what for? I don' ever remember getting nothin' from her.
Ol' lady? Tha' don' sound right.
Maybe at least a card—put it right in with Margaret's stuff when it gets mailed—
jus' don' say nothin' 'bout it to the ol' man.
But how do I sign it? Wha' do I say?

He planned with Sing Lee to not work the second Saturday morning from then, so he could leave early for downtown. That was the place for him, he decided. He did not want to just trudge about from one local store to another to make selections and purchases. Staying in his own neighborhood for his first Christmas shopping trip did not seem right to him. It would be humdrum, not interesting or exciting. Every day he happily anticipated the moment when he could set off on his buying spree. He thrilled at thoughts of being propelled along hectic, crowded streets, through exciting stores, in touch with happy people who felt the same excitement. He hoped it would be snowing, just lightly, whitening everything and everyone freshly and brightly.

But it did not snow. The city lay under mounds of soot-tinted snow and rime-slicked sidewalks and streets. Cars slid into other cars and horns tooted angrily and blared and drivers yelled and raged. Mickey hardly noticed, ignoring conditions, traipsing cheerily through the hurly-burly of countless shoppers in countless stores. It was a new experience for him, an adventure. It only ended when he reached home, exhausted, with a different happiness than before. His shopping list had been altered several times as he discovered one affordable thing after another that he thought would make a better gift than he had first written. Finally, he forced himself to settle on a choice for each name on the list and started comparing prices, looking for *bargains,* a word his father used so often.

Heading north on rattling subway cars, switching from one subway line to another, from express train to local, he draped his legs over two shopping bags compressed into the small space beneath the long bench seat, pressing his calves against the bags for the feeling of security. Reaching both hands down between thighs, he tightly clutched two sets of bag handles, protecting against theft as his head drooped tiredly, chin on chest, dozing fitfully, worried about his treasures, but unable to keep awake.

It was fifteen minutes into darkness when Mickey reached home and dark rooms, not finding even a note as to what his father was doing or his whereabouts. He was disappointed. He emptied the shopping bags, carefully strewing contents into sorted heaps—*The Kelseys right here—and this package is for Mr. Lee—I hope he likes it—and two presents for Aunt Ellen—an' here's Margaret's stuff—plus one card for each person on top o' the pile—an' somethin' for the ol' man! GOT to remember that one, or there could be trouble!*

Two days before Christmas, Mickey added a second gift for Sing Lee. He had already gift-wrapped a carton of Camel cigarettes in red and green paper with holly-leaves-and-berries design. Sing Lee had been the person who was the most difficult for gift decision-making. The cigarettes were finally chosen because Mickey could not decide on anything else. Though he believed it was Sing Lee's almost constant Camel-smoking every day that made him cough so much, Mickey nonetheless prepared a carton of ten packages of cigarettes as a gift.

He decided on the second gift when the wizened Chinese itinerant peddler who stopped at the store every ten days or so parked his gaudy panel truck directly in front of the Sing Lee Laundry as Mickey stared through a circle he had wiped clear in the window condensation when he heard a loud engine rumbling on the street. The truck was painted a bright lime-green color and was emblazoned with a highly detailed fire-breathing, wild-eyed, red-eyed, different-darker-color-green creature that covered the complete side of the vehicle, taking up most of the space top to bottom, with its convoluted tail curling round onto the back door, and front legs spread across the driver's door, with fearsome-looking, splayed, clawing talons on the side of the engine compartment cover. When Mickey examined the small delivery truck closely after he went outside, he discovered the same creature on the other side. *Wow! This mus' really look like somethin' great when it's rollin' along on the streets!* Mickey had not yet seen the delivery van when it was moving. It had either pulled up to the store unseen, as had happened this time, or it was already parked when Mickey arrived or did not leave until after he had left to make a delivery or had gone home.

The truck was a veritable small warehouse on wheels. Goods were crammed onto tightly stacked shelves from floor to ceiling on each side of the interior and blocking the rear double doors. The merchant, How Chin, had to probe with a flashlight beam to find many items not visible in the dim light of a small ceiling bulb behind a dirty glass shield.

But he seemed to know the precise location of every item. Mickey had learned that on the several occasions Sing Lee had him help the old man bring Oriental food delicacies and gewgaws from the truck into the store onto the wide store counter. The two Chinese, in lilting, sing-song language, would discuss items, handling each piece; the merchant cajoling, Sing Lee nearly always reluctant to buy. Occasionally Sing Lee was eager or the merchant was successful. In the first visit by the peddler, Mickey had been puzzled by changes in tone of their foreign words, by their changing moods, surprised at their hostility. Nasal sounds turned shrill sometimes, sounding vehement, becoming smoother as they spoke softly again, then worsening to anger, shifting back to calmness. Most items, even food packages, seemed to stir them each to vigorous verbal battles, another ritual of changeable emotions. In their second set-to on that first day, Mickey hesitantly spoke to them in the midst of an excited back-and-forth torrent of words. They both looked puzzled as he tried to calm them, weakly pleading that they lower their arguing chatter from a boil to a simmer. Sing Lee laughed loudly, saying something to the other man, whose eyes widened, looking at Mickey, amused. "Ah—" he said, with a slight bow to Mickey, nodding his head up and down, a slight smile growing, spreading into a grin. Then he laughed, letting it slip into a giggle, covering his mouth with a hand, embarrassed by laughing at the boy's helpful attempt, appearing ashamed at making the boy feel embarrassed. Sing Lee looked intently at Mickey. When he spoke, Mickey was so accustomed to his speech pattern that he no longer seemed to hear mixed-up *r*s and *l*s and did not notice missing words. He understood Sing Lee perfectly.

"My friend apologize. He sorry he not understand that *you* not understand our ways. He is not angry at me—and you must not worry about me. This man is not going to hurt me—and I am not going to hurt him. We have been friends for a very long time. It is only—it is—in our country—in our little town—and in the street markets even in big cities—is custom to do what we do here at this time—here in my store—custom not to buy at first price—not to sell at first price. It is honorable to discuss cost of something—the price of something—difference between the two—then understand between two people true value of something. Do I say it right so to have you understand we are really friends? I have known How Chin many, many years. Our parents are from two close villages in China.

"It is only that he sells—and I am buyer."

But Mickey did not bargain with How Chin. Standing outside the merchant's truck, ready to help carry wares into the laundry, Mickey saw a stack of familiar-looking boxes in the shadowy interior. "How much is that?" he said, pointing to a shelf in the truck. "One of those yellow boxes there with Chinese writing all over it—says Lichee Nuts in English." Sing Lee kept a yellow cardboard box of lichee nuts near his ironing machine, regularly popping a brownish, dried litchi fruit into his mouth as he worked. Mickey said, "Mr. Chin, I wanna buy Mr. Lee a box of those for a Christmas present. So don' tell him I got it, okay?"

"They two dollar fifty cent each box."

"I'll buy one."

"They very good. Come from China. They not grow in this country."

"Tha's okay. I wish I had enough money left to buy two boxes for Mr. Lee. They're his favorite. He's always got a box next to him when he's working. Seems like he's forever eatin' 'em."

"I must charge so much for them because I *pay* very much too."

"I un'erstand, Mr. Chin. But it's Christmas. I don' mind paying that price—Mr. Lee's a nice man."

"They very hard for me to get. Merchant who brings from China say I must always buy six box each time. Very expensive for me. But—they very best lichee nut in world—and come only from China." The merchant's "lee-chee" was pronounced "ree-chee."

Mickey dug into his trouser, shirt, and jacket pockets, finding money. "I still wish I could get him two boxes—but tha's all right—I got him somethin' else besides this anyway, Mr. Chin."

How Chin, sitting on his haunches inside the truck, shuffled his feet to move forward, closer to Mickey. "If sell lichee nut for less I not make enough money. Then it not smart for me to keep lichee nut in here for many customer—it not good business—it too expensive for me. Then it hard for customer all over big city to get lichee nut. Must go far to Chinatown—take much time—and pay more too."

Mickey was amused. "Mr. Chin, it's okay. I got the money." How Chin squinted, shaking his head slightly from side to side, tugging a box from the tightly packed stack. "I let you have this for two dollar—for your important holiday."

"But Mr. Chin, I said I got enough—" He put out a palm with two bills and coins in it.

The peddler stared at Mickey. "You must learn to save money every time you can." How Chin plucked the two bills from the extended hand, leaning further forward on his haunches, beckoning with a scrawny forefinger. "I give you *two* present—this box for your gift to your friend. You save fifty cent cash—*and* I have give you free lesson *how* to save cash—make money."

A wondering look showed on Sing Lee's face when Mickey gave him two gift-wrapped packages, saying, "Open the long one first. But you prob'ly already guessed what it is—from the shape."

"But I not Christian. This not my holiday. Many of my people are Christian, but I Buddhist."

"That's okay, Mr. Lee. You know what Christmas means. I like you and wanted to show you I did. So I figgered you ought to be one of the people to give a present to, along with a few more I'm givin' to others."

Sing Lee carefully undid the wrapping. "Thank you. I smoke Camel aw-ra time. You velly nice to do this."

"It ain' nothin' really. But that other one is the one I think you'll really like. It made me feel kinda special gettin' it." Sing Lee was even more careful opening the second gift, smiling slightly, then smiling widely.

"Ah—I see yellow—and now I read Chinese printing." Mickey felt extraordinarily happy. "Ah—aha—lichee nut—very *good* lichee nut. How Chin always have this kind with him when he drive to here."

He looked at Mickey, his brownish face uncharacteristically expressive, brown eyes open wide, showing pleasure. "You even maw nice to do this."

Later, Mickey stood at the Kelsey door, listening to footsteps on the other side, responding to his third bell ring. Only Mr. Kelsey was home. He stood looking sleepily down at Mickey. "Oh—hello. I couldn't think who might be at the door. Guess I must have dozed—while I was doing this." He softly shook the newspaper in his hand.

He was surprised when Mickey handed him three small Christmas-paper-wrapped packages. "Two of 'em are one fer Martin and one fer Daniel—an' this little one is for Mrs. Kelsey." When he had wrapped the gift he was certain she would guess what it was because of the shape and aroma but he was also positive she would like the best-smelling soap he could buy. Mr. Kelsey folded the newspaper and tucked it under an arm. Taking the gifts, he turned and picked up an envelope from a small table. Mrs. Kelsey had written Mickey's name on it in her large, swirling, graceful handwriting.

"Thanks, Mr. Kelsey—an' Merry Christmas—an' tell the others I said the same for them, too."

Their gift pleased him, but he wished it was not money. *I'll spen' it an' have nothin' to remember! I know she thought it was nice—but I don' know what to spen' it on. I don' wanna end up buyin' my own present jus' so's I can have somethin' to remember the Kelseys an' this Christmas.* He promised himself he would not spend the crisp five-dollar bill. He would keep it in the bill-size gift folder printed with a Christmas design, signed separately *Martin* and *Daniel* and *Mother Kelsey.* Every time he would lift the flap he would see each one's handwriting.

I know what I'll do! I'll keep it all in my wallet—always have it fer an emergency. An' they'll always be with me. If I gotta use it, the Kelsey family will be the ones that rescue me.

Mickey was disappointed by the start of Christmas Day. He felt no excitement. *At leas' Margaret was here las' Christmas an' there was somebody to talk to and we swapped presents—even if she was a jerk an' doin' dumb stuff most o' the time. An' las' year Aunt Ellen was wit' us later to make that little turkey an' stuffin'— an' a pie!*

But the ol' man ain' said nothin' yet today. I don' know what we're gonna be doin'—if we're doin' anythin'.

He was disappointed that not even a small Christmas tree decorated the small rooms. His father had said they could not afford one. Mickey thought about buying a few tree-decorating items with his tip money and putting them up, but he worried about angering his father, remembering last Christmas when the angry man ripped decorations from the tree and threatened to break up the small evergreen and throw it out on the street for trash pickup, all because of something Mickey and Margaret both had done to infuriate him—and Mickey could not even remember what triggered that rage. He did remember it was one of the rare instances that Margaret figured in blame. Only Aunt Ellen's arrival calmed his father's destructive rage. *An' she made him go to the store for some things for her cookin'. I guess she got him outta there to make him cool down. She never did say. Good thing he went, too. I mighta got another lickin'. Even when he got back he wasn' good company at all—an' Aunt Ellen finally went home mad herself. I sure don' know what made him like that on Christmas Day.*

As soon as his father came sleepy-eyed from his room Mickey eagerly wanted to give him gifts. "Hold on a few minutes, dammit! I'm not awake yet. You know well enough it takes me ten or fifteen minutes to get going. I'm damn tired from these long hours I've been putting in. And I'm not done yet. I have to work today." Mickey was stunned.

"You don't have to look like that. I don't need to be downtown until eleven o'clock. I got an okay to be late because it's the holiday." He pulled aside an edge of the drawn window shade in the front room to peer outside. "Looks like rotten weather out there." His father put together a pot of coffee and set it on the stove to percolate, plodding to the bathroom to wash and wake up fully. Mickey sat glumly in a front-room chair, leaning heavily against the back, legs sprawled, hands jammed into bathrobe pockets, staring at the window shade, mentally grousing about the rotten weather.

When he sensed his father was about done with his wake-up bathroom routine, Mickey started putting dishes and utensils on the kitchenette table, then stacked his two similarly shaped and wrapped flat, oblong gifts in the space between their opposite seating places, then moved them closer to his father's side. Mickey watched him as he made a small stack of whole wheat toast, at the same time heating a saucepan half-filled with milk, then gather the coffee pot, the toast, and items from the ice box, moving everything to the table. "Let's eat first. I have to get ready to go."

Mickey's throat tightened. He felt his eyes burn. Glumly, he watched his father prepare the breakfast he enjoyed best—chunks of toast crammed tightly into a large, deep bowl of warm milk. "I was brought up on this for years back on the farm when I was a boy," he had said many times. Mickey slowly broke his own two slices of toast into a shallow bowl, watched a glob of butter melt, spreading across the milk surface, yellowing the whiteness. He ate less than half, staring blankly at the milk-swollen pieces of bread. He sensed his father was looking at him.

"Might as well get on with this," his father said. "It's getting late for me. I've got a long subway ride ahead of me." He curtly said a thank-you for Mickey's Christmas present of gloves in one flat box and a lightweight scarf in the other. He got up from the table, going into his room, returning with a thick, rectangular package wrapped in dark-green paper. "I thought you could make good use of this." He put it on the table between them. Mickey slowly reached for it.

The dull-colored package was heavy. He needed a second hand to lift it easily. *Geez!—another darn book! Why else should it be so heavy?* He carelessly tore the wrapping loose. *A dictionary? Darn! Biggest one I ever seen—'cept for the one in the school library.* He riffled the pages.

"Well," his father said, "what do you think? That certainly should be a big help to you, oughtn't it?—now that you're in high school."

"Yeah—it's swell. Jus'—" His eyes burned more. "Yeah—nice." His throat stayed tight. He did not look at his father when he asked, "You gonna open the card?"

"Oh—yeah—sure," the man answered, putting his coffee cup down hard on the saucer. Mickey wondered if his father was going to give him something that Margaret might have sent him—or maybe even something from his mother, too— now that Margaret was with her and maybe reminded her to do. But his father only opened the envelope flap, pulled out the card, looked at it quickly, said a quiet thank you, and put it on the table, quickly turning away, moving to a chair back where his jacket was draped. "You'll have to do the dishes. Start on them now, while I get ready for work."

The days between Christmas and New Year's Day passed slowly and drearily. Schools were closed for the long holiday vacation. Mickey slept later each morning, his father not bothering to wake him when he left for work. He had told his son, the first night, "Read some good books now that you've got time, instead of that trashy stuff you're always looking at when I'm not around. I told Mr. Lee you could get to his place earlier every day to help him out, not just hang around here or anywhere else doing nothing. Besides, you'll probably make more tips that way. I can use the money."

New Year's Eve was no special event for Mickey. In the morning his father told him to get home right after he finished working for Mr. Lee, and to stay home. Then he surprised Mickey by a longer explanation than ever before. "I just might be going to a New Year's Eve party at a good friend's house. I made a deal with my boss to get off at ten o'clock tonight at the garage downtown, but then I still have a half-hour subway ride. I haven't seen some of the people who are going to be there for a few months—and I haven't been to a New Year's party since I can't remember when. So it's going to be a grownups party—that's why you're not going. Anyway, you can take care of yourself for one night—you're fifteen years old. I was taking care of myself at your age, and even earlier too. Just stay the hell out of trouble, you hear? And that means you stay home all night. I don't want you out on the streets at midnight, or even before then. Hear?"

Mickey turned the radio on early in the evening, planning to listen to Guy Lombardo usher in a new year at midnight. He contemplated a long subway journey to Times Square for the raucous celebration for Father Time's farewell. He knew he would enjoy the excitement. He had never been there for such a huge, crowded celebration but he had seen plenty of newspaper photographs and read many news accounts. However, his father had said he *just might* be going to a party, not that he *positively* would be going. *Yeah—he said* might, *I know he did— an' that only means maybe.* He tried to remember his father's tone of voice when he said that. *Was he just trying make me think he wouldn' be here tonight so he could catch me at somethin'?*

Mickey puttered about in the small apartment, reading mystery story magazines, dozing in a chair, listening to mystery and adventure radio tales, thinking about the Kelsey brothers, doing bits and pieces on a model airplane that he only worked in when his father was not at home. Just after eleven o'clock he fell soundly asleep in the front room chair looking at a comic book and listening to the turned-up radio and missed the increasingly loud Times Square crowd calling out the Ten—Nine—Eight—Seven—Six—Five—Four—Three—Two—One count bringing in a new year.

Sing Lee worked steadily, producing bundles and more bundles for the neighborhood, but none for the Kelseys. Mickey longed to see the profusion of gifts he was sure they had been given by generous parents and relatives. Each time he passed their door he listened for sounds. One afternoon he rang their doorbell on an impulse to see Martin and Daniel, but no one answered. Not until late Saturday afternoon, as he trudged uphill, did he see a light behind the drawn shade of their living room. He wanted to rush to the apartment. He thought about going back to the laundry to ask Mr. Lee if he could go ask the Kelseys if they had any laundry to be picked up. Instead, he made himself keep trudging up the hill, heading home, anticipating seeing the brothers and their mother after school on Monday.

But on Monday, after a long day at the far high school, reluctantly attended that day, Sing Lee told Mickey that Mr. and Mrs. Kelsey and the two boys had delivered their laundry later that past Saturday—after unpacking from their week away from the neighborhood on a vacation in Connecticut. "It first time I meet the mister and her two sons. She ohn-y come in by huh-self when we first start do business. They he-ah ohn-y haf hour after you go 'way. The missus say they go visit fami-ree—they go because boys not in school aw week rike you—and they aw not see those people for hoe year."

"Is anything ready for them yet, Mr. Lee? I can go over there the first thing."

"Oh, no," Sing Lee said. "Be-faw they bling things to be done I have much other wuhk. So I must do other wuhk first. I aw-rus do in order things come into store. Is fair that way. And the missus say that fair for her too; they have other to use."

It was almost that full work week before Mickey spoke to Martin and Daniel, then only briefly, as he stood in the corridor and they stood, smiling at him, behind their mother. She said, "We all very much appreciated your thoughtfulness. Your gifts were so kind. I loved mine. But the boys are so busy with their homework, I really can't have you in to visit them. But it will be soon when you can. And I do have this for you." From behind her back she gave him a large paper bag, top twisted closed. It had an aroma of her cooking as she purposely brought it to his nose. "Brownies, oatmeal cookies you like so much, vanilla wafers, and some macaroons—I know they're your favorite—all baked this afternoon. I knew you'd be making a delivery."

Another week went by before he talked with the two boys. For ten minutes they chattered excitedly, Mickey urging them to describe their gifts, putting off their persistent question, "What did you get?" Finally, reluctantly, he answered, "A dictionary. A great big one. It's beautiful. I can really get smart with it."

"What else?"

"Well—nothin' yet. But I haven' seen my Aunt Ellen for a long time. I'm sure she hasn' had the chance yet to give me her present. I think she's outta town visitin', a long ways away. Yeah—my father said she hadda go see someone who's been sick for a while.

"An' not only that—my sister's gonna send me somethin' soon. My father said he already sent mine to her—quite a while before Christmas."

"What did you do Christmas Day? Go visiting?—have Christmas dinner somewhere?"

"Well—nah! My father hadda work—hadda go in early. So I jus'—kinda hung aroun'—readin' things in my new dictionary—learnin' all kinda new things an' words—an' listened to the radio—to the story 'bout Scrooge an' Tiny Tim. But tell me some more 'bout *your* things—that you two got."

At the door, as he left, Mrs. Kelsey said, "I must have you come by and chat with Martin and Daniel for a longer while. It will do each of them a world of good. They've both been studying so much they need someone to talk with besides each other."

Twice the next week Mickey spent a quarter to a half hour with Martin and Daniel, arranging with Sing Lee to make the Kelsey delivery last, lingering with the boys when he felt his father would not be home when he got there tardy, or hoping he would not notice a late arrival because he dozed in a chair with his newspaper.

Late in the following week, Mickey made the second delivery to the Kelseys. Icy winds blew harshly from the northwest, across the frozen river, hurling sleet and snowflakes through venturi tubes of narrow streets. Mickey shivered in the long apartment building corridor. Twice, three times he pressed the Kelsey doorbell button. He could hear trilling on the other side of the door—"I'm coming, I'm coming"—as he juggled two large bundles of shirts in the crook of an arm. It was warm in the dimly lighted hallway, but Mickey could not feel it. The chilling wind had quickly penetrated the worn plaid lumberjacket on the short, rushed trip from Sing Lee's shop. Fiercely propelled sleet had beat on the back of his bare neck as he hurried up the hill and across the street, numbing flesh that now tingled, then burned as circulation was restored by the warmth. His spirits soared as Mrs. Kelsey hurried him into the apartment. "Just look at you. You look terrible—look frozen. Your hair is stiff with snow and ice. Your face is blue—and it's red—besides being frosty white. Why aren't you wearing a hat?—with something that pulls down over your ears. And where's your scarf? Surely you must have one. It certainly doesn't do much good leaving it at home." Mickey detested wearing hats of any sort since enduring women's stockings converted into skullcaps to train hair to lay down flat.

Mrs. Kelsey took his bundles, saying, "You stand right there a moment. I have just the thing for you," disappearing, reappearing in seconds, waving a thick bath towel. She briskly rubbed his thawing hair, then told him to finish the job himself. "And go in to see Martin and Daniel, that is if you have time to stay. Their homework's done. Now they're working on their blessed model airplanes again. Seems that's all they want to do—make flying models—talk airplanes—talk flying. Saints be praised—I hope they don't want to be aviators, the way they talk. That Lucky Lindy fellow from a dozen or so years ago is their hero, along with all those others flying across oceans and flying across this big country—one after another— always trying to out-do the next fellow—and now women are doing the same thing!"

She stood arms akimbo on her full hips. "Oh, well, I'm not going to be able to stop what's going to be, I guess." Mickey kept rubbing his hair dry, almost as vigorously as she had, slowing as she watched, smiling at her. "But I do know," she said, "what I can do this minute—and that's get something started that will warm your insides. Get along with you now. Go see the boys. But first straighten your hair. Do you have a comb?" He mumbled that he did not.

"You'll have to use your fingers to make it look something decent. Here, let me get it started for you. Then finish it using the hall mirror over the little table here," she said, pointing.

The battering cold was forgotten. Mickey had already said good-night to Sing Lee as he left with the last deliveries, all in the same building, first to the Goldfarbs on the sixth floor, then down on the elevator to the Kelseys. He had no homework to do. The whole week's assignments had been done on time. He need not hurry.

47

It was a good thing that sometimes I did have a better time for myself.

That's the way living should be—just like it was with those people, the Kelseys.

It's too bad that after what happened I didn't get to see them anymore.

48

Mickey vaguely heard the Kelsey's doorbell ringing, and paid little attention to the subdued b-r-r-i-n-g-s. It was only another bit of background sound. The intermittent short rings abruptly switched to insistent clamoring. The Kelsey brothers looked up from what they were showing Mickey, first looking toward the sound, then the three boys looked at one another. They heard Mrs. Kelsey pad along the lengthy hallway, past the closed door of the brothers' room calling out to the bell-ringer to be patient, that she was coming as fast as she could. The boys chattered about what a nuisance the bell-ringer was, making all that fuss, then went back to closely examining the dope application Martin had just made on the delicate tissue paper fabric of the upper wing of a model Spad fighter used in the World War.

There was a soft knock on the door, then Mrs. Kelsey put her head into the room. "Mickey, the person at the door is looking for you. It's your father. You'd better see him right away."

"Are you kiddin'? Wha's he comin' here for? How'd he know I'm here?" As he started from the room, she put an arm about his shoulder, saying softly, "I'm sure it's all right—but you have been here for more than two hours—" looking at her watch— "closer to three." She looked at him again, compassion in her eyes. "It's really my fault. Twice I was about to remind you that you might be expected at home, but I got distracted with all that cooking I'm doing and paying house bills in between." She squeezed his shoulders in both her hands. "I wish I had reminded you. But I'll explain whatever needs explaining to your father."

"It's okay, Mrs. Kelsey. I left a note at home sayin' I'd be late. I did that after school before I left for work. You won't hafta say nothin' to him."

His father, scowling, arms folded across his chest, leaned against the opposite wall in the corridor as Mickey closed the Kelsey's door behind him. He stood looking at his father, worried about the scowl, not knowing what to do next, thinking he should just start walking out of the building and to home.

"How late is it?" his father said.

"Whadda ya mean?"

"How *late* is *late* is what I mean—like the *late* in your note." His father's scowl intensified. He still leaned against the wall, looking casual in his pose, but his voice was a growl.

"Geez—I dunno—a little while—I guess."

"Give me a better answer than *that*, damn it!"

"I said I dunno—maybe an hour—a little more. I was doin' fun things with those boys makin' a model plane—an' Mrs. Kelsey gave me a sandwich."

"Fun?—and I'm sitting at home wondering? The *one* night I get in early?"

"*I* didn' know you'd be home early. How was I *s'posed* to know? You're always workin' or away some place." His father pushed away from the wall, stepping close to Mickey, rolling his hands into fists, putting them on his hips, snarling questions and statements. The growl grew louder and higher-pitched in the echo-chamber hallway with terrazzo flooring, with smooth walls and high ceiling, every surface bouncing even slight whispers angularly about.

Mickey stood petrified, without answers, infuriating his father more. The man circled the boy, growling, hissing, snarling, questioning, accusing, demanding; threatening that it was time Mickey got the worst thrashing he ever had, that it was long overdue. Mickey squeezed his eyelids tightly together. He tried to block his ears from inside his head to shut out raging sounds. He tucked elbows into his sides, crossing wrists one atop the other, pressing fists hard into his stomach. He pulled his head and neck down into hunched shoulders, stiffening every torso and arm muscle against a smashing blow. His father's infuriation seemed worse each second, with each revolution circling the boy. Mickey's responses were only mutters, his mind confused, throat tight, hurting. Images flashed in his brain. He shuddered at the recall of almost-forgotten wild shakings and thudding blows in the Weinstein drugstore.

Mickey only heard the rough voice, not listening to words, furious that his father was creating such a disturbance outside the Kelsey's door, making enough noise for the two brothers to certainly hear. Mickey imagined them pressed to the other side of their hall door, curious, listening—and Mrs. Kelsey hearing, too; afraid she would not have him in any more, afraid his father had made him lose his only friends. *Wha's makin' my ol' man do this?*

Mickey not listening enraged his father more. "I'm fed up with your stubbornness!—and your laziness!—and your always thinking only of fun! You answer me! Hear?" They were only more words Mickey blocked from being heard. His head seemed as if it would burst. It ached and pulsated with pounding blood driven by a racing heart. The skin of his face, the skin on the top of his head, and his ears, the back and sides of his neck, everything burned with rapid, exciting flushing of blood.

A thump between his shoulder blades made him stagger forward several steps, but he stayed in the tensed, slightly hunched posture. The voice was louder, deeper. Mickey's mind kept shutting it out, or at least making it unintelligible.

Now the man stood in front of him, looming like a colossus in the weakly lighted corridor, clenching Mickey's chin with strong, pressing fingers, forcing his head up. "You'd better answer, if you know what's good for you!" The squeezing fingers hurt his jaw. The excruciating pressure on lower teeth made them feel as if they would break loose. "Open your damn eyes! Look at me when I talk!" Mickey tried to shake his head loose, jerking it up and down, side to side, then trying circles, but the thick, powerful fingers and the thick, strong wrist kept it mostly immobile. His mind screamed: *I didn' do nothing!—STOP IT!*

He clawed at the crushing grip, again trying to twist his head violently, to tear loose from the painful grasp. He heard the voice get louder, angry sounds bouncing along the sterile hallway, from wall to wall to floor to ceiling, rushing from one end to the other and back, pounding at his ears. He was sure his brain was going to spew from his forehead. The front of his head felt ready to crack in a second, then explode in the next second.

Mickey kicked his feet, lashing out with them, flailing frantically, thrashing at his father's legs, aiming toes for where he thought shins were.

Simultaneously, with a sharp, pained cry from his father when a foot smashed a shin, Mickey felt himself lifted by his chin, shaken, then hurled away. He slammed into both the wall and the floor at almost the same instant, his back taking the brunt of impact. Mickey was stunned by whiplash motion of his head knocking against the wall. He twisted onto his hands and knees, got to his feet clumsily, then raced along the corridor toward the stairs leading to upper floors.

An apartment door opened, someone stepping partly into the hall, tentative, loudly calling out, nothing that Mickey understood. He bounded through the seemingly endless, shadowed hall, straining for the stairs, hoping for strength to run up them quicker than his father, hoping he would be safe somewhere up there. Mickey, somehow in the din, heard footsteps pounding, making louder, harder noises than his own light weight made. A voice boomed in the hall: "You stop right where you are! Hear me? Goddam it! I'm telling you!"

Mickey stumbled on the lower treads, falling clumsily, banging and scraping both shins through trouser and high-stocking fabric, scraping fingers and palms, clambering wildly up the shadowy stairwell. He twisted his head, even as he scrambled and fell and scrambled. *Jesus!—jus' like with that fuckin' nigger kid all over again!*

A dozen steps up he stumbled again, tumbling, rolling disjointedly down the short flight. His father reached him as Mickey landed at the bottom, frustrated, pain seeming to envelop the boy completely, terrified by the looming, dark figure. He pulled himself into a tight ball, striving to be as small as possible, as compact and invulnerable as he could be, waiting for destructive pummeling, waiting to be disposed of by a single smashing blow, as done to a cockroach.

His mind stormed.

He uncoiled, springing to his feet, whirling, looking, lunging. He balled his right hand into a fist. He tasted bile rising in his throat. He swung his arm blindly, feeling pain in the thumb, shooting through his wrist muscles, starting into his lower arm. His whole hand numbed. The fist rebounded from the man's thick forearm. Mickey's eyes focused on a shirt button above his father's belt buckle, pulling his arm back first to get more force. He lashed out more vigorously, more angrily, plunging the fist at the button. Mickey was not aware he had balled his other hand into another fist and did not realize for a couple seconds that he had also brought that small weapon around in a sweeping arc. Then he was aware and surprised that he was striking back at an assailant, at his father. Enraged, his eyes swept up to look at his father's face.

His father's intense scowl clearly showed his anger, but he had a puzzled look also. He stood dumbfounded. Mickey flailed at him harmlessly, but Mickey's rage was generating unknown strength in his mind and body. Staring at the face as he pummeled the midsection and arms and wherever else he could strike, Mickey saw puzzlement abruptly turn to sneering, then saw the colossus pull back its arm slowly, cocking it to end the confrontation.

Before the backswing was completed, afraid of what was about to happen to him, desperate, using savage strength, Mickey swung his fist upward mightily, driving it unerringly into the center of the face. The aquiline nose was an open target. He hit it squarely. In the instant before contact, over his hurtling fist, he could see eyes widening. The face did not seem able to move, to dodge safely. Then Mickey could see the pounding fist flatten the fleshy part of the nose, rupturing tiny veins in the nostrils that rapidly leaked blood. Astounded by his bravery and unexpected speed and strength, Mickey pulled back the fist, snorting and grunting at his victory, driving the fist at the same target, hitting it with staccato thumps, sporadically alternating with blows by the left fist. Equally astonished, relatively unharmed, but with his nose now gushing blood, his father stood dumbly for instants, confused, not reacting, not defending, not warding off speedy strikes.

His bewilderment swirled into madness. Mickey had never seen that look on his father's face before. He knew various intensities of wrath and rage and fury in those eyes, but nothing matching this. The face got darker, the scowl distorting it more than Mickey thought possible. His father looked at fingers he had moved to his nose, testing reality, smearing the fingers red, making guttural noises at the sight of his blood. In a brief, still moment they looked intensely at each other.

He's gonna kill me for beltin' him!—for makin' him bleed!

Mickey saw a long, dark leather razor strop whirl through his mind, held by one end in his father's hand, with something glinting, something metal, a large round metal circle, swinging in a slow-motion deadly arc. The man had, in another place, in a basement room, become embroiled in another rage at his boy. Without a second thought, driven by an urge to punish, he had grasped the dangling end of a double-thickness sharpening and honing strop for his straight razor, snaking it off the nail protruding from a door jamb, where it hung by a large metal ring. Without turning the weapon to hold it by the end with the heavy metal ring, he let fly with powerful strokes. It had taken days for the broad swaths made by the thick leather and other marks by the large metal ring to fade from Mickey's torso, arms, and legs.

Mickey shook his head, shaking the image away, then darted to one side of his father, under an upraised arm, running headlong toward the other end of the corridor, past widely opened apartment doors with curious, worried people only edging into the corridor to see better, staring at the commotion, then turning to watch as the boy ran by. He ran blindly at the start, gasping, struggling to focus his eyes, screaming in his mind, telling himself countless things to do. He stumbled. He scampered. He shrieked short, low yells of fright every several pounding steps along the claustrophobic hallway. Movement was getting difficult. Feet were hitting each other and scuffling along the floor. An agonizing thought struck him! *There's TWO doors to get through!* He had no idea how close his father was.

He fell against the thick all-glass door, both hands clawing at a horizontal metal push bar, finally roughly forcing it down to release the latch, hurling the heavy door wide, almost falling down in the large vestibule.

I did it!

But there was the second door—thick, wood, heavy, with thick translucent glass in the top section—and it sometimes stuck. The top of his head seemed spinning so fast he thought it would come undone somehow, spilling all his brains out, leaving nothing for thinking, for getting himself out of his predicament, now the worst in his life. *Where is he? Where's my ol' man?*

He spun into a forward-moving complete-circle turn, to not lose progress toward the last door barrier, hoping to see how close his father was. Mickey stopped the turn, standing stock-still.

I ran shit-scared fer nothin'!

The figure still stood at the far stairs, appearing to be hunched forward, as though staring through the shadows. Mickey felt an overwhelming relief, grateful he was not pursued closely. Beyond the full-length, full-width, thick, solid-glass door in its closed position, the figure's shouting did not reach his son, sounds only bouncing back at him, echoings that made the figure even angrier. The leaking blood, running into his mouth, agitated him, discoloring fingers of both hands as he tested his nose. However, it was a lesser irritation than his son's impulsive act toward him, and the boy had not stopped his running, had ignored warnings to stop. The man lunged forward, determined the boy would not get away.

Mickey, seeing the figure running, leaped down the vestibule steps, two at a time, jerking open the heavy wooden street door, flinging it wide, surprised it worked so easily, surprised at his surge of strength. He plunged recklessly down outside stone steps, into darkness. *Jesus, I musta really been in there long—bein' this dark out here!*

On the sidewalk he looked frantically along the street in both directions, lighted weakly from widely spaced light poles. He did not know what to do next. He squinted into darkness in both directions, at both sides of the street. Everything was still. To the right, down the short part of the hill, not far away, was the dark, forbidding river. *Maybe I could go hide in the park.* Up the hill, almost a full block to go, the whole borough spread straight ahead and to the left and to the right. *A million hidin' places if I go that way!*

The building door, up the flight of stone steps behind him, sounded a menacing, heavy thump. *Shit! I let him catch up to me!*

Mickey spun about, tensing, putting his arms high, crossing them at his face, hunching forward to protect his midsection with elbows pressed to his body. Tears started involuntarily. He looked up. "Please!—I didn' mean—"

The steps were empty!

The automatic door-closer, so often to blame for keeping the door from being opened easily, had pulled the heavy door shut solidly. The thump of the closing would ordinarily have escaped notice, but with no other street sounds to override it, with no distracting thoughts to divert attention, the thump was obvious to panic-stricken Mickey, and frightening.

No hulking figure, standing at the top of the steps, glaring. No furious eyes No twisted face. No bloody nose. Nothing charging at him in rage. But was there a shadow on the cloudy glass?

Jesus—ya fuckin' dummy! Get your ass movin'—he's comin' through there any fuckin' second!

He sprang to the left, charging pell-mell up the shallow hill, toward brighter lights on the north-south avenue. Before the crest he slowed, stopped, looking down the grade. The street was empty. He ran again.

49

"Hey, buddy—you sleeping?" The sudden voice from behind him was startling. "More of the alphabet just got called. Maybe it's your turn."

"Naw—I'm not sleeping."

"You looked it," the voice of the unseen person went on. "Legs stretched out, chin hanging on your chest. I could never sleep like that, looking so uncomfortable. Being like that for long would break my back. Me—I gotta have something flat to stretch out on—anything."

"Nope—I wasn't sleeping. And I don't think I'm ready to go in yet. What did they call?"

"N through R."

"Nope—not me—I'll be in the last bunch."

"Then it looks like you can go back to what you were doing. Sorry I woke you up."

"I wasn't sleeping. Just thinking."

50

Light bothered Mickey's eyes. He put a hand across them, to gain darkness, to keep something away, but he was not sure what the something was,

"—with your two cousins—"

then tilted the hand up, making a shield against the ceiling light. He looked about. It was

"—this bed—"

a small room. The light from the ceiling came from a small bulb in a round upside-down glass shade that bounced weak, yellowish light to the ceiling and the rest of the space in which Mickey found himself. He was puzzled. *Wha' the heck is—?* Ahead of him were two, long narrow windows, extending from a few inches above the floor to within a few inches of the ceiling. Two metal-frame beds were to the left and right of the windows, against side walls

"—understand, don't you?"

with the heads flush against the window sills. A woman's voice

"—not long—really—"

to one side behind him kept sounding as Mickey wondered about the room. Outside, through windows without curtains or drapes, it was dark. *The shades are all the way up. At this time of night?*

"—as soon as possible—"

There were pale squares of light in a building in the distance, beyond a blackness that filled the lower half of both windows, but he could not tell how far away the lighted squares were.

Mickey looked down, staring at his shoes, wiggling his toes inside them. He felt chilled. He could feel that the hole in his sock at the right big toe had gotten larger. The floor was covered with light-hued linoleum; not white, sort of a light tan color. A dark solid-brown braided rug was spread between the beds. His eyes moved to his chest, to dark fabric covering it. He had on a brown, waist-length leather jacket with a long, shiny metal zipper on the front. He patted the soft material, tugging the jacket down by the knitted waistband. He held out his arms, looking from one long sleeve and knitted cuff to the other. He wondered

"—you know—if it had been possible—"

where he had gotten it.

"—that you do understand me?"

The trousers looked different. So did the shoes. He looked out the window, staring at the pale squares of light from the building in the distance. *Why are the shades up? So late at night? Must not care 'bout anybody lookin' in.*

"—all so quickly, I didn't have much chance to—"

A hand lightly touched him, but he stayed absorbed in determining how far away the squares of light were.

"—really do the best we all can—"

Tha's a different woman!

The new voice puzzled him more. He became more aware of the coolness of the room. He studied furniture, the floor, the brown rug, windows, the rolled-up shades at the window tops, the far panels of light.

"Are you listening to—"

He rolled his eyes up to look at the ceiling,

"Leave him be for a minute; he'll be all right." *Tha's a man's voice.*

then looked at the side walls. They were both the same color, and they matched the color of the space between the windows and all the walls were the same color as the ceiling and they all nearly matched the linoleum and the two bedspreads matched everything else. There was nothing on the walls. *Ain' nothin' but tha' brown rug in here for any kinda color. No pictures?*

Who does this place belong to?

The voice of the first woman murmured on, sounding tense to Mickey, nervous-sounding, seeming uncertain about what to say. The second woman again said something. *She talkin' to me?* He concentrated. Words seesawed between the two women, behind Mickey, close by, gradually taking on clarity, meaning. *Askin' if I mind stayin' here—a little while.*

The other one's sayin' it's all settled. What's settled?

Mickey turned slowly, away from the distant lights he no longer cared to guess about, turning his back to the tall windows and the two beds. He kept his eyes from focusing too quickly on what was near, making himself first stare into a long distance, then bringing his vision back in to nearness and on figures facing him some three feet away. Two women looked at him, frowning, anxiety in their eyes. One woman was his height, the other shorter. Both were plain-looking, with no makeup, dark hair streaked with gray. The straight, untended hair of the shorter, plumper woman was parted in the middle, hanging straight, ending slightly below her ears. The gray was in streaks. The other woman, dressed in a floor-length bathrobe, center-parted her hair too, but it was longer and she braided and coiled and pinned it low at the back of her head. They took turns saying reassuring words. The shorter, plumper woman seemed fidgety to Mickey.

A middle-aged man was in the doorway, behind the women. His gray-striped brown hair was smoothly combed straight back from the brow—the same style as Mickey's. The man leaned against the door opening, one arm high on the jamb, the other arm bent at the elbow, shirt sleeves rolled-up, hand on hip. He looked relaxed, noncommittal. Two boys, younger than Mickey, stood in front of the man, one to each side, watching Mickey with deep curiosity.

The shorter, plumper woman stopped talking. Her eyes flicked up and down, from her intertwined, nervously working fingers to Mickey's face, but only at his forehead, back to her fingers; up and down again; then once more. She did not look into his eyes. The other woman talked positively, quietly.

"We'll all do the best we can to make things comfortable while you stay. The boys will share one bed. You'll have the other. You just take it easy—take your time—everything will be all right." Mickey wondered who the people were, what he was doing in the room. Both women were saying things again, but their voices were only droning sounds to Mickey. He was exhausted, feeling wobbly. He wanted nothing more than to sit on a bed, have the droning stop.

The talkative, self-assured woman turned to a small, low chest of drawers in a corner, slid open the top drawer and lifted out neatly folded pajamas, handing them to Mickey. She wordlessly shunted everyone from the room, closing the door softly behind her, smiling slightly at Mickey.

He looked at the folded pajamas in his hand. They felt cooler than the room did. He threw them on the bed to the right. He angrily swiped at the long dangling string-pullcord of the ceiling light, jerking it mightily. As the light went out, he felt the pullcord break and he let it fall to the floor. In the darkness he fell heavily onto the bed along the left wall, sprawling on his back on the bedspread. His body tightened. He beat his chest with fists. He raised his shoe-covered feet high above the coverlet and brought them down together with fury. In seconds he was asleep.

Mickey twitched and twisted as a sudden, terrifying, roar broke into his unconsciousness, then he sprang violently into an upright seated position on his bed, letting out a loud, short yell. His bed was shaking; the whole house was shaking; his whole body was shaking—*Oh shit!—he's comin' to get me! What's he doin' to make all that racket? Where the fuck am I? Shit!—shit!—shit!*

Mickey twisted about, eyes drawn to the ceiling-to-floor window at the head of the bed. Past the windows, in the outside darkness, less than fifty feet away was a monstrous black snake-looking thing rushing and roaring from right to left, its belly even with his eyes, its back high above the window top. Flashes of light on the side of the thing zipped by in a flash. *It's a train!—a friggin' train! Nobody said nothin' 'bout a fuckin' train!*

The eight cars of the passenger express from New York to Boston roared and rattled along eastward, pulled along by a huge, hard-working, noisy, steam locomotive, the whole train rushing through night blackness at sixty miles an hour. A wall of air being violently pushed aside in the headlong rush made a whooshing, roaring sound of its own that mixed with the train's intrinsic metallic cacophony of high speed. A sound that began distantly from the dark quiet room in which three young boys slept quickly grew louder, fiercely impinging on silence. Noisy bangs and slams and screeches spread widely as the hurtling leviathan worked to stay on schedule, vibrations and sounds reaching out to pound at less fragile things along both sides of its path. Sturdy factory constructions barely reacted to the train's passing, but wood frame buildings convulsed noticeably. Ceiling and wall cracks started or separated a little more. Loose things on shelves shook. Sleeping pets hunched themselves into tighter coils. Sleeping people who had long grown accustomed to train passings hardly noticed any disturbance. If they reacted somehow they seldom remembered it in the morning and never felt as though sleep had been disturbed.

At two-thirteen a.m. the express rushed along on the high viaduct that coursed through the industrial part of the city and passed by Mickey's bedroom window—frightening him half to death, as he recalled the next morning, without saying anything about it to anyone else at breakfast—then there was an absolute silence. Seconds later he could hear the soft breathing of someone in the other bed, then things seemed normal, except for the darkness, except about the bed in which he sat, except about who was in the other bed. He remembered two boys someone said were his cousins; and he remembered a woman handing him folded pajamas; and he remembered running on a sidewalk up a long hill.

At two-sixteen a.m Mickey was again soundly asleep, exhaustion mercifully erasing the quick terrible moments with the train from his mind, mercifully shutting down his consciousness so he could sleep after a long period of turmoil.

In what seemed only few seconds more he was awake, in darkness. Insistent knocking got louder before he realized he was not dreaming. Those were real sounds, not just banging noises in a pestery dream. A muffled voice somewhere was saying something between the thumping sounds. He realized he was on his left side. Everything was black. His eyes were closed. He opened them but still everything was black. *Fer chrissake! What the hell is this? Oh, got it—I'm in a bed!* A muffled voice said "Boys—it's time to get up." Mickey was mystified.

He put his head outside the bedcoverings—a sheet, two light blankets, and a thin, fluffy comforter. He faced a wall, a light tan color. His whole face instantly felt coldness. *Where the hell am I? What's all this stuff on me? This ain' my bed!*

His ears felt coldness. He remembered a train during night. *That friggin' thing scared the livin' shit outta me. They shoulda tol' me 'bout it! Least I wouldn'a been so shit-scared—maybe.* He twisted about in the bed to look at his surroundings, to solve his sudden mystery, and saw another bed. He remembered flopping down on the bed he was in, that he had his shoes on when he did it. It seemed like it was only a few seconds ago. He concentrated on his feet. *Nah—I don' have no shoes on right now—an' I got pajamas on. When did all that happen?*

The muffled voice again said "Boys—it's time to get up." Mickey raised up, pushing the bedcovers down slightly, propping himself on both elbows. The room was lightening with daylight. Beneath the pajama fabric his shoulders felt the coldness of the air in the room. "Yeah, yeah! Okay—be right up!" *Where the hell am I?*

"Okay, Mickey," a woman's voice said on the other side of a closed door. "Breakfast is almost ready. Wake the boys up. Tell them to hurry down to get dressed."

Wha' boys? Who's she talkin' 'bout? He remembered tossing folded pajamas on the bed in which he now was. He remembered two boys standing next to a man. He threw back the covers and twisted about to sit with his feet on the braided rug. The room coldness swept over him. He wanted rub his hands all over his arms and shoulders and chest to chase away the chill, but first he had to find out something. He got up and hunched over the other bed, over what seemed to be a shapeless mass under the bedcovers. He lightly grasped what he guessed would be a shoulder and shook gently, then more firmly when he was sure it was a shoulder in his grip. A grumbling, muffled voice said, "Okay, okay, Mom—I'm awake—we're awake—we're getting up. Be right down." Covers were thrown back and in the weak light of an outside street lamp two faces stared at Mickey, and he stared back. The three of them wordlessly scrambled out of beds and quickly dressed in the cold room.

At the kitchen table, the middle-aged man with several narrow stripes of gray in his pompadour-combed hair spoke to Mickey matter-of-factly, but his manner was not unfriendly. "I'm your godfather—your mother's brother—your uncle. Being your godfather is one of the reasons you'll be staying with our family for a while, until things get settled." Mickey sat quietly, looking at the bowl of hot oatmeal cereal. With a spoon he poked at the mound rising out of the warm milk. "It's all right," the man said, "you can go on with eating while I say a thing or two."

One long edge of the large table was against a wall. The man sat at one end, Mickey at the other. "In a minute I'll leave you to your breakfast. I don't have a lot to say." Mickey stirred the cereal and milk together, watching little steam vapors break from inside the hot oatmeal.

The two boys in his room last night sat along the open edge of the table, scooping cereal and milk from their bowls, adding more butter to toast slices their mother had already buttered. Occasionally, one or the other glanced at him. The woman moved from the stove to the table, sitting between her sons, placing a long oval platter of wavy bacon strips and fried eggs on the table, close to the man.

The man said, "It's a godparent's duty to help a godchild when help's needed—God's help. So you'll be here for a time until your mother can take you in."

My mother, huh? Won'er wha' she's like?

"She and your sister live where there's only room enough for them—"

How much room is that?

"—only a very small apartment. Your mother wants you there—with them. She has wanted you there ever since Margaret has been living with her. She wanted you there from the very beginning. She wanted you both from the very beginning, from the day you were each born—"

Yeah? Well, where was she until jus' now?—jus' yesterday, I guess it was.

"—but things just did not work out for her. As I said, she wanted you with her when she got Margaret. But there just wasn't enough room in her place for both you children. So she did the best she could at the time. She at least took care of one of you—and it happened to be your sister. She had to make a choice that no one should ever have to make.

"Do you understand what I am saying?"

Mickey nodded that he did.

"Son, I don't mean to talk this way at breakfast. Meals are to nourish one's self, both body and mind, not to overwhelm someone unpleasantly." Mickey nodded again that he understood.

"With that said, you just dig in at whatever's here. You must be famished after your experience. We'll talk later—you and I—and your aunt.

"One last thing, I promise. Your aunt here, she and your mother were best friends all the time they were growing up themselves. Your aunt can be a big help.

"Let her be helpful." He scooped up hot oatmeal with a tablespoon, blowing at steam, cooling the heaping spoonful, then looked at Mickey.

"Oh—call the boys' mother Aunt Margaret. Your sister's named for her. I'm Uncle Pete.

"The boys are Hal—he's the oldest—and Pete Junior is a year younger."

Mickey heard nothing from his father, and he asked no questions. No explanation was made of how he arrived in the small austere second-floor bedroom of a badly aging house in a grimy section of an industrial city. After a while he stopped wondering. How or why or when or anything else did not seem important. He just knew that things were different, and that was good enough.

For a long time Mickey saw little of his mother—the shorter, plumper woman of the two he had turned to face on a mystifying night. But it regularly occurred to him what it was that had surprised him most at that moment—he had not *recognized* her. He had never even seen a picture of her in any of the many small apartments in which he and his sister and his father had lived since he was about nine or ten years old—as far back as he could remember, not even in any of the several photograph albums his father had. It was three weeks—as best as he could remember—before he saw her after that nighttime scene in the new house. Then it was only for a few minutes, and all he remembered was that she said something like "Hello" and "How're you doing?" He did not remember her even leaving, not even saying good-bye. Had she really left without saying good-bye?

It was a long while before Mickey felt as though Margaret was his sister. He saw her only briefly in the first three weeks after their long separation, next at Christmas months later, then only occasionally for a long while after that. She seemed to only be another girl, not a sister.

Mickey realized, in a short time, that his new circumstances were a black-and-white contrast to his recent way of living. Day-to-day life was not going to be the same. He bridled inwardly at the new confinement, greatly agitated at the start—though he tried to not let these new grown-ups see it—then less and less angry, then only occasionally annoyed. Now there were two adults in his life every day, and for a major part of each day, except for when they were at their jobs and he was attending school; and every morning and every afternoon and evening, and during every night there were the same two boys.

And he lived in a house, a real house, not just another apartment, even if the house was in a section of the city with factories nearby, one as close as a half block, and there was a big moving company warehouse also only a half block in the other direction; and even if outside his bedroom window there was the above-street-level viaduct that was the roadbed for four sets of railroad tracks that went for several miles through the city. Apartments were all he had ever known as living quarters; some of them cold-water flats, with kerosene space heaters for warmth, a couple early places with small coal stoves in a living room, and better apartments had steam heat. It did not make any difference to him that his new bedroom had no heat in it, that the three boys had to move quickly after they got out of bed and rush down stairs into the kitchen so they could take turns changing in the bathroom between the kitchen and the closed-off front room that they called the parlor—he had never heard anyone call their living room by that name, though he knew what a parlor was.

After a delay of several days, school records were transferred from one state school system to another state's system—records more detailed than Mickey had expected, with a chronology of absences and tardiness and with subject grades and teacher comments, usually negative.

Mickey's guardians were prepared when high school officials said that one of them had to appear at their offices to discuss his entry into a new school system. Aunt Margaret went with an embarrassed, guilty-feeling Mickey, embarrassed because he had a good idea of what she would learn. "She's going with you," Uncle Pete told him, "because she knows more about these things—and she has already made arrangements with her boss at work for a morning off to get you enrolled."

Aunt Margaret was astonished when Mickey's records were shown to her. With well more than half the freshman year completed, the principal was reluctant to admit Mickey.

Uncle Pete was surprised—but not angry, not even seeming annoyed; he just sat quietly, occasionally slightly shaking his head from side to side in mild wonder, occasionally glancing at Mickey, who kept his eyes down—when Aunt Margaret told him, as they sat at the kitchen table, what had happened with the principal.

Well, yes, the principal understood that the boy *had* satisfactorily completed eighth grade, but then there's the matter of the freshman year being so far along now and getting in now the boy might not be able to keep up with classmates considering how much time he had already lost and seeing how low his New York City grades were, and with all the Fs he already had, he probably couldn't—but it was right, ma'm, that he has to be in school *somewhere*—that he just can't spend the rest of the school year not doing anything about his education. Well, he agreed, the boy would be enrolled as a freshman, but said that he *had* to admonish the guardian *and* the boy both that, in light of the transfer record, the boy's advancement to sophomore depended on *superior* attendance *and* no failing grades in any subject *and* good marks for deportment.

Mickey went to school each day because of the strict notice and close adult supervision; because he did not want to make trouble; because he thought he might be sent back to his father otherwise. *At leas' I got two other kids aroun' a lot so I can do things with somebody.*

The boys were affable and quiet types. The older, Harold—Hal—was two years younger than Mickey, though almost the same in height and form, but not with the same strength. Pete Junior, was a year to the day younger than Hal. The differences in age meant little to Mickey. They were the only two boys in the small neighborhood, and Mickey had quickly been told the roaming range Hal and Pete Junior were allowed by their parents. The three boys were occasional companions for brief wanderings after school, three o'clock to five-thirty, when the adults returned from work in different places in the city.

That the two boys were "family" had not, in the full sense of the word, occurred to Mickey. The term *first cousins* was only a vague description, giving him little understanding of who they were other than two boys he was getting to know better, slowly, learning to accept and to like despite how different they were from most boys he had known. *Well—I'm sorta bein' forced into it, I guess ya could say. Might as well make the best of it, huh? Mick?*

Mickey investigated his new environment in small measures as he walked the blocks between house and schools, but he did not go far afield from the customary route that took fifteen to twenty minutes to stroll. He knew Hal and Pete Junior would always reach their house at a certain time, that they were never detained after school for an indiscretion, that they never tarried along the way home. He subtly tried to involve them in small explorations when he discovered they knew little of their neighborhood's farther reaches, and knew even less about the city. Neither of them had ever explored a backyard or a building alley. He was surprised when they could not give answers about what was where, or about how far or close anything was. He planned quests to take them throughout the neighborhood, but their timidity was irritating. One or the other always was hesitant, talking about riskiness in doing what was proposed, or claiming inability to do what Mickey suggested because of a sore foot or a pain in a shoulder or a headache or a back or something else not feeling right.

Bullshit!

Always bullshit excuses!

However, he never said the profanity to them. He quickly understood that it was useless to intimidate them with obscenities. Their strict upbringing would win out. The boys were much like the Kelsey brothers, reared in a small world, with quiet, firm guidance; each brother satisfied with the other and with their parents, despite occasional unnoisy squabbling between the boys out of parent earshot; each boy happy with going to school every day and with doing homework; unconcerned about what went on outside their limited mobility range, with little adventurousness in their natures.

Mickey tinged each tale of a new close-by exploration of his with mild excitement, carefully describing what surrounded the two boys, what they had *not*

yet seen—but certainly *should* have, he told them, by *this* time. "Geez!" he once
said, "you guys have never done anythin', have ya?" He wondered to himself what
their two lifetimes must have been like all the time so far in their small confines.
Borin'! I'd bet my ass on that!

One afternoon, on a sunshiny, warm, late spring day, Hal surprised Mickey
when he said, "Can you take Petey and me somewhere with you? But first we have
to do some homework and want to be mostly done with it when our Ma gets
home, and so it'll be all done by the time Pop is there."

Mickey did run-of-the-mill things in the limited time they had for their first
excursion; led the two boys thorough streets with names they did not know,
showed them grocery and hardware stores, showed them a hobby shop with
innumerable plane, boat, and car models in the front window. He took them past
small and large factories with signs bearing names Hal and Pete Junior had only
heard.

On two other days, close together and less than a week later, Mickey suggested
going somewhere—he did not know *where* yet, but it did not make any difference
to him he said; they would find *some*place, *some*thing to do. Hal firmly said,
"No—too much homework!" Mickey saw Pete Junior's disappointment each time,
but Mickey said nothing to persuade Hal.

The first time Hal said *no* to going along, Mickey remembered the school
admonition about grades. That was one reason for not trying to persuade Hal. He
stayed home with the two boys, doing his own homework assignments. He was
finding school work easy enough to do and was most interested and did best in
history, geography, civic studies, and general science. The least interesting to him
was mathematics, and he was especially confused by and disinterested in algebra.
*Wha' the hell am I ever gonna do with this algebra crap? Doin' numbers is somethin' I
can see doin'. Ever'body's gotta know how to add an' subtrac' an' stuff like that, but who
does this junk? I never seen nobody doin' it anyplace I ever been! I never saw either of
the Weinstein brothers doin' anythin' that needed friggin' algebra!*

The second time he asked and they again stayed with studying, he had only
brief, simple history and geography assignments, did them quickly, and went for
a slow-paced walk in warm air, a couple blocks north, turned right and went
through the train viaduct underpass, heading for the harbor area. In the school
library he had seen a city map and was intrigued when he discovered a waterfront
area. *That oughta make some good exploring territory!*

Wind and flood tide made the smell of salt water air strong. But not long after
entering the edge of the newly found area a five o'clock factory whistle sounding
loudly a few blocks away deterred him from further venturing. He had twenty
minutes to get to the house, to wash and sit down with a schoolbook, ready for
Aunt Margaret, always the first home, minutes before Uncle Pete.

Occasional roamings for the trio enlarged geographically and lengthened in
time, but the boys were always home on schedule, appearing industrious when the
adults returned from work. Hal saw to that, and Hal diligently prevailed often
enough because he did not want Pete Junior's grades to suffer because of less

attention to schoolwork. When Hal firmly won a discussion and made an unhesitating decision, Mickey sometimes joined them—once in a while willingly enough but usually reluctantly, depending on his mood and degree of restlessness—and spent time with homework, but more often, he roved on his own, swearing the brothers to secrecy about Mickey having gone off from the house.

Hal persistently argued, "It's getting close and closer to the end of the term. We do want to go see things with you—we really do. We've talked about it—how you've shown us a lot. But we both want to do good in school. Not because we *have* to. We *want* to—and we *like* school."

More bullshit!

Mickey's work in school barely was passing. Twice different teachers quietly told him at the end of a class that he had failed a brief quiz, in both cases missing a passing mark by one wrong answer. Soon after the second notice, the principal had Mickey stop by at the end of a day and talked with him briefly at the school office front counter to caution him about maintaining passing grades or he would not be a sophomore. "This is only a reminder, son. The next time I will have to let your folks know. It's the school system."

Mickey halfheartedly glowered at Hal.

But—well, school ain' as bad—isn' as bad as it used to be, I guess. Maybe I'll get to like it if I go long enough!

"Okay, Hal—if tha's how ya feel. But I foun' somethin' you really oughta see." Pete Junior's eyes widened. Mickey paused before adding, "Maybe someday soon we *all* can go there. Boy, you oughta see what it is."

"Yeah," Hal said, "soon maybe. Don't get all excited, Petey. Start studying!"

Mickey had discovered a monolith structure during a solitary out-of-the-way meandering from school, a mile from home. It was at the street side of a huge jumbled lot—a block-square field of razed buildings; with some deep foundations and low sections of brick walls not yet completely reduced to small rubble; huge piles and large and small clusters of bricks and mortar; door frames sprinkled everywhere; hundreds of windows turned into millions of pieces of glass.

A hundred-foot-high, circular, brick smokestack, twenty feet in diameter at the base, towered above everything for several blocks of two- and three-story small factories and warehouses. To Mickey's eyes it was a magnificent construction, the first time he had seen such a thing from a close vantage. It had loomed suddenly when Mickey wandered aimlessly around a street corner, a long half-block away. He crossed the roadway to the sidewalk lightly littered with rubble, walking slowly toward the smokestack, even more slowly than he had been meandering before, awed by the close view of the tremendous tapering height. Closer, stopping to stare, he saw countless circular rows of bricks, up and up, changing from distinctly reddish bricks at ground level to a darker red hue—with brick and mortar detail no longer visible to the eye—to a solid mass of dark color at the top opening that had not spewed waste for a long while. He approached closer, tipping his head back more with each step, eyes on the small-looking top, feeling a slight dizziness as he focused on the silhouette. It seemed to be wavering. He stopped moving, shading his eyes with both hands, his neck aching, wondering which way to run if the wavering top suddenly tumbled down. He kept staring up. *Hey—don' worry! It's jus' the moving' clouds that make it look like the top's waving aroun' up there!*

Wow—ee!

Look at it go!

He studied the base of the smokestack, walking slowly again, moving closer. Its circumference was about six feet from the sidewalk. At ground level, a ten-foot high circular section of corrugated metal conduit protruded from the side of the stack base, boarded over where the metal had been burned through with a cutting torch during building demolition. The short horizontal section was all that remained of a tunnel through which had run pipes for carrying boiler room wastes from a factory building toward the sky.

Mickey reached a small, decrepit wooden door that hung inwardly on one hinge. Two rusted metal signs were fastened to the tilted door: DANGER! in foot-high faded red letters; below it KEEP OUT! in six-inch-high red letters, equally faded.

Mickey moved into gray light, squeezing through a narrow opening. *Shit, this is easier than gettin' through them narrow openin's at the bottom o' subway gates in stations without 'tendants!*—clambering over fallen bricks that held the door fast in its tipped position. Brilliant sunlight entered the top of the stack, darkening as it spread down, deadened by the thick layer of grime coating the interior. As his eyes adjusted to the dimness, he saw a series of steel rods bent at two corners, each shape embedded into the wall, regularly spaced one above the other, forming ladder rungs, used for inspecting the interior chimney surface for soundness. Far overhead, Mickey saw the sky as a small spot of grayish-blue. *Holy geez! Look a' them steps! What a heckuva feelin' it mus' be to climb to the top of this thing!*

The damn thing is higher than that roof I went off to the clothesline pole! He shuddered at that sudden vividness.

Several days later, with two idly curious cousins in tow, after promising an adventure that he kept nameless, Mickey led the way into greater dimness than he had been in on his first visit. He wondered if he should have come back with two younger kids. Along the route from home he kept them mystified, even after turning the corner and the smokestack appeared suddenly in full, towering view— neither boy commented on what Mickey thought was a majestic construction— even after standing on the sidewalk six feet from the broken wooden door listing in the corrugated metal conduit. Neither Hal or Pete Junior understood his intent when he pointed up. "Here it is. Great!—ain' it? Wait'll ya see the inside!" The brothers looked uneasily at each other.

The sky was becoming more overcast, darker than when they had left home, now carrying the threat of a sea-borne storm sweeping across Long Island's narrow land mass and Long Island Sound waters. "C'mon, follow me—an' stay close, okay?" Mickey led them across the broken glass and fallen bricks, threading through piles of debris, and past the DANGER and KEEP OUT signs.

The round stack interior was gloomy, mysterious; depressing the brothers' spirits from the elation of a soon-to-be-experienced adventure they had felt at home and along the way. Little light seeped down from the port high overhead. Mickey tried re-exciting the boys with the mystery and adventure of what they were doing. Trepidation, however, made them nearly speechless. When they spoke, they had to repeat their words. Mickey was unable to decipher their mumblings. Their disappearing eagerness and confidence eroded even more as they penetrated the murkiness.

Pete Junior wanted to be the last to enter, but Hal acted as rear guard, herding the wary youngster ahead of him, more as a sense of protection than because of his own reluctance. "Spooky, ain' it?" Mickey said, softly. Pete Junior blurted, "Do we have to stay in here? There's nothing to see—nothing to do."

"That ain' true, Petey," Mickey said, voice tinged with enthusiasm. "Look up there. Look hard. See? There's a ladder on the wall. Betcha it goes all the way to the top!" He looked at their faces. They were both shadowed masks, both frowning.

"Imagine—" Mickey kept talking softly, "goin' all the way up an' lookin' outside. From up there I'll betcha could see a hunnert miles." Pete Junior shook his head from side to side vigorously. Hal stared at Mickey. "Petey can't do anything like that! Going up there? It would be too scary for him—and it's too scary for me, too! I wouldn't want to do it!"

"I know—I know," Mickey said. "I was jus' thinkin' what it would be like—an' I was really meanin' *me* when I said 'bout goin' up. I don' think I could go all the way up there either." Hal shook his head up and down slightly, saying, "That's a pretty hard thing to do—for anybody."

"I was jus' showin' ya," Mickey said, "what it's like to see somethin' diff'rent—to know diff'rent kinds o' things—so you could have stories to tell—so you won' be 'fraid o' things."

"We going now?" Pete Junior said.

Mickey sighed. "Okay—we'll go find somethin' else to do—an' we'll head home in a little while."

Floor rubble clunked as it was moved by clambering feet going for the listing door and full daylight. "Wait a secon'," Mickey said. "I wanna try goin' up a few steps on that ladder." He moved over the clutter to the wall, looking up for the first rung. "You guys wanna wait in here? Wait outside if you want?" He heard whispers between the brothers. "In here," Hal said.

Mickey jumped up several inches, keeping his eyes on the hard-to-see ladder rung, and clutched at the rough metal step with both hands, hoping it would not pull loose. Hanging onto it grimly, he poked a hand upward several inches for the next rung, then moved his lower hand up to the third rod, flailing his legs, struggling until he put a knee on the bottom rung. He grunted with satisfaction when he got into position with both knees on the first step. He found another rung overhead, lifting himself to get both feet solidly on the lowest step. With tight grips on two separate rungs, after jerking and twisting each to test for secure fastening to the brickwork, Mickey shook his body up and down to positively test the security of the first rung, and decided to keep testing the perches as he progressed upward.

He quietly sighed in relief, not wanting the boys to hear. Below, he could still dimly see their faces. With a deep breath, he started climbing slowly, steadily, jerking each rung, trying to pull one loose, starting to hope one would jiggle a little bit. He was beginning to feel less sure of himself, to wonder if his scheme was such a good idea. He carefully kept track of his movement up the rungs—*fourteen—fifteen—sixteen*—stopping with both feet on the twentieth. *Holy geez! I did it!* Looking down, he could not see either boy. *Won'er if they're still here inside?*

He climbed five more rungs, exhilarated that he had gone at least as far as twenty steps up into near darkness, then decided he could go another five—*at least!* Up he went. *Twenty-five!* They were easy to do. *Hey—why not five more?* He tested each rung vigorously as he climbed *Thirty! Now I'll jus' do five more—jus' fer good measure!* Again he went up. *There—thirty-five!*

He calculated how far he had risen. *There's gotta be at least a foot between each o' these steps—so that's thirty-five feet right there—an' that first step hadda be 'bout five or six feet up the wall. Wowee!—I gotta be forty feet up in the air!* He gripped a rung at chest level more firmly. He peered into the gloom below but saw nothing but blackness. He thought about calling down to Hall and Pete Junior but decided it might make them think he was nervous.

He looked up. *The light at the top is gettin' brighter. I'll bet it really would be a great sight from up there.* He felt like he was back on his own in the big city, back doing one of a zillion zany adventures that most of the kids he knew were always doing.

Yeah—tha' was great—but I better not keep doin' this with these guys bein' aroun'. Boy, if I get hurt or somethin' they'll be the ones in a heap o' trouble.

He moved down slowly, counting, smiling as he felt a foot on the twentieth rung, then on the fifteenth, then on the tenth. From that perch he could see the two faces peering up, watching him closely. On what he calculated to be the bottom rung, he slid a sneaker-covered foot down along the brickwork, searching for one more rung, but there was none. With both feet on the last step, he lowered his hands rung by rung until he was in a tight crouch, hands clutching the third rung up, then let himself drop, hoping the floor was flat where he would land, that he would not twist an ankle or fall clumsily. He touched down lightly, turning as Pete Junior clapped hands. Hal said, "That was pretty good."

"Now I wish I'da gone all o' the way up," Mickey said, exulted. "I coulda done it—jus' to see what the outside looks like from up there."

Hal spoke quietly, squinting up the stack. "I know Petey can't make it up, but maybe I'll try going a little way. Okay?"

Mickey smiled as he braced his back against the dirty wall, surprised at Hal's new and unexpected willingness, lacing fingers together to make a step below his waist for Hal's start in reaching the first rung with his hands. Pete Junior stared up at his brother climbing slowly up into the gloom, disappearing; waiting nervously until he could not keep from calling out, "Hal?—you all right?"

"It's okay." Hal's voice sounded hollow, echoing. "I'm high enough I can't see anybody from up here. I'm on my way down."

Pete Junior applauded when Hal landed on the ground awkwardly, grunting heavily. "My turn—huh, Hal?"

"What? What do you mean, your turn?" Hal's voice was angry. "Naw—you shouldn't go up there! It's too scary—too hard to do. I don't want you getting hurt!"

"Why would I get hurt? *You* didn't get hurt. I'd just do it the way you told me to. I'd be all right."

Hal stared at the smaller boy. "Because I'd be the one in trouble if—"

"There's not going to be any trouble. Just let me get up and go a couple of steps. You could still watch me in the light that's up there. I just want to see what it's like. *You* did."

"Darn you, Petey. Always—well—remember, don't look down!"

Mickey and Hal gripped wrists to make a platform between them, lifting Pete Junior high enough to reach the third rung with his hands, making it easy for him to put his feet on the lowest step. He pulled himself up hand over hand. As he rose into deep shadows, the two watchers heard soft, fearful moans. Nonetheless, Pete Junior climbed. "My feet are on step number ten, okay? I'm coming down now, okay?"

Pete Junior was the most voluble on the trip home for supper. By nature, both boys were generally subdued, not talkative, but throughout the entire walk home they were the liveliest Mickey had seen them. He congratulated them, cautioning that they ought not describe their adventure at home, even hint at it. Their parents might not approve of such wandering, he warned. *Might not? Shit!—they'd kill me if they ever foun' out!*

As much as they tried to stay calm, at supper Aunt Margaret asked Pete Junior what had gotten into him and Uncle Pete said he had never seen Hal so talkative.

Two Saturdays later, after an early lunch, the three boys were given permission to go to a baseball diamond in a park a dozen blocks away from home. "But," Aunt Margaret said, "be home by four o'clock or so—four-thirty at the latest. I'll be canning all afternoon and we're having supper early, because, as a treat, father is taking us all to a movie that's showing at seven o'clock tonight."

Halfway to the ball diamond Mickey suggested it could be more fun if they all explored down by the docks. He added, "Think of what could happen there!" Hal shrugged his shoulders, seemingly indifferent, facing Mickey squarely, making sure his back was to Pete Junior, covertly holding a fist in front of his chest, making short thumbing motions at Pete Junior, a step behind. "Gee," Hal said, "I don't know."

Pete Junior spoke up. "Hey, I know you're saying that because of me. But let's all of us go—me too. We could have another good time like that. They all agreed on visiting the docks.

Mickey took them to where he had not himself been before, wending through blocks of industrial buildings with open windows letting out sounds of banging and clanging and clicking and whirring and buzzing and thumping. Where they could manage it, they peered into openings to see what things were making such sounds. They wandered aimlessly, getting to a broad inlet that poked in from the bay, almost touching a broad asphalt roadway fronting a long row of warehouses. A hundred-foot-long wood pier extended out into the water. Tide was at full ebb. Much of the inlet bottom was exposed; dark, oily; sloping down gradually from the shore for half the pier length before the deeper, dredged part of the inlet began. At the far right side of the inlet a dredging barge floated, crane and clamshell scoop poised for Monday morning.

"Hey," Pete Junior said, excited, "there's a big tugboat out at the end of the pier. Can we go look at it? I've never seen a real one, just pictures—and in the movies. It's big, isn't it?"

A deck hand answered Pete Junior that they could not come aboard—even though it was all right with him—because he didn't know if the captain would have said they could come if he was here—but he's not—that he was sorry he had to say no. They walked slowly along the pier back to the roadway.

"This is a little like the piers I used to fool aroun' on back where I came from," Mickey said. "A bunch o' us guys—a big bunch—we did all kinda great things— had good times—" He leaped up onto a rope-tied cluster of three thick round pilings, the flat tops three feet higher than the pier planking, pretending he had lost his balance, waving arms about comically. Then he stood erect, looking over his shoulder to the bay, remembering the wide river and the many piers on which he had been. He looked down at Hal and Pete Junior. "But this is only a *little* like those. The tops o' ours were higher above the water—a lot higher—an' the water was always plen'y deep—deep enough so we could do some swell dives cuz the pilin's all stuck up way above the dock." He jumped down to the planks.

Twenty feet before the road, as Mickey and Hal talked about what they could all look for next, Pete Junior hopped onto a stubby, rope-bound cluster of two pilings with broad, round, flat top surfaces. He stood easily balanced, looking at the backs of the two boys walking away from him.

"Hey!—look!" he yelled.

The two boys glanced over their shoulders as they kept moving. "Petey!—get off!" Hal shouted, as he spun about to face Pete Junior.

"Jesus Christ!—" Mickey said loudly, as he turned too. "You better watch it. Those things are slimy a lot o' times!"

Pete Junior lofted himself up lightly, leaping to another piling group three feet away, closer to the other two boys. The slight loft was gracefully done and Pete Junior agilely landed atop the flat-topped poles, smiling, looking first at Mickey's eyes, then at Hal's. Pete Junior wriggled his body, waved arms, and did dance steps. Mickey laughed and applauded and shouted "Copy cat!"

"C'mon, Petey—get off there!" Hal moved a step to his brother. Pete Junior's eyes widened as his feet moved faster on the slippery, slick-oil-film wood of his new perch; his body wriggled more, his arms moved in larger, irregular arcs.

"Holy shit!" Mickey yelled. "He ain' kiddin' now!"

Pete Junior's fingers clawed at air for six feet, plunging, flailing arms wildly, body vertical, legs pumping as though riding a bicycle. He WHUMPED into thick, slurpy, oily black mud coated by foul-smelling slimy residue of bilge fluids pumped overboard by dockside vessels, sludge that resisted inward and outward motions of slowly flooding and ebbing tides.

Pete Junior was sunk almost to his knees in the muck, yelling loudly, frantically, terrified by the grip on his thin legs, out of reach of the pilings, where even a slight touch on them could have eased his fright. Mickey was surprised at Hal's calmness at his brother's plight, expecting him to panic, to act dumbstruck. Mickey turned away from Hal and moved to the edge of the pier and knelt, stretching an arm to the whimpering boy. Their hands could not connect. Mickey turned to give instructions to Hal, but he was at a warehouse door, pulling a long board from one of several empty crates stacked against the building.

Pete Junior clawed strenuously at Hal's board extended down to him, missing each time. With one off-balance grab he pulled a foot from the quagmire. He fell forward, a beseeching look on his face turned up to his brother. PLOP!

He kept his head up, snatching wildly at the board with both hands, splashing rainbow-colored oily water, grabbing the board, nearly jerking it from Hal's hands at the moment Mickey laid hands on the board to help. The two boys hauled mightily, tugging the contorting body, helping pull the second leg from the sludge. "Hang on, Petey," Hal yelled. "We'll pull you in to shore where we can reach you better."

Pete Junior slid across the surface as they pulled, pushing uselessly with his feet, scrambling futilely for shore. Mickey's and Hal's efforts were awkward as they maneuvered round two other sets of pilings until the hapless victim's thrashing feet finally struck firmer footing. Pete Junior stumbled up onto the pavement, gasping, exhausted, falling spread-eagled on his back. "I'm okay!—I'm okay!"

"Geez—ain' he a mess!" Mickey said, smiling. Hal, glowering down at his brother, said, "You sure you're not hurt?"

"Nah—it's okay—I'm okay. I'm just all wet—and all dirty." He sat up, water draining off, oily slime streaking his clothing, gobs of mud sticking here and there. His hair was bedraggled and matted. Mickey said, "You look like a wet, sick puppy, Petey." Pete Junior smiled. "Yeah—but I did it, didn't I?"

Hal suddenly said, "I know how we can get him clean, clothes and all." Keeping the sodden boy between them, Hal led Mickey a mile and a half to the city-owned salt water beach, explaining to Mickey, "Our folks take us here three or four times every summer." In a cavernous public men's locker room and shower Mickey, said, "Nice goin', Hal! Good thinkin'," lightly punching Hal's shoulder in approval. "Great—now we're outta trouble at home!"

Mickey and Hal stripped to their undershorts and stripped Pete Junior naked, tossing all their clothing and sneakers in a heap in the portal between locker and shower rooms. Pete Junior was embarrassed by his nakedness, worried strangers might enter, but Hal was insistent. "Don't be so dumb. Only a few people are out on the beach. The water's too cold for real swimming. Anybody out there's just getting some suntan. Nobody's coming in here. Besides—think of the trouble we'd all be in if you showed up at home looking like you did." Hal turned on the shower, twisting handles to get the water hot enough to dilute and wash away the heavier oil. Mickey searched trays at each shower head, finding small remainders of two soap bars. Hal started soaping and scrubbing his naked brother's head and back. Mickey yanked doors open of locker after locker and found a towel left behind. It looked clean enough to suit them.

As Hal helped Pete Junior lather, scrub, and rinse, Mickey soaked all their clothes under another shower, striving hastily, soaping everything, rinsing, soaping, rinsing, soaping, rinsing, until the soap broke into small slivers, hoping no foulness remained.

When Pete Junior glistened, Mickey and Hal each quickly and light soaped and rinsed their bodies and heads with the last trace of the soap used on Pete Junior. They pulled on wet underwear and trousers, gathered up other wet clothing, sneakers, the towel, two baseball gloves, a ball, a bat, and walked along the warm sand toward the long breakwater of craggy boulders at the beach's west end. They found a distant place out among the boulders near the end of the breakwater where they stripped to undershorts and laid out clothing flat on hot dry rocks to dry in the bright sun.

They joked and laughed and exaggerated events, creating a larger adventure; the best one yet, the brothers said; nothing like they had ever tried before—for *darn* sure! Prowess and antics and reactions were excitedly told and retold for half an hour in the refreshing onshore breeze and rejuvenating sunlight. Pete Junior's frowns disappeared. He seemed to glow with an after-pleasure stirred by thrills of his episode. Hal, warming to his brother's elation, seemed different to Mickey.

Checking clothing and footwear for smells, and satisfied no trace remained of oil or slime or sludge or filth, the three boys dressed, then hurried to the small park and ball diamond to carry out a scheme developed on the breakwater. Two hours later, sweat-soaked, faces, hands, and clothing streaked with infield dirt and blotched with outfield grass stains, they trudged home triumphantly.

In the warm kitchen, the boys' mother—busily working at simmering pans and pots—said, a moment or two after the trio had entered, she thought something smelled strange. Hal said it might be the creosote that park workers were putting on every piece of wood that was stuck in the ground, and they were doing it at the same time everybody was playing ball. "One of us must have accidentally got some of the stuff on us by touching something that just got swabbed. Or maybe something from one of the benches got on one of us. There were wet paint signs on all the benches—but it wasn't really *paint* on them—it was some kind of dark wood stain—and you know how that stuff smells when it's new, Mom—but the wood was dry—I made sure of that, with Petey being with us—but you know how that smell stays around, Mom—from the stuff that Dad has done—"

"My, my, Hal—you certainly are going on, aren't you?" his mother said patiently, peering into a pot as she stirred. "I don't know when I've heard you so talkative." She lifted the lid of a deep pot and slowly stirred the contents. "Well, then, Hal," she said quietly, "knowing what the workers were doing, you should have seen that everyone was more careful." She stood up straight, facing the boys, smiling. "Now, you boys wash up for supper and the movies." Mickey's peripatetic exploits included Hal and Pete Junior less often from then. He did not want to be the cause of them getting into troublesome situations. He liked the two boys. Hal taught him what he knew of playing baseball and the rules of the game, and he helped Mickey with homework. And Pete Junior always seemed excited by seeing and doing new things, however slight. The three of them went to an occasional movie on a Saturday morning, but Mickey made sure they returned directly home, despite once-in-a-while mild urgings by the two boys, especially Pete Junior, to explore. All in all, the time they spent together away from home dwindled.

The school year ended. Mickey's attendance, owed to a mixture of supervision and increased willingness to go to school, plus attention in class and to homework, resulted in passing grades and promotion to sophomore. With the final report for the school year carried home for signature, he nervously apologized for the C grade. "Mickey," Uncle Pete said, "it's all right. It's only fair of us to expect that you at least *pass*. This C grade means you learned as much as an average student is expected to learn. You're intelligent. You're smart. You've got a lot of time ahead of you. You'll be better than a C student. We already know that."

When summer vacation started, Mickey asked his aunt and uncle when he might be going to live with his mother and sister. They were evasive; one day soon it might be possible, perhaps very soon; he would have to be patient; his mother was trying to work things out to have it be real soon, she hoped, they said.

Twice that late spring and early summer, on prearranged afternoons, his mother came by the house. The same routine was followed each visit. They rode a bus downtown, ill-at-ease with each other, speaking awkwardly, not knowing what to say, speaking more in fragments than in whole sentences, speaking with lots of hemming and hawing, with lots of *ers* and *uhs*.

On the first bus trip she asked about Hal and Pete Junior and their parents; how everything was going—in general, as she put it. "Uh—pretty good—I guess." She asked about high school and his studies, about how he was doing, if he liked the school. "Okay—uh—I guess." She told him things his sister was doing, how good she was doing with her roller-skating—"Tha's good—yeah—"; how worried she was about her interest in boys—she was such a young girl to be thinking so much about boys—"Yeah—uh, huh—"; how very good she was doing in school— "Uh, huh—" He could not bring himself to ask her directly why he could not live with them, instead of staying with some aunt and uncle a dozen blocks away, even as much as he liked them; why he could not at least visit them once in a while, say every two weeks or so, maybe every week.

Wha's so hard 'bout that?

Downtown, they walked slowly past blocks of retail stores, window-shopping. On their first visit she bought him a sleeveless argyle sweater as a gift. In his mind he was not certain he would ever wear it—it was such a pattern of large reddish

and brown diamonds—*How'm I gonna look in this thing?—like some dumb ol'
smarty-pants know-it-all school kid?*—but he thanked her; and he did wear it, after
a couple weeks, and came to like it as a favorite piece of clothing for school.

On their second visit to a crowded and busy downtown, Mickey admired
a pair of bright red canvas ankle-high sneakers with white laces and trim. She
dug through a worn coin purse from her pocketbook, finding a dollar bill and
several coins, adding them to his ninety-five cents so he could have the bright
footwear.

On that trip she bought him a Dixie cup of ice cream from a street vendor
and they slowly walked back to a bus stop. The return stroll took longer on both
visits. She tired easily because of her great weight. She clutched a rumpled
handkerchief to repeatedly wipe perspiration from her forehead and forearms and
hands.

Homeward, on each ten-minute bus ride, it was more difficult to talk, and
each spent much of the time gazing out a window, not really seeing things along
the way. Mickey each time again wanted to ask why they lived apart, but kept
silent, resolved to be patient, as Uncle Pete had advised. When the bus reached the
stop two blocks from where he lived, from where they would go in opposite
directions, she continuing on the bus, they said awkward good-byes, without
touching. On the second visit, nearing the stop, he wanted to blurt questions
about her and his father, but did not. Then he decided this time he *would* ask
about living with her and Margaret, but did not. Pain in his throat made him want
to cry. He glared at his reflection in the bus window. *A guy from where you're
from—a big city kid—who was in the Hell Raisers—ain' gonna cry on no bus—in
fron' o' people—in fron' o' his own mother!—Jesus!—you're fifteen years ol' now! almost
sixteen!*

Mickey became closer with the two boys and their parents. He settled into the
family routine. He wandered less. He became better at throwing, catching, and
hitting a baseball. Sport became more interesting. He started listening to baseball
games on the radio in the kitchen, though Hal told him he should not be listening
to the radio when he was doing homework. He found that he was wanting to *help*
Hal and Pete Junior, at whatever it was that the two boys were doing or wanted.
The family's life was his life, except for going to church.

Early on, asked by Aunt Margaret what religion he had been raised in, what
church he wanted to attend, he answered Protestant; that he did not want to go to
church for a while, if he did not have to. "It's all right," she said. "You take your
time. There'll be time enough later to talk about it, if you want to, when you feel
better about everything."

Each Sunday he was allowed to sleep late, awakened a few minutes before the
family left to walk several blocks to church, and asked to please to set the kitchen
table for the weekly special breakfast for them all. He enjoyed the task,
remembering how Mrs. Cartwright and Mrs. Kelsey fussed over every item being
just so at special meals. But more and more he felt disappointment at not going to
Sunday service with others.

In midsummer, disappointed by his second visit with his mother, he said to Aunt Margaret, "Would it be all right if I could start goin' to church on Sundays with all o' ya?" She showed her surprise, and smiled. "Of course. Next Sunday?"

"An' I been thinkin'," Mickey went on. "I oughta do it right. I should take some lessons—catechism lessons I guess they are—an' be like you people—be a Catholic." Aunt Margaret smiled again.

Father Auberge was a native of Canada; middle-aged, tall, corpulent, red-nosed, with thick, long all-gray hair that never seemed fully combed. His speech was slightly slurred, it seemed to Mickey when they first met. He wore eyeglasses with dark tortoise shell rims. His French-accented English was easy enough to understand except for the occasional slurring, but the gist of what he said was not always clear to Mickey because it was liberally laced with Latin words, terms, and phrases, and with occasional French-Canadian utterances that Mickey eventually suspected might be mild oaths since he used them when he seemed to be upset about something.

By the end of the second weekly hour and a half meeting in the priest's parish house study, Mickey was persuaded Father Auberge was a drinker. He acted the same as had a parent of two past friends. The first time they met, Father Auberge, slowly, carefully, and unsteadily strolled into the large room carrying a metal cup shaped like a wine glass. He kept the cup by his chair as he lectured, from time to time sipping from it. "My doctor says," he later told Mickey, when he noticed the boy steadily watch his movements each time he picked up the cup, as he drank, and as he put it down, "this light wine is as good as anything else for joints that ache. I decided what better way to take it than from this cup resembling a mass chalice. For me, it's a constant reminder that I serve the Lord." The priest had the small goblet in hand each time he entered the study for Mickey's catechism lesson.

The Thursday afternoon meetings with Father Auberge became a tribulation for Mickey. He was quickly interested at first when the priest began recounting the nearly two thousand-year history of Catholicism. And he was pleased with Father Auberge's gift—actually paid for by Aunt Margaret's special contribution to the Parish Fund, unknown to Mickey—of a catechism book with Mickey's name inscribed on an illuminated plate on the inside front cover. He was eager to learn something new, and this, a special course in something he essentially knew nothing about, would help in becoming part of his new family. He wanted to know the meaning of the religion that was so different from that to which he was accustomed, that had so many mystifying rituals, said in so peculiar a foreign language.

However, he lost his enthusiasm soon. Mickey questioned many of Father Auberge's statements, bristling at the priest's repeated sonorous incantation—*"Have faith, my son!"*—each time he was dissatisfied with garbled readings and lecturing by the priest and asked explanations. Before the second week's lesson was over Mickey realized the futility of questioning and arguing.

"You told me incest was horrible, after telling me only a little bit about what it was—but I figgered out what ya meant—and tellin' me that terrible things that will happen to mankind because of it goin' on today. But why were there no terrible things because of it in the beginning?—when everything first got started in the world."

"I don't understand what you mean," Father Auberge said, lifting the small chalice, sipping from it.

"Adam! Adam an' how he got here on Earth I can maybe unnerstan'—a little—cuz—like you said, 'Have faith!' So, then I have faith, and maybe believe there was a real miracle in the very beginnin'—that Adam was created just like *that*, like easy as snapping fingers—an' s'pose there really was Eve coming from Adam—you know—the rib? Okay—so I have faith and believe that—that *tha's* how the world got started—so simple—cuz of a miracle. Then Adam an' Eve have a son—like in the usual way—an' I awreddy *know* how *that* is—'cept they didn' have nothin' to use like people have today to keep from—well, you know what I mean, I guess—talk 'bout 'n accident, huh? Those two not even knowin' wha' they're doin' when they're doin' it or knowin' nothin' 'bout babies at all—cuz there was no babies anywhere—an' then later on Adam and Eve have another son—an' all tha' time they still don' know—"

The priest's forehead above the small chalice was getting red. Mickey sensed that he was saying something wrong, at least according to the priest. "Oh, oh—sorry, Father—I didn' mean ta joke."

Father Auberge peered over the goblet rim at Mickey, finished with a sip, holding the cup near his lips. "Yes?"

"Well—Cain kills his brother Abel—an' Cain gets sent away to live someplace besides Eden—an' then Cain gets a wife—and gets married, I guess—did people in those days get *married?*—I ain'—I *haven'*—seen nothing' yet—*anythin'* yet in all this readin' 'bout the word *married*—"

Father Auberge kept peering over the goblet rim, but moved it to rest on his lower lip, and slowly raised it to let wine slowly drain into his mouth.

"—an' the two of them have a son who later has his own son—an' then later *he* has *his* own son—an' so on an' so on—you know, father an' son an' father an' son—"

The priest lowered the small goblet to stop the wine from going into his mouth, but kept it pressed to his lip. He nodded at Mickey, slowly, to show he was listening.

"—then there's more children later on, huh?—for Adam an' Eve?—sons an' daughters for 'em—"

Father Auberge kept nodding, slowing the up and down movements.

"—then I read somethin' 'bout it came to pass that men began to multiply—meanin' there was a lot of 'em after a while, I guess—an' those guys—the *men,* I mean—saw the daughters an' liked 'em an' took 'em as wives—I don' know what *took* means; married 'em, I guess it means—"

The priest's nodding stopped, but the cup remained on his lower lip. Mickey saw that Father Auberge's eyes had narrowed behind the eyeglasses. He was squinting.

"—but I don' unnerstan' where Cain's wife came from—I didn' see anythin' 'bout her in what I read—an' I jus' know that there was only one female aroun' at the time, as far as I could find out—an' that was Eve—an' we know who she was—"

The priest drained the goblet quickly, then thumped it harshly onto the table by his chair. He hoisted himself awkwardly up from his overstuffed chair, glowering at the wall above Mickey's head. "I see you need to have more faith— but we don't have any more time for this particular subject today."

The time for that particular subject did not come again, though Mickey finished the series of catechism lessons. However, Father Auberge never came back to the point where he had thumped down his wine goblet and Mickey thought it best to leave the matter alone. He decided to do the least that needed to be done to become a Catholic so he would feel better about going to church on Sunday mornings with the rest of the family. Aunt Margaret and Uncle Pete both urged him to attend with the family while he was taking instruction, but he said he wanted to do the whole thing the *right* way, and the two grown-ups said nothing further; and Hal and Pete Junior were admonished to say nothing, so Mickey would not feel embarrassed. Ultimately, on a Friday evening Aunt Margaret was Mickey's sponsor at his baptism by Father Auberge, and she was the only family member with him. Mickey wanted it that way. The next evening she saw to it that he left home on time for the walk of four blocks to keep an appointment with the priest for a private confession so that Mickey's first church attendance the next morning would include a holy communion rite. "Then," Mickey told his aunt and uncle, "I'll be able to call it special—knowin' I did it right."

Kneeling in a pew in the dimly lighted church, head down, eyes cast upward, he watched Father Auberge come through a door at the side of the altar and walk slowly along a side aisle toward the confessional, steadying himself by tracing fingers along the wall. In the dark booth, Mickey sensed that the priest had been drinking more than sacramental wine. Mickey fumbled his way through the ritual statement, saying general things, carefully avoiding his thefts and his lascivious thoughts and the Buddy-and-Patty episode and the under-the bridge escapade and hurting Aaron's attacker and sneaking rides on the subway and into movies and playing hooky and forging his father's name and countless other sins and Father Auberge mumbled that he should say three Hail Marys and an Act of Contrition.

Sunday morning, as he knelt at the altar railing, he felt he was now part of the family when he took part in a First Communion ceremony with several younger children. Afterward, Uncle Pete shook his hand, then the brothers did, too. At breakfast Aunt Margaret smiled during almost the entire meal.

At the end of July, Mickey turned sixteen.

School started again on a misty, cold Tuesday following the Labor Day holiday. Mickey liked the learning he had done in his first extended period of attending school classes. He began his sophomore year with interest. This school was different than the last. Distinctions were not traded on to create cliques or rankings or castes or pecking order. After school each day he wandered less. He studied more, finding it easier and more enjoyable to do. By the end of September he felt a new assurance. *I can tell I'm gonna get better grades this year!*

He talked with his aunt and uncle at the kitchen table after one supper, explaining how much better he felt about being with them and the boys, about school, about grades, about working part time to earn some pocket money. "I know where I can get a job two days every week, after school is over, on Tuesday an' Thursday, four o'clock to six o'clock, an' eight o'clock to noon on Saturday mornings. It's a safe job, an' an easy one—bein' a shelf stocker at that big new grocery store on State Street—one of those new *supermarkets.* It's on the way between here an' school—an' it jus' got finished bein' built las' week. You oughta see the size o' the place—ten times as big as any other grocery store that you ever saw—maybe twen'y times bigger! It's got *everythin'* in it!"

Uncle Pete slowed Mickey's talkative pace by not answering immediately. Aunt Margaret looked at her interlaced fingers resting on the edge of the table. Then Uncle Pete said, "Your aunt and I have talked about this sort of thing. We've been expecting it would happen one of these days. We know you can't be spending all your free time with boys as young as Hal and Pete Junior. Later on a few years difference in ages won't make a difference between friends, but right now, at this time in your life, you need friends nearer your age. And you're going to need spending money to do things.

"You go ahead and go down to City Hall tomorrow after school—you get your working papers. But you've got to keep your grades up. Understand?"

"Sure I will—sure—an' thanks—thanks a lot—but can I give ya—say, half o' what I make every payday?—you know—to sorta help out a little—for me stayin' here an' all."

"You don't have to do that, Mickey," Aunt Margaret quickly said.

"Yeah—maybe I don'—but I *wanna.*"

"Certainly. We understand," she answered.

Each Tuesday and Thursday afternoon and Saturday morning for weeks Mickey reported to the warehouse at the rear of the gigantic retail grocery store. The assistant manager assigned the dozen after-schoolers, individually and in pairs, to widely dispersed sections of store shelving. His aim was to keep them busy, keep them from adolescent jabbering, keep them from horseplay and rowdyism. He had them unpack cases of canned goods, boxes, bags, and bottles, had them stamp prices on individual items, and had them fill in empty shelf spaces on store shelves. Each stocker used two-wheeled hand carts or four-wheeled flat-bed, castered trucks to lug cases from the bowels of the huge warehouse, rushing through aisles, hurrying to replenish assigned shelving areas as fast as possible, not to please the boss as much as to congregate with other boys.

There were other tasks; unloading trucks at the receiving platform, stacking cases almost to the ceiling to make space for incoming shipments from trailer trucks, or moving stock from one location in the warehouse to another site for one reason or another. Often, the quickest, highest-volume transfer method was to form a long human chain of stockers for passing cases to one another in the manner of levee workers passing bags of sand to stem a flood, or like old-time firefighters with their bucket brigades of water in small portions to douse large fires.

One afternoon there was a new stocker in the queue that turned a corner, the line snaking to move cases of soups and vegetables. The new boy faced Mickey from a close distance, on the opposite side of a path of travel of rapidly moving heavy cases, tossed from one stocker to the next in quick succession. Mickey had not see the boy before. He stood at the point of the line that made a ninety-degree bend. Mickey stood opposite, facing him, the first one after the bend.

The other boy was taller, dark-skinned, dark-haired, muscular. His lips were a thin line, compressed as though he was angry. His eyebrows were pulled together, pinched above his nose, creating a pronounced vertical furrow. He had dark eyes. The whites did not appear white. Upper and lower lids were close, in a continual squint. He said nothing when he first saw Mickey; he just squinted. The intense look stifled Mickey's impulse to say any greeting.

Almost as soon as everyone was in position the flow of heavy cases started. In a straight line it was easy to get ready for the weight and impact of each case passed along, moving from one set of hands and arms to the next. Heads bobbed up and down or feet shuffled at a sudden or off-balance load on arms. Gasps and grunts popped along the line from efforts of catching, swinging, and tossing cartons.

Mickey was positioned a step away from the ninety-degree bend, the only corner in the long line from the truck at the dock edge to the high stacks being formed; a step from the new boy, who, with a quick movement, threw up his dangling arms, toward the line that Mickey could not see around the corner. A brown rectangular form landed on the other boy's outstretched palms. Effortlessly lifting the case in a smooth rising arc, he pivoted at the waist, toward Mickey, tossing the carton vigorously. Mickey's eyes widened. *Holy—ya coulda tol' me it was comin'.*

The box thudded onto Mickey's palms and forearms. He grunted at the sudden impact, struggling to not drop the case, shifting it awkwardly for a grip so he could pass it to the left. Rid of the load, he glared at the new boy at the corner, but he stared away from Mickey.

The next case came at Mickey as abruptly as the first, in the same belligerent way, causing him as much difficulty. The next case, too, and the next several, were delivered as harshly. Mickey breathed hard at his effort of keeping the flow going, but his movements had to get quicker, to keep pace with the new boy, who took case after case from someone around the bend, receiving it with his sharp hands-up motion, then, in much quicker pivots, snapped the box to Mickey, raising it for a pushing toss. Mickey kept ready, slightly reaching, tensing for the thumping impact, grimly watching the boy's movements. The boy stopped in the midst of his motion to toss. The chest-high carton tipped forward from his fingertips, starting to rotate, then fell. Mickey lunged forward, saving it from thudding onto the cement floor, balancing himself quickly—*Wha's this sonofabitch doin'?*—passing it safely along.

The next two dozen or so cases moved along with ease and regularity. Mickey's eyes did not meet the other boy's; he was always looking in another direction whether Mickey glanced at him or peered at him steadily. Then Mickey decided he should not try to get his attention, have eye contact with him. *He's taller'n me— stronger too—no gettin' away from that! Looks mean! Reminds me of Tony Minelli. Prob'ly jus' like him—always spoilin' for trouble!*

There I go—'fraid again!

I'm sick o' bein' afraid o' guys like this—an' like Tony!

The transfer job was done. Mickey moved further ahead in the line as it filed from the warehouse back into the store to carry on with stocking shelves. He asked a boy, "Who's this new kid? What's his name?"

"Bruno."

For the next two weeks Mickey heard talk of Bruno bullying other boys, but it was always a case of someone hearing it from someone else. The bullying seemed only to be wisecracks and insults. No one said anyone got beat up on, or hurt, not even pushed or jabbed. However, Mickey kept his distance from Bruno. Once, when he heard Bruno had been really nasty and was getting nastier each day, Mickey did not go to work the next afternoon, knowing it was likely that other trucks were due to be unloaded by a chain gang. In school he argued with himself. *See? You're so worried that you're puttin' your head up your ass! Now it's easy, ain' it? That way you won' see him—huh?*

Ain' that right?

Working far inside the warehouse, late on a Friday afternoon, Mickey looked for six cases of mushrooms for the assistant manager. He had said, "You stay 'til you find those six damn cases. This paperwork says they came in this week—and the boss put them on tomorrow's sale. He's already got them in the newspaper ads showing in large pictures. He says find 'em!"

Mickey was lucky. He found them quickly, only by chance turning left into an aisle rather than turning right into another aisle. He piled the six errant cartons on a hand truck. *Five minutes to put all these other cases on the floor back up on these stacks, an' two minutes to get his mushrooms out front—plen'y o' time left to be outta here on time.*

He had only hoisted one carton from the floor back onto its stack when he sensed someone behind him.

"I been sent to help cuz it's close to quittin' time." Mickey twitched at the suddenness of the voice in the quiet. He did not want to turn face the voice. *It's fuckin' Bruno!—shit!—oh, shit!* He did not answer, keeping his back to the other boy, seeing only Bruno's legs as he half-twisted himself, bent down, and lifted cartons from the floor, pushing them above his head to wherever one would fit. On one twisting bend he saw Bruno had moved, facing him, standing with a case in his hands. He shoved it at Mickey.

Mickey took it, pulling and lifting. For an instant it felt that Bruno had not relinquished his grip. Then the case came free and Mickey tossed it up onto the stack. Turning to Bruno for the next box, he stretched his arms out to have it put into his hands. Bruno effortlessly extended the heavy case, then let it drop. Muscles in Mickey's lower back tensed and strained and stretched painfully as he doubled forward, struggling with the sudden weight. In his mind he swore at Bruno as he slowly lifted the case atop others.

Turning back for another, he saw it being shoved at him, held so a corner formed a triangular point. It caught him in the midsection, thumping violently into a thin bundle of muscle and nerves below where ribs joined. As the blunt corner drove into his solar plexus, he doubled over, trying to pull himself back from the projectile. He did not completely dodge the quick thrust. He clawed at the bulk, shoving it away, but not in time. Quick, sharp pain stimulated tears. Mickey saw a surprised look in Bruno's eyes as the case was shoved back into his own abdomen. He stumbled backward, his eyes widening as he tripped over cartons on the floor. Trying to push the box aside with both hands, he could not use them to break his unexpected fall. His buttocks thudded solidly on the cement floor. He kept rolling backward, snarling with rage as his back scraped across cement. He floundered about, then scrambled in confusion onto all fours, wildly trying to orient himself, growling and grunting in frenzy. Mickey stood stunned, paralyzed by indecision. His mind screamed: *You asshole!—you fuckin' dummy!—you hadda knock him on his ass! You're fuckin' done fer!—you stupid!—*

Bruno leaped up, raging, eyes on Mickey, rushing, clenching him in a powerful bear hug. Mickey protected his face with crossed arms, expecting a punch instead of the sickening squeeze. His eyes shut tightly. He felt himself hurled free, spinning, thrown ferociously to the floor. Before he stopped tumbling, arms wrapping his head, he felt himself being lifted by the front of his shirt, fabric gripped so tightly at his throat he gagged for breath. A fist smashed into his face when his hands slipped down to claw at the collar, hitting above Mickey's nose, between the eyes. The fist smashed again, striking the corner of his mouth. Flesh inside caught between upper and lower teeth, making him squeal in pain. The grip at his collar was gone. He was roughly shoved away, stumbling backward blindly, arms crisscrossing his face, trying to protect himself better, pulling them in tighter, pressing hands tightly over each ear. A fist caught him above the left ear. He squeezed his head with hands and arms. Severely dazed, he felt hands biting into his shoulders at each collarbone. He was shaken violently, painfully, powerful hands tightening, fingers pressing more sharply. As nerves were pinched and twisted, excruciating pains shot through his neck and shoulders, flashing lightning strokes up into his head, down his upper arms, through his chest, ranging across his shoulder blades, and many parts of Mickey's body felt numb. He spun about roughly, feeling his feet leave the floor. His legs jerked like a berserk puppeteer's dangling, flailing marionette. He thumped heavily onto something solid, sprawling face down over full, unyielding cardboard cases of canned goods, hands behind his head, bent arms covering ears. He felt a box corner strike below a cheekbone. He squeezed his closed eyes tighter at the new pain. Fireworks went off behind his eyelids, changing from white explosions to reddening flashes, redder and redder. Whistles and squeals sounded in his mind, worsened by sudden booms that made him shudder. Red swept over everything, dulling sounds, stopping them. Red swirled quicker, dissolving into an enormous whirlpool, lightening in color, darkening, spinning into black, solidness, stillness.

Mickey's mind shuddered. His body shuddered. He tensed, dreading Bruno's next violence, feeling tremors attack one part of his body after another. He heard his own sobbing and snuffling. His mouth hurt. A place above his left ear hurt. He moved his head, covered by arms, scraping his cheek on coarse cement. He peered beneath an arm, raising it slightly, eyes searching, raising the arm higher, fearfully expectant, eyes sweeping the aisle, rolling warily and slowly onto his side, then onto his back, expecting a thudding foot or fist. Bruno *was* gone.

Mickey sat up slowly, testing for specific points of pain besides the general injury he felt. He leaned against cartons, fingers probing various hurts. He rose slowly, unsteadily, suspicious that Bruno had only hidden, that he lingered out of sight, ready to spring out when he saw Mickey relax, but Bruno *was* gone.

It seemed to Mickey that an age had gone by since he started searching for mushrooms, but the large-face warehouse clock over the door into the store showed six minutes to closing time. He rubbed a handkerchief across his face, hoping no injury marks showed, that his eyes were not red. He restacked the fallen mushroom cases onto the hand truck, wheeled it out front, and left it standing by the bare shelf, ready for cans to be price-marked and put up the first thing in the morning before the store opened for customers.

Mickey walked to the front of the store, avoiding aisles with the few remaining customers, and went to the timeclock near the manager's cubicle, getting to the card rack quicker than he expected, happy that no one else was there yet. *Some kids an' reg'lar help mus' be workin' overtime a little bit. Good! Now I won' hafta answer any dumb questions about marks on my face!* Seconds seemed an eternity before the clock mechanism tripped to show the hour.

He left the store by the front entrance, walking past cashiers and the assistant manager, keeping his head down as he held hands high over his head, letting the lightweight baseball jacket wriggle down his arms as he grunted good-nights. He was thankful no one paid attention as he passed, some offering their own good-nights.

Mickey slowly walked eight blocks, feeling aches, limping slightly. Spreading evening grayness, under a thick, low overcast, depressed him even more, depression turning to anger. *That sonofabitch! Wha' did he come after me fer?* Mickey thoughtlessly struck out with a fist, striking at a mind's-eye image of Bruno, crying out in anguish and pain when the fist glanced off a rough brick surface. Shreds of flesh were torn away from knuckles. The raw, bloody marks burned agonizingly when he pushed the bony joints between his lips and soaked the wounds with spittle. *You dum' bastard!*

Why dintcha paste the sonofabitch when he was in fron' o' ya?

Ya wouldn'ta got hurt any worse than ya jus' did to yaself.

Instead, ya gotta hit a dumb ol' fuckin' wall!

He stopped in the doorway of a closed store and squeezed the damaged fist with his other hand. He muttered aloud, spewing vile threats at Bruno. He railed against himself, growling what he *could* have done, what he *should* have done. He snarled more threats at Bruno.

In anguish, pain everywhere in him becoming more evident, he slumped to his knees, head sliding down a grimy plate glass window. He curled tightly, crying, his body heaving. He sensed all Bruno's strikes again. *Ya gutless shit! Ya never even hit him back! Not even once!*

He shivered and sobbed in the doorway. *I gotta get home for supper!* He got himself upright, leaning against the window heavily, suddenly pulling away, afraid he would crash through, in among the male and female mannequins wearing bathing suits.

He went into a small restaurant, going directly to the men's room, and washed away dried blood on his chin that had leaked from his mouth. He crumpled paper towels and soaked them under running cold water, applying the sodden mass to his swollen cheek and puffed ear. He took another large water-soaked wad with him to keep coolness and pressure on the same place until he reached home.

He stepped up his pace the next three blocks, suddenly rejuvenated by a determination. *Next time that friggin' Bruno ain' walkin' away without a mark! A good one—right across his fuckin' nose!—jus' like wit' my ol' man!*

At the supper table he scoffed at the blue mark on his cheek and the swollen ear. "It ain't nothin'—it *isn't anything*! The kid nexta me stockin' cans on a top shelf knocked some over while I was squattin' on the floor puttin' stuff away on the bottom. Them cans—*those* cans—they caught me right here—an' here! Wow!—they sure hurt for a second."

Saturday morning Mickey reluctantly entered the store an hour before public opening, wary of Bruno. He put on an apron, stuffing china-marker grease pencils and a carton knife in the chest pocket, and went to his stack of mushroom cases, nervously peering round each aisle corner and along the aisle. He heard joking and laughter of other stock boys in nearby aisles as he kept to himself, doggedly cut off case tops, took out small cans, and scrawled large red price numbers on their small tops, regularly looking left and right for Bruno.

Mike Kendall sauntered along the aisle, stopped by Mickey, and quietly said, "Hear what happened to Bruno yesterday?"

"Uh-uh. No. What?"

"He got fired—jus' before quitting time."

"No kiddin'. For wha'?"

"The boss came 'roun' a corner and saw Bruno come out of the warehouse looking real mad 'bout something and then go down an aisle and go right up to Billy Sweeney and punch him in the mouth—for no reason at all—and knock Billy on his ass—and before the boss could say anything Bruno *kicks* Billy—right in the balls!"

"Honest?"

"I'm surprised you didn't hear the racket!"

"I was way into the warehouse—gettin' these mushrooms—an' the door was closed—an' all the other guys were gone by the time I came out. Nobody up front said nothin' 'bout it when I left—an' I wen' right past 'em on my way out, too. Tha's funny, huh?"

"So, the boss runs and grabs Bruno—and Bruno turns on him, getting ready to poke him—but it turns out the boss was a boxer in college and had a few pro fights later on. He didn't belt Bruno—that was a good thing for Bruno—but it was easy enough for the boss to keep from getting hit by a really pissed-off Bruno. Then Bruno right away sees who he's up against and quits throwing punches. The boss fires him right on the spot, grabs him by the back of the shirt collar, and walks him right up to the cash register, pulls out money, pays him off, and hustles him right out the front door—and I mean *hustles*. Wha' do ya think o' all that?"

"Well—I guess Bruno musta had it comin'. I heard some stories 'bout him—"

Mike Kendall walked away, saying, "Yeah, me too. Well, I gotta get goin' now. I'm lucky today. I got the cereal an' bread shelves to take care o'—all light stuff."

"Yeah," Mickey said. "I'm lucky today, too."

51

*B*eing rid of Bruno was more good luck for me.

Why was I always running into guys like him? Even when I was keeping my nose clean?

All I ever wanted was—well, it wasn't that much.

Ari, though—he was different.

52

Mickey wandered, slowly. If someone had been watching it would have appeared he was moving aimlessly, but he had an ultimate destination in mind. A first-baseman's mitt dangled from his belt by the glove back's hand strap.

As one of the last boys hired in the early autumn at the SUPER Food Market, he was in the first half dozen let go when there was less food to put on shelves. Other part-time jobs were hard to find. He was left with the time after school until five-thirty to himself, with homework assignments mandated as having first call on his attention. Today there had been none. The school year was nearly over. Teachers were less demanding. They had already determined who was promoted, who was not.

When Mickey passed the last row of buildings on his walk from home, and the park and fence became visible, he groaned quietly in disappointment. No baseball players were in the large park with a baseball diamond in each corner. Along the square perimeter of the city's large recreation park was a high chain-link fence, a barrier against wildly thrown baseballs and most foul balls sent askew by hard-swinging batters. He leaned disconsolately against the cool metal, peering through the large openings, wondering what to do next, what to do in place of idly fooling around alone in the park with a baseball diamond at each corner.

He watched a figure enter the park through a gate at a far corner, diagonally opposite. The figure propped a bat against the fence near home plate, set down a water pail, trotted along the base paths, from home plate to first, second, third, and home, then ran them twice more, faster each time.

The figure, small at that distance, trudged to the pitcher's mound carrying the water pail, placing it to one side of the raised infield position. Mickey, squinting hard, focusing intently when the figure momentarily removed a baseball cap, saw it was a boy, appearing to be near his own age. The boy bent over the pail, stood erect, then moved to the pitcher's mound. His body went through contortions of a pitcher making a throw—arm moving through a wide, vertical circle, from his waist, then in front of his chest, down, round in a sweeping arc, coordinated with a lifting, kicking, stepping leg, arm aimed at home plate, swinging sharply across his body in a follow-through motion, all in easy movements. Mickey could see a white object hurtling at the fence backstop. *He's pitchin'—to nobody!*

The boy, hunched over forward, peered at the backstop, then moved to the pail, bending, standing straight, going back to the mound, going through a second curling, twisting, exploding gyration. Another white object flew from his coiled, twisting, snapping, sling-shot arm. After his second rhythmic body-wrenching movements, Mickey realized the water pail was a bucket of baseballs, for systematic hurling at imaginary batters.

Mickey walked along the fence for a long block, turning at the corner, walking the second side of the square park toward the other boy's backstop, studying his pitching form as he diligently hurled ball after ball at imagined strike zones. He seemed skilled. Mickey's envy increased as he walked the fence, getting closer, seeing more clearly. He thought of his own limited ability. He could throw a ball anywhere to the infield with reasonable accuracy and good form but not with the other boy's speed. Several years of sporadic stickball-playing with long lengths of broom handles and tennis balls in New York city streets had honed basic skills, but throwing much heavier baseballs was more difficult. Mickey wished he were bigger, stronger.

He passed the high backstop, entering the ball diamond through a narrow chain-link door, unfastening his belt to slide off the mitt, pulling it onto his left hand, lightly tapping the glove pocket with a fist. The boy on the pitcher's mound stopped, peering at Mickey, eyes shaded darkly by the bill of his cap. Mickey pointed at the bat leaning against the fence. "Want me to be a batter?" The figure on the mound nodded. "OK—hit some easy ones back to me." In a few throws and swings Mickey knew he was not as good a hitter as the other boy was a pitcher.

The boy on the mound was skilled, and patient. Mickey was eager and hopeful. In the next hour they took turns pitching. Mickey's efforts were more like tosses and high lobs, without the grace and precision and speed and accuracy of the other boy's realistic baseball pitches. They each relaxed, Mickey more skeptical, each expecting nothing more than a brief period of baseball practice.

The boy said his name was Ari—"I'll explain it later, maybe." He coached Mickey in batting stance and swing, at times stopping his pitching motion to walk to home plate and position Mickey's arms and feet and hips and shoulders and head and elbows and knees, to help swing more smoothly, to make contact with pitches more often. Ari tried initiating Mickey into the art of pitching, but Mickey was an awkward, self-conscious athlete. Only his batting improved slightly.

They agreed to meet again in two days at the same diamond for more practice. Ari said he lived close enough to the park to throw a baseball from his second floor outside porch to the pitcher's mound. He pointed across the street to a three-storied gray-painted frame house with green trim, with a wide outside front porch on each floor. "That place is more than forty years old. My parents rented the top floor when they first came to this country. Ten years later, working hard all that time, they bought it—that *whole* house. All the kids in our family were born there—none of them in a hospital."

Ari said his name was short for Aristotle—that his parents were Greek and Rumanian—from the old country—but he didn't like anyone to call him that—he thought it sounded funny—sounded so funny in this country—especially the way his parents said it, like in Greece: Ah-rist-oh-*tell*-ee. The way people in this country pronounced it sounded badly enough to him—Air-is-*tottle*—but he disliked the other one more. So he shortened it himself to Ari, saying it like Harry without the "aitch" sound. "I really don't mind the name, because it was given to me for two reasons—one for a respected uncle in my family, and second for the famous Greek philosopher. But *I'd* rather be Ari."

Mickey was excited as he walked home for supper, wondering, at first, why he felt so elated. He thought about the past hour. Ari had been serious in his instruction, but not so intense that he lost patience at Mickey's unskilled efforts. He would smile slightly in amusement, but not laugh, at Mickey's ball handling and batting. When Mickey stopped watching Ari watch him, when he kept his eye on the ball—Ari coaching steadily—throughout a batting swing or as it bounced to him on a sharp hit from Ari's precise hitting, he played better. Then Ari steadily called encouragement and praise, or slapped his glove palm in applause at a sign of improvement. *I could get to like this guy—if he don' turn out like some o' the others.*

Ari was several months younger than Mickey and he should have been a grade behind in high school. When Mickey asked him about them being in the same grade, Ari seemed embarrassed, but then he explained. "The school skipped me a grade once, when I went from sixth to eighth," he said, shrugging his shoulders. "It was after they talked to my parents—both at once—at school.

"You should have seen how nervous they both were when they got a letter from the school principal asking them to make an appointment for discussing something very important. They letter didn't say *what* it was about—just *very important.*

"At first the letter made them mad, especially my Ma. They said official letters in the old country were always about *terrible* matters. They were sure I was in trouble. And *I* thought I was in trouble. But I couldn't figure out why.

"To make a long story short, my mother walks over to Pop's barber shop when she gets the letter in the morning—and they call the school right away from there. My father talks to the principal's secretary who says she doesn't know why the principal wants to see them. But she says he has some time early the next morning. So off they go the next morning. *But*—the night before, after I got home from school quickly to do a lot of studying, they're asking me all kinds of questions, asking me if I was in trouble, asking me what was wrong.

"Anyway—I said I was going to keep this short, but I'm not doing it—the principal just wanted to tell them I was being promoted past seventh grade right into eighth. The teachers said I was a very good student and I could do eighth grade work easily, so why should my time be wasted in seventh grade?

"I thought my Ma would never stop kissing me."

Hurrying faster to the park for their practice, Mickey thought more—*This guy won' turn out like the others. He's more like Walter Cartwright.*

He looked far across the park, peering at people on the diamonds, a game going at each, then made his way through players of different teams on back-to-back outfields instead of walking the long way round. He spotted Ari on an upper tier of low bleachers. Ari saw him and started down the seats as though walking down stairs. He called out someone's name on the playing field. "Hey, let my friend work out in the infield, OK?" The first baseman waved and moved away from the bag.

Ari gave Mickey time; he was patient. And he did not get resentful as Mickey improved. He said, "You're never gonna be great, buddy—but you'll get good. You're halfway there now—and we've only been doing this a little while."

One night, late—the boys' bedroom now crowded with three beds with barely leg room between them, with Hal and Pete Junior asleep for more than two hours—Mickey turned restlessly in his bed.

I've got a friend!

I do!

Ari listened, cajoled, scolded. He made Mickey angry, then coaxed him into calmness. He defended Mickey's thoughts when Mickey questioned himself. Sometimes he agreed with Mickey's self-doubts. Once he agreed when Mickey said he felt like an asshole because of something he had done. Mickey got angry because of the quick agreement, but in minutes they laughed together, Mickey nodding thoughtfully when Ari explained why he agreed.

Ari also asked Mickey's help, and he admired Mickey's talent for easily following song melodies on the radio—whistling, humming, lah-dee-dahing from a very first note—saying that he himself could not carry a tune in a basket. Time after time he expressed amazement at Mickey's spelling ability, testing him incessantly. Ari deferred to him in history and geography, but he was disappointed that he could not excite Mickey with the wonders of mathematics, at which he did so well himself.

Mickey's wonder at his good fortune grew. *I never knew nobody like him. An' his folks—they treat me like a son!*

Three weeks and a dozen warm-ups on the baseball field later, Ari's mother—short, plump, smiling—pulled Mickey gently by the wrist, tugging him from the back porch into her deliciously odored kitchen, guiding him to a white-painted chair at a white-painted table. "You are just in time. I have a spinach pie ready to take from the oven."

Aunt Margaret was a good cook of plain French-Canadian food from her side of the family and plain Irish food from Uncle Pete's side of the family—soups and stews and meat and potatoes and other vegetables—but Mickey quickly grew fond of the joyful diversity of aromatic, spicy, flavorful Greek and Rumanian foods and cooking by his best friend's mother.

I've got a best friend—finally!

Damn! Whoopee!

DAMN!

They were the same height when they measured themselves back-to-back, and when Ari pushed upwards to make their heads touch at the same point. But Mickey always looked taller because his natural stance was erect. Ari's posture was hunched, making him look like his torso sloped forward even when supposedly sitting straight in a chair. Standing, he looked ungainly, his head always seeming tilted up, or a little sideways, always appearing to be looking up, eyes peering intensely from recesses shaded by nearly straight, almost continuous eyebrows, separated only by small gaps in thick short hairs nearly blending between his eyes, curving down to the bridge of his nose. At first glance it seemed he had a single broad band of black over his eyebrows, across his forehead, temple to temple.

His nose was large; lips dark and full, that smiled readily, unevenly, showing even, white teeth. He had a low forehead, usually covered by uncontrolled, thick locks of curly black hair. His posture made normal-length arms seem awkward and longer than normal. His and Mickey's weights were consistently within one or two pounds of being the same, but the way Ari carried himself lent an image of thickness and belied his great agility, which he so ably demonstrated each time he taught Mickey about the intricacies of basketball playing and ball handling.

Ari could laugh explosively or chuckle. He seemed to always have a retort for someone who wanted to be a psychological opponent, often coming to Mickey's aid. He was an honor student who bemoaned Mickey's woeful attitude about school. But he never denigrated Mickey. He remained a friend.

Ari was astounded by Mickey's tales of risky escapades in quest of fun and daring; amused that playing hooky—a thought that had rarely occurred to him, an act he had never done—was so simple a matter; horrified and angry at Mickey's HR Club initiation rituals. He shook his head in disbelief throughout Mickey's relating his harrowing subway encounter with the colored boy and telling about the near-deadly bus ride.

"Pal—I don't know how you got to make it this far. You've got *some* kind of luck, I'll tell you."

"Yeah," Mickey said, "I know."

"Maybe it's cuz—" Mickey wondered how to say what he thought. "Maybe cuz I was s'posed to meet ya—so we could be friends."

Ari smiled. "I think you're right."

Time passed quickly for Mickey, and happily; much of it with Ari. Mickey's metamorphosis continued. His existence became a satisfying steadiness, without boredom. He celebrated Ari's seventeenth birthday in late April in Ari's kitchen, with a spinach pie—made especially for Mickey, Ari told him—followed by a large round cake with seventeen tall candles. The dozen family members and friends in the large kitchen applauded and cheered loudly, and his mother kept wiping her tears with an apron corner. Ari's father ceremoniously poured small glasses of potent Greek liqueur and Ari was toasted. Mickey's eyes watered as the clear fluid seared his throat. Ari's father smiled proudly, and his mother did, too, letting happy tears flow. In July Ari joined Mickey in his family's small kitchen for Aunt Margaret's birthday cake baked for Mickey's seventeenth birthday. "I invited your mother," Aunt Margaret told Mickey, "but she said she has to work. She did say she was putting a card in the mail—and said your sister had to be in a roller-skating contest."

Mickey matured to a B-student in his junior year, capable at mathematics, learning enough to pass, but remaining generally disinterested in school subjects. Ari taught him the rules and tactics of football and they went to school games. Ari continued befuddling Mickey with his agility and quickness on a basketball court, whirling dribbling, skillfully fending Mickey off as he tried stealing Ari's ball from his quick hands; darting with flashing feet and fast moves to block Mickey's basket shots or to whirl in quick arcs and circles, swiping at the ball, almost always penetrating Mickey's defense, artistically lofting and sinking the stolen ball for another score of his own.

Mickey enjoyed Hal and Pete Junior, but it was not the same friendship as with Ari. Ari was a great joy in Mickey's life—but Mickey could never bring himself to use those simple words to his best friend. *Boys don' talk like tha' to each other!*

53

I wish Ari was here now.

Hm—I wonder how those words would sound to Ari? Kind of mushy? For two guys?

Well—anyway—at least now I know how to say them.

A voice called out: "The rest of you people get your things together. It won't be long before you're in here."

I thought I'd never get to be doing this—and now it's only a few more minutes. But it really didn't take too long, all things considered, once I got the letter. Son of a gun!

54

It did have a sloppily imprinted, reddish ink, rubber-stamped sender's return address in the upper left corner, every character streaked and blurred. *They must have been in a real hurry to get this in the mail to me.* Only three characters— streaked and curved from someone's hurried swiping motion as envelopes were apparently hastily rubber-stamped one after another—were easily understood: 126.

In place of a postage stamp a forbidding message was printed in black small block letters:

FOR OFFICIAL USE
PENALTY FOR PRIVATE USE, $300

Mickey's name and address had been carefully handwritten, by a woman, from its appearance.

Look at this—it's here. Wonder if I'll still be able to go ahead with my other plan because of this?

For a long time Mickey had not thought much about everything in the newspapers and on the radio. When the trouble had started nearly three years before, nothing directly affected him, so why pay attention? There was a lot of discussion in school civics classes, but the whole thing was far away. It all seemed like just so much more history, and it would all probably pass away soon anyhow. He had not really comprehended the President's speech on the radio as the family gathered at the kitchen table at Uncle Pete's insistence. "It's going to be more of the same," Uncle Pete had said quietly, "but worse this time. I'll guarantee that!"

Mickey felt that he had a lot more to think about than places thousands of miles away in every direction. He did not even know anybody who might be in any of the places—*'cept that ain' countin' Tom and Bobby Monahan—those two cousins on my mother's side, because I hardly know 'em. I know their names an' we met 'em once—that's it.* He could never remember what Bobby was doing, but he sometimes heard about Tom flying in China, and he remembered that someone at a family gathering had said, "He's certainly been over there for quite a while— almost from the beginning." *I wonder if he flies over that town where Mr. Sing Lee was from?*

He would occasionally hear that another of the boys who used to be at the YMCA a lot had gone into the army or the navy. Then he heard about someone else he used to see at school. Mickey's friend Ken asked him one afternoon, at the Y, if he had heard that Arnie Pierce had been killed when the destroyer he was on was sunk by a Japanese submarine. "Ain't that a switch, Mick?" Ken said. "It's supposed to be the other way around—you know what I mean?—the tin can chasing the sub and doing it in with ash cans."

Mickey remembered Arnie—one of the kids always swimming at the Y pool. Once, as a lifeguard, Mickey had to help Arnie while he was swimming when he got a stomach cramp and a leg cramp in the center of the deep end of the pool just after Mickey came on duty.

Mickey liked being a Y lifeguard on boys' swimming sessions because he was the only boy allowed to wear swimming trunks. They were meant to be an authority symbol for boys who, after testing and instruction, were selected for staff lifeguard status. Best of all, in his mind, he no longer had to swim naked like all users of the Y's swimming pool, boys and men.

The day he helped Arnie he thought the other boy was joking, thrashing about only to pretend trouble. Arnie was like that. Mickey sat on a bench along the tiled wall, twenty feet away, smiling, amused by the antics. *He's not gonna keep pullin' that crap on me—the wise-ass son of a bitch!* He rescued Arnie when the yells and gasps and grunts became real for him, pulling Arnie by the hair, holding his head up out of the water, slipping him along on his back for ten feet through the water to the safety of the ladder. Arnie sputtered and yelled he was being hurt by the scalp tow, but Mickey yelled back at him. "Shut up! I'm saving your ass, dummy!" In seconds, Arnie was out of the pool. He threw an arm about Mickey's shoulder. "Thanks, pal—I was gettin' scared out there."

Suddenly, Ken's words so clear in his mind, Mickey felt soberly different. What had not meant anything at all to him, for so long, that he did not really understand, that he did not think about, or care anything about, thumped his mind. *Arnie's dead? Someone I've talked to? Somebody I touched?—saved from dying? And now he's dead from really drowning—but nobody was around to save him that time.*

Others in school left abruptly—quitting—to enter military or naval service, and Mickey and Ari talked about what they might do, what they should do. Ari said, "I'm ready, if I have to, just like you are, Mick, but I don't know when I'll get called, or even if I will. If things keep going the way they are, we keep on winning in the war, neither one of us might have to go, pal. So I just keep on working away at that part-time job in the shirt factory and helping Pop at the barber shop. I'm positive we'll both get to graduate first. It's almost the end of the term. There can't be that much of a hurry so that we'd get pulled out of school so close to graduating."

On an early-May afternoon, not saying anything even to Ari beforehand, Mickey went to a U.S. Navy recruiting station, saying to the chief petty officer that he was ready to enlist as a sailor because he had heard the navy took people in at seventeen, that he could go now because he would be eighteen in July; but the CPO said he would have to wait until the navy called on him later; it had all the people it needed for now—besides, it would not take him right now anyway, not *this* close to his high school graduation.

Mickey then learned that the U.S. Marines also took recruits at age seventeen. The tall, husky sergeant wearing a green woolen uniform in the downtown recruiting office said all Mickey had to do was bring a written consent of a parent or guardian and the Corps would be happy to review his application.

Uncle Pete said, "It's not up to me. I'm sorry. I *am* your godfather, but I'm not your *legal* guardian. I don't have authority to give consent. Everything is really up to your mother."

His mother stirred cocoa in a saucepan. "I was so surprised when I opened the door and saw you standing there. You're getting so tall! I can't believe it." Mickey sat quietly at the table in the small area she said was a kitchenette, that he thought really was part of the living room. *I'm not that tall! I'm still shorter than most of the guys my age—except for Ari; we're about the same height. It's just that you haven't seen me that much; that's why I look bigger.*

"It's too bad your sister isn't here—so you two could visit. She's off roller-skating again. Seems like all she wants to do is spend her time at that skating rink. I worry a lot about her—her being a sixteen-year-old now. It's worse than when she was fifteen—and fourteen." She poured cocoa into his cup. "If she wasn't doing so well in school, I'd make her stay home more and study. But what can I do? And she does deserve to be with her girlfriends.

"Oh—you said I needed to sign something. What could there be that I would have to sign?" She cried when she saw the application for the Marine Corps. "You're *only* a *boy!*"

Mickey pleaded that he would soon finish high school, then turn eighteen during the summer vacation. "Then I'd get taken in anyway, and have to go where I was told. But if you sign this I get what I want, get to go into the Marines as soon as school ends.

"What difference does it make to you anyway?"

He watched her slowly frown. Her lips rolled in, leaving a thin line. He was sorry he had said it so harshly, said it at all. Her hand trembled scrawling her name. Feeling ill-at-ease, standing by the apartment door, looking at his mother, Mickey folded the paper and put it in a shirt pocket. "I'll be all right." He opened the door. Seated at the table, she looked at him intently. He said, "I'll see you."

Mickey was disappointed when the big sergeant accepted the application but said there would be a waiting period until the Corps' quota from this city was called. "At that time, son, you'll take a physical, get sworn in, and be on your way to basic training."

"How long will that take? I mean getting called for the physical?"

"Don't know."

"But I thought there was a war on. A lot of my friends sign up and they're gone in a week—a lot of times it's less.

The sergeant shrugged. "The Marine Corps is different. There's nothing I can do." He turned his broad back to Mickey and rummaged in a file cabinet drawer.

Dispiritedly, Mickey endured the final weeks of school, finishing as a B+ student, math still the least interesting subject, still affecting his improved average. He could not bring himself to the same level of excitement of other seniors for the graduation ceremony. He paid little attention as teacher and student speakers droned about the past and the future. He was impatient as the line of students seemed to take forever to pass across the auditorium stage and each received a thin imitation green leather folder containing a diploma. His excitement only rose when the students cheered and whooped and hollered at the close of the ceremony. Mickey, Uncle Pete, Aunt Margaret, Hal, and Pete Junior found one another in the milling crowd and Mickey's hand was shaken several times, and Aunt Margaret kissed him on a cheek. Then he sought Ari and found him with his family and there were more handshakes and congratulations. Ari began working full-time at the shirt factory and talked to his supervisor about something for Mickey to do, who got a job and was assigned to Ari to be shown what to do and work with him every day, unless either of them was needed elsewhere. It was uninteresting work, often monotonous, sometimes irksome, more so for Mickey than Ari. But Mickey felt good about contributing to the family resources instead of just living with them and not paying rent and eating their food without helping pay for it and relieving them of having to buy whatever he needed for clothes and shoes and for an occasional movie.

Each day, after work, Mickey looked expectantly for a letter from the U.S. Marine Corps. He had not told Ari about his application; Ari had said the navy was the *best* choice, in his opinion; well, at least for himself, anyway. Mickey was not sure if Ari might be disappointed. *I don't think he would, but maybe I just won't mention it—just in case it doesn't work out anyway. They might never even call me up, so then there'd be nothing to explain, okay?*

The time the two youths spent together amounted only to time in the shirt factory. Working hours lengthened as military and naval orders increased. The company added a ten-minute rest break in the afternoon in addition to the same break that had always been allowed to workers during midmorning. Stacking dozens of hundred-foot lengths of fabric one atop another for the pattern cutter soon became more tedious, more uninteresting; a boy on each side of the table trotting alongside it, each grasping the long metal rod through the cardboard core of the bolt, rolling a layer out in one direction, reversing direction, doing the same, reversing direction, doing the same, repeating, repeating, repeating, until the stack of cloth was a foot or more thick.

If I have to work while I wait to be called I wish I was doing something better than just making shirts! I haven't learned anything in this place except how to hold a cigarette—and I don't smoke!

NO SMOKING signs were liberally posted in every area of the shirt factory, including the men's rooms. It was an absolute rule that no smoking was allowed anywhere throughout the second floor loft—for insurance reasons, for safety reasons, and because three of the bosses did not smoke and thought no one else should. During the half-hour lunch time, workers who smoked went outdoors to have at least one cigarette. As soon as the klaxon sounded, announcing the morning and afternoon break times, there was a rush for the stairs at either end of the loft so men and women and youths could have at least a few puffs of a cigarette.

However, strongly addicted smokers schemed, ignoring the major fear of getting caught smoking in the work area and being fired. Smokers willing to defy the company rule stayed away from obvious bathroom congregating places and being easy prey for surveillance. But the addicted smokers were determined to smoke, even if on company property during company time. Veteran workers finally found a place for men to "sneak a smoke" and a firm informal rule was quickly implemented that only two people at a time could use the location—*no ifs, ands, or buts about it.* If two people were already in place, a hopeful smoker would have to leave, to try later. An overwhelming yen would be replaced by a disappointing frustration.

Mickey was surprised that the bosses had never learned about the hideaway—he was told it had been used "forever." *I'll bet they do know about it and just look the other way. They know the guys make sure everybody sticks to the two-at-time rule—and know that the guys don't screw off from work too long at a time. And I guess the bosses don't worry about the insurance rule too much, as long as the workers stay happy—and be careful.*

The secret place was in the large scrap room by the men's washroom, between stacks of large bales of pattern shreds and behind big mounds of pattern shreds waiting to be baled. Some worker, years before, developed the knack of holding a cigarette so that a sitting smoker who might doze would not drop it accidentally, perhaps starting a killing fire. Clandestine smokers happily passed the knack along, eager to conspire against others who did not want them to smoke.

The trick was to grip the cigarette deep in the vee between two middle fingers of a hand, sitting with a forearm resting on a knee or a thigh. In the dangling hand, natural pressure of the two middle fingers against each other firmly gripped the cigarette, even if a smoker dozed. The smoldering cigarette burned slowly and the ember progressed to the finger grip and singed fingers, bringing back consciousness.

For nonsmokers wanting a nap, the knack was also a form of alarm system to keep from falling asleep and being away from a work place for too long—light a cigarette, grip it properly, position himself comfortably, out of sight, and get six or seven minutes of light sleep.

Ari was the one who gleefully passed along the trick to Mickey. "I know you don't smoke—but it's a swell way to grab a catnap." Mickey was surprised at Ari's out-of-character advice. A year later Mickey remembered the clandestine tip and made use of it.

Mickey abruptly quit the shirt factory job to work in a machine shop that made carbine rifle parts. His decision surprised Ari. A thoughtful look came over his face. "I don't know how we're going to practice baseball and basketball much now," Ari said.

"Yeah—I know—but I feel I want to do something better than just making shirts. This other place makes rifle parts for soldiers and marines. I kind of feel they're needed more than shirts are."

It was much more tiring work, standing for hours at one position at a large bank of drill presses, shifting weight from one leg to the other, periodically straightening his back to escape the insidious slouch that became painful after a short while, workers elbow to elbow, mounting rifle bolts in a fixture, drilling the same set of holes in every bolt, taking bolts from a tray on one side behind him, putting them in a tray on his other side and behind. Each day, in minutes, his fingers looked like prunes, shriveled by continuous immersion in the thin, cold, white cutting fluid that poured steadily over the spinning drill tip and the bulky drilling fixture from a copper tubing nozzle. However, the money was good, especially for a seventeen-year-old—and there were a lot of other boys about his age, as well as a lot of older men who had been doing this sort of work all their lives and who were too old for military service—and there were some young women drill press operators—some of them good-looking, and some of them *really* good looking—and some of them operated bigger, more complex machines.

Several days before his eighteenth birthday he got home from work and Aunt Margaret was sorting mail at the kitchen table. She quietly said, "There's something here for you, Mickey—a postcard."

Boy, what a rundown neighborhood! Mickey had expected the place to be in a better area of the city, expected it to be somewhere bright and shiny, downtown, with all the latest equipment, something like shown in the movies. But this *was* both the street and building number in the telephone directory when he looked it up to verify it, and the sign over the door *did* read the same as included in the postcard's curt imprinted message notifying him of his duty by law to report for draft registration as soon as possible, that he had to do so on his birthday at the latest, between the hours of 8:00 A.M. and 4:00 P.M., under penalty of law, except if his birthday is on a Saturday or Sunday or a legal holiday, and then he must register on the next following day, during the same hours, and to do so at:

SELECTIVE SERVICE
DRAFT BOARD NO. 126

Up one long flight of dimly lighted stairs was a large, oblong, high-ceiling loft, with floor-to-ceiling windows at left and right ends as he entered. A long row of folding tables paralleled the long windowless brick wall opposite the door, and old people, their backs to the wall, sat on hard-seat, straight-back chairs or on folding metal or wood chairs, filling in form questions being answered by young men sitting on hard-seat, straight-back chairs or on folding metal or wood chairs, on opposite sides of tables, their backs to Mickey. In clusters to each side of the door were groups of tall, gray metal filing cabinets. Squeaky drawers were pulled open and pushed shut by old people putting folders in and taking them out, and other old people moved slowly about the room, tending to tasks.

Mickey saw all this in three to four seconds, leaning through the half-opened door from the dim landing at the top of the long stairs. No one paid attention to him. He stepped fully into the room, firmly and loudly shutting the door behind him. No one looked up as he looked about.

Mickey walked across the wide space, to an empty folding chair opposite a plump gray-haired lady sorting papers and making notes on a long yellow lined pad. He stood between the chair and the table. The woman made what looked to him to be illegible squiggles on the pad with a pencil.

Look at her—just ignoring me!

She could say hello—or something!

She tore the sheet from the pad, put it with other scattered loose papers, put the sheaf at the left front corner of the table, and looked up.

"Hello."

She looked at his postcard. "You're early—a couple *days* early at that—and early in the day, besides. Most boys wait until the last day they can—and some of them even wait until almost the last minute of the day, thinking we'll tell them to come back—but we stay right here after the door closes and see that they get registered like they're supposed to."

Young boys? She knows I'm eighteen. That's not a young boy anymore! Old people always think everybody's young if you're not at least the same age as they are!

She pulled a long blank questionnaire from a tray and started asking questions. Mickey sat in the wobbly folding chair, giving answers, repeating answers. The woman leaned over the form, mumbling questions, often asking them a second time, scrawling the answers on blank lines or making **X**s in small squares. As she labored over the forms, Mickey looked about. There was nothing of what he had expected; no patriotic posters; no flags or red-white-and-blue bunting; no posters warning that loose lips sink ships, no other ominous warnings of any sort, nothing that gave him a sense of starting a great adventure.

The woman diligently ran a fingertip over every question number on both sides of the form, occasionally asking something, confirming an answer. "I *have* to ask some of these again, young man. It's very necessary. We've been told there can be a lot of trouble later if the questions aren't answered right. The government knows you'll be coming home some day, and it doesn't want to waste time seeing that you get out of military service. Here—sign—right there." He did.

The woman said something he did not hear. He leaned forward. "What did you say?"

Leaning back, she breathed a sigh. "I said you'll be hearing from the government in a little while."

That's it? That's all there is to it? You don't tell me when I go? What outfit I'm going into?

What do I do about the Marines?

She put his questionnaire on top of the stack at the corner of the table. "That's all you have to do today." Mickey leaned against the back of his chair, studying the woman, wanting her to say something about what was ahead of him. She squinted at him through her glasses. Mickey looked to both sides of where he sat but the old people and the other young men were busy with forms. Looking over his shoulders, people searching file drawers kept sorting through folders. Mickey felt a crashing wave of disappointment sweep over him. He was angry his waiting was not over, that he still did not know more than when he climbed the stairs. He stood up angrily, spinning about, charging across the narrow-planked wood floor, jerking open the door. He turned to the woman, trying to think of something to yell out to the room. She was bathed with sunlight that had broken through the outside overcast, filtering at a low angle through street windows at one end of the hall. Sun-sparkled dust hanging in the still air of the loft softened the early morning brightness that fell on her and the table as she studied a sheet of paper. She looked up at Mickey, adjusted her glasses upward on her nose, then turned her eyes down.

Damn!

But it isn't her fault!

Mickey closed the door quietly.

Aunt Margaret handed Mickey the long white envelope as soon as he entered the kitchen. She turned from the stove and slowly took it from an apron pocket. "This is yours."

"Thanks." He read the front, seeing his name written in large curving letters, staring at the smudged return address.

"Uh—yeah—I mean, yes, ma'm—thanks. I'll look at it after I wash up." He put it the letter in a hip pocket.

Aunt Margaret pursed her lips in mild anguish as he turned and went into the bathroom, thinking she was right about what the letter contained, since she had taken a closer look at the return address, and judging by his long, thoughtful look at the letter. She turned back to the stove.

The boys' bedroom no longer had bare walls and ceiling. They were festooned with pictures and suspended model airplanes. The bureau was stacked with books and magazines. So were the chairs. Aunt Margaret had long since surrendered to the increasing interests of the boys.

Mickey kicked off his sneakers, using one foot against the other. He slid across the bed, leaning his back against the wall, feet pulled back, knees up. Resting arms on knees, he looked steadily at the envelope. Newspaper headlines flashed in his mind, black-lettered banners that once had meant nothing to him. He remembered newspapers stories from all over the world.

What's it like?—being so far away?—from home?

He saw himself rescuing Arnie Pierce in the swimming pool. Ken's story about Arnie and his navy destroyer made him shudder.

What must other things be like?

Getting hurt?
Dying? Being dead?
Now Mickey had *his* letter.

It seemed to singe his fingertips. He stared at his handwritten name for a long moment, then started to rip open the flap, but stopped. He dug through trouser pockets, pulling out a penknife. He carefully slit the envelope open along the top. The unfolded sheet read:

Greeting: Having submitted yourself to a local board composed of your neighbors for the purpose of determining your availability for training and service in the land or naval forces of the United States, you are hereby notified you have been selected....

55

A young lieutenant at the front of the room, with gold bars on his shirt collar points, stood on a chair held steady by a young sergeant. Everyone in the room stood, looking at him.

He said, "I want each of you to raise your right hand. You are to repeat the United States Army enlistment oath after me, each of you saying your own full name—first name, then middle name, if you have one, then last name—after the word *I* at the start of the oath. You are all to speak loudly enough to be heard. In a few minutes you will sign enlistment papers containing the oath. Gentlemen—

Michael's voice, at first, sounded hollow to himself, and he was not sure it was loud enough to be heard, though everyone else's voice seemed clear to him. He spoke more strongly, in unison with the others:

> I, Jason Michael Young, do solemnly swear or affirm that I will support the Constitution of the United States against all enemies, foreign or domestic; that I will bear true faith and allegiance to the same; and that I will obey the orders of the president of the United States and the orders of the officers appointed over me, according to regulations and the Uniform Code of Military Justice. So help me God."

"Now," the lieutenant said, "you are members of the enlisted ranks of the United States Army. Lower your hands. The sergeant will give you further instructions." The lieutenant stepped down from the chair and walked from the quiet room.

I'm not a damn kid anymore!

To hell with you, Tony Minelli!

—and fuck you, Bruno!